"You are the wizard's wizard, man! *You have turned Mars into New Jersey!*"

Even in the general alarm of the moment, Kit had to snicker. "Could have been worse," Ronan said under his breath as he looked around. "I could have done it the other way round."

"This is the place where that old radio version of *War of the Worlds* happened, isn't it?" Kit said. "The one they did on Halloween way back whenever it was, and they pretended it was happening in New Jersey somewhere, instead of England."

"And it's not even the *right* New Jersey!" Darryl said. "It's New Jersey *now!* Look over there—" He pointed. Off to their right, across the street, was a big handsome blue building with a long, peaked roof. On the opposite side of the road in front of it stood a pole with road signs that said ROUTE 629 and TO NJ TURNPIKE. Farther down the pole were posted an ad for an Internet café and a faded picture of somebody's lost dog.

Darryl was looking at the big blue building. "Bet you that was the mill once," Darryl said. "Look, I was right! There's the old millstones. They've got 'em sunk into the ground so cars won't ruin their lawn when they turn the corner. There's where the water came out past the mill. *But no Martians!*" He started laughing again.

"I wouldn't be too sure about that," Ronan said, very quietly.

Diane Duane's
Young Wizards Series

DIANE DUANE

A Wizard of Mars

GRAPHIA

Houghton Mifflin Harcourt

Boston   New York

Graphia and the Graphia logo are trademarks of
Houghton Mifflin Harcourt Publishing Company.

For information about permission to reproduce selections from this
book, write to Permissions, Houghton Mifflin Harcourt Publishing
Company, 215 Park Avenue South, New York, New York 10003.

www.hmhbooks.com

The text of this book is set in Stempel Garamond

The Library of Congress has cataloged
the hardcover edition as follows:
Duane, Diane.
A wizard of Mars/by Diane Duane.
p. cm.—(Young wizards series; bk. 9)
Summary: Young wizards Kit Rodriquez and Nita Callahan manage
to wangle their way onto an elite team sent to investigate the
mysterious, long-sought "message in a bottle" that holds the first
clues to the secrets of the ancient Martian race.
[1. Wizards—Fiction. 2. Mars (Planet—Fiction. 3. Fantasy.] I. Title.
PZ7.D84915Wji 2010
[Fic]—dc22
2009023851

ISBN: 978-0-15-204770-2 hardcover
ISBN: 978-0-15-205449-6 paperback

Manufactured in the United States of America
DOM 10 9 8 7 6 5 4 3 2 1
4500285590

Contents

... Mars, why art thou bent
On kindling thus the Scorpion, his tail
Portending evil and his claws aflame? ...
Why planets leave their paths and through the void
Thus journey on obscure? 'Tis war that comes,
Fierce rabid war: the sword shall bear the rule ...
(*Pharsalia*, Marcus Annaeus
Lucanus: Book 1)

The one departed | is the one who returns
From the straitened circle | and the shortened night,
When the blue star rises | and the water burns:
Then the word long-lost | comes again to light
To be spoke by the watcher | who silent yearns
For the lost one found. Yet to wreak aright,
She must slay her rival | and the First World spurn
Lest the one departed | no more return.
(The *Red Rede*, 1-8)

Truth is always late, always last to arrive, limping
along with Time.
(*The Art of Worldly Wisdom*,
Baltasar Gracián, §146)

Terra Cognita

★

THE PROBLEM, KIT THOUGHT, scowling at the paper, *isn't the basic* shape, *so much. It's what to do with the legs...*

He briefly glanced up from the pencil sketch he'd been doing in the margin of his notebook and looked wearily up at Mr. Machiavelli, his history teacher, as if he'd actually been paying attention to anything the Mack was saying. It was hard enough to care, this time of year. *One more week till school's out. One more week!* — and especially late on a Friday afternoon, when the air-conditioning was broken.

Again! Kit thought. He was sweltering, along with everyone else in the place. Only little, balding Mr. Mack, strolling back and forth in front of the blackboard and holding forth on Asian politics of the 1950s, seemed untouched by the heat and humidity. He paused to write the word "Pyongyang" on the board, pausing in the middle of the process to stare at the word as if not sure of the spelling.

Oh, come on, Mack, give us a break: who cares about this stuff right now?! But the Mack, as the whole class knew too well by now, was unstoppable; the heat slowed him down no more than cold or rain or dark of night probably would have. People names and place names and endless dates just kept on rolling out of him, and now he turned to the blackboard and started writing again. . . .

Kit let out a sigh and glanced at the air vents at the back of the room. Cold air should have been coming out of them, but right now they were emitting nothing but an occasional faint clunking noise as somewhere in the system a feeder vent kept trying and failing to open. The school system was having budget troubles, which meant that some equipment that needed to be completely replaced wasn't even getting maintenance. But knowing this didn't make the heat any easier to bear.

People in the back of the room were fanning themselves with paperwork and notebooks. Kids sitting by the open windows were leaning toward them, courting any passing breath of air, and (when Mr. Machiavelli wasn't looking) panting obviously, as if it would help. Without stopping what he was saying, Mr. Mack had paused to flip open a book on his desk and peer down at it: he shoved a bookmark into it and turned back to the blackboard, starting to write something else. *How can this not be bothering him when he's got a whole suit on?* Kit thought. *Doesn't he have sweat glands??*

The cooling system clunked several times more, to no effect. Kit made a face, glanced at the clock. It seemed hopelessly stuck at twenty past two, and the class wasn't going to let out until quarter of three ... which from where Kit was sitting felt like at least a year away. *I can't stand it anymore. And anyway, none of them'll notice —*

Very quietly Kit reached down into the book bag beside his desk and pulled out his wizard's manual. At the moment, the manual looked like his history textbook — which was perfectly normal, since earlier this year Kit had stuck a chameleon spell on the manual's exterior, causing it to imitate the proper textbook for whatever class he happened to be in.

Kit turned idly through the manual's pages to the one that held the spell he'd first crafted to do repairs on the school's cooling system, back when it broke down during the hot spell in April. He'd had to use the spell several times since, and he'd had to rework it every time, because engineers from other schools kept coming over to work on the system — and every time they did, they disrupted whatever quick fix Kit had managed to implement the last time he'd done the fix-it spell. *Gotta get in here sometime during vacation and do a real fix on the whole system,* Kit thought. *Otherwise things'll get even worse when the cold weather comes around ...*

The words of the spell, in the long, curved strokes and curlicue hooks-and-crooks of the wizardly Speech, laid themselves out before him on the manual page. Hovering above them, faint and hardly to be seen, was the shadow of the camouflage page that any casual, nonwizardly observer would see if he or she looked at the book.

There was of course no question of saying the spell out loud in a situation like this. *Gonna be kind of a strain doing it on the quiet,* Kit thought. *But this heat's just too much. And what's it like on the other side of the building, where the Sun's hitting? The kids over there must be dying. Let's just call this my good deed for the day . . .*

He closed his eyes for a moment, working to make the requisite "quiet zone" inside his mind, and then opened his eyes again and started silently reading the words of the wizardry in the Speech. Slowly the wizardry started to work: a silence started to fall around Kit as the universe seemed to lean in around him, listening to the spell.

In the growing silence, Kit watched the room around him seem to fade, while the normally invisible layout of the cooling system now started to become visible, glowing like a wireframe diagram that stretched out and away from the history classroom. Kit didn't need to go hunting through the system to find the source of the problem: he knew where it was, and anyway, the locator functions of the spell would have shown him the duct near the heart of the building, just this side of the heat pump in the school's engineering center.

Kit peered at the duct in his mind, concentrating on the source of the problem — a vent shutter that looked something like a small, boxy Venetian blind.

"Okay," he said silently in the Speech. "What is it *this* time?"

The guy came again, said the vent shutter buried deep in the duct, *and he tightened those bolts up too much* . . . "Said" was of course not the best way to put it — inanimate objects don't communicate the way organic ones do — but to a wizard like Kit, who was good at communicating with such objects, the way the information passed was enough like talking and listening to think of it that way.

The wizardry showed Kit the bolts that the vent shutter meant: a series of them, up and down each side of it, fixing its shutter hinges to the inside of the duct. "Got it," Kit said silently. "Okay, here we go —"

He turned his attention to the bolts. "Come on, guys, lighten up. You don't need all that tension. Just let yourselves unwind . . ."

Half of wizardry was persuading people, creatures, or objects to do what you wanted them to: the rest of it was knowing what words in the Speech would get the intention across . . . and by now, Kit knew the words entirely too well. Slowly, the wizardry showed him the bolts loosening up one by one. "Not too much," he said in his mind. "We don't want the shutter to fall out. Yeah, that's it . . . just like that."

The last bolt rotated a quarter turn. "That's the ticket," Kit said in his mind. "That should do it. Thanks, guys . . ."

With one finger Kit traced a series of curves on the desk, the "unknotting" routine to undo the Wizard's Knot that fastened most spells closed and started them working. The wizardry obediently unraveled: the glowing wireframe of the duct structure faded out as the classroom faded in around Kit again. And from far away in the building, echoing down the air vents that led into the room, Kit heard something go *clunk*, just once — the vent's shutters, locking into the correct position. After a few moments, a breath of cooler air started sighing out of the vent.

Kit let out a breath of his own. It was tough to conceal the effects of doing a spell, even a minor one like this: he felt as if he'd just run up a few flights of stairs, and it was now taking some effort to keep his breathing regular. For the moment, all Kit could do was shut his manual and pick up his pencil, his hand shaking with a fine muscle tremor born of the brief exertion. But the air was cooling already. *Worth it,* Kit thought, *even for just twenty minutes . . .* He glanced again at the sketches in his notebook's margin, the topmost of which showed a single slender tower rising from a forest of smaller ones, all surrounded by a barren, otherwordly landscape. The tower in particular was fuzzy around the edges, with erasures and redrawing: rendering architecture wasn't Kit's strong suit. But the figures he'd drawn farther down the page were better, especially the —

"Not too bad," said a voice over his shoulder. "Better put some more clothes on her, though, or you'll lose your PG-13 rating."

Kit froze as the laughter of his classmates spread around the room.

Mr. Mack's hand came down and picked up the

notebook. "Actually, as regards the draftsmanship, not bad at all," his history teacher said. "I'd rate her babe quotient at, oh, an eight or so. Make it eight-point-five for her, uh, attributes." More snickering went around the class. Kit's face went hot. "But as for the content . . ." Mr. Mack gave Kit a disapproving glance. "Not sure what it has to do with the aftermath of the Korean War . . ."

"Uh. Nothing," Kit said.

"Nice to see that you realize that, Mr. Rodriguez," Mr. Mack said, wandering back up to his desk and dropping the notebook on it. "So maybe you'll exculpate yourself by filling us in on the continuing significance of the thirty-eighth parallel . . ."

Kit swallowed hard. This kind of thing was so much easier to do on paper: the shufflings and mutterings and under-the-breath comments of his classmates routinely filled him with more dread than being locked in a closet with the Lone Power. "It's the border between North and South Korea," he said. "Both sides have it heavily fortified. It's also one of the few land borders you can see from space, because there's normal city light on the southern side of the line, and it's almost pitch-black on the north . . ."

Slowly his throat got less dry. Kit went on for a minute or two more about famines and political tensions, trying to remember some of the really good stuff that would have been just a couple of pages back in the notebook right in front of him if he hadn't been drawing in it. Finally Mr. Mack held up a hand.

"Enough," he said. "Ms. Simmons, maybe you'd

pick up where the artistic Mr. Rodriguez left off. What effect is the UN's food-aid effort likely to have on the North in view of the present political situation?"

"Uh —"

Kit had little amusement to spare for poor Delinda Simmons's ensuing struggle to find an answer. Between doing the spell, trying to hide it, and then having to try to recall notes he'd taken two weeks before, he was now stressed to breathlessness. He concentrated on acting like he was paying attention, while being grateful Mr. Mack had let him off the hook so soon — he'd seen some of his classmates go through scenes of torment that had lasted a lot longer.

At last Mr. Machiavelli held up a hand, with just a glance at the clock. Kit glanced at it, too: somehow it was still only two thirty. *Boy, you don't need wizardry to get time to run slow, sometimes . . .* "All right," Mr. Machiavelli said. "Were this an ordinary day, you'd all have to sit here and suffer through me doing a recap of what the work required for next Friday was going to be. But, lucky you, for you there *is* no next Friday! Where you'll all be by then, since classes end on Tuesday, I neither know nor care. Me, I'll be up on the North Fork, wearing a really beat-up straw hat and helping an old friend prune her grapevines — not that any of *you* will care. What you *will* care about, of course, are your final grades."

A great stillness settled over the classroom, broken only by the sighing of cool air from the vent. Mr. Mack turned toward his desk, flipped his briefcase up onto it, and opened it. "These exams," he said, "as you know, are sixty percent of your final grade. As usual, there'll probably be questions and comments from some of your parents." Mr. Mack drew himself up as tall as was possible for him: maybe five feet two. "But you, and they, should know by now that there aren't going to be any changes. Whatever you've got, you've brought on yourselves. So, those of you who have recourse to inhalers, get them out now ..."

He brought out a pile of papers, stapled together in six-sheet bundles, and started to work his way up and down the aisles, starting from the leftmost row. Kit sat there with his palms sweating, grateful that at least Mr. Mack wasn't one of those sadists who called you up to the desk in front of everybody to get the bad news.

In the first row, subdued mutters of "Yes!" or "Oh, no ..." were already going up. A couple of seats behind Kit and to the left, his buddy Raoul Eschemel-ing got his paper and looked at the back page, where Mr. Mack usually wrote the grade. Then he raised his eyebrows at Kit, grinned at him, at the same time making an "OK, not bad ...!" gesture with one hand.

Kit swallowed as Mr. Mack came to his row, gave Gracie Mackintosh her paper, gave Tim Walenczak, in front of Kit, his ... and then glanced down at Kit, shook his head slightly, and walked on by. "I'll see you after class," Mr. Mack said.

The sweat all over Kit went cold in a flash. Some kids in the class broke out in either a low moan of "*Uh*-oh ..." or some really nasty laughs that were badly smothered, on purpose. Kit went hot again at the laughter. There were some junior boys and a senior in here who resented being tracked into this class with the smart younger kids; these guys were constantly ragging Kit about his grades being too good. *As if something like that's possible where my folks are concerned!* Kit thought. But nonetheless, he could just hear them: *He's a geek, just a nerd, it comes naturally, he can't help it . . .* Or else: *teacher's pet, little brown-noser, who knows what he's doing to Mack to get grades like this . . .* They were just the normal jeers that Kit had long ago learned to expect, and it didn't take mind reading or any other kind of wizardry to hear them going through those kids' brains right now.

Kit could do nothing now but sit there as students all around him got their papers while his own desk remained terrifyingly empty. *Oh, no. Oh, no. What's going on . . . ? What have I done now . . . ?* And the tragedy was that he had no idea. He racked his brain for anything that made any kind of sense, as the last papers in the right-hand row went out.

Mr. Mack made his way back to his desk. "Not a brilliant result, all told," Mr. Mack said as he closed his briefcase and put it aside. "Workmanlike, in many cases. Dull, in a lot of others. You people need to get it through your heads that spitting a teacher's exact words back at him in an essay, or adding material that's plainly been plagiarized from encyclopedias and online sources, won't cut it . . . with me, or the much tougher teachers to follow. None of your results exactly shone, and none of your results were utter disasters . . . with a very few exceptions."

The silence was nearly as profound as the one that had leaned in around Kit earlier, but this one was more unnerving. Kit felt eyes all around the room resting on him in scared or amused conjecture.

He looked over his shoulder. Raoul hunched his tall, blond, gangly self down against his desk and rolled his eyes at the others' reaction. The look he threw Kit was sympathetic: Raoul, too, had had a grade slump earlier in the year, and his own dad and mom had taken turns tearing strips off him about it ever since, invoking not getting into college and "a ruined résumé" and other dire threats if he didn't shape up. Ever since, he and Kit had been studying together, and they'd both thought they had the course material down pat. *Well, one of us did, anyway . . .*

Mr. Mack glanced at the clock. It suddenly said two forty-three, and now Kit found himself wishing desperately that time would slow down again. "Well," Mr. Mack said, "I'm sure you're all thinking we've all seen enough of each other for one year. For the moment, I'm inclined to agree with you. So all of you just get yourselves the heck out of here!"

This invitation was immediately followed by a muted cheer and the concerted shriek of chairs being pushed back as the bell went. Everybody who hadn't already leapt to his feet did so now and plunged toward the door: the classroom emptied as if it had been turned upside down and shaken. Kit stood there and watched everyone go . . . then finished stuffing his manual and other books into his book bag and went up to Mr. Mack's desk.

"Well," Mr. Mack said, glancing up from Kit's notebook. "Any thoughts?"

This gambit was one of the Mack's favorite ways to get a student to say something dumb, allowing him scope to verbally torture the unfortunate victim for many minutes thereafter. Kit was determined not to let this happen. "Okay, I shouldn't have been drawing," he said. "I should have been paying attention."

Mr. Mack put his eyebrows up as if resigned at so quick a surrender. Kit had seen this maneuver, too, and what came of it: he refused to rise to the bait. For a few moments there was silence as each of them concentrated on outwaiting the other.

Then Mr. Mack glanced at the notebook. "It's a thoat, isn't it," he said.

Kit followed his glance, surprised. "Uh, yeah."

"Not a lot of people still read those books," Mr. Mack said. "Burroughs's style has to seem antiquated these days. But you can't fault his imagination." He looked down at Kit's sketch of what had to be a very large creature, to gauge by the scale of the humanoid being standing next to it. "What made him decide to put so many legs on these things, I can't imagine. I could never assemble a clear picture of a thoat in my head no matter how I tried."

"If you sort of divide the legs into two sets —" Kit said.

"Six and two, huh?" Mr. Mack said, studying the drawing. "With the six in the back grouped for better traction? You may have a point." Mr. Mack glanced up at him again. "But it's possibly still an effort that might better have been saved for your art class."

"Uh, yeah . . ."

He glanced across the page. "And that would be the calot, I guess. Another nice solution for the multiple legs. Nice tusks, too. You wouldn't want to get on the bad side of that thing. And as for *her* . . ." Mr. Mack said, glancing down at the sketch again with a critical eye. "Well, you've put more clothes on her than Burroughs did. This rendition owes more to Victoria's Secret than the descriptions in the original . . . so let's let the inappropriateness issue ride for the moment."

Kit blushed fiercely. "Now about your test," Mr. Mack said. "You and Mr. Eschemeling have been working together. Pretty hard, I believe. So I was curious about . . . let's call it a discrepancy in your performance on the final."

What have I done to deserve this? Kit thought in despair. *I worked so hard! I really studied for this, it should have been all right, I should at* least *have passed —*

"Especially since there's nothing wrong with your ability to discuss the material, even in front of your admittedly unsympathetic classmates," Mr. Mack said. "That was a nice touch, by the way — that bit about being able to see the border from space. I saw that picture myself, some months back. It brings you up short."

Kit didn't feel inclined to mention that he hadn't seen the image as a picture: the difference was clearly visible from the surface of the Moon when the weather on Earth was right. "The light on one side, and the darkness on the other . . ." Mr. Mack said. "A striking image. Too bad things aren't usually quite so simple, especially over there. Anyway, no question that your work's improved the last couple of months. You've been trying a whole lot harder than you were before."

And this was true . . . which was why Kit couldn't understand why he was standing here alone without a test paper in his hand. *Mama's going to go so ballistic with me, we'll be able to use her to launch satellites! I can't* believe *I* —

"The problem might lie in the way your concentration comes and goes without warning, kind of like it did just then," Mr. Mack said. "But we'll chalk that up to end-of-term antsies, huh?" Then he grinned — an expression that Kit had rarely seen on Mr. Mack's face before. Kit didn't know if this was cause for alarm, but he was alarmed enough already. "Now, then —"

Mr. Mack popped his briefcase open and pulled out one last test paper. Kit instantly recognized his own handwriting on it.

"I thought I'd spare you the embarrassment of dealing with this in front of the class . . ." Mr. Mack said softly. "Don't think I haven't noticed that some of our older participants have issues."

If Kit thought he'd been sweating before, he now found that his pores had been holding out on him. Mr. Mack looked at him with a thoughtful expression. "And so," he said, "I didn't really want to give them a chance to make your life uncomfortable all summer because of" — he held up the test paper — "this."

Kit gulped and reached for the paper, shaking slightly. At the bottom of the front page, circled, was a number: 99%.

Kit's eyes went wide. "Ninety-nine?" he said. "*Ninety-nine!*"

"Best mark in the class," Mr. Mack said. "Congratulations."

Then it hit Kit. "Ninety-nine??" he said, flipping the pages to look at them one after another. "*Why not a hundred!?*"

Mr. Mack looked at his watch. "Possibly one of the shortest bursts of gratitude on record," he said. "Kit, I had no choice. You misspelled 'Pyongyang.'"

Kit was so torn between relief and completely unreasonable disappointment that all he could do was say "Oh."

"One 'o,' one 'a,'" Mr. Mack said. "I checked. Sorry about that. But your essay was terrific. Best I've seen in a long while. You're showing at least a few of the warning signs of falling in love with history."

Kit said nothing, partly from embarrassment at being praised, and partly because he suspected Mr. Mack was right, and he didn't know what to make of that.

"So you can tell your mother, who I know was giving you grief," Mr. Mack said, "that whatever else you've done in your other subjects this spring, you've passed history with flying colors, and I'm really pleased with you. She should be, too. Tell her to get in touch if she wants any more details."

"She will," Kit said.

Mr. Mack smiled slightly. "So did mine," he said. "Mothers . . . Go on, get out of here. Enjoy your summer."

Kit stuffed the paper hurriedly into his book bag and shouldered it. Mr. Mack closed his briefcase with the air of a man shutting a whole year into it, and good riddance. Then he glanced up. "Unless there was something else? Of course there was."

Kit gave up any hope of ever being able to put anything over this particular teacher. "Yeah. Uh — *How do you not sweat like that?*"

Mr. Mack looked briefly surprised, and then laughed out loud. "The phrasing's unusual," Mr. Mack said. "I take it you mean, how do I not sweat? And the answer is, I *don't* not sweat."

Kit raised his eyebrows.

"But I *do* waterproof the insides of my clothes," Mr. Mack said.

Kit stared at him. Mr. Mack laughed again, then, the sound of a sneaky magician giving away the secret to a really good trick. "It's a Marine thing," Mr. Mack said. "We used to do it on parade. We spray our shirts with that anti-stain waterproofing stuff you use on upholstery. It's good for giving other people the impression that you're not quite human."

His voice as he said this was so dry that Kit burst out laughing. But a moment later he stopped. "You were in the Marines?" Kit said, and found himself looking at Mr. Mack with entirely new eyes. This little guy, just barely taller than Kit's mama, with his bald head and his red tie with little blue galloping ponies on it, a different tie every day — *"Korea?"*

Mr. Mack shook his head. "Oh, no," he said. "A lot of other places. But Korea was well before my time."

Kit looked at him; this time it was his turn to look thoughtful. "The way you talked about it, though. The dark, the light —"

Mr. Mack shook his head. "If a historian needs anything," he said, "it's an imagination. The dates, the place names, the battles . . . they're not what's most important. What matters is thinking yourself into those people's heads. Imagine how the world looked to them — their sky, their sea. Their tools. Their houses. Their troubles. That's how what they did starts to make sense. Along with what we do in the same situations . . ."

He paused, looking surprised at himself. "Sorry. It's a passion," Mr. Mack said. "But I can recognize the signs in someone else. Watch out: it'll eat you alive. Other lives, other minds . . . there's no getting enough of them." He gave Kit a cockeyed look. "Why are you still here? Go away before I give you a quiz."

Kit grinned and left with as much dignity as he could manage. The dignity broke down about three yards down the hall, as he caught sight of Raoul, trying to look like he was leaning casually against a locker, waiting for Kit. Kit didn't know whether to try to look cool or to scream out loud. Screaming won. He pulled the paper out again, waved it in Raoul's face.

Raoul snatched it out of Kit's hand. "Do you believe this, Pirate?" Kit yelled. *"Do you believe this?!"*

They started jumping up and down together like the acrobatically insane. "Ninety-nine! Ninety-nine!" Raoul promptly turned it into something like a sports chant. *"Nine-ty-nine! Nine-ty-nine!"*

People wandering down the hall that crossed this one stared at them, vaguely interested by the actions of the certifiably mad — meaning anyone who would still willingly be in the building after the end of the last period. "But what did *you* get?" Kit said as they headed toward the doors at the end of the hall.

"Eighty," Raoul said.

Kit suddenly felt bizarrely disappointed. "How'd *that* happen?"

"I messed up the essay," Raoul said. "But I did okay on everything else. It's not a bad grade. My mom'll get off my case now."

"Mine, too," Kit said, "I hope. But wow . . . what a relief. I thought I was dead!"

"*I* thought you were dead!" Raoul laughed that crazed laugh of his as they went down the hall to the paired doors that led to the parking lot. They each hit one door and burst out into the hot, humid summer air, laughing.

"This day could not *possibly* get any better," Kit said.

"Oh, come on," Raoul said, "stretch your brains. Anything could happen . . ."

They saw Raoul's mom's slightly beat-up red station wagon come swinging in through the parking lot gates. "So listen," Raoul said, "my dad says we're having a big barbecue party next week, for his birthday. Next Thursday. You and your folks and your sister, you're all invited. Can you make it?"

"I'll find out."

"Okay," Raoul said, as his own mom pulled up. "Text me later!"

Kit nodded, waving at Raoul's little blond mom as he got into the car. The first thing Raoul did was fish around in his pack and show his mom the test paper: she grinned, and Raoul flashed a grin of his own at Kit as his mom drove away.

Kit let out a long breath as he glanced down at his own paper one more time, then put it away. His nerves were finally settling down, which was a good thing, as he was also still tired from doing that spell. He wasn't so tired, though, that he wasn't going to immediately call the wizard with whom he worked most closely and do a little gloating.

He pulled his wizard's manual out of his backpack, flipping it open to the rearmost pages, the messaging area. Some pages were covered with stored messages, all seemingly printed in the graceful curvilinear characters of the wizardly Speech; but any one Kit touched with a finger would seem to rise up out of the page, the writing increasing in size for easier reading. He flipped through the back pages until he found one that was blank, ready to take a message — and then stopped. In the middle of a page that had been blank earlier in the afternoon was a single line of text, and it was glowing fiercely blue and pulsing alternately brighter and fainter — the sign of a message that had just come in and hadn't yet been read.

Kit peered at it. There was nothing there but a time stamp — JD 2454274.123287 — and these words:

We've found the bottle. Meeting this afternoon. M.

The breath went right out of Kit.

Holy cow . . . Raoul was right!!

"*Yes!*" Kit shouted. He slapped the manual shut, shoved it back in the book bag, and jumped up and punched the air some more. And then, because right in front of the school would have been a bad place to do a teleport, he ran off across the parking lot, grinning, to find a more private spot.

Gili Motang

NITA CALLAHAN SAT on the flat, warm stones at the edge of the koi pond, her eyes closed, looking for something.

After a moment, she saw it. *Shadow,* she thought. *A shadow across the Sun. Just for a few seconds.*

But when?

She waited: and then she knew.

"Now," she said, and opened her eyes.

The water rippled at her in the summer breeze, the surface of it dazzling in the bright and uninterrupted sunlight. Nita winced.

"Oh, come on," she said under her breath. "Come *on!*" She looked up at the sky overhead. It remained stubbornly clear.

"That won't help," said a small voice from the water.

She frowned and refused to answer. Above and beyond the trees that surrounded Tom Swale's yard, very slowly, a single little puffy cloud could be seen cruising toward the low, late-afternoon Sun. It seemed to be in no hurry. If clouds had feet, it would have been dragging them.

Nita scowled harder. *Hurry up!* she thought in the Speech. *Come on, get a move on!*

But merely thinking something in the Speech doesn't turn the idea into a spell . . . especially since wizardry is mostly about persuading creatures and things to do what you want, not ordering them around. The cloud actually seemed to slow up. Then, finally, almost reluctantly, it started to pass in front of the sun.

Nita grinned. "Awright!" she said, looking down into the fishpond. "That's the best one yet! I only missed it by half a minute."

One of the koi, the one with the silver-coin scales, looked up out of the pond at her. "Fifty seconds," Doitsu said.

"Or about fifty-five seconds too long," said another voice, a human one, from behind her. "Doesn't count. Try it again."

Nita let out an annoyed breath and turned. "You guys are just being mean!"

"An oracular who predicts the future a minute late is possibly even less effective than one who gets it wrong all the time," Tom said, straightening up with a groan from the flower bed where he'd been working. "And will probably get a lot more frustrated."

"Hey, thanks loads," Nita said, and slumped against the fishpond's rockwork.

"You'd hardly expect me to start lying to you at this late date," Tom said, amused.

Nita gave him an annoyed look. "Let's see *you* do any better!"

"Me? Why should I?" Tom said, frowning down at the next flower bed. "This is *your* gift we're trying to sharpen up."

"And, anyway, it's too hot!"

"True," Tom said, "but nothing to do with the business at hand. Come on . . . give it another try."

Nita wiped her forehead; she was sweating. "It's no use," she said. "I need a break."

Another koi, a marmalade-colored one, put its head up out of the water. "You need to concentrate harder," said Akagane. "You can't be in that moment unless you're in *this* one."

"Blank your mind out first," said Doitsu.

A third head came up, splotched in red and black on silver-white. "Pay more attention to the news," said Showa.

Nita rolled her eyes. "None of you are helping!"

"It's not help you need," Tom Swale said. "It's practice. You think anybody learns to see futurity overnight?"

"Forget the future," Nita said. "I can barely see the present!" She leaned back against the rocks behind the koi pond, rubbing her eyes: beams from the low sun piercing through the trees were glancing off the pond's surface, and the glitter of them made her eyes water.

"The news'll help with that, too," Tom said. He

was sweating; even in a T-shirt, the humidity that day was enough to make anybody miserable.

"And it's not *the* future," said Showa, back-finning toward where the rocks overhanging the pond made a small waterfall. "*A* future."

Nita sighed. "But how can you tell you've got the right one?"

"You can't," said Akagane as she rose to the surface in Showa's wake. "At least, you can't tell for sure, or very clearly."

"You can get a feeling," said Doitsu, just hanging there in the water and fanning his fins. "Or a hunch."

"But what if you're wrong?"

Doitsu made a kind of shrug with his fins. "You try again. Assuming you haven't blown up the world or something in the meantime . . ." And he submerged.

The other two koi sank down into the water as well. Nita sighed and leaned back, watching Tom as he walked over to another of the plant beds, squatted down beside it, and then let out a long, annoyed breath. He reached down in among some of the plants, pushed broad green leaves aside, and sighed. "Guys," Tom said in the Speech, "how many times do we have to have this conversation?" He picked something up, looked at it. It was a slug. He shook his head and tossed it off to one side, into another leafy bed. "Those are *your* strawberries" — *fling* — "over *there!* These are *my* strawberries" — *fling* — "over *here!*"

Nita gave him a crooked smile. "That can't be real good for them . . ."

"Slugs are resilient," Tom said.

Nita watched another one fly through the air. "Yeah. I see how they bounce . . ."

"Do I hear a criticism coming?"

Nita restrained herself, but wasn't quite ready to stop teasing Tom yet. "Isn't it weird that a Senior Wizard can talk the sky into hitting things with lightning but can't talk a bunch of slugs out of eating his strawberries?"

Tom sighed. "Lightning's a lot easier to talk to than slugs," he said. "Not that you're so much talking to the slug as to its DNA . . . which has been the way it is for about a hundred million years. Strawberries are a relatively recent development, to a slug. But then, so are human beings . . ." He grinned then. "Anyway, I live in hope that they'll get it eventually. But enough of you being on my case. Or just you. Kit's running late. Where's he gotten to?"

Nita rolled her eyes. "That'd be the question, the last couple weeks."

Tom glanced up. "He's missing Ponch, huh?"

Nita shrugged, not sure how to describe what was going on. Kit's dog had been getting increasingly strange for a long time, but last month he had gone way beyond strange, right out of life and into something far greater. Kit wasn't exactly sad about what had happened, but he was definitely sad at not having his dog around anymore. "It's complicated," Nita said. "I don't think it's just about Ponch. But he's been away from home a lot . . ."

Tom straightened up again and gave Nita a look that was slightly concerned. "A lot of that going around right now . . ."

Nita sighed. "Tell me about it. But his sister Helena's coming home from college in a couple of weeks. *That* has to be on his mind. And then there's Carmela. He's having trouble dealing with her lately."

Tom pulled off his gardening gloves and tossed them up into the air: they vanished. "Yeah, well," he said. "First time off the planet, and what does she do but stride out into the universe like she owns the place and blow up the Lone Power. I could see where that might make Kit feel a little surplus." Tom strolled back to her, his hands in his pockets. "Does Carmela seem any different?"

"No. Or yes," Nita said. "But that might just be because of her PSAT scores."

Tom put his eyebrows up. "Worse than expected?"

"Better," Nita said. "It's screwed up her college plans. She thought she was going to take it easy and go to the community college in Garden City. Now all of a sudden her pop and mama and her guidance counselor are giving her all this stuff about CalTech and Harvard . . ."

Tom gave Nita a wry look. "Interesting problem. But otherwise it sounds like you're telling me that, though her PSATs might be an issue, shooting up a major interstellar transport center and being dragged halfway across the known Universe hasn't particularly cramped her style."

"No. And that's what has me worried. Tom," Nita said, "tell me she's not turning into a wizard!"

He laughed one big laugh. "Would it break your heart if she was?"

"Mine? Not really. *Kit's?* That's another story."

"Not that I could do anything one way or the other," Tom said, "if the Powers offered her the Oath and she accepted it. It'd be out of our hands. But wouldn't you think it's kind of late for her to become a wizard? You know how it goes. Onset in humans is usually between twelve and fourteen . . ."

"Except for people like Dairine," Nita muttered.

"Yes, well," Tom said, straightening up with a groan and massaging the small of his back, "your sister's the exception to most of the rules I know. How's *she* coping, by the way?"

Nita shook her head. "I don't know. It's hard to work out what's going on with her sometimes. All she'll say is that she's looking for Roshaun."

Tom nodded, heading for the French doors at the back of the house. Nita got up from the edge of the pond and followed him in. "What's your take on that?" Tom said.

Nita shook her head as she stepped into the relative cool of the living room. *That he vanished in a cloud of moondust while he was doing a wizardry that had one end stuck in the core of the Sun, and he's probably dead, and my sister's in denial?* she thought, but refused to say out loud. On the kitchen table, Tom's version of the wizard's manual was stacked up several volumes high. "What's it say about him in *there*?" Nita said.

Tom put up his eyebrows. "You haven't looked in your own manual?" he said.

"Well . . ."

"Scared to?"

Nita gave him a look. She had of course been scared to. Finding out the truth would have forced her into a position where she would have had to start working out what to do about Dairine.

Tom shook his head. "You know," he said, going over to the sink to wash his hands, "if I looked in there for an answer, and then told you what I was shown, it *might* not be data that from your point of view would necessarily be definitive. Or even useful. Has that occurred to you?"

"No," Nita said.

"Well," Tom said, "when you do get around to looking, tell me what you see."

Nita rolled her eyes, as she'd been hoping to get Tom to do the scary thing for her: she'd had more than enough of being scared in the last month or so. *Great. Now I get to go back to being just too chicken to look* . . . "And by the way," Tom said, turning off the faucet and reaching for a dish towel hanging over the door of the cupboard under the sink, "you're blinking."

"Huh?" Nita said, and then glanced to her right. "Oh, yeah —"

There in midair beside her, a little pinpoint of blue light like a star was flashing on and off. "I really should hook up a sound to this," Nita said, reaching out to the little light and pulling it straight down in the air. "I did this wizardry the other morning real early, and I didn't want to wake anybody up while I was testing it . . ."

A vertical slit of darkness opened in the air, exposing the inside of the otherspace pocket in which Nita kept her wizard's manual and various other useful objects while she was out and about. She reached into the darkness, felt around for a moment, and then came out with her manual.

Nita started paging through it while Tom opened the fridge and rummaged around. "Message?" he said, coming out with a couple of cans of cola.

"Yeah. Uh, got any fizzy water in there?"

"Sure. Thought you were the big cola fan, though . . ."

"I'm off the sugar for a while."

"Don't tell me," Tom said, coming out with a bottle of mineral water, "that you're starting to worry about your weight! *Completely* inappropriate for you at your age —"

"Huh? Oh, no, no, it's just that I keep getting these . . . Never mind." Nita trailed off, partly on purpose, as she flipped the manual open to the back pages where the messaging wizardries and messages were stored — no way she was going to get into acne-and-body-image issues right now with a wizard of a completely different sex, seniority, and order of importance. On the rearmost page of the manual, one block of text was alternately glowing dark and fading. Nita peered at it. Then she snickered.

"Kit's getting ready to go to Mars," she said,

putting down the manual for a moment and opening the mineral water to take a swig. "What a surprise!"

Tom chuckled as he popped open his can of cola. "Kind of the flavor of the month with him, isn't it . . . ?"

"More like the flavor of the year." Nita read down the message and tapped the reference link at the bottom of it: another message, the one that had caused Kit to send her the first, appeared in the first one's place. "He's got Mars posters up in his room, and little Mars crawlers on his desk, and half the Mars books in the school library *aren't* there: they're stacked up on his bed . . ." She grinned. "Hey, this is great. Mamvish got in just now! We've been talking to her a lot by manual this last year, but we've never seen her in person. Kit's gonna be buzzed to meet her finally."

Nita shut her manual and put it away in the otherspace pocket again, "zipping up" the little blue light to close it again. She pinched the light; it went out. "Which is probably why he ran straight over to Gili Motang without waiting for me . . ."

Tom smiled at Nita's annoyed expression. "Well, maybe it's understandable," he said. "Mamvish is heavily in demand all over this side of the galaxy: normally we don't get to see so senior a wizard out this way unless it's something to do with worldgates. If the Powers' own Species Archivist has come out to our neighborhood in person to check up on something, that's definitely a hot topic. So if Kit wants to go do the fanboy thing, well, so will half the other wizards on the planet." Tom paused. "And now that I think of it . . ." He got up and went back to the fridge.

Puzzled, Nita watched Tom open it again and start rooting around. "I guess there really *are* no accidents," he said, coming out with a very large plastic bag full of tomatoes. Tom shut the fridge and handed the bag to Nita.

She looked at the bag, and then at Tom again. Tom grinned at her. "When you catch up with Kit," he said, "make sure you take that with you. It's been so hot so early this year, the backyard's getting overrun with these." He sighed. "And in another week it'll be the zucchini. I've really got to check in with the global warming intervention group . . ."

"*Tomatoes??*" Nita said. "What kind of spell uses tomatoes?"

"And tell Mamvish we send our best," Tom said. "I'd love to go see her myself, but I have to get back to work. Carl and I and all the other Seniors are still hip-deep in the on-planet cleanup from last month's business."

"I feel for you," Nita said, not entirely sincerely. "Tom, there are a ton of these! My arms are breaking!"

Tom just laughed. "So levitate them."

The spell to make them float would have cost as much energy as just carrying them, or more. Nita just gave Tom an annoyed look, boosted the overstuffed bag up from the bottom, and shifted it to her other arm. Tom picked up his cola again and went over to the table, gesturing at the stack of manuals. Several of them picked themselves up off one in the middle of the stack: Tom pulled it out, and the others settled back onto the stack once more.

"Obviously our manuals will update with a précis of what you all decide to do about whatever she's here for," Tom said, sitting down. "Especially since Mamvish won't have come all this way just for fun. But do me a favor and drop me a note to fill in any details you think we should know about."

"Okay," Nita said, and shifted the bag to the other arm again. Tom was already paging through his own manual, wearing a distracted look . . . which frankly didn't surprise Nita, considering what all the wizards on the planet had been through of late. *So why hang around and pester him? Let's go find out what the tomatoes are good for.*

She hefted the bag again to resettle it over her hip, then wandered out of the house and over to the fish-pond again, peering in. One of the koi came drifting up to the surface: it was Doitsu. "Hey," Nita said. "I forgot to ask you:

"Wha'd you think of the mealworms?
Did they satisfy
That deep-down desire for 'yum'?"

Doitsu gave her a look and just hung there in the water, fanning his fins and saying nothing.

"Okay," Nita said. "See if I go out of my way to bring *you* stuff from the bait shop again."

Doitsu eyed Nita from under the water. "The

mealworms were lovely," he said. "But your scansion's execrable. 'Wha'd'?"

Nita rolled her eyes. "I'm just getting the hang of this! Cut me some slack."

"When you can construct a haiku without apostrophes, sure," Doitsu said. "And not a moment sooner. If you're going to be an oracular, you've got standards to maintain. So get out there and make me *not* want to spit in your eye." And he vanished down into the water again.

Nita shifted the bag of tomatoes to the other arm. "I'm getting trash-talked by *fish*," she said under her breath. "Something's wrong with this picture." She sighed and took the flagstone path around the side of the house, heading for home.

It wasn't too long a walk, which was a good thing: though she kept shifting the tomato bag from hand to hand, both her arms were still killing her by the time she got close to her house. As Nita came down the sidewalk in the early sunset light, she looked at her front yard — all covered with ground ivy, and with the single big maple tree standing up out of the middle of it, shading everything — and thought, *Why does it look so little these days? And the house, too.* It was a standard enough bungalow for this neighborhood — white-shingled, black-roofed, two stories, with the attic partly converted — but lately it had seemed much smaller than it had this time last year. As Nita walked up the driveway, the memory of the vast main concourse of the Crossings Intercontinual Worldgating Facility came back to her unbidden, illuminated with its strange sourceless night lighting, its tremendously high roof-sky seemingly absent and the whole con-course open to the huge, pulsating, many-colored stars of its home planet's neighborhood. *After you'd been there as much as I have this last month, anything'd look small,* Nita thought. *That place has got to be the size of New Jersey. Well, Rhode Island, anyway . . .*

She went up the stairs to the back door, expecting to have to let herself in: but the inside door was open. Nita opened the screen door, braced it behind her so it wouldn't slam, and dumped the bagged tomatoes on the drainer by the sink as she went through the kitchen. "Daddy?"

"He had to go back to the shop for something," came a voice from inside, and Nita grinned then, because it wasn't her sister's voice coming from the living room but someone else's entirely. "He'll be back in an hour, he said."

Nita went through the dining room into the liv-ing room. There Kit's older sister Carmela was sitting on the floor amid a heap of cushions and a scatter of TV remotes. Nita looked at the remotes in bemuse-ment: she couldn't remember their TV as having quite *that* many. There was the VCR remote, sure, and the one for the TV, and the —

"Ohaiyo gozaimas'!" the TV yelled at her as she entered.

Nita stopped still. *Oh, no . . .* she thought. "'Mela," she said, "you didn't —"

"I brought our remote over," Carmela said, and stretched her fluffy-sweatered self out among the cushions, toying with her single long dark braid. "Dairine said it might be smart to train your TV to get the alien cable channels, the way Kit did with ours. This is bargain-shopping season, after all! And we don't want to freak out the visitors at home . . ."

Nita perched briefly on the arm of her dad's easy chair behind Carmela and looked at the TV. It wasn't nearly as fancy or new a model as Kit's new entertainment-center TV was, but all the same it was showing a channel-listing page as sleek and modern as anything Kit's set could boast. And as Carmela punched the "scroll" button, the online guide shifted through page after page after page of channels that didn't exist anywhere on *this* planet. The entries on the scrolling pages were all in the curving, curling characters of the wizardly Speech, which many worlds used as a common language of discourse. "Wait a minute," Nita said. "*What* visitors?"

"Ooh," Carmela said, "you mean you haven't heard? Guess who's coming home from college!"

"No, I did hear," Nita said, easing herself down off the easy chair to flop down among the cushions, "but I thought that wasn't till July . . ."

Carmela shook her head until her braid flopped around. She punched the remote, which immediately changed the TV Guide channel to one of the many thousands of alien shopping channels available to users of GalacTrans or whatever other unearthly "cable" provider Carmela had hooked them into. "Nope," she said, watching absently as some alien being apparently made entirely of wreathing chartreuse smoke did its best to demonstrate the virtues of what Nita thought was some kind of household appliance, maybe a food processor. It picked up one indecipherable "accessory" after another with tendrils of green smoke, waving them around. "That whole thing blew up," Carmela said, leaning back and briefly looking at Nita upside down. "Helena had a fight with her boyfriend, so no Paris for *them!* She's already cashed in the plane tickets. She's going to come back next week and stay here until her college choir's trip to Romania or wherever they're going . . ."

"Slovenia, Kit said," Nita said.

"Whatever. At least she'll have fun with the vampires!"

Nita shook her head. "No vampires," she said. "Some undead, yeah, and some confused Goth wannabes. But there haven't been real turn-into-a-bat-and-flap-around vampires since 1652."

"Really? What happened in 1652?"

"Some other time, okay?" Nita said, increasingly distracted by the chartreuse-smoke creature, which was now pouring itself rapidly into what looked like the container of the food processor and pulling a lid down over it. A second later, a tentacle of green smoke came curling out of the container and punched one of the buttons on the processor's front. The tendril was abruptly sucked back into the main mass of the creature as many peculiar things started happening inside the container at that point, including small lights flashing like sparks inside an outraged microwave. "So when's Helena's trip?"

"August the first," Carmela said, shaking her head. "Gonna be tough at home till then, Neets." She raised her eyebrows, looking at Nita out of the corner of her eye. "*I* know," Carmela said. "Let's do a road trip. Let's go over to Ireland and see your buddy Ronan!"

Nita rolled her eyes. "He is *not* my buddy!"

"Yeah, and isn't it wonderful," Carmela said. Her real intentions, Nita thought, couldn't possibly be as predatory as her smile made them appear. *I hope!* "But isn't it August when everything gets crazy in Ireland? It did last time . . ."

"Believe me," Nita said, "what happened then is *not* a regularly scheduled event." She sat there for a moment more watching the TV, where the "blender" seemed to have stopped — at least the flashing and smoking going on inside it had. The mist creature came out, not yellow-green now, but pink, and waved its tendrils around: a long line of number-characters in the Speech, probably the "food processor's" details, started flashing on the screen. Nita shook her head. "I came in late," she said. "What's this about?"

"It's a portable wanjaxer," Carmela said. "On sale, it looks like. Which is all right, except I don't know if I really want to get into wanjaxing. I mean, I'm as broad-minded and tolerant as the next girl, but there are all these *color* issues . . ."

Nita rolled her eyes. Carmela had been spending a lot of time lately studying alien lifestyles, and her attempts to explain some of the finer points could take hours. "Forget it," Nita said. "You see Kit before he left?"

Carmela looked at Nita in shock. "*You* didn't? You mean he just ditched you and ran off halfway around the world?" Carmela paused. "*Is* it halfway?"

Nita frowned, considering. "I'd have to look it up. How'd you know where he went?"

"The remote told me," Carmela said. "It loves Kit, but it's no good at keeping a secret. Are you, cutie-bunny?"

She reached down to the remote on the cushion beside her and tickled it under its infrared emitter. Nita was startled to see it arch its little "back" and emit a small electronic purr. She thought back to her conversation with Tom, and then put aside the thought that Kit's original specialty had been getting inanimate objects and mechanical things to do what he wanted. And now Carmela... *Naah, it's probably still just something to do with Ponch. Everything here got really strange because he was getting really strange. It'll take a while for things to calm down...*

"Anyway," Carmela said, "he's kinda forgetting his manners, if you ask me." She leaned back among the cushions. "You two've been working on this Mars thing for months and months now."

"Well," Nita said, "it's really been more him. Not that I'm not interested. But I have stuff of my own to take care of." She stretched her legs out.

"Yeah," Carmela said, "I've noticed. And not your water-based project that you've been so sneaky about, either. Oh, yeah, I noticed ... don't give me that look. All those magic conference calls all of a sudden with you and Miss Thunder-Fins the Humpback!

But this is how many times now that you were 'too busy' to come shopping with me? Three? Four? And you looked cranky, not happy like when you've been working with S'reee."

Nita looked briefly morose. "Dairine . . ." she said. "She's been out a lot lately, and my dad's been giving me grief about keeping tabs on her. Suddenly I'm supposed to be my sister's keeper."

"You'll need a whip and a chair for that," Carmela said.

Nita made a face, since this was true. "How much did Kit tell you about the Mars thing?"

Carmela rolled her eyes most expressively. "Nothing, as usual. He's started acting like he owns all the wizardy stuff in the world, Neets! You'd think there wasn't enough to go around."

Nita laughed, maybe just a little evilly. "Don't think that could have anything to do with *you*, could it?"

"Me?" Carmela actually batted her eyelashes. "However could that be? He's just jealous because *he* never got a chance to blow up a worldgating facility. First Dairine, now me — he's just feeling like he's missed an opportunity."

Nita grinned, for that thought had crossed her mind. "Come on," she said, getting up. "I need to change."

She headed up the stairs: Carmela came after her. "But anyway," Nita said at the top of the stairs, turning down the hall toward her bedroom, "you know how he keeps going up there."

"Kind of hard to ignore," Carmela said, following Nita into her bedroom and flopping down on her bed while Nita went to her dresser and started pulling open drawers. "He sheds all this red dust all over the place when he comes back. It's all staticky: it gets all over the CDs and the DVDs. They get scratched. And he's always wrecked the next day. He's started using it as an excuse not to do his chores."

"Tell me about it," Nita said, rolling her eyes. She came out with a pair of very worn and faded floppy jeans, and then with a short-sleeved pink cropped top that she held up against her while looking in the mirror.

"Dairine again . . . ?"

"Same problem, different story," Nita said, chucking the pink top back into the drawer: it was the wrong shade to work with what little was left of her spring tan. "Those big transport wizardries really take it out of you unless you can get somebody to help you pay off the energy debt. Anyway, Mars — Kit's not the only one who's had Mars on the brain for a long time." She picked up another top, a white one, and held it up against her.

"Why? Are they going to invade us?" Then Carmela paused for a moment, getting a curious look. "Now that you mention it — who lives there?"

"Nobody," Nita said, shaking her head and dumping the white top back in the drawer. "So isn't it funny that you think somebody there might invade you?"

Carmela looked surprised. "Well, you know how it is. All the movies and old stories and stuff about invaders . . ."

"'From Mars,'" Nita said, looking over her shoulder. "The words almost seem to go together for a lot of Earth people. Weird, huh?"

"I guess," Carmela said. "You mean, it shouldn't be weird?"

Nita shrugged, turning back to the drawer and rummaging through it. "Well, think about it. 'Invaders from Venus'? 'Invaders from Jupiter'? You don't take them seriously. The language itself is giving you some kind of hint." She came upon another top, a light green one, and held it up against her. "And it's not just because Mars is the most Earthlike planet in our solar system, either. There's just something *about* Mars. People have been interested in it for a long time, because of that. So wizards have been interested in it for a long time, too. There are all kinds of things about it that're weird." She picked another top out of the drawer, another pink one, and held it up against her, too. "For one thing, it doesn't have a kernel."

Carmela blinked. "What?"

"A kernel. Everything's supposed to have one. People, things, atoms, planets. It's like, if a body's or a thing's the hardware, the kernel's the software: the rules for how it runs."

Carmela considered this. "So a kernel's kind of like a soul?"

"No. But souls can get hooked up to them. Anyway, a planet's kernel usually just bops around inside the planet, doing its own thing and keeping the gravity and such working right. If there are wizards on the planet, one of the strongest ones gets told to keep an eye on the kernel and make sure it keeps working right." Nita dropped the pink top back in the drawer.

"But there's no people there, you said. So no wizards —"

"Not now," Nita said. She put the green top down on the dresser and shut the drawer. "But once upon a time . . ."

"There *were* people?"

"We don't know," Nita said. "But everybody *feels* like there should have been."

"Whoa!" Carmela said, sounding both amused and skeptical. "Sounds kind of vague for you, Miss Neets. You're usually Hard Science Girl."

"Yeah, well, everybody's vague about this," Nita said, sitting down on her desk chair and pulling off her shoes. "Mysterious stuff, and nothing in the manual to tell us what happened." Then she wrinkled her nose and got up again, opening a different dresser drawer to get at the socks. "But when a species feels the effect of a neighboring planet this strongly, it usually means they've got past history."

"What? Like somebody there invaded us before?"

Nita pulled off her old socks, put on a new pair. "Not necessarily. Maybe they could have . . . or they meant to. But it never happened." Then she grinned, looking up. "Or else it *did* happen . . . and we're all Martians."

Carmela gave Nita a very wide-eyed look. "¿*Que*?"

"There are lots of meteorites from Mars lying

around on Earth," Nita said, getting up and feeling around under her dresser for her favorite beat-up sneakers. "Some people think that life here might have been started by some little bug on a shooting star that survived the ride in through the atmosphere. Splashed down into a nice warm sea ... and then umpty million years later ..." She grinned, gestured around her: her bedroom, her clothes, her teen magazines. "Us ..."

"And what do wizards say about that?" Carmela said.

Nita shook her head. "Jury's out," she said. "The manual doesn't normally tell much about a species' origins until the species has already discovered a lot of the truth itself. Culture-shock issues ..."

"*I* wouldn't be shocked," Carmela said, sitting up and folding her legs under her. "As far as I'm concerned, half the people in school act like Martians already."

Nita snickered, wandering over to the door of her room and chucking the used socks out at the laundry basket in the hall. They bounced off the wall and went in. "But lots of people *would* be bothered," Nita said. "Worldview stuff, religious stuff ... Hey, look, even wizards are only human. We're not all perfect at having both the real *and* the true in our heads at the same time without them blowing each other up! Especially since both the real and the true keep changing all the time." She headed back to the dresser to pick up the jeans and the top she'd decided on. "But some people think that finding the truth for themselves is cooler than just sitting around with what people tell them is true. They think it's okay to find out where you really came from, even if at first it gets you upset."

Carmela sat quiet for a moment. "You know," she said, "if people here found out there really *were* Martians . . ."

Nita bent down for her sneakers. "They'd freak," Nita said, heading for the door. "And they'd do it big. Even if the little probes we've sent there don't find anything bigger than germs, some people will still freak, because they think we're — they're — the most important things in the universe, all the life there is." She snorted.

"Yeah," Carmela said. "Sker'ret would laugh all his legs off at that one."

Nita put her eyebrows up, leaning against the doorsill. "How *is* our favorite centipede?"

"Busy," Carmela said. "The Rirhath B government's still cleaning up the Crossings, and Sker's having himself a party being King of the Alien Worldgates while his Esteemed Ancestor grows in his new legs and claws and brains and things." She grinned. "Sker'ret says he needs me to come help get their shopping mall cleaned up."

"Cleaned *out,* you mean," Nita said. The planetary government of Rirhath B had settled a considerable reward on Carmela for "services rendered" in the liberation of the Crossings Worldgating Facility . . . and Carmela had chosen to take her reward as shopping vouchers. Nita guessed that a whole lot of the Crossings' shopkeepers were rubbing their hands, claws, or tentacles together at the prospect. "*That* trip I'm taking with you, no matter *what* Dairine does . . . But anyway, the freaking's gonna happen eventually, no matter what we do . . . because no matter who goes looking for life, sooner or later they'll find it. And as far as wizards here go, it looks like the Powers That Be have decided that if we're old enough to be asking serious questions about the fourth planet, we're old enough to be told. But only because we didn't just ask and then run away to play. We started going there and digging around."

"How long has this been going on?" Carmela said.

"Since the 1770s . . ."

Carmela banged the side of her head with one hand a couple of times in a my-ears-are-malfunctioning gesture. "Sorry! I thought you said since the Revolutionary War . . ."

"'Melaaaaa . . . !" Nita said, laughing, and headed out of her bedroom, making for the bathroom just down the hall. "There were wizards here then!" She pushed the bathroom door shut enough to change clothes in privacy.

"What, in New York? And they went to *Mars?*"

Nita pulled off her school pants and pulled on the jeans. "There were wizards all over the world, just like now. And sure they went to Mars! Everybody here was all hot on Mars around then, not just wizards. William Herschel started it. It was in all the papers. There were drawings and everything." Nita snickered. "Though most of them were of completely made-up stuff that was never there . . ."

"Okay," Carmela said with a sigh, as Nita sat down on the edge of the tub to put on her sneakers. "I am very weirded out now. Not that this is even slightly unusual, but no one has any pity on *my* mental health . . ."

Nita grinned as she pulled off her old top, for Carmela's mental health was more robust than most people's. She put on the lighter top, bent down to retie one loose sneaker-lace, then straightened and glanced at herself in the mirror. And paused, startled, for there was another figure behind her, looking at her over her shoulder in the mirror: taller, as slender as she was, but extremely pretty, far more so than —

Nita blinked. The other reflection was gone.

Now what the heck was that? Nita thought. *And who has hair that color?* For the long, flowing, waving hair of the person she'd thought she'd seen had been the richest and most vivid sky-blue imaginable.

Nita stared into the mirror for a second more. There was nothing to be seen but her and the black-and-white tiles of the wall on the far side of the bathtub. *I've been watching too much anime,* she thought.

"You fall *in*, in there?" Carmela called.

"No . . ." Nita said, and reached for the mouthwash, looking suspiciously at the mirror. This was one of the unfortunate aspects of changing wizardly specialties . . . assuming that she *was* actually changing one, not just adding something on. Everything got so unsettled: you saw things, heard things, sensed things that at first didn't make any sense. *Later* they did . . . but usually too late to help you sort out whatever the present problem was. Nita took a gulp of mouthwash, rinsed, spat, turned the faucet on to rinse the sink, and looked in that mirror again. Nothing but herself, and the memory, the shadow of a shape, fading already. Sapphire-blue hair, black eyes, profoundly deep. A fierce look: uncompromising, alien.

And afraid . . .

File it away, Nita thought. *Stick it in Nita's Big Book of Odd Oracular Imagery, and have a good long look at it later. Bobo?*

Got it, said the voice she was only slowly getting used to hearing in the back of her head, and even then not every time she spoke to it. There were unnerving, ambivalent silences sometimes when Nita spoke to the peridexis, her own personal "online" version of the wizard's manual. It didn't always answer. Nita wondered if this was because it knew she wasn't entirely happy with it being inside her . . . though she'd been happy enough a month or so ago, when for a little while it was all the evidence of wizardry she'd had left. *And if I don't trust it completely . . . does it trust me? And if not, why not? This is all so bizarre . . .*

"You *did* fall in!" Carmela said from the bedroom.

"*No!*" Nita said, briefly annoyed, and put the cap back on the mouthwash. She smoothed her top down and went out of the bathroom, leaning against her bedroom's doorsill again.

"Come on," Nita said. "I'll show you. Anyway, Kit's over there, and you know you want to go make him crazy . . ."

"It's what I live for!" Carmela said. "Let's go." She stood up and stretched. "What's summer wear for Mars look like?"

"A force field. But that's my problem. Anyway, we have another stop first." She eyed the sweater Carmela was still wearing, a leftover from an unusually cool morning. "Better dump the angora," Nita said, pulling open one more drawer, rummaging again, and coming up with a T-shirt that was too big for her, but about the right size for Carmela. She grinned and waved it like a flag. "You won't need it where we're going."

Carmela gave her a look, got up off the bed, and grabbed the T-shirt out of her hand. She vanished into the bathroom: a few moments later she was back in Nita's room again, though she was still fussing with the T-shirt in a dissatisfied way. "So now what?"

"Just come stand over here by the window." Nita snapped her fingers, and her otherspace pocket popped open in the air beside her. She reached into it and felt around.

Oh, you don't need that . . . said the voice in her head.

Let's just say I like to check my figures, Nita said silently to the peridexis, riffling through the manual. *Besides, I like to be extra certain, because it's Carmela I'm transiting as well as me. Kit would be cranky if I got his sister stuck in the Earth's core.* Then she snickered. *Then again, maybe he wouldn't . . .*

"And what is so funny?" Carmela said. "Besides the way this tent fits?"

"Everybody should have a few floppy shirts," Nita

said. "Don't distract me." She flipped through a few pages and found what she was looking for, the manual's "persona" utility. "What's your birthday again?"

"November sixth," Carmela said, knotting up the T-shirt into a more fashion-conscious configuration above the waist of her jeans. She peered over Nita's shoulder, watching the way the Speech-characters on the manual page shifted and changed as she spoke. "Look at them jump around! Is that analyzing my voice?"

"And your brainwaves, and a lot of other things," Nita said. "It makes a shorthand version of your name in the Speech: that gets pasted into the spell. What was the last book you read?"

"*Gulliver's Travels,*" Carmela said, watching a new layer of characters appear and nest themselves in among the first group, shoving them around in various directions and changing the colors in which they appeared on the page. "The uncensored one. Hey, what do you mean 'shorthand'? Is it safe to put shorthand *anything* in a spell?"

"Safe enough for this," Nita said, watching the Speech-characters knit themselves into a little thorny circlet on the page, bristling with attachment-spurs that would hook into the larger spell. "We're not going out of atmosphere, and less than fifty-eight thousand miles total. Not enough for significant error to build up." Then Nita wrinkled her nose. "Wasn't that kind of gross?"

"What, the book? Come on. I don't know why that parents' group keeps trying to ban it. You'd think school kids had never heard that people pee." Carmela snickered. "Maybe the grownups are just trying to keep word from getting out."

Nita smiled slightly as the diagnostic fitted another level of meaning into the long sentence-acronym it was assembling from the data that came with Carmela's physical presence. All kinds of information about her were being summed up and pulled into the construct: it'd be interesting to analyze it all in detail later on, though some of the information was already giving Nita second thoughts. "Your favorite color is *this* shade of yellow?" Nita said, putting her finger on one part of the Speech construct and pulling that set of characters off to one side, out into the air. She had to wince at the little bead of light that came to life at the tail end of the character chain. It was a particularly eye-watering shade of citrus yellow-green.

"This week, yeah," Carmela said. "Next week, who knows?"

Nita shrugged: at least the routine was picking up its data correctly. "Okay," she said, and let go of the character string: it snapped back into the circlet where it belonged. "Great — we're set. Two seconds . . ."

Nita turned back to the center of the manual. "Gating circles, please?" she said in the Speech. The manual fell open at the place where she stored her transit circles. "Thank you . . ." She reached into the page and pulled one out, an on-Earth transit routine that had her own Speech-name and the transit's starting location, her bedroom, woven into it already. With a flick of her wrist she dropped it to the floor around the spot near the window where the two of them stood. Then Nita turned back to the page where she'd generated Carmela's shorthand name. Carefully she lifted the long string of glowing characters out of the page and dropped it near Carmela, where there was a receptor socket ready to take it in the larger transit circle.

Carmela looked down at it all suspiciously. "Are you sure this is safe?" she said.

Nita gave Carmela an amused look. "*This* from somebody who let a *TV remote* install a worldgate in her bedroom closet? Spare me. And you should really have Sker'ret check that . . . he's the expert." Nita shut the manual, looked at the spell that lay burning on the floor around them, and started to say the words of the Wizard's Knot that would fasten the spell closed and start it going.

You're forgetting something. . . .

Nita's jaw dropped. "Oh, wow, you're right!" she said. "'Mela, wait right here. Don't touch anything!" She jumped over the edge of the spell-circle and ran downstairs.

Nita trotted through the kitchen, shut and locked the back door — something else she'd forgotten — and then picked up the plastic shopping bag of tomatoes from beside the sink. *You're welcome . . .* said the peridexis.

Nita rolled her eyes. "Everybody gives me a hard time," she said, heading back upstairs. "Thanks, Bobo . . ."

In Nita's bedroom, Carmela was standing there with her arms folded and an *I'm-waiting-patiently,-*

what-do-you-mean-*don't-touch-anything?* expression on her face. "Does your invisible friend possibly have a secret identity?" she said. "A *cute* one?"

Nita gave Carmela a look. "You behave," she said, "or I'm going to let your mama and pop know just what they're trying to turn loose on the poor unsuspecting nerdboys of CalTech."

"Please," Carmela said, sounding unusually fervent even for her. "Just do that, and I'll fall at your feet and kiss them forever."

"Yet another image I didn't need," Nita said. She looked down at the transit spell and began, once more, to speak the words in the Speech.

The world always seems to press in all around to hear a spell being spoken. As Nita said the words, and heard the merely audible sounds of the everyday world go quiet under the pressure of that larger regard, she started to become strangely aware of something else: the sense that the spell itself was reacting strangely to something in the circle with her. *The peridexis,* she thought. She'd noticed this before, recently, when heading out for off-planet work — Carmela's presence in the spell merely added an unusual edge to the effect, as the peridexis shifted its presence to adapt to her. As the spell pressed in with more force around them, Nita wondered for the umpteenth time how she was going to get used to having what seemed to be wizardry itself in her head with her. It wasn't all a bad thing: she'd kept a little of the increase in power which all Earth's younger wizards had experienced during the recent crisis, when others had lost theirs much sooner. But she couldn't get rid of the idea that there was something about all this she wasn't understanding yet, and she needed to get to grips with it pretty quick. . . .

The silence leaned in around them, becoming total. Light started fading as well, leaving the two of them, for the long, strange stretch between one breath and the next, marooned in an odd daylight darkness. For that little time, Nita and Carmela were all that seemed to exist: and of the two of them, Carmela seemed much less concerned about it all, standing as casually there in the spell-circle as someone waiting for a bus. Nita turned slightly to read and say the last words of the spell, feeling the world resisting them. It always resisted a little at the end of a gating: no matter how sweetly you persuaded one place to let *you* stop being where you were while *it* stayed the same, the local physicality hung onto you and complained to the last. *What's funny,* Nita thought, *is that I never really noticed it until now. Was I always in too much of a rush? Am I just hypersensitive because of this change-of-specialty thing? Or is it the peridexis? Whatever —*

She pushed through the resistance, said the spell's last word, and added the final syllables of the Wizard's Knot to make it all come real. Reality, finally becoming resigned to the wizardry, surrendered. Everything went black: then not quite black, but the deepest possible blue —

Heat: that was the first thing that made an impression — heat that even at dawn still pressed in all around and briefly took your breath. Nita glanced around to make sure that Carmela was all right, for in the direction they'd been facing, the sky was still fairly dark. Then Nita groaned and put the tomato bag down on the indefinite-colored, sandy ground, massaging the arm that had been holding it for what now felt like about a century.

They were standing on an elevated outcropping of land near the edge of an island in a sea that, in the growing dawn light, was already a surprisingly vivid deep blue. Ahead and to their right, the black balsalt cliffs of the island's northern peninsula dropped sheerly down into the water. In those cliffs' shadow lay a kind of patchy, glowing pallor — the biolumi-nescence associated with the offshore coral growth. Soon enough, Nita knew, that glow would fade as daylight grew and the native reds and violets of the corals asserted themselves. As she watched, a delta-winged shadow slid across the green-white glow — some passing giant manta, out hunting early.

"Whooo," Carmela said, turning around very carefully, for they were a good way up from the stony beach below.

"Hold still," Nita said. "I'll make a light." She held out a hand and said the sixteen words of a wizard-light spell. The light popped out of nothing in the air, burning small and hot and blue, and Nita got out her manual. "I need to check that everybody's where I think they are . . ."

She glanced at the messaging page in the back of the manual, comparing the coordinates laid into one message to the terrain below. A map came swimming up out of the glowing text, showing the cliffside, the path leading down from it, and the beach on the island's northwest tip. There Nita saw a little cluster of blue-light pinpricks, one circled in red. "Yup," she said, and shut the manual, shoving it back in its other-space pocket. "There he is. Let's go."

Nita made a downward-pressing gesture with one hand, and the little sphere of light sank down to shin level, illuminating the path before them. "Down this way. Take your time: you wouldn't want to slip . . ."

They made their way down the path, the light going before them and growing slightly paler as the dawn light all around grew stronger. North of the cliffs, the island's slope to the water grew gentler, creating a spot that more resembled a beach, though not the kind that would have been pleasant for sunbathers. It was strewn with boulders of every size, though they were smallest down by the water. Here and there some small scraggly tree, scrub tamarind or beech-pine, pushed its crooked, wind-twisted way up between the boulders.

"Okay," Carmela said as the path switched back again, and for a little while they walked more or less toward the swiftly brightening eastern sky. "So geography was never my big thing: I give. Where on Earth are we?"

Nita snickered. "Half the clues are right in front of you," she said. "I should make you guess."

"Juanita Louise," Carmela said, "you are a real pain in the gnaester sometimes . . ."

"Carmela, *what* did I tell you about the 'L' word?" Nita said, as they turned another switchback curve in the hillside trail. Nita hated her middle name and was still trying to figure out how Carmela had discovered it, as Carmela wouldn't tell her. "It was Dairine, wasn't it?" she said. "That little —"

"Not her, Miss Neets," Carmela said, looking smug. They turned another switchback curve, and Nita, paying too much attention to Carmela's expression, banged her left sneaker-toe against an unexpected rock. "Ow, ow, ow . . . !" she said, putting down the tomato bag hurriedly and hopping briefly on the other foot.

"See that," Carmela said. "The world's punishing you for being cute with me. *Ooooh . . .*"

Nita stopped hopping, grinning at Carmela's reaction to something Nita had seen before when wizardly work had taken her and Kit close enough to the equator — the shortness of dawn and sunset twilight, and the bizarre way that sunrise and sunset just seemed to happen, *bang,* all at once. The Sun didn't quite leap up over the horizon, but it seemed a very short time between the moment the first burning splinter of the Sun's upper limb broke the water and the one when the whole blinding disc, veiled in furiously silver-burning clouds, rose over the eastern sea. The water of the bay beneath them came alive in a storm of glitter.

"Welcome to Gili Motang," Nita said.

"This is really cool," said Carmela. "Except for the temperature."

"It'll get worse, but I don't think we're gonna have time to care."

The last turn in the path had brought them around to look back the way they'd come, so that they were now gazing straight down into the hot, blue waters of the Molo Strait. From that direction the dry southwest wind was blowing hard, and big waves rolled up the southerly-facing beaches; the crash of the surf could be much more clearly heard when you were facing into it. "Pretty," Carmela said. "So where *is* Gili Motang exactly?"

"Indonesia," Nita said as she put her stubbed foot down, wriggling her toes inside her sneaker. She picked up the bag of tomatoes again. "Our visitor has a project going here. Or not going, and she keeps coming in to work on it. Did Kit tell you who he was coming to see?"

"Some important wizard," Carmela said. "Kit's really impressed with her; that's all I know. 'Manfish'?"

"Mamvish," Nita said as they negotiated one last switchback on their way down the hillside. "She's really old . . . in our years, anyway. She's spent three thousand years or so saving species that're about to be destroyed: getting rid of what's threatening them, or else moving them to new homes. 'Rafting,' it's called. Some species she's even been able to save *after* they've been destroyed."

"That must take some work!"

"She's got the power to pull it off," Nita said. "Tons of it. What's fun is that even though she's such a big deal, she's still kind of a goof."

They came down onto the stony, broken ground at the bottom of the hill. Carmela tsk-tsked at the rocky beach as they made their way along the base of the hillside. "Not much good for swimming . . ."

"No," Nita said. "Especially not if you have trouble with sharks . . ."

Carmela laughed. "Like you wouldn't!"

"Not these days," Nita said, smiling. "No." She changed the tomato bag over to the other hand as they came around the pointy end of the hillside where it dropped to the water.

Another small, half-circle rocky bay was revealed on the right as they made their way down among the fractured sandstone boulders that had rolled down the cliff. The strand of the bay was boulder-strewn too, and small dark shapes — human figures — sat on the biggest rocks near the water. Near the base of the cliff, not far away, stood a long green-golden shape that had to be fifty feet long.

"What *is* that?" Carmela said. "Hey, it's a dinosaur!" And she started to head straight down-slope toward it.

"Uh, no," Nita said. Then she caught a motion out of the corner of her eye. "'*Mela, watch out!*"

She flung an arm out in front of Carmela. Carmela stopped so suddenly she nearly fell over forward onto the seven-foot-long Komodo dragon that was suddenly blocking their path.

"Whoa!" Carmela said, and stumbled back. Nita grabbed Carmela's arm to steady her as that blunt, oblong head swung toward them.

Yum, the Komodo dragon said. Its tongue went out and waved around in the air, tasting it for their scent.

"You really wouldn't like eating us!" Nita said in the Speech.

"Yeah," Carmela said, also in the Speech. "We're probably both full of additives."

The dragon looked from Carmela to Nita and back again. Its tongue went in and out a few more times. *What's an additive?* the Komodo dragon said. *Is it nice?*

Very carefully, Nita handed Carmela the bag of tomatoes, acutely conscious of how the dragon was following her every move. "No, they're really un-healthy . . ." The moment she had both hands free, Nita took hold of one of the charms on her bracelet, the one with her shield spell set up in it. Komodo dragons could move like lightning when they wanted to, and could rip an arm or a leg off you before you knew what was happening. *If this guy tries something cute, I'm gonna have to adjust this spell on the fly so it works for two of us —*

"You should really go inland," Nita said. "There are all kinds of nice goats and things for you to eat up there, much nicer tasting than us."

"Seriously," Carmela said. "Just go on back there in the forest and take a seat, and your server will be with you shortly!"

The dragon looked peculiarly at Carmela, and its tongue went in and out several times more. Nita held her breath.

Finally the Komodo dragon turned and lurched

away, uphill, toward the scraggly forest above the beach. Nita let out a long breath and shot Carmela a look. "You've been spending too much time in those restaurants at the Crossings!"

Carmela shrugged. "Being nice never hurts . . ."

"You've got that right, anyway," Nita said. "Let's get down there before we have to have that conversation with one of Mister Dragon's buddies."

The two of them headed downslope to where the track gave out. Shortly they were picking their way among the cracked yellow boulders toward the group on the beach. "Neets," Carmela said, "I hate to tell you this, but there's another dragon down there."

"Where?"

"Under the dinosaur."

Nita peered ahead. "It's okay . . . I think it's too busy to notice us. Anyway, don't you see someone familiar?" She took back the bag of tomatoes.

"Who?" Now it was Carmela's turn to peer. "Where do you — *Ronan!*"

Carmela took off toward where that tall, slim shape was lounging on top of a big boulder in black jeans and a black T-shirt, and doubtless paying the price for it in this weather; but he looked as casual as if he were sitting on a block of ice. Nita grinned as she negotiated the rocky stretch between herself and the wizards sitting on the rocks by the edge of the bay. Kit was there in T-shirt and baggies, perched on an even bigger boulder than the one where Ronan Nolan had stretched himself out. Nearby, on a lower, flatter stone, a smaller shape sat cross-legged — younger, much darker, wiry, in swim trunks and a floppy white tank top: Darryl McAllister, one of the newer wizards of Nita's acquaintance, a neighbor from over in Baldwin. The three of them were watching yet another Komodo dragon, bigger than the one Nita had spoken to, and also keeping an eye on the huge, shimmering, golden-green shape bending down over the dragon: one that, to Nita's way of thinking, seemed much worthier of the name.

If someone had stood an African elephant next to that great shape, the elephant would have been taller, but the saurian, sheathed in a handsome, pebbly, gleaming hide, would have been much bigger. Though Mamvish's shoulders stood no more than twenty feet from the ground, they were nearly ten feet apart, and each leg was as thick as the trunk of the forty-year-old maple in front of Nita's house. Those legs bent twice, in a double elbow — one of them bending backward about eight feet from the ground, and the second one about four feet above it. Each leg ended in a six-toed paw, as broad compared to the leg as the foot of a cat, and each toe had a massive, metallically glinting claw retracted partly into it. The hind legs were like the front ones, though the hip joints were higher than the shoulders, and the tail that trailed away behind them lashed and coiled, gesturing more expressively than any Komodo dragon's tail could.

At the other end, the saurian's long, oval head peered down at the smaller one of the Komodo dragon sitting between her huge forefeet. The massive jaws in that huger head opened, exhibiting teeth that gleamed like pale metal, and a broad, black tongue. Around the words that she spoke, like the breath behind them, came a low, moaning hiss like a house's central heating system complaining of too much pressure in the radiators. But the voice itself spoke the Speech in a surprisingly high register, like a flute's or clarinet's. As Nita got closer, she could see how subtly changing colors ran and shimmered underneath the gemmy bumps and pebbles of the hide, shifting slightly with the words and the volume at which they were spoken.

"Let me put it again in a way you can understand," the voice said . . . while sounding as if its owner wasn't sure this could be done. "There's nowhere else for you to live in these seas! The two-leggers are encroaching on your territory. No matter how well the ones who come here right now are treating you, sooner or later some will come who don't mean you anything like as well. You'll have nowhere else to go! And there are much better places for you to be, with no two-leggers, with nothing but people like you — people who're interested in you and want you to live somewhere safe! If you'll just let me show you —"

The Komodo dragon between Mamvish's feet looked up at her and opened its mouth, emitting a similar hiss, though a much smaller one. By way of the Speech, Nita heard it say, *I'm hungry.*

Mamvish rolled her eyes in frustration. This was worth seeing, since it wasn't just the eyeballs that rolled; the entire socket containing each one went around in a large and wobbly circle. "You can eat anytime," she said. "Please pay attention. We're talking about something *important* here —"

A juicy little deer would be nice right about now, said the Komodo dragon . . . and it turned ponderously around and lurched away out of Mamvish's shadow and up the beach, toward the underbrush that sprang up under the eaves of the forest.

Mamvish watched it go. "You stupid, *stupid* things," she hissed, "why do I keep wasting my time?" She stamped all her feet in annoyance. "It's your *lives* I'm trying to save here! Your whole *rijakh*'d *species'* lives! . . . And all you can ever think about is *food!* If you came home with me, you'd be superstars; your species would be comfortable and safe forever! And now I wonder why I'm bothering trying to take creatures home who're so *merthakte* dumb! Powers that Be in a *bucket,* have you ever seen the like of these people? Time after time you come umpteen thousand light-years to make them the offer of a lifetime, and every time they ignore you; they don't have the brains to come in out of the Sun; they —"

The tirade went on. Somewhat distractedly — for Mamvish was using a completely new and interesting subset of words in the Speech — Nita made her way over to the boulder where Kit was perching. As she scrambled up beside him, Nita found herself wondering whether there was a separate "bad language" section of the wizard's manual, and why she'd never thought to go looking for it. *Am I really that much of a geek? Oh, god.* Kit was looking elsewhere, as if embarrassed. Darryl was listening with fascination: Ronan had leaned all the way back on his boulder with his hands under his head, his eyes closed. *Because of Mamvish, or Carmela?* — for Kit's sister was sitting there, trying to keep her attention evenly divided between Mamvish and Ronan. For the moment, Mamvish was winning.

"What *took* you so long?" Kit said under his breath. "You missed *everybody.* Half the wizards we know have been here, and a lot we don't."

"Want to understate some more? Half the wizards on the *planet* have been here!" Darryl said from the next boulder over. "A real mob scene. And some real heavy hitters. Check this out!" He scrambled over toward them, holding out the WizPod he used these days to carry his wizard's manual. "Jarrah Corowa was here, and she even gave me her autograph!" He pulled a glowing page sideways out of the WizPod and into the air, showing Nita the tracery of Speech-characters there.

"Wow!" Nita said, for a wizard's autograph, depending on how much of the wizard's personal information it contained, could be worth a lot more than just a keepsake of meeting someone who was famous for their way with a spell. "Nice going!"

Kit rolled his eyes in a good-natured way at Darryl's excitement. "Fang was here, too," he said.

Nita let out a breath, sorry to have missed an old friend in wizardry, the orca who'd sung the part of the Killer in the Song of the Twelve. "How is he? He came way out of his way to get here."

"Not all that far. He and his family swim the Pacific this time of year: he's over here working on typhoon steering or something. He's fine, and he was asking about you. *And* her." Kit threw an annoyed glance in Carmela's direction. "On another subject, is it just barely possible that we can go anywhere on this planet these days, or any other, without *her* coming along?"

"Funny," Nita said. "I was going to ask whether it was possible *you* might go anywhere that *I* could come along."

Kit stared at her. "What?"

"I was late because I was waiting for *you!* I hung around Tom and Carl's for half the afternoon!"

Kit looked stricken, as if this had never occurred to him. "But you said you were going to talk to the fish."

"I was!" Nita said. "But I didn't go there *to* talk to the fish! I went there to blow some time until *you* were going to turn up after school — which you never did! Oh, no, you just heard the word 'Mars' and forgot all about everything else, and ran straight off here!"

"Come on, Neets, you know I —"

Would you two ever just take it to telepathy, Ronan said silently, *or else save it for later? She's starting to run out of steam again.*

At least the hissing was dying down. "Why?" Mamvish was saying to the sky and the Earth and whatever else might have been listening. "*Why* do I keep coming out to this dust speck of a not-particularly-interesting world out at the farthest possible edge of all that's bright and beautiful to talk to these idiotic creatures who make a pt!walnath look assertive and a Zabriskan fontema look smart? I *ask* you."

Then she fell silent. Mamvish looked around her, a little guiltily. "I'm sorry," she said, "very sorry. They're just so —"

"Clueless?" said Darryl. "Lackwitted? Like you called them the last time you lost it?"

"Dim?" said Ronan. "Pitiful? Like you called them half an hour before that?"

"All right, it's not kind to describe them so," Mamvish said, sounding contrite. "They're as the One made them. If they won't be saved, they won't. But I just keep hoping they'll change their minds... though I'm starting to wonder why I bother."

"Because you're a wizard?" Nita said. "And it's what wizards do?"

Mamvish swung her huge head in Nita's direction... and then froze. Both those eyes suddenly went forward and trained on Nita with tremendous directness: and Mamvish's nostrils flared.

"*Cousin,*" she said. "Are you carrying what I *think* you're carrying?"

Nita held up the plastic bag. "You mean these?"

Mamvish suddenly lurched toward Nita as single-mindedly as the Komodo dragon had.

Nita hurriedly scrambled down off the boulder, headed for Mamvish, and started to carefully empty out the tomato bag onto the stones. "No, no, it's quite all right," Mamvish said. "I don't mind a little roughage..."

Nita dropped the bag and the tomatoes as Mamvish

lumbered forward. A second later, the tomatoes and the bag were gone. So were some of the stones — deafeningly crunched up, shattering and splintering. Everyone stared. Mamvish's eyes rotated in her head in opposite directions in what Nita very much hoped was delight, and the shimmer under her skin ran suddenly tomato-red.

"You are my *friend!*" Mamvish said, using the Speech-word *thelefeh,* which was a much closer and cozier usage than *hrasht,* or "cousin." Nita was charmed, and began to see some use in having carried that bag halfway across the planet. "And this is unquestionably one of the best worlds in this whole part of the galaxy," Mamvish said, straightening up after a moment. The place where her jaw jointed pulled back and back into what her species apparently used for a smile; Nita started wondering if Mamvish's head might actually come apart. "Thank you so much for bringing those: I didn't think I was going to have time to get any, this trip. Do forgive me; I missed your name —"

"You didn't miss it," said a voice from behind her. "She was late."

"Stow it, Ronan," Nita said. To Mamvish she said, "I'm Nita."

"And of course I know you, *thelef',*" Mamvish said, lowering her head so that one of her eyes could look into both of Nita's. "We've spoken often enough via manual. I'm sorry if I moved quickly, there . . . It's really hard for me to help myself around these things. It's something to do with the bioflavinoids . . ."

"You should grow them at home!" Nita said.

"They're not the same," Mamvish said, sounding sorrowful as she hunkered down on the rocky beach again. "There's something in the water here. Or the air. Or the spectrum of this particular sunlight. Tomatoes are just happiest on Earth . . ." She sighed. "But it doesn't matter. They're a tremendous compensation for other slight annoyances." One eye glanced back toward the Komodo dragon, which was disappearing into the brush up near the cliff. "And, after all, who knows if I'd ever have found out about Mars at all without the tomatoes?"

"Tomatoes are all very well," Ronan said, sitting up and stretching himself in the sunshine, "but as for these folks, you should just move them. If they don't have the smarts to agree to leave on their own, then change their minds for them —"

"Don't tempt me," Mamvish said, waving her tail in annoyance. "Unfortunately this issue goes right to the heart of the Wizard's Oath: 'I shall change no creature unless it, or the system of which it is a part, is threatened.'" She looked around her. "And they are. These are the only ones left of these creatures, except for the few hundred on the other island, and those few others scattered about the planet in zoos. But if I change their minds for them, will they still be the creatures they are?" A long, deep fluting sigh came out of her. "Never mind. They're a problem for another day . . . though one that has its resonances with what we're about to start."

Nita opened her mouth, but Carmela, sitting up on that boulder, put up her hand and starting waving it around like some back-of-the-classroom kid desperate to be called on. "Excuse me," she said in the Speech, "but what *are* we about to start?"

Nita threw a glance sidewise at Kit. He was covering his face and groaning softly. One of Mamvish's eyes was suddenly regarding Carmela; the other one was looking in what seemed mild confusion from Nita, to Kit, to Darryl, to Ronan. "Has this planet gone *astahfrith* without my noticing?" she said. "I *have* been busy . . ."

Nita snickered, for this was probably an understatement. "No," she said. "We still have to hide our wizardry, mostly. But there are people who're in on the secret and aren't freaked by it. Mamvish, this is Kit's sister Carmela. 'Mela, this is Mamvish fsh Wimsih fsh Mentaff."

"Hey," Carmela said in the Speech, "Life says, 'hi there.'"

Mamvish's eye actually tried to lean farther out of her skull in Carmela's direction. "And It greets you by me as well. You're not a wizard, though . . ."

"Don't need to be," Carmela said, sounding utterly certain. "Too much work. I'm just a tourist training to be a galactic personal shopper."

This was all news to Nita, but she tried to keep her grin restrained and out of Kit's sight: his reaction to Carmela's ever-growing ability with the Speech had been becoming increasingly pained.

Mamvish looked unfocused for a moment, or as much more unfocused as one could be expected to look when her eyes were already pointing in different directions. Then she said, "Oh! You're the one who shot up the Crossings during the intervention last month."

"That would be me," Carmela said. "But Neets was there first. And our colleague with all the legs."

"Sker'ret is a great talent," Mamvish said, "and an invaluable resource. His people have been instrumental in your world's development, you know that? At least as far as worldgates go. It's good to see that you're so well connected."

One of Mamvish's rear legs came up to scratch behind where one of her ears might have been, had she had any on the outside. "Meanwhile, I don't see why you'd need to be excluded from this. Especially since you came with the bearer of the tomatoes." She beamed at Nita, then turned back to Carmela again. "From your own world's point of view, Mars is a 'situational location of interest.' Wizards here have been trying to find out why for some centuries now. And even the outer worlds feel echoes of something that happened . . . and have nothing further to say." She tilted her head, looking thoughtful. "So plainly there's something going on here that we need to know about before we move forward."

"And what are we moving *toward*?" Carmela said.

We. Nita could just feel Kit start fuming quietly. "Waking up the Martians, dummy!" Kit said.

"Well," Mamvish said, swinging one eye in his direction, "that's the question we'll be examining. Local catastrophes have killed too many species in the past — peoples we could ill afford to lose. My job's to prevent the loss of worlds that have something special to offer the universe, to keep species or planets that have made unusual contributions from being completely lost — and, occasionally, to get back lost worlds that aren't as lost as we think they are."

"Like Mars . . ." Nita said.

"Yes," Mamvish said. "And sometimes, as seems to have happened in this case, we get a little help from the species in question: they leave us data about what happened to them."

"A message in a bottle," Ronan said.

"Yes. In this case, the 'bottle' we've located seems to have been emplaced some five hundred sixty thousand years ago."

Nita blinked at that. "Wow. There were just human ancestors around then. It was — what, the really early Stone Age?"

"The Lower Paleolithic, as I understand your usage," Mamvish said. "Any knowledge or memory your most distant ancestors had of Mars is lost. But worlds have different kinds of memory than the beings that move on their surfaces. Whatever humans know about Mars, the outer worlds have different knowledge about it: troubled recollections. We have to go carefully at first." The eyes rotated again in the head. "But the risk may be worth it. Some of the most dangerous 'lost' species have brought us some of the greatest gifts once they've been revived."

Carmela was looking dubious. "Am I completely misunderstanding you, or are you actually talking about bringing them back from the dead?"

"Well, there's dead and there's *really* dead,"

Mamvish said. "Of course we couldn't do anything about the second kind. However, there are a hundred different kinds of stasis, soulfreeze, matter seizure, and wait-just-a-minute that species across the galaxy have invented to stave off entropy's Last Word. Many species have seen a catastrophe coming and found ways to archive or preserve not just the news about what happened to them but themselves as well. In Mars's case, the first steps have been toward finding out whether there *were* ever Martians — because your whole species seems to have some kind of unfinished business, or unstarted business, with Mars. If Martians did exist, the next step would then be to find out what happened to them. Once we know that, we can start working out how to re-evoke them — in a limited way, just to find out firsthand what happened to them. From there we can make the determination as to whether it's wise to revive them wholly. And then —"

"We bring them back," Kit said softly.

"Maybe," Mamvish said. "We've got a lot of steps to go through before that. And the first one will be to —"

Nita suddenly felt as if something had kicked her in the chest. The breath went right out of her, for no reason she could understand, and she gasped in reaction. At the same moment, "I'm so sorry I'm late," said another voice, a female one, out of nothing. "What did I miss?"

They all turned — Nita last: she was still having trouble finding her breath — and stared. Standing there among the rocks of the beach was what looked like a slender little housewife in her thirties, wearing a flowered housedress and flip-flops. She had boldly highlighted shaggy blond hair, a blinking, placid baby in a patchwork-patterned shoulder sling, and a yellow parakeet sitting on her shoulder.

Mamvish hurriedly put down the scratching foot, stood up, and inclined her head to the woman. "Irina," she said, "this is more than a pleasure!"

Nita and Kit stared at each other, and Darryl's eyes went wide, and even Ronan, for all his usual overlay of unconcerned coolness, sat up straight. *Is that who I think it is?* Nita said silently to Kit.

Look at the way Mamvish's acting. It has *to be —!*

"I'm just passing through," said the Planetary Wizard for Earth, and the baby chuckled and reached up to pull on her hair as she smiled around at them all, then at Mamvish again. "I heard you were going to be in the neighborhood, Archivist. I thought I'd wait until the excitement died down, and then drop by and pay my respects."

"Planetary," said Mamvish, bowing her head more deeply, "don't be respecting *me.* I'm just migrant labor."

Irina laughed; the parakeet fluttered its wings and scolded her, a little scratchy noise on the hot, sunny air. "And I'm just a housekeeper!" Irina said, reaching up a finger to the parakeet: it nibbled her nail. "Sure, the house is bigger than some. But it's the empty house next door that's really got me interested. I hear you've finally found what you were looking for —"

"We were about to go up to the site to look at the

find," Mamvish said. "Do you have time to accompany us?"

"For a few minutes, surely."

Mamvish put her head up and cocked one eye at the Sun. The other stayed trained on the ground, as if she was looking for something. Nita watched this with interest, suspecting that Mamvish was about to cast some kind of transit circle —

Shadow fled outward from Mamvish and ran swift as a blast wave across the ground, past the rocks on which they were all sitting, out toward the sea and up the face of the cliff. In that shadow, Mamvish glowed. The green-gold shimmer under her hide was replaced by darkness in which burned a great complexity of characters and sentences in the Speech, writhing and coiling about one another, flowing out onto the darkened ground. The shadow beneath them now filled with those words and characters, and as Mamvish stretched her head upward into the air, the sound of the surf behind them was drowned out by what seemed a whole chorus of voices chanting in the Speech, like a great concord of wind instruments: Mamvish's voice, but seemingly multiplied many times over, as if she was somehow reciting all the different parts of the spell at the same time.

Nita tried to breathe and found she couldn't. The spell held her in place, and she couldn't move a muscle, not even to look sideways to see how Kit was taking it. All around them, instead of the inward-leaning, listening silence that normally meant a wizardry was starting to work, Nita started to hear something astonishing —

more voices, seeming to join in with Mamvish's fluting one, all speaking the Speech together with her from out of some great echoing depth, a great chorus of intention, elation, even excitement —

Then the silence fell, abrupt, unexpected: and the sea was gone, and the sky was a dark hazy russet-golden color rather than blue. Nita let go the awed breath she'd been forced to hold, looking around her at a world that had gone a dusty ochre, shading to rusty charcoal at the edges.

Nita slid down off the boulder, took another breath. Since her eyes weren't boiling out of her head in the hyperthin air, and she hadn't half frozen since they got there, it was plain that Mamvish had taken care of the group's atmosphere needs. But Nita still felt wobbly. That huge wash of Speech and wizardly power left her feeling like she'd been run over by a truck, and as if all the spells she'd ever cast by herself or just in company with Kit were weak little things by comparison. She leaned against the boulder, gulping, and tried to get her composure back.

Kit, still up on the boulder, was gasping and trying to hide it: Ronan was shaking his head like someone who'd been punched. Carmela, sitting beside him, had unbraided her hair and was braiding it up again — a sign that Nita had learned to read as meaning that 'Mela was unnerved. Only Darryl was standing there casually looking around him, seemingly unaffected. Nita saw Mamvish, noting this, rotate one eye toward Irina, who was fanning herself with one hand like someone who'd broken out in a sweat. Irina said nothing, but Nita suspected that a few thoughts were passing between them concerning why so young and relatively inexperienced a wizard should be untroubled by what had just happened.

Good, Nita thought. *Something we don't have to warn her about.* Nita had been concerned about the appropriateness of one of Earth's precious few *abdals* getting involved in off-planet wizardly work: but if Irina didn't do anything about it, then it definitely had to be all right. Nita let out a long breath and looked up at that strange butterscotch-colored daytime sky, which shaded down toward deeper tints of apricot and warm brick red at the horizon. Southward of where they stood, the dust was thick in the sky, softening a horizon that was usually much sharper, hiding the view of the distant foothills.

Nita swallowed, smiled. It had always been wonder enough just to step out of a gating circle onto this ancient and alien soil, to stand gazing up into this unearthly sky and see that smaller, cooler, pinker sun. Nita had been here often enough, over the last year or so, to almost get used to that marvel. But today there was something new that sharpened this view, lent an edge to the feel of the place. The clue they'd been hunting had finally been found. Now every shadow, every rock, seemed to be hiding a secret.

Life . . . !

Syrtis Major

"WHAT TIME IS IT HERE?" Irina said.

"About halfway through the sol," Mamvish said, glancing around. "Am I right — that's the name your people use for the Martian day? Excellent. Anyway, it's late autumn here: we're just north of the planet's equator."

Looking around, Nita smiled wryly. The only way to tell that fall was here was by the angle of the Sun and the slight warmth remaining in the atmosphere — meaning that the outside temperature was only about thirty degrees below zero. Feeling less shaky now, she pushed away from the chilly boulder she'd been leaning against and peered south toward the highlands. This part of Mars's northern hemisphere was dominated by flat country, the crater-pitted remnant of old lava flows. Southward the highlands would start to pile up into far more spectacular and mountainous terrain, dotted with terrible crevasses and ancient volcanic peaks. But all that was well over the horizon. Here everything was relatively flat, darkened by the local green-brown sand and dust — except for the features lowering over the site to which Mamvish had brought them. On every side, immense charcoal-dark dunes of windblown basalt sand had piled up — stretched out serpentlike across the plain, half a mile or a mile long, as sharp-edged as any desert dune on Earth. But in the lower gravity, these dunes towered nearly five hundred feet high, casting long, cold shadows across the plain in the light of early morning.

The others were getting down from where they'd been sitting. Nita threw a glance at Kit, saw that he was all right, and went over to where Carmela was standing, gazing around with her hair braided up again, a look of astonishment on her face. "Aren't we inside a force field or something?" Carmela said. "How come I can feel the wind?"

"I told you," Nita said, "Mamvish has power to burn ..." Whenever Nita and Kit had come here on their own, or to work with the other wizards involved in this effort, they'd both worn personal force fields that hugged them close, keeping the Martian atmosphere out and their own carefully calculated air supplies in. But Mamvish had built her wizardry very differently, so that it matched the temperature and oxygen content of Earth's air exactly but still transmitted the forces of the thin exterior atmosphere as if they were one and the same. It would have been an incredibly difficult wizardry to structure, and Nita could imagine the kind of power necessary to run it. *The same kind of power that can pick you up off one planet and drop you on another between one breath and the next without it even looking hard . . .*

"Why's everything this khaki color?" Carmela said, as she and Ronan and Darryl came over to join Nita and Kit near where Mamvish and Irina were looking around. "I thought this was supposed to be the *red* planet."

"Because we're in the middle of Syrtis Major," Kit said. "That big dark eastern-hemisphere blotch that everybody used to think was a sea, with canals running into it. There were a lot of volcanoes here, so the ground's full of this green stuff, olivine, that formed when the lava cooled." Kit looked around like someone who just needed to see a few landmarks to be sure where he was. "This isn't really a crater we're in: it's what's left of one of the calderas where the lava came out. It's called Nili Patera." He looked over at Mamvish. "And the bottle is —"

"A few hundred meters south," Mamvish said. "Síle and Markus get the credit for finding it. They were working this site all this week . . ."

"Who're Síle and Markus?" Carmela said, bouncing up and down in place to get the feel of the gravity, which was only about a third of the Earth's. Each bounce took her several times higher than she'd intended, and Nita kept having to reach up and grab her and pull her back down.

"A couple of the other wizards on the project," Kit said. "Síle's from Ronan's part of the world —

she's at college studying computer science in Paris. Markus is in the German army: he drives tanks."

"They were the ones who called me in," Mamvish said. "Markus's unit had to go on active service yesterday morning to help with the floods in the south of his country. Síle stayed here and kept running the spell routines that she and Markus had been working on, till something came up that required her to head home and go out on errantry yesterday evening. She called me in just before she went on active status."

"It's a shame they can't be here," Kit said. "They've been working so hard on this for so long . . ."

"As have about twenty other people from your planet for whom this is a special interest," Mamvish said. "But they don't grudge missing the action, as long as there *is* action." Her tail swished with excitement. "The rest of your team will get here when work and errantry leave them time. Meanwhile —"

"Where is it?" Kit said. "*What* is it?"

"It's where you said you thought it might be," Mamvish said. "Hidden under one of these dunes. But time passed, the wind blew, the dune moved . . . and now it's not hidden anymore. As for the what — now we'll find out. Over this way . . ."

They all headed southward. Nita saw that Carmela seemed to have recovered her composure and had gravitated back toward Ronan, who was gliding along a foot or so above the surface, with only the occasional very practiced and casual bounce: he looked as unconcerned as if he were walking across some park back home. *Looks like he and Kit have been up here*

*working in one-third g an awful lot. Maybe more than
I thought . . .* But projects of her own had been keeping Nita busy lately, and what she told Carmela had
been true: the Martian project had been far more Kit's
passion than hers for some months. Not that she hadn't
come up every now and then to see how things were
going. But mostly they *hadn't* been. Until now, Kit
and all the other wizards he'd been working with had
found nothing at all. . . .

He and Darryl and Ronan were now bouncing
along together, talking hard as they came up beside
Mamvish. Carmela had dropped back, succumbing to
the fascination of where she was and looking intently at
the sandy ground, the dusty rocks, the alien dune-vista
between her and the horizon. Irina, too, had paused to
pick up a rough dark-green stone and look closely at it.
The baby hanging in front of her patted the rock with
one hand and crowed as Nita came up next to the two
of them. "Irina —" she said very quietly.

"It's about Darryl, isn't it?"

Nita went hot with embarrassment. "It's all
right," Irina said softly, turning the rock over in her
hands. "He can be away from Earth for short periods,
and his function as a channel of the One's power into
the world won't suffer. But I think you'll find that he
won't care to be away much longer. For those of us
who've become important at the planetary level, the
Earth whispers in our ears when it's uneasy at our
absence. And the whisper's impossible to ignore."

Irina tossed the rock to the ground and gestured
with her head toward the others. She and Nita started to

bounce after them, and the baby shouted with delight as they went, while the yellow parakeet scolded them noisily, finally taking off and flying on ahead, quick as an arrow-shot in the low gravity. "Besides," Irina said, "while Mamvish is here, nothing's going to dare interfere with him, or you, or anything else that's going on."

"Yeah," Nita said. "I couldn't believe that spell. And she did it so casually. What her power levels must be like —"

"Well, yes, but it's not just that," Irina said, even more softly than she'd spoken about Darryl. "She's unusual even as wizards go. It wouldn't be in the manuals, but it might be useful for you to know: she's an Abstainee."

Nita's eyes went wide. "She had her Ordeal and the Lone Power *didn't show up?*"

Irina nodded, smiled. "It even sent her a message saying It wasn't *going* to turn up. She told me once," Irina said, with a somewhat cockeyed look, "that It said It had a headache."

Nita shook her head, not knowing what to make of this. "I bet *that* doesn't happen often."

"Galaxy-wide? Eleven times in the last five centuries," Irina said. She looked ahead toward where the others had stopped in the shadow of one more black-sand dune, a very perfect crescent with the open side toward them. "And as usual, the question is: do her power levels come from being an Abstainee, or did the Lone One decide not to get involved because of her power levels . . . ?" Irina shook her head. "It may not matter. But she's good to have around for backup . . .

and no wizard alive knows more about this particular kind of work than she does. I'm glad she's here. Especially since this is such an odd place, some ways . . ." Irina gazed toward the northern horizon for a moment as they went. "I have to come up here two or three times a year to make sure the planet's operating correctly in the absence of a kernel, and afterwards I always go away wondering why the manual's so short of information about exactly what's happened here. Now, though, what the Mars team has found may mean the silence is finally about to break a little . . ."

Shortly they caught up with the others, who were all standing around a little irregular outcropping or bump of dark olive-colored stone, just four feet or so high. It jutted up deep in the shadow of the crescent dune, and just a foot or two clear of where the steep, smooth sweep of dark, gritty sand on the dune's inner side came down to the ground.

"It's under that?" Kit said as Nita and Irina caught up with the others.

"Inside it," said Mamvish.

"And you're sure whatever's in there isn't something contemporary?" Ronan said. "Like that alien tourist beacon Nita's sister found up on Olympus Mons when she passed through on her Ordeal? Not some practical joke?"

Mamvish tilted her head one way and the other, the gesture her people apparently used for "no." "Many sites that wizards have investigated here over the last three centuries have had a scent of old wizardry about them, but never anything this concrete. And the survey spell identifies what's emplaced here as being at least five hundred forty thousand years old. Even Earth's earliest wizards didn't venture this far for many thousands of years after that . . . so I think we're safe enough from practical jokes. Anyway" — and she gestured with her tail at Kit — "Kit is probably the most Mars-crazed of the whole team, and he's the one who's always been after everybody to keep on looking here, even after previous searches came up blank."

"Why, Kit?" Irina said. "What seemed so special about Syrtis?"

Kit shook his head. "I don't know. It was just a hunch to start with." He looked around him. "But Syrtis Major was the first feature on Mars that anyone on Earth really noticed, the thing that's most obvious from space. It just seemed like a good place to start."

"Hunch or no hunch, Kit seems to have a feel for this place," Mamvish said. "Why argue the point? No one knows why any wizard's good at any particular specialty. The Powers may know, but it's not information They seem interested in sharing." She shrugged her tail.

"How come all the sensor spells the team was using before didn't turn this up until now?" Nita said.

"Because it was built to hide its nature," Mamvish said. "An extremely elegant piece of wizardry, exactly mimicking the structure and composition of its surroundings. For a long time, before the dunes advanced into the crater, all the spell had to pretend to be was this chunk of rock . . . and it did that perfectly. But then the dunes came in, and the wizardry had to adapt itself to mimicking not only rock, but dust and sand of a different composition and structure. The adjustment took a while, since the spell had only limited running power available to it. And when the dune moved away again, the spell had to adjust again. A dust storm moved through here the other night: in the wind, the dune moved just far enough westward to reveal the outcropping, and the wizardry started to adapt again. But Síle was still here, up north by the canyon valley you call Huo Hsing Vallis, running the new survey spell she and Markus had designed . . . and she detected the chameleon spell and what it was protecting before the wizardry had time to reset and hide it all again."

"Well done, that woman," Ronan said. "She always was the stubborn type."

"Sometimes stubbornness pays better dividends than high power levels," Irina said. "Well, shouldn't we take a look at it?"

"This is your job, I think," Mamvish said to Kit.

Kit suddenly looked abashed and shy. Nita had to hide her smile.

"Go on," Mamvish said. "You're the one who predicted the location. Pull it out of there and let's see what it is."

Kit nodded, knelt down in front of the outcropping, put his hands up against it, and very slowly and carefully recited the fourteen syllables of the Mason's Word, which has power over stone and the mineral elements. Then he leaned inward. Slowly Kit's hands sank in through the surface of the brown stone, up to the wrists, then up to the elbows. He looked absently upward, like anyone feeling around for something he can't see, and then his eyes widened.

"It's pretty big," he said. "Round, I think. Kind of beach-ball sized . . ."

Very slowly he pulled his arms back. His face tensed. "It doesn't want to come," he said.

"The spell would resist," Mamvish said. "That's its job. Keep pulling —"

Nita watched as the sweat popped out on Kit's forehead. She could feel his nervousness, catch a flicker of stressed-out thought: *Please don't let me drop it, don't let anything bad happen to this thing, we've been looking for so long —*

Then Kit sat back on his heels, hard, gazing down at what he held. For a few seconds the ancient chameleon spell refused to entirely let go, so that what Kit held looked like nothing but a rounded, gritty, green-brown boulder. Then, gradually, the seeming fell away. Revealed in his hands was a shining blue-green metallic object, strangely shaped: a sort of blunt-ended capsule or stretched sphere, about two feet long.

"Wow . . ." Nita said, and then realized that her heart was pounding. All the others let out breaths of surprise and satisfaction as they peered over Kit's shoulder. Only Kit was completely silent, kneeling there with the thing braced on his knees and staring at it in wonder.

And, way down in the pocket of her jeans, Nita's cell phone rang.

Kit looked over his shoulder, his expression surprised and annoyed. Nita said a word that was *not* one she'd heard Mamvish using earlier and pulled her phone out, checking the ID on its display. It was her home number. *If it's Dairine, I swear when I catch her I'm gonna grab her and shove her head down the* — But the phone, having had its caller ID tweaked with wizardry, helpfully added: DAD CALLING.

"Oh, no," Nita moaned, for she suspected she knew what he was calling about. "Oh, no. I'm sorry, I have to take this . . ."

She flipped the phone open, acutely aware of everyone watching her, and flushed with embarrassment. "Hello?"

"Nita," her dad said: and that was an immediate sign of trouble — both in terms of his tone of voice, which was annoyed, and the fact that he'd called her by her name rather than one of the usual nicknames or pet names he used. "Where are you?"

"I'm on Mars, Dad. Please, can this wait a little while? Because I —"

"No. I need you home right now."

"Daddy, I —"

"Five minutes."

She knew that tone of voice, and there was no arguing with it, not if you wanted life to continue in anything like a normal way. "Okay," Nita said.

Her dad simply hung up.

Oh, he sounds so steamed about something, what can have him so mad . . . ?

I bet I know.

She started to get mad herself as she folded up the phone and put it away. "This is so *unfair!*" she said.

Mamvish gave her one of those amused Senior-like looks that suggested that the concept of "fairness" was something Nita should have gotten past by now. Nita sighed. "I have to go," she said to Carmela. "I'm really sorry —"

"Don't be," Carmela said. "It's no problem. I'm sure Kit will drop me off as soon as he's done here. Won't you?" And Carmela turned on Kit one of those bright of-course-you-will looks that dared him to say anything different.

Nita saw Kit's face work through annoyance, frustration, and an imposed calm that suggested he didn't want to look like an idiot by protesting too much. Behind him, Ronan was gazing innocently at nothing in particular, and Darryl was watching all this with acute interest.

"Sure," Kit said.

Nita reached for her charm bracelet, feeling for the single charm, like a thin ring or empty circle, that held the preset transit spell that would take her home in a hurry. She said the few words in the Speech that took the "safety" off the spell, and as she pulled the bright line of light that was the transit spell out of the charm, Kit threw her an apologetic look. "I'll log everything we do," he said. "Get back as soon as you can —"

"Depend on it," Nita said, dropped the transit circle glowing on the dusty brown-green ground around her, and vanished.

Kit let out another long breath as the others gathered around to look more closely at what he held. He looked up at Mamvish and Irina. "What is it?" he said.

"Well, as far as the shape goes," Irina said, peering at the object, "it's a superellipsoid. A superegg, some people used to call it, or a Lamé solid: the three-dimensional object you get when you rotate a super-ellipse around its axis. Not as resistant to force as a sphere, but it's less likely to be mistaken for something natural." She reached out a hand, touched it.

Bizarrely, Kit flinched, even though he'd touched the object already. But nothing happened. "It's weird," he said. "It looks like metal, but it's not cold. Even with Mamvish's environment field covering everything here now, it should still be cold . . ."

Ronan and Darryl and Carmela all came to crouch down around Kit and carefully touch the superegg. Kit got a sudden image of cautious ape relatives reaching out to a tall black monolith, and had to smile.

"Seems like it's in no hurry to crack open," Mamvish said. "But then some of these bottles have long-duration 'time locks' on them, or routines that analyze the finders as carefully as they'd like to analyze the find."

Kit reached sideways into his otherspace pocket, hanging near him in the air as it always was, and pulled out his manual, putting it down on the ground beside him and flipping to one of the sensing-routine pages in the rear section. He was shaking and couldn't understand why. *It's not as if I've never seen anything alien before!* Kit thought. *But this is different. This is stranger. Isn't that weird? The closer to home an alien thing is, the harder it hits —*

He looked at the manual. It showed him a diagram of the superegg, but very little data appeared beside the image, and no information about whatever might be inside it. "It *is* made of metal," Kit said. "But there's plastic in it, too. And wizardry . . ."

Irina looked over Kit's shoulder at his manual. She reached down to touch it, and a few extra lines of information appeared in the Speech, but nothing more. She looked surprised. As Mamvish, too, gazed down at the manual, her huge tongue flicked out, wavering over the manual as if tasting the air around it.

"This object's cloaked," Mamvish said.

"Even against someone with our authorizations?" Irina said. "That would take some doing."

"So it would," Mamvish said. "But we have little data on how powerful the wizards were who worked on this world." Her tail lashed. "At least I don't get any sense of this interference being something of the Lone Power's doing . . ."

Irina frowned. "That's an impression that could be faked."

"Yes," Mamvish said, "but as you say, against one of us? What are the odds?"

Irina raised her eyebrows, shrugged. "Admittedly, low. But there's a first time for everything . . ."

"I can feel something," Kit said, turning the superegg over in his hands. "Like there's just a little fragment of power in there — a splinter."

Mamvish put her tongue down against the superegg, let the tip of it rest there for a moment. Symbols in the Speech once again whirled and glowed in her hide, but they were faint and vague. "Yes," she said. "I feel it, too. A fragment of a spell, or a collapsed and compacted sequence of a wizardry, no more. And it's not active."

"Like it's on standby," Darryl said.

Mamvish tilted her head sideways, a "maybe" gesture. "It could be. If there's a complete spell held inside, it may have been set to stay dormant for a while after this artifact was found."

"In any case, I can confirm your surveyors' results," Irina said. "This object's very old indeed, and nothing like the kind of spell that Earth wizards were doing half a million years ago, even at what were then their highest levels of organization. Structurally, and in terms of the complexity of the outer shell alone, this is completely different. It feels alien to me."

"Aren't you going to try to get it open?" Carmela said.

"We'd have to have a clue as to how," Irina said. Once more she reached down to touch the superegg, running her hand slowly across its surface. "To use wizardry to operate on an object, you have to know what it is, what it's made of . . . and working that out may take us a while. *Come on,*" Irina said in the Speech, and the sudden burst of power in the words her soft voice spoke shook Kit as if someone had struck him. But the power was all persuasiveness. "*Tell us your secret. You've been alone so long already — isn't telling about yourself what you want to do, what you're all about? Who set you here? What are you for? We're here to listen . . . !*"

Nothing. Kit shook his head, wondering how

anything inanimate or otherwise could be unmoved by such power directed at it. But the egg just sat there in his lap, mute.

"Plainly this is going to take more analysis," Mamvish said with a sigh. "Well, it's the usual thing: nothing worth finding out about comes easy . . ."

"What's that?" Ronan said suddenly.

Everybody looked at him. "That sound," he said.

Kit realized he, too, had been hearing something in the background, a low, hissing noise like static from a radio in the next room. But now it was sounding closer, or as if someone was turning that radio up. Everyone looked in all directions.

"There," Mamvish said, both her eyes swiveling to look almost directly back the way they'd come.

Kit's view was blocked by her bulk: he stood up to see. Then his eyes went wide. In the distance, maybe half a mile away, a tall, dark, twisting shape was wobbling across the landscape toward them, kicking up dust as it came. It was vague, soft-featured, amorphous — but it was getting less vague every moment as that hissing noise got louder.

"Dust devil," Ronan said, peering past Mamvish. Beside him, Carmela watched its approach open-mouthed, her attention distracted from Ronan at least for the moment.

"Saw one of those on the TV news the other night," Darryl said. "It looked smaller . . ."

"They can be a mile high," Kit said, for the moment almost oblivious to the superegg he was holding. "The winds inside are almost as fast as an Earth tornado's . . ."

"Now there's a question," Darryl said. "If a tornado hits you here and picks you up, what happens then? Does Mars have an Oz?"

"It's not very likely to hit us," Mamvish said . . . and then trailed off as the dust devil swerved and headed right toward them.

To Kit's slight satisfaction, Carmela gulped. "Mamvish, your shield thingy'll keep that out, won't it?"

"Wouldn't matter much if it didn't," Kit said. "You might get some dust in your hair. The air here's so thin, it could hit you square on and not hurt you."

The dust devil was still running right at them, as unerringly as if it was on invisible tracks. Mamvish half turned, lifting her head, and her hide darkened: under it, symbols and phrases in the Speech began to twist and flow. Kit sucked in a breath and held it at the feel of the power building around her. *She's really something,* he thought, once more frozen in place as all the others were. *But no, not* all *the others* — Irina straightened up and came around Mamvish's side. The parakeet fluttered away to perch on top of the stone outcropping, and Irina's baby looked up into her face with a strange, silent composure, as Irina went up to stand by Mamvish's head. She hadn't said a word out loud in the Speech, but Kit could see the air around her hands trembling with some force that rippled the air like heat.

The hissing grew louder; the dust devil wobbled

only a little from side to side as it came at them, blocking half the horizon away with a whirling russet wall of dust. The Speech-symbols under Mamvish's hide blazed as she reinforced her shield-spell, but she didn't otherwise move. Then the whirlwind of dust blew right over them.

For a moment they were caught right in the center of the vortex. The hiss became deafening. Kit, standing there with the superegg in his hands, tilted his head back and found himself looking up at a view that even few wizards would ever have seen — the dark golden radiance of the Martian noontime sky, but just a circle of it, completely walled around by the upward-widening, brick-colored cone of a dust devil's heart. The breath went out of him in wonder. But he was feeling something else as well, and couldn't understand where it was coming from. *I've seen this before! But that's crazy. Where could I ever have seen this?*

The moment passed as the dust devil did. A second later it was behind them, wobbling away across the Martian landscape again. Mamvish's wizardry released them, and they all turned to watch it go.

"What a mess," Carmela said. Kit had to admit that she had a point. The outcropping and the ground around it, which had been fairly clean after the dune had been blown back, were now almost entirely buried in the finest possible red dust. Much more of it was piled nearly ten feet up the face of the black dune.

Darryl whistled softly. Irina, the air around her hands gone quiet again now, clucked softly to her parakeet, which had taken to the air. It flew back to her, sat on her head, and shook its feathers out, raising a small red dust cloud of its own.

"Well," Mamvish said, looking after the dust devil as it wandered away toward the horizon, "*that* was unusual . . ."

"You really think so?" Irina said. "You'll be telling me you believe in coincidences next."

Mamvish tilted an eye back toward Irina. "Not as such," she said, "of course not. It's safe to say that we've been noticed. But by what?"

"The planet?" Ronan said.

Irina threw a thoughtful look at him. "If Mars had a Planetary, we could ask him, her, or it," she said, "but it doesn't." She sighed. "One more mystery."

"Best we take them one at a time," Mamvish said.

Kit hefted the superegg, which was getting heavy. "Let's start with this one," he said. "What do we do with it?"

"Well, we'll have to keep trying to find a way to get it open," Mamvish said. "Bottles like these usually lead to more of the same: the more of them you can open, the more you can find out about the species that left them for you, and why they left them. Some of them are just memorials. Some are cries for help. And some species foresee their own demise and leave you information about how they tried to stop it. If you can make sense of those, you can start working on a way to bring them back."

"Assuming," Irina said, giving Mamvish a wry look, "that bringing them back is a good idea."

"Well, of course!" Mamvish said. "It's not a

course of action anyone rushes into. You need a lot of information before you reconstitute a lost species. Some of them are lost for good reasons. And you have to think about the effects of a reconstitution on the nearby planets." She looked at Kit and the others. "Your world's now technologically of an age to notice what's happening here. If a new species suddenly turned up here, humans would be asking why."

"They'd be doing a lot more than that!" Ronan said. "They'd be going completely spare."

"Whether aliens would be reconstituted *here* is an entirely different question," Mamvish said, waving her tail. "We've got a big galaxy, and plenty of completely uninhabited systems with suitable planets. Relocation is always a possibility. But that's a question for later in the process."

"Which you'll need to continue without me, unfortunately," Irina said, "as I need to get back to what I was doing at home. Let me know how you do with your analysis on that." She nodded at the super-egg. "What'll you do with it?"

"Re-emplace it for the time being," Mamvish said, looking at the outcropping. "If there seems to have been some kind of local reaction to its removal, better to minimize the effect for now."

Irina nodded. "As for you folks," she said, glancing at Kit and Ronan and Darryl, "just a word. Our cousin Mamvish is as busy as any Planetary would be, and her expertise is in demand. So you want to pay careful attention to whatever advice she gives you in this intervention. If there's the slightest chance that you don't understand or can't handle any problem that comes up, call her right away." She looked thoughtfully at Kit. "I've been watching this project for some time, from a distance. Tom and Carl have told me that you were to be trusted with it ... that you were possibly even vital to it, if only for your commitment and all the time you've been spending on it: and this development suggests they're right."

Kit tried to keep the grin of pride off his face. He was only partly successful. Irina smiled, too, but her look was still serious. "Naturally I trust my Seniors' judgment," she said. "But, regardless, since Mamvish seems to think you should be taking a leading role in what starts happening here now, I want you to be very, *very* careful what you do." Irina gave Kit a look that suddenly had a slight edge of frown on it. "When Tom and Carl briefed me on what you've been working on here, I naturally took a long look at your history as a wizard. *All* your histories," she said, glancing at Ronan and at Darryl. Then she turned her attention back to Kit. "So far in your career you've shown a certain talent for gambling successfully with your own skin in crisis situations. But this work won't be like that. This is likely to be one of those extended projects where when things go wrong, they start so small that you miss the early warning signs. Whatever happens here will inevitably affect Earth sooner or later ... so I expect you'll behave accordingly."

"Yes, ma'am," Kit said, sounding very subdued.

"All right," Irina said. "And now that all that's said —" The sudden grin that flashed out was as excited as Kit's would have been. "You're on the cutting edge of something very unusual, very special. Enjoy it! And keep us posted."

She turned away and strolled back over to Mamvish. "Don't forget, now," Irina said, "let me know right away if there's anything you need."

"Cousin, I'll do that," Mamvish said, and bowed her head again. Kit put his eyebrows up, for the word wasn't quite the casually friendly relationship-word *hrasht* that one wizard used to another in the ordinary course of business. It still spoke of a close kinship, but it was more nuanced, and echoes of the overshadowing attention of the Powers That Be hung over it.

Irina patted Mamvish on the flank, waved to the rest of them, and then she was gone.

A leading role . . . ! Kit thought. *A leading role!*

"Yeah, well, you heard her reading you the pre-riot version of the Riot Act," Ronan said under his breath. "So don't get cocky."

Kit threw Ronan a smug look that suggested the advice might already be a bit late. Ronan rolled his eyes.

"Is she really the most senior wizard on Earth?" Carmela said. "She doesn't look old enough."

Kit winced in embarrassment at someone as sketchily informed about wizardry as Carmela making such judgments . . . even though the thought had crossed his mind as well. Mamvish, though, cocked an indulgent eye at her. "Seniority," Mamvish said, "takes many forms. Irina is quite special. No one understands the Earth the way she does: and as a result, it listens to her." She waved her tail in a way that to Kit somehow communicated a strange level of concern. "If for some reason the Earth needed to be destroyed in a hurry . . . *she'd* be the one that the Powers would talk to."

"She takes care of the Earth's kernel?" Darryl said, awed.

"She may occasionally *be* the Earth's kernel," said Mamvish. "Certainly she's the planet's foremost geomancer: and when you possess and exercise power at so central a level, the difference between what you do and what you are does start to blur." She waved her tail again, turning as she did so.

Another brief storm of Speech-characters broke out under Mamvish's hide, and the newly deposited red dust went sliding away sideways from the outcropping and the dune, blown there by a more concentrated and focused wind than the one that had dropped it there.

"Let's tuck the egg back in where we found it," Mamvish said to Kit. "It'll be safe enough here. Your manuals, and my version of the Knowledge, have stored all the data we acquired from the egg today. The rest of the investigative team will now have the data, too. Our next task is to work out how to open the egg, or read its interior, so that we don't lose any potential clues to just what happened on this world."

"You mean," Carmela said, "maybe the species that lived here destroyed themselves or something?"

Mamvish waved her tail uncertainly. "It's too soon to say. When both the planets and the species in a given system have such ambivalences about another of the system's worlds, it could be an indicator that something catastrophic occurred. But with so little information in the manual to guide us, we have to be careful not to jump to conclusions."

"Isn't it kind of weird that there *isn't* anything?" Darryl said.

"Not at all. Sometimes the Powers That Be purposely conceal information for one reason or another — but in this case, They tell me They've done no such thing. Which leaves us with other possibilities. The Lone Power might have interfered, causing that information to be hidden. Or the species in question may itself have found a way to redact the data, for reasons of their own." Mamvish waved her tail again. "We'll take our time and find the truth. Meanwhile, I've got other business to take care of . . . so let's seal this up and call it a day."

Kit nodded and went to kneel in front of the outcropping again. He put one hand on that cold brownish stone and said the Mason's Word, feeling the stone go soft under his skin. Then carefully he slipped the egg back into the heart of the outcropping.

When it was completely concealed, he paused for just a moment more with his hands on the smooth alien metal, unwilling to take his hands away: he thought he felt the egg tingling slightly in his grip. *Am I imagining that?* But a moment later the sensation had faded. *Probably something to do with using the Mason's Word: you always get a little fizz, something to do with the gas atoms in the oxides or nitrates or whatever coming unbound . . .*

Kit pulled his arms out of the stone, stood up, and dusted his hands on his pants. As usual, the gesture was fruitless: there always seemed to be more dust to get rid of. "Yeah," Carmela said, "and when you get home, make sure you stay away from the DVDs until you've washed up . . ."

Kit silently gritted his teeth. *I can't wait to dump her,* he thought. *And then we have to find a way to keep her from tagging along everywhere we go, or this thing's gonna turn into a disaster . . .*

"So," Mamvish said. "Keep doing what you're doing, cousins: and keep me informed. I'll leave the shield here to protect what we've found. *Dai stihó!*"

And she was gone, without the slightest movement of the air inside the shield.

"Now there goes a professional," Ronan said, shaking his head in admiration. "Irina's right: we're lucky to have her around." He stretched, glanced around. "Meanwhile, I've got to get back myself. Conference call tonight?"

"Yeah," Kit said. "Put a note in my manual — we'll set a time. Big D?" He glanced at Darryl.

"Any time after dinner's fine," Darryl said. He waved and vanished, making a careless pop in the air.

Ronan rolled his eyes again. "Sloppy," he said. "See you later —"

A second later Ronan, too, was gone, more silently. Kit looked at Carmela. "Well," he said, "let's get you back." He reached into his otherspace pocket and pulled out the ready-set transit spell he used to get back to his bedroom from Mars. Uncoiling the long sentence in the Speech, he ran the glowing line of light through his hands until he found the part he was looking for. "We need to put your personal info in this," he said. "Now, how much do you weigh this week?"

His sister glared at him. "Could you start with a more tactless question?"

"Sure. Your IQ?"

Carmela glowered. Kit grinned as he dropped the spell to the ground, and it stretched into a circle around the two of them and joined one end to another like a snake biting its tail. His hands were still tingling slightly as he started reciting the first part of the transit spell and the world started to go silent around them.

It was strange that even as the silence built and the universe leaned in to listen to what Kit wanted, he could still hear that hissing, the dust whirling by. . . .

Wellakh

Nita appeared as quietly as she could in the shade of the sassafras trees at the "wild" rear of her backyard. In between the bigger trees were tall thickets of smaller sassafras and wild mulberry scrub, screening the space from any possible view from the houses behind or to either side: but right now, the possibility of any neighbors noticing her was the least of her worries. Nita glanced up through the leaves at the late afternoon light, letting out a long, annoyed breath. *Since when do I appear out here like someone who's afraid to go in the house?*

She slipped out from under the trees, heading up between the flower beds of the garden. Close to the house, not far from the chain-link fence and its gate, a tall, broad-crowned rowan tree stood in the middle of the yard, all covered with white flowers: an old rope swing hung from one branch. As she walked under the rowan, a long, leafy twig dropped down toward her: she put up a hand absent-mindedly and high-fived it. "Liused . . ." she said in the Speech.

Sounding a little under the weather, the tree said.

"Ask me in an hour or so and I'll give you a more detailed weather report . . ."

She opened the gate to the driveway. Her home life had once seemed so much more casual. *Where's your sister, dear? She's on one of Jupiter's moons, Mom. . . . Oh, well. I guess that's all right. Just as long as she's not creating life again.* After the shock of discovering that their daughters were wizards, Nita's mom and dad had eventually become almost relaxed about it all. But along with her mother, those days were now gone. Her dad had become much more the heavy parent in the last six months. *You have to expect some changes,* her counselor, Mr. Millman, had said. *People handle their love and their loss in a hundred different ways. The results can be annoying until you understand what's going on.* Though Nita was starting to understand, the annoyance was a long way from abating. In Nita's dad's case, she suspected his new sternness about wizardly doings was because he knew the tendency toward wizardry had come down to his kids through his side of the family, and he was feeling as if this was somehow all his fault.

If only I could brainfix my dad and make him think that everything was just fine with Dairine. Well, Nita *could* brainfix him, but it would be the wrong thing to do, would be in complete contravention of the Wizard's Oath, and would make her feel like a criminal. Nor was it any consolation that psychotropic spelling, the wizardries that could be used to change people's minds about things, were such a nuisance to work, had such a horrible backlash on the wizard who worked them, and worked for so short a time before everything went back to the way it had been before. The irony wasn't lost on Nita that a wizard could so easily change concrete physical matter, but practically had to sweat blood to change something as immaterial as someone else's thought.

Or if I could only clone my sister. Make an extra one who'd stay home and behave, so Dad wouldn't notice what was going on with the real one . . . Then Nita groaned, not believing she was seriously *having* this idea. The last time there'd been a cloned Dairine around, during her sister's Ordeal, the complications had been nearly endless. *One of her's enough for any universe! Or the whole sheaf of them. Besides — a Dairine that hangs around behaving all the time? Instantly identifiable as a fake.*

She paused on the back doorstep, trying to devise some kind of strategy for handling her dad. His stern moods could be hard to derail —

"You could come in, you know," said a voice from the kitchen, through the screen door. "It's not *you* I'm going to ground."

That sounded promising, but it didn't seem smart to relax just yet. Nita went in.

Her dad was rooting around in a cupboard next to the stove; a full coffee cup stood on the counter. "Are we out of sugar?"

"We just got a whole bag last week," Nita said,

leaning against the counter. "Is sugar why I came all the way back from Mars? We were just getting to the good part!"

"And you can go back," her dad said, coming down with a crumpled-up, near-empty bag of store-brand sugar, "as soon as you sort things out here at home."

"What 'things'?"

"Your sister," her father said, "was missing from school today."

Thought so. Nita rolled her eyes. "Daddy, there's only two days of school left before summer. You know that she —"

"I *don't* know that she," her dad said, sounding annoyed, letting the cupboard door fall shut and pulling a spoon out of the silverware drawer, which he hip-slammed shut. "And I really dislike getting these calls from school telling me she's nowhere to be found, after she promised she'd stop cutting classes to run all over the galaxy!"

Nita went into the dining room and flopped down in a chair. *This is* not *my fault, why am I having to deal with this?*

"So where is she?" her dad said. "Did she mention to you where she was headed?"

"No. I have no idea."

"It's not just that she wasn't at school," her dad said. "She also hasn't done her chores. The kitchen was a mess when I came in, and the garbage didn't go out this morning. And after I had a big thing with her last week about not leaving the planet before she's done her work at home! For a few days it looked like she was going with the program. But now . . ."

Nita buried her head in her arms. *This is a disaster. I can see it coming now: here goes my whole summer . . .*

In the kitchen, the spoon clinked in the cup for a few moments: then her dad followed Nita in and sat down beside her. He turned the mug around and around on the table between his hands. "Honey, your mom was always better than I was at knowing what was going on in Dairine's head . . . or at least having a clue." She could hear from his voice that it cost her father something to make this admission. "I don't have her to help me out now. So you're going to have to step into the gap and give me a hand."

Nita wanted to laugh helplessly, but this didn't seem to be the moment. "I can check the manual to find out where she is, sure. But as for figuring out why she does what she does day by day, by reading her mind or something, it's not going to happen, Daddy! It's easy to keep someone out of your head if you know they're trying to listen. And even when you *can* hear somebody's thoughts, you can't always tell what the thoughts mean to *them.*"

Her dad looked frustrated. "Then what use is mind reading?"

"Not a lot," Nita said. "Talking still works best. Which is what wizardry's about, to begin with."

"Well, talking's not working real well with Dairine at the moment," Nita's dad said. "She keeps telling me she'll stay in touch, be back home for meals . . . and then it doesn't happen. This has to stop . . . and *you're* going to see that it does."

"Me? How? I can't do anything about —"

"Oh, yes, you can. To begin with, you can find her and get her back here. And then you can find a way to make sure she behaves." Nita's father frowned. "I don't want to play the bad guy here, but I can't spend every day of the summer wondering where she is and what trouble she's getting into! I have a right to some time off, too — an afternoon or an evening when I don't have to be worrying about her. This kind of behavior isn't fair to *me!*"

He looked at Nita. She let out a breath. "No," she said, "I guess not."

"Thank you. So I want to know from you every day where Dairine is, until I can start depending on *her* to let me know. And you go nowhere on any given day until you've satisfied me as to where she's going to be and whether she's okay."

Nita heaved a heavy, exasperated sigh and stood up. "You want her back here right now?"

"Yes."

"And then I can get back to what I was doing?"

"Yes."

"Then I have to do something first," Nita said.

"Do it. Then bring her home for dinner."

Nita went slowly up the stairs, wearing a frown that she suspected looked much like her dad's. *I hate this. And it's not fair to me. But there's no way out. And he's kind of right —*

At the top of the stairs, she paused, looking out

the window that overlooked the next-door neighbor's front yard. *So treat it like a challenge from the Powers . . . because maybe it is. Figure out what to do, and maybe the rest of the summer won't turn into a horror story.* Nita let out a breath. *Think of Dairine as just another intervention, one more problem to be solved.*

Then Nita swallowed — because whether she liked it or not, there was one step she had to take before she could start solving this particular problem.

In her bedroom she sat down on the bed and pulled her manual out of her otherspace pocket. For a long moment Nita sat hunched over, holding the closed book in her hands, looking at the scuffed blue buckram cover, then flipped the book open and paged through to the directory that listed wizards and their status.

She didn't have a bookmark for the page she wanted, but then she'd never had cause to look up information about the world of the wizard in question: he'd just turned up in her basement while she was off on exchange. "I need the pages for the star system containing the planet Wellakh . . ."

The book in her hands riffled its own pages hastily from right to left, kicking up a little cool breeze. Nita smiled. "Can I get you to do this all the time when it's hot out?"

The pages instantly laid themselves out extremely flat, open and still. "Okay, don't get all annoyed," Nita said under her breath, amused, and glanced at the open pages.

Wellakh's golden-yellow star displayed in the

first of a set of images on the left-hand page. The right-hand page filled with data about the system and its one inhabited planet: a precis of local system history, details about the species inhabiting the one inhabited world, and other general information. Nita read quickly through it, shaking her head; the planet's history had been difficult. *Not that anyone couldn't tell that from clear out in space,* she thought, looking at the image of the planet. Half of Wellakh was dappled with blue seas and lakes, much of its terrain red-golden with the planet's idiosyncratic vegetation. There were even snowy mountains here and there. But the other half of that world was flat and scorched-looking, a slagged-down desolation. *What would it have been like growing up there — knowing that anytime, your sun might get cranky and pull the same stunt again?*

Nita touched the listing again. "Show me all wizards native to the planet for the last hundred Wellakhit years."

The picture of the planet dissolved, replaced by a couple of columns' worth of listing. Nita glanced down it, turned the page to see two more columns there. But that was all. *Just a few hundred wizards. Not a lot for a world with a population of over a billion: mostly a pretty peaceful place. But the troubles they've got are big ones. And for the worst ones, they need a very special kind of wizard . . .*

Nita started running down the list. *Ke Nelaid, ROSHAUN . . . 'See det Nuiiliat'? Oh, I get it, that's the clan name the whole family's listed under . . .*

Under *det Nuiiliat,* a long list of wizards in that

family went right down the page. In fact, half the wizards on the planet were either in this family or related to it. Nita swallowed as she came to "Nelaid" . . . then realized this wasn't the wizard she was looking for, but his father. *Ke Seriv, NELAID. Residence* — The address initially displayed in the Wellakhit language, then re-rendered itself in the Speech. *Sunplace, the Borders, the Scorched Zone, Old Continent. Position: Sunlord-in-Abeyance. Power rating: 28.8 +/-.5.* Nita's eyebrows went up: that was a very high rating, certainly higher than Tom's or Carl's. *Physical status: Corporate. Mission status: Presently unassigned; political considerations.*

But this wasn't the name Nita was looking for. *I missed it: on Wellakh they change their names depending on who their father was . . .* She glanced farther up the column, and a little shiver of pain went through her as she found the name she'd resisted looking up for so long.

Ke Nelaid, ROSHAUN. Former residence: Sunplace, the Borders, the Scorched Zone, Old Continent. Position: Son of the Sunlord, son of the Great King, descendant of the Inheritors of the Great Land, the Throne-Destined. Nita grimaced at the huge weight of words, which Dairine had immediately reduced to "prince." Then Nita looked down at what she had been avoiding, the single line underneath the description.

Physical status:

And she stared at the blank space after the words. There was nothing else there.

But that doesn't make any sense —!

Nita scanned up the column again to other older names. The majority of their physical status listings showed the single long, curved-back streak of Speech-charactery that meant one thing: *Recall.* Nita had seen it often enough in the listings of wizards from Earth, both those whose lives had been lost in the line of duty and those who had died in other circumstances. The implication seemed to be that once you were a wizard, maybe you never stopped being one unless you really wanted to — and even after you were dead, or what passed for dead in the Real World, the Powers That Be nonetheless considered you to still be on some kind of duty. It was, in a strange way, reassuring.

But this . . . this *is just strange.*

The listing did have some unusual descriptions of physical status. One, attributed to one of Roshaun's great-great-grandmothers, was *Indeterminate.* A couple of others said *Exhaled.* Nita blinked. *Whatever* that *means!* But the complete lack of a physical status for Roshaun left Nita bemused. She reached out to the listing and touched a different name, feeling the small sizzle of power that spoke of active wizardry indwelling in a self. All the names had it, dead or alive. But when she touched Roshaun's name —

No sizzle: a feeling as if the manual page was nothing but ordinary paper. *It's as if not even the Powers That Be are sure what's happened to him. How can* that *be? I don't get it.*

And if even They *don't get it —*

Nita let the manual's pages fall forward on the finger that held her place. *Whatever it means . . . it*

*also means that Roshaun's not dead! Or not dead yet.
Or something. And whatever else I might think about
what Dairine's up to, at least she's not nuts, or in
denial. She's looking for somebody she's got at least a
chance of finding. Maybe the smallest chance imaginable ... but still a chance.*

Nita spent the next few moments just getting
hold of herself ... for she'd been shaking, afraid of
what she was about to find. *Which just goes to show
that I should've done this a long time ago. Maybe I
could have saved myself this grief with Dairine!* The
shock of relief was almost as hard to bear as the shock
she'd braced herself for, that final awful certainty
from which there would have been no retreat.

Finally she flipped the manual open again, riffling
through to the section holding the directory for
Earth. Nita had a quick-reference "bookmark" page
installed at the front, showing names of wizards she
knew well or had worked with either frequently or
occasionally. The name she was looking for was
almost at the top. *Callahan, DAIRINE R. Present
location: Sunplace, Old Continent, Wellakh.* Nita
raised her eyebrows. *Okay ... but doing what?* she
thought. *Arrival time: JD 2454274.10012. Power rating, 5.45 +/- .55 ...* Nita eyed her sister's power level:
it was lower than she'd ever seen it. *Then again,
what's this supposed to be?* She looked curiously at the
listing beside it, one she couldn't remember having
seen before. It said, *Under augmentation: augment
level 3.2 +/- 2.2.* She frowned. *That's a new one.
What's she up to?*

She put her finger on the listing. "Coordinates, please?"

They displayed on the page. At the same time, a voice said in the back of her head, *You know, if you'd just ask me, I'd do the gating and take you there.*

"Bobo," Nita said, "I appreciate the offer. I just want to make sure I don't lose the hang of doing it the hard way."

You're just a glutton for punishment, the peridexis said.

"You and I are going to have to sit down — as much as you can sit, anyway — and have a long talk about —"

How we can be talking at all? Bobo said. At least he didn't sound injured. *I guess I wonder myself. But go on, do your spell the hard way . . .*

Nita jiggled the charm bracelet on her wrist until the gating charm came up. Out of it she pulled a long, blue-glowing thread of spell, a single word-character in the Speech. This she drew down until it touched Dairine's entry in the manual, hooking to its location parameters. Then Nita let go of the strand of light. When it snapped back into the charm, it pulled with it a whole new chain of characters, swallowed them up, and blazed, ready to go.

Nita stood up and shoved the manual into the waiting otherspace pocket. Then she pulled on the charm again, and that long line of glowing blue light slid out: she dropped it on the floor, where it went a fierce molten gold and stretched into a circle of Speech-words, ready to knot itself up in the Wizard's Knot.

Nita looked down at the glowing words and slowly began to speak them, turning as she spoke.

The room went silent. Darkness pressed in. As she completed the spell and pronounced the syllables of the Wizard's Knot, everything went dark.

Moments later she found herself standing on a terrace of some smooth, glittering dark-golden stone. Behind her, in a sheer stone wall, was a series of tall, glassy doors, like the entry to a school or the front of a theater, leading into some dim, hard-to-see interior.

Maybe fifty yards in front of Nita, the terrace ended in a meter-high railing that followed the terrace's curve hundreds of feet along to either side and out of sight. Out past the rail she got a glimpse of wide gardens far below, fading off into a barer landscape. Glancing from side to side, Nita saw that the terrace itself was cantilevered well out from the surface of the huge, relatively smooth needle of stone behind her, in the base of which the doors were set.

Nita tilted her head back, trying to see the top of the peak above. *A few hundred feet, maybe* — It was hard to tell. The blue-green sky was full of clouds: as she watched, one drifted straight into and around the top of that needle of stone, obscuring it. More terraces were visible above, staggered around the surface of the uprising spear of stone, up to the cloud and past it.

Nita glanced around, wondering where to go from here. Her transport wizardry had built into it a typical so-called "decent interval" offset; you'd be deposited somewhere within, say, a hundred meters of the person you were seeking, but the wizardry wouldn't drop you right into that person's lap. *So let's see . . .* Down the right side of the curve, nothing was visible but featureless, shining stone. To the left, though, maybe fifty yards down, Nita spotted a single small door, all by itself. *But wait. Not a door. That's a gate. It's got bars —*

Nita reached sideways and retrieved her manual from the otherspace pocket — for when a wizard was visiting a world where wizardry was practiced in the open, his manual was his passport — and walked toward that gate.

Above her, that cloud moved away. On the stony spire's far side, the sun came out, throwing a long path of shadow down the wall, over the gate and Nita, and out to the terrace's edge. But as she got close to the gate, she saw a light as intense pouring out of it, streaming in a narrow bar-striped ribbon out across the terrace.

Nita stared. *Oooookay,* she thought. *Unusual.* She walked slowly to the gate, tucking her manual under her armpit, and reached for her charm bracelet, pinching one small glassy lens-charm between finger and thumb and saying a few words in the Speech under her breath. A fragment of spell-shielding ran up and over her free hand and nearly to her elbow, like an oven mitt of thickened air. She wiggled her fingers to make sure that it felt right, and then stuck the shielded hand into that light.

Nothing happened. *Just sunlight?* Nita thought. *Weird, unless there's a window on the far side of the mountain* — She shook the shield-spell back down her arm: it vanished. Then she peered around through the bars of the gate.

Her mouth dropped open. *Sunlight,* she thought. Inside the gate was a huge, domed, circular room nearly as wide across as the entire width of the spire of stone. Inside it, floating maybe three feet above the floor, was a sun.

Nita leaned against the gate, staring at the burning, dark-golden globe that hung there. It looked to be about fifty feet in diameter. Blobby black foot-long sunspots sailed slowly across its surface, the fiery red-gold plasma they pushed through getting all torn up by their magnetic fields. Plasma writhed and stretched away from the surface in bright filaments as the sunspots plowed stubbornly through it like inkblots with a mission. Elsewhere, sticking up off the surface like fuzz off a ball of yarn, spiky prominences licked into the upper reaches of the star's atmosphere, frayed at their ends, fell back again. If you held still, you could just see the star's rotation, as slow as watching sunrise. As Nita watched, movement off to the right caught her eye as someone walked around the side of the great globe and stood with her back to Nita, looking up at it.

What the heck is she wearing? Nita thought. There was no mistaking Dairine, especially in that small sun's light: it made her red hair look even redder than usual. When Nita had seen her this morning, Dairine had been been wearing floppy jeans and a cropped T-shirt. She might still have them on, but it was hard to tell, as she also now wore some kind of silky floor-length tunic in a dark honey color. Dairine half turned, pushed up the sleeve of the tunic — *yeah, the jeans and the top are still there; what a strange look!* — and thrust her arm into the sun, almost up to the shoulder, where she stood feeling around under the "star's" surface like someone trying to find something hidden at the back of a dark cupboard.

And as Dairine felt around inside the sun, her glance fell on Nita.

Dairine's eyes went wide: she froze. *That's my cue*, Nita thought. *Is this open?* She pushed the gate experimentally. It swung open under her push.

Nita walked in and started across that broad shining floor toward Dairine. Dairine took her arm out of the sun, shook it, folded her arms, and stood watching Nita come.

This was a sure sign that Dairine was in a snotty mood and ready to be tough to deal with. *Now it's just a question of how to handle it.* Nita kept walking, letting her attention move to that huge, slowly turning ball of energy. The energy was real; as she got closer, the heat from the "sun" was increasing, though it was nothing like what a star would genuinely have emitted. *It's a simulator*, Nita thought. *Maybe even a real-time mirror of Wellakh's own star —*

Another shape came out from behind the star-globe: a man. He was taller than all but the tallest human beings would be — slender, narrow-shouldered, wiry, with very long hair as red as Dairine's. He wore the same sort of long, light tunic Dairine was wearing, though his was several shades darker, with

nothing under it but a sleeveless vest and long, loose
trousers of a similar silky material, almost exactly the
dark fiery amber color of that star.

As Nita got closer she spotted something else
unusual that Dairine was wearing besides the tunic.
Around her neck was an oversize torc of red-gold
metal, with a smooth, egg-shaped, egg-sized stone set
in it — paler than the metal, slightly paler than the
color of the star. In its depths, as Nita got close, she
saw a glow that shifted and moved, echoing the stretch
and snap of the prominences on the "star's" surface.
Every now and then the glow dimmed as a miniature
sunspot slipped by under the surface of the gem.

Dairine, hostile-eyed, watched Nita coming as
the man walked around the side of the "star" toward
them. Nita paused and waited for him to approach.

His walk was easy and graceful, but his expression
suggested that the outer calm concealed a tremendous
tension. Nita found herself being examined by very
immediate green eyes, shadowed under heavy brows.
The Wellakhit's face was a sharp one, high-cheekboned,
eyes slanted, so that it was easy to get the impression of
some cool and thoughtful predator looking at you. As
he got closer, Nita picked up on something else: a sense
of sheer power that transmitted itself right across the
empty air. She concentrated on hanging on to her composure as he came, for she'd never felt anything quite
like this before from a being who worked with wizardry and was also mortal. *Most immortals spend a lot
of effort covering up their power,* she thought, *so we
ephemerals won't get too freaked. And mortal wizards*

don't flaunt their power: it's rude. But *this* wizard possibly had reasons for handling his aura differently. On Wellakh, where there were relatively few wizards, Nelaid ke Seriv was very senior indeed: if not actually the Planetary — for some worlds had none — then the next thing to it on Wellakh, a person of crucial importance to the planet's well-being and a power to be reckoned with. *Which is probably why it annoys him so much that some of his people keep trying to assassinate him. And why he walks around with his aura hanging out, so anybody in range gets reminded what they're in for if they cross him . . .*

As he came, Nita's eyes went back to that flaming hair of his. It wasn't just almost the same shade as Dairine's: it was *exactly* the same shade. *That is beyond strange!* And at the back of Nita's mind, the thought stirred that, in a wizard's world, there were no coincidences. When something looked like a connection, it was smart for you to pay attention —

Later. When she judged that Nelaid was close enough, Nita executed the half bow that she'd found worked well with most bipedal humanoid species. "Senior," Nita said, having considered which of ten or twenty terms of address would be most correct, "in the Powers' names, and on Their behalf, greetings from another jurisdiction."

"Young cousin," he said, a response correct if not precisely comradely, "in Their names, and on Their business as always, welcome."

"What are *you* doing here?" Dairine said.

Nita didn't even spare Dairine a glance. Protocol dictated otherwise: you always greeted and briefed the most senior wizard first. This also left Nita with a perfect way to outflank Dairine's temper. "Sir, I'm sorry to interrupt whatever's going on, but we have a family situation that in my judgment overrides what my manual indicates is an elective exercise on my sister's part. With your permission —"

Nelaid nodded, a gracious gesture of agreement, and turned away as if to examine the star-simulation. Nita went over to Dairine. Under her breath she said, "You look like a Jedi knight who lost the bathrobe's belt."

Dairine rolled her eyes. "I live for your fashion bulletins."

"Your continued life is just what we're talking about. At least your home life. Dad wants you back there right now."

"You came all the way here to tell me *that*? You can just go back, thanks."

The dismissive, cutting tone made Nita flush hot. As she opened her mouth, "Your pardon," Nelaid said, "but a matter has arisen that requires my intervention. If I may be excused —"

Surprised by the very status-neutral language, Nita caught the oddest look from Nelaid, a slight narrowing of the eyes. Then he vanished without so much as a breath of wind, the effortless displacement of a wizard who had long since perfected the art of teleporting in or out without anyone being the wiser. *Especially whoever's trying to murder him this afternoon . . .*

Nita turned back to Dairine. "What exactly are you doing?"

"Practicing. Or I was until you butted in." Dairine turned away.

"Practicing what?"

Shrugging out of her overrobe, Dairine glared at Nita. "Messing with the energy management of a live star," she said. "What are you, obtuse?"

She's trying to get me mad, Nita thought, *and that'll be her excuse to blow me off.* "Cruel question for someone you know hates geometry," Nita said.

Her sister's mouth quirked as she folded up the robe. Nita kept her own face still. "Dair, you ditched school."

"Like everybody else wasn't ditching it today," Dairine muttered, turning away. "Like it's such a big deal. Some schools are more important than others."

"Won't argue," Nita said. "But you and Dad had an agreement. If you'd let him know what you were going to do first, you might have been in less trouble than you are now. Now you've got a mess to clean up. The least you can do," Nita said as Dairine opened her mouth to say something angry, "is let me help you get out of it so you can get on with business."

Dairine paused. "What?"

Nita laughed, thinking, *This is the way to go, keep her off balance . . .* "You think I enjoy watching you get in trouble? There's nothing in it for me. And it screws up my schedule. Let's keep this brief so we can both get back to what we were doing, okay?"

Dairine stared, caught between bemusement and suspicion. "Are you all right?" she said. "Have you flunked something?"

"No! This isn't about anything but me helping you cover your butt, because it looks like you need help with that right now."

Dairine scowled, but now at least the scowl suggested that they might be on the same side of the argument. "All right, how?"

"We're going to bug your manual," Nita said.

Dairine's eyes went wide. *"Oh, no, you're not!"* she said. *"Nobody* but me messes with Spot!"

"Of course somebody does!" Nita said. "All the time. *Wizardry* messes with Spot every second of the day."

Dairine gave her a strange look.

"All Dad wants is to know where you are, and that you're okay," Nita said. "There are two ways that can happen. He can make me run after you constantly and report in on everything you do. I mean *everything.* If he doesn't like something you're up to, I'll have to haul you out of it . . . which is probably going to make us kill each other by the end of the summer. You'll be sick and tired of me butting in on you every five minutes, yeah?"

"Yeah —"

"And I'll want *you* dead because having to keep tabs on you will ruin *my* schedule and drive *me* berserk. Since killing each other would get the Powers That Be cranky with us, let's try something different. Remember the translation spinoff we arranged with

Tom last month, so Dad would have access to the manual info about Filif and Sker'ret and Roshaun when they came to visit?"

Dairine nodded, but couldn't cover the wince of pain on hearing Roshaun's name. Nita pretended she hadn't noticed. "We'll do the same deal," Nita said, "but instead we'll hook the output from your daily manual precís into it. Dad can read it on the computer, or even his cell phone."

"He won't understand half of it," Dairine said, scowling.

"Not my problem," Nita said. "You get to explain stuff to him when you get home every day. He'll calm down even more when you're telling him about what you're doing."

"It's gonna be a nuisance," Dairine said.

"Not as much a nuisance as being grounded."

Dairine grinned. "Like he could."

"He couldn't. But Tom could." The amusement fell out of Dairine's expression. "You know he and Dad talk every few days! One word from Dad to Tom, and unless you're officially on errantry, your butt's going to be stuck on Earth till the two of them agree otherwise." Dairine opened her mouth. "And the Powers That Be wouldn't countermand Tom unless there was something big going on! Till we hit the local legal age, They're mostly on Dad's side."

Dairine stared at the polished floor. "I don't know," she said at last, looking toward the simulation. "This has kind of a Big Brother sound to it . . ."

"Or Big Sister?" Nita said. "Yeah, it does. But it's

the best deal we're going to get from Dad right now. And since Bobo *is* wizardry, and the Powers That Be run him, he can't do anything bad to you or Spot." Nita glanced around. "Where is he, anyway?"

Dairine gestured with her head toward the star-simulator. To Nita's considerable surprise, a small shadow, like a rectangular sunspot, materialized near the bottom of the slowly rotating globe: and then a dark oblong shape extruded itself from the shadow and dropped toward the shining floor.

The shape put out legs in midair and landed on them, bouncing slightly as it came down. Then it came spidering over to Dairine and Nita.

"Wow," Nita said, "he's had another upgrade." When she'd seen Spot only that morning, he'd looked as he had for the last couple of months — a little silvery laptop about the size of a large paperback book. Now, though, he'd gone wider, leaner, and shining black. Set into the back of the closed lid, matte black against the sleek gloss of the rest of the carapace, was what could at first glance have been mistaken for the fruity logo of a large computer company: but this apple had no bite out of it.

"Very slick, guy!" Nita said to him. "Nice look."

Thanks, Spot said. As usual, he was no more verbally forthcoming with Nita than with anyone else but Dairine. But he did sound faintly pleased.

Dairine let out a long breath. "I don't know about this," she said under her breath. "Bobo's kind of your tool."

Nita burst out laughing. Dairine looked at her

strangely. "What? What's so funny?"

It took Nita a few moments to get the laughter under control. "My tool! Oh, please. Like I can order wizardry around and tell it what to do! Please let *that* happen." She got down on one knee. "Spot," she said, "have you been following this?"

Yes.

"Will this solution work for you? You're the one who'll be the source of the raw data. Bobo'll just be managing the spinoff for Dad: he'll feed the massaged data to the computer at home."

Maybe with text-message alerts when something new comes in, Bobo said at the back of Nita's mind. *Copied to e-mail . . .*

Nita rolled her eyes. *Not only do I have the spirit of wizardry living in my head, but it's a* geek *spirit.* She turned her attention back to Spot.

He turned one eye up to look at Dairine. *Okay with you?*

Dairine shrugged. "If we're going to stay on track with what we're doing here, sounds like it has to be."

Okay, Spot said, and trundled off back under the simulator. There he levitated up into the body of the surrogate sun, vanishing in the glare of its chromosphere.

Nita shook her head. "How hot does it get in there?"

"Not too bad," Dairine said, and sighed. "A couple thousand degrees K. The temperature's scaled down, like the exterior, for practice. Wizards here usually scale themselves way up in apparent size to work with Thahit. Seems it perceives us better that way."

Nita nodded. "Okay. Look . . . thanks for working with me on this. Why don't you go get changed and we'll head home and deal with Dad before he gets too crazy. The sooner we disarm him, the sooner life gets back to what passes for normal."

Dairine nodded, moved away. Then suddenly she stopped and turned: and the strange, hard look on her face made Nita wonder if she was going to have to do this bout of persuasion all over again.

"One thing," Dairine said.

Nita tried to stay calm. "Yeah?"

Dairine came back to Nita almost reluctantly. "When you came after me just now," Dairine said, "you checked your manual first, didn't you? To see what happened to Roshaun."

Nita froze. Dairine's voice had gone expressionless and flat, and hearing it sound that way scared Nita: the last time she'd heard that tone from her sister had been just after their mom had died. *How do I handle this? What do I say?*

"Yeah," Nita said. "I did."

Dairine stared at her. Then she whispered, "What did it say?"

Oh, wow, I was afraid of this! Either she hasn't looked, or she has and doesn't believe what she saw. And if whatever I say is the wrong answer, now I get blamed for whatever I found. "Uh . . . Something weird. Something really — vague."

Dairine's face was simply frozen. Nita didn't dare move. *Oh, no, I'm dead now . . .*

But suddenly her sister was hugging her hard, her face buried in Nita's vest. "Oh, wow," Dairine was saying, "oh, *wow,* I was so scared, I thought that he — and then I thought I was crazy; it didn't make any sense. But if you saw it, too, then it's true, he's not, *not* dead, he's *not* —"

Nita was bemused, but for the moment the safest course seemed to be to just hang on to Dairine while her sister got herself under control. "It's okay," she said, "it's okay" — while very much hoping it actually was.

After a moment Dairine pushed her away, turning her back to wipe her eyes. "Come on," Nita said, "let's get moving. Go change."

Dairine nodded and vanished.

Nita turned away from the slowly rotating star — then jumped. In complete silence, Nelaid had reappeared behind her and was standing with hands clasped behind his back, looking past Nita at the simulator.

That ironic gaze shifted to her now. Nita popped out in a sweat. The effect was similar to being in the principal's office, except that in this case she hadn't been called: she'd walked in and told the principal to his face that whatever he was doing, he needed to stop it while she dealt with business. "I'm really, really sorry," Nita said. "If I could have, I'd have waited till she got home. But my dad —"

Nelaid held up a hand, closed his eyes. It was a gesture Nita had seen other humanoid species use as the equivalent of a headshake. When Nelaid opened his eyes again, his expression was milder, if no less ironic. "She is, I take it, a trial to you."

Nita rolled her eyes. "You have no idea."

"I might," Nelaid said. "I had a younger brother once. He should have been Sunlord when our father left the body. But others had different plans for him. And my father, and me."

In the précis on Wellakh, Nita had seen references to the political instability of the world: but the phrase "frequent assassinations" can sound merely remotely troubling until you find yourself discussing the reality of it with one of the targets. Not certain how to respond, Nita kept quiet.

"She reminds me of him," Nelaid said, looking at the simulation of the Wellakhit homestar as it gently rotated. As they watched, a single loop of prominence arched up out of the leftward limb of the star, strained away from it, snapped in two; the ends frayed away and the separate jets fell back to the sun's surface in a splash of plasma.

"Of your brother?" Nita said.

Nelaid closed his eyes again. When they opened, Nita was sorry she'd said anything: the grief and pain in Nelaid's eyes flared as the prominence had, brief and fierce. Then the look was swallowed back into that look of carefully controlled irony, and might never have been there at all. "Is she in difficulty at home?" Nelaid said.

"Some. It'll be okay when we get back. Our dad just needs to know what Dairine's doing."

And then the idea hit her. "I wonder —" Nita said, and stopped. *Where do I go from here? There are too many ways this can go wrong —*

Too late: Nelaid was waiting. "It might make our father happier," Nita said, "if he knew for sure that she had someone keeping an eye on her. Someone —"

"Older?" Nelaid said. "More responsible?" He smiled. Again there was pain in the smile, but it was distant enough, Nita thought, that Nelaid could now also find it funny.

"A father figure?" Nita said, taking the chance.

After a long moment's stillness, Nelaid nodded. "Perhaps, when the present problem is settled, he and I might speak. At his convenience."

Nita bowed to Nelaid, and not one of those all-purpose half-bows, either. In the middle of it, the air went *bang!* behind her as Dairine reappeared. "You drop something?" her sister said.

Nita straightened, catching a glint of humor in Nelaid's eyes, but this hid itself as quickly as the pain had. "No. Where's Spot?"

Spot popped out of the air between the two of them. Nelaid looked over Nita's head and said to Dairine, "You did moderately well with the last exercise, but you have much work to do yet before it's perfect, and perfection is what's required. Let me know when you're at liberty to deal with the situation."

Dairine bowed, too: a somewhat cursory gesture, but more than most entities would get from her, no matter how many planets they virtually ruled. Nita pulled the transit circle out of her charm bracelet, dropped it to the floor, nodded goodbye to Nelaid, and activated the spell.

A few blinks later they were standing in their

backyard. The long afternoon shadows were not too far along from where Nita had left them. "Go upstairs and sort yourself out," Nita said as they headed toward the house. "Be quiet about it. Then come down. Don't make him come up after you. Okay?"

"Will you cut it out? It's not like I don't know how to handle him!"

Nita caught her sister by the shoulder. "Handling's not what he needs right now. Just play it straight, so we can both get back to business. Please?"

Dairine gave her a quick look of rebellion — but that was all, a moment's indulgence of habit — and vanished.

Nita sighed and headed through the gate, up the driveway, and into the house. Her dad was still at the dining room table, working on another cup of coffee: he looked surprised to see Nita come in the door.

"She'll be down in a minute," Nita said, and flopped into a chair.

Her dad blinked. "Just like that?"

Nita shrugged.

Her dad stared down into his cup, looked up again. "You think I was a little abrupt with you before?"

Nita said nothing, just gave him back one of his favorite expressions, a wide-eyed look with the eyebrows right up.

Her dad laughed, a brief, embarrassed sound. "Sorry about that."

"It's okay."

He was looking at the table again, a little unfocused. "Roshaun," her father said, sounding reluctant.

"Just what happened with him up there on the Moon?"

Nita shook her head, wishing she had more clarity on the subject. "He vanished."

"But wizards vanish all the time."

"Not like this," Nita said. "It was a lot more . . . final."

"But not final enough for Dairine."

"No. Dad —" There was no way to say this that wasn't going to pain both of them, so she just said it. "Even for humans, there's dead, and then there's *dead* dead. Other species handle mortality other ways. They have to: their souls are different shapes from ours. But no matter what shape your soul is, when you're a wizard, weird things can happen to change the way things work . . ." She shook her head. "The only thing I'm sure of is that Roshaun's not dead the way *we* think about dead."

"And so Dairine actually has some chance of finding him?"

Nita nodded. "If anyone can, yeah. But he's still lost. And all this time she's been spending on his home planet . . . I think she feels like she owes a debt to his mom and dad. Like she got Roshaun involved with our planet . . . and then Nelaid and Miril lost their son because of what she did."

Her dad sat silent for a moment. "It's honorable, what she's doing," he said at last. "But at the same time — Nita, she's *eleven!* And she needs a lot of watching."

"So that's just what you'll be doing, whenever you want," Nita said. "And she's going to explain everything you see. It'll be the next best thing to standing over her shoulder, watching." And Nita grinned. "Might be more data than you want."

"I wouldn't bet on that," her dad said. But as he leaned back in the chair, he looked more relaxed.

Nita stood up. "So am I off the hook?"

Her dad's look was meant to be stern, but Nita wasn't fooled. "For the moment. We'll see how this works out."

Nita went over and hugged and kissed him, because he was really being very good. Then she headed for the back door before he changed his mind.

"By the way —"

In the kitchen doorway, hearing the stairs creak as Dairine came down them, Nita paused. "Yeah?"

"I keep meaning to ask you. What *is* on Mars?"

"Besides a rock with your cell phone number carved on it?" Nita grinned. "We're not sure. But we're gonna find out."

"Well, all right. But don't get us invaded, now . . ."

"*Daddy!*"

He gave her a mischievous look. "Well, you can't blame me. It's kind of the first thing that comes to mind, isn't it?"

"Yeah," Nita said. "I know."

And she vanished.

Nili Patera

IT WAS DARK. KIT FOUND himself staring at his bedroom ceiling, his eyes wide open. He was wide awake, but he couldn't think why.

He lay there on his back under the covers for a few seconds, listening to the house. It was still, devoid of any of the little middle-of-the-night sounds that it made as the weather got warmer. And one other sound was missing, from the braided rug by the side of his bed: a small, faint whistling snore.

Kit sighed. *Ponch,* he thought. But his dog's midnight snore was a sound he would not hear again. He turned his head on the pillow, peered at the digital clock on the front of the clock radio. *3:38.*

Which is what time on Mars? He closed his eyes again for a moment, trying to do the math for the time at Nili Patera. But math was no match for the image of the green-brown sandy soil under his knees, and the strange shining blue-green superegg in his lap. He could just feel the faint sense of some quiet power running under the surface of it, mute, waiting. *That was it,* he thought, pushing himself up on his elbows. *It wasn't ready. It was waiting for something.*

And what if it's ready now?

Kit sat up in the quiet, gazing into the darkness, his heart pounding as if he'd been running somewhere. It was weird. Then, *No, it's not,* he thought. Kit had had a lot of trouble getting to sleep when he'd finally gotten home and turned in. He'd been as wired as if he was seven years old and the next day was going to be Christmas. *Well, what do I expect? I was on* Mars. *I actually touched an alien artifact that someone left there. I felt that it was* alive —

And waiting.

He looked again at the clock. *Mamvish said we should do some analysis first,* Kit thought. *Irina said, take your time . . .*

Kit sat there for a few moments, listening to his heart pound. Then he threw the covers off, got up, and went to the desk by the window.

The manual was there where he usually left it when he was home. *Analysis . . .* Kit thought. He flipped the manual's cover open and paged through to the Mars project section, then tapped the open pages so they'd glow in the dark.

The only new things on the main project page were the manual-generated précis of what the group who went up to Mars yesterday had found, and beside it, a few "read, noted" symbols from research team members who'd flagged the entry to let other team members know they'd seen it. Kit shook his head, unbelieving. *Twenty-six other wizards working on this project and* nobody *has anything interesting to say?* Kit thought, frowning. *Even just 'Hey,* wow*? Come on, people . . . !*

He let out a frustrated breath and flipped on through to the part of the master directory he'd book-marked. *I wonder, is Mamvish around —?*

He found her name halfway down the page, as usual, with that astonishing power level noted next to it — a four-digit level, when even the most powerful wizards on Earth usually only went as high as three. Even Irina's level wasn't as high. Yet at the same time, the level of respect Mamvish had been showing Irina suggested that, at the more elevated levels of practice, sheer power wasn't everything. *Even if you could blow up a whole planet all by yourself —*

It was a creepy thought. Wizardry was usually about keeping things alive, or at least in one piece. *And* why *would the Powers That Be want someone to blow a planet up?* Kit thought. *Especially their own?* A sudden image came to him of Irina, standing alone in some desert place, terrible power building around her, while her face held still and cold, and her eyes —

Kit shivered. *Now, where'd that come from?* he thought. *Catching something from Neets, maybe —* He shook his head, glanced down at Mamvish's listing again. Next to the short version of her name flashed a small knotted symbol that was Speech-shorthand for *Occupied: on assignment.* Next to it was a long string of symbols indicating that Mamvish wasn't anywhere near this solar system, since the light-years-from-your-location symbol had a tens-of-thousands aug-mentor suffix on it. *Halfway across the galaxy, it looks like. And busy. Dammit . . .*

Kit leaned back in his chair, tipping it back on its back legs and rocking for a moment in thought: then sat forward and turned some more pages in the manual. *It's quarter of nine where Ronan is,* he thought. *He must be up by now!* But the "status" part of Ronan's listing, when he came to it, was grayed out, a sign that the person was unavailable for some routine reason, usually sleep. *I can't believe it. How can any sane person sleep late after what we were doing yesterday?*

Kit folded his arms on top of his manual and put his head down sideways on them, frustrated. Again he found himself gazing at the oval braided rug where Ponch could always be found between bedtime and morning, lying on his back, snoring, waiting for Kit to get up and feed him. *I wish he was here,* Kit thought sadly. *I'd just say, 'Come on, Ponch, let's go to Mars!' And he'd jump up and spin around a few times and run out the door, ready to go . . .*

Then Kit let out a long breath. He was a wizard, not a magician: and in a wizard's world, there was no use wasting your time wishing for things you couldn't have. You went on to the next option — by getting up off your butt and doing the necessary work. *Even if there's no one else to do it with . . .*

Kit stood up, glancing down at the manual. *Neets . . .* But he could just imagine what she'd say if he woke her up at four in the morning after the afternoon and evening she'd had. Kit flipped over to the fast-messaging area in the back of the manual and had another look at the terse message she'd left him about the results of the phone call from her father, and her annoyance on coming back to Mars when everything was settled to find that everyone else had left. *Talk to you tomorrow AFTER LUNCH,* the note ended. He could practically see her scowling.

Well, she'll be over it after she's had some breakfast and some time to relax. Kit straightened up, shivering: it was a while since the central heating had been on, and the room was chilly. *I'll jump up to my usual spot, then go check on the superegg from there. It'll take less energy than doing a whole new custom transit.*

Very quietly he pulled clothes on — jeans, sweatshirt, down vest — and then the hiking boots his pop had given him for his last birthday, when the family had driven upstate for the weekend and walked the Appalachian Trail through Bear Mountain State Park. Those boots had been getting more than Earth dirt on them the last few weeks, and the abrasive sand and dust of the much-eroded Martian surface was in the process of wearing the leather down to a nice beat-up patina. He finished lacing up the right-hand boot, rubbing the leather thoughtfully: it was dry. Even though Kit always took enough air with him to Mars for a given visit, plus twenty percent in case of emergencies, that air tended to get very dried out while it was there. So did anything else inside the air bubble with him. *Better find the neat's-foot oil and leather wax for these things when I get back. Don't want them to start cracking.*

Kit picked up the manual and paged through it again, then whispered the thirty-eight words of a spell macro he used when he wanted to get in and out of the house quietly: one small subroutine that put an inch-thick layer of hardened air between him and the stairs, as a cushion for his footsteps, and another subroutine to ask the downstairs back door if it would please unlock itself in absolute silence.

He made his way quietly downstairs, through the living room and into the kitchen. Just a faint line of light showed by the back door where it had eased itself open — a little crack showing Kit that the dimness outside was paling toward dawn. There, just behind the door, Kit paused for a moment, looking at something hanging on one of the coat hooks behind the door — a long, slim, faintly blue-glowing cord with a loop at each end, dangling down half-hidden behind one of Kit's winter jackets. It was a spell made of fishes' breath and other hard-to-source ingredients: Ponch's wizardly leash, the only leash that had been able to stay on his dog and keep whoever was walking him connected to him when he'd started walking between universes. *I really should roll that up and put it away . . .* But he hadn't been able to do that just yet: it would have been an admission of how completely his dog was gone. Kit sighed, touched the doorknob. *Thanks,* he said to the door and its locks.

No problem, they said in chorus. *Know when you're coming back?*

"Not just yet," Kit said in the Speech. "Go ahead, lock up again, but real quiet." He stepped out, pulled the door closed behind him; both locks snicked back into place.

Kit went down the stairs into the carport and paused by his dad's pet project, the Edsel Pacer that he'd been restoring forever. Part of the problem was that parts for a car made in 1958 were getting hard to come by. But more to the point, Kit's pop was in the habit of taking a lot of overtime at work so that the family could afford things he thought they needed to have, like the new entertainment center, so mostly the Edsel sat here waiting patiently for him to summon up the energy to work on it. Every now and then his pop came out and waxed it, or oiled whatever metal was exposed so that it wouldn't suffer, or installed some long-sought part that had finally come in from somewhere around the country. The relationship was becoming a guilty one on Kit's pop's side, no matter how often Kit explained to his pop that the Edsel didn't really mind.

"Hey, guy," Kit said, leaning against the right front fender and looking down into the headlight on that side. "You doing okay?"

I'm fine. Any news on the replacement tail-lights yet?

The car's resigned tone made Kit grin. "I hear they actually shipped," he said, walking around to the far side of the car and carefully opening the front door.

He slipped in and sat down on the broad bench-style front seat, bracing the door so that it would fall closed quietly. "Should be here next week."

Great! Where you going today?

"The usual place," Kit said. He reached out and punched one of the radio buttons on the Edsel's dashboard. In immediate response, the transit spell he'd installed inside the car a couple of months back came alive around him, a glowing tracery of Speech-characters seemingly shining up from just underneath the surface of the seat's leather. The closed environment of the car did a good job of muffling the air-implosion noise that went with a teleport, and it was hard enough to see into the Edsel that Kit felt comfortable vanishing in there without adding the energy outlay of an invisibility spell on top of the transit. "We all clear?"

He could feel the Edsel looking around it, though as with most inanimate objects, Kit wasn't sure what it was using to do the looking. *All clear. Be careful!*

"All the time," Kit said. He reached down to the glowing lines of the transit spell, braced himself, and said the word to activate it.

The next moment was never entirely comfortable. No one travels a hundred fifty million miles in a breath without his or her body complaining about the stresses and strains of bypassing lightspeed and numerous other natural laws. Kit felt, as usual, as if he was being squeezed unbearably tight on all sides, and the pressure got worse and worse — until all the pressure abruptly went away, and almost all the breath whooshed out of his lungs. That, too, was typical for a private transit to Mars: it took a fraction of a second for his life-support wizardry to analyze its new coordinates, recognize them, and kick in.

Kit swallowed and opened his eyes, starting to gasp as the usual reaction to doing a biggish spell set in. He was right where he was supposed to be, sitting on his usual "landing rock," perched on the rim of the ancient caldera-crater of the extinct volcano Elysium Mons. Kit sat there waiting for the breathlessness to pass, and concentrated on blinking until his eyes worked right again.

He had originally chosen this spot for its spectacular view. Though not as high or huge as its more famous cousin Olympus Mons, Elysium Mons stood up steep and splendidly isolated in the northern-hemisphere lowland plains of Elysium Planitia. The cone of the old volcano alone was taller than Mount Everest. But underneath the mountain proper lay a great uplift plateau that ancient stresses had pushed some three kilometers up out of the crust; so the spot where Kit now sat towered at least forty thousand feet above the dark-sanded plain. Off to his left, twenty miles south and east at the edge of the pedestal, the little crater-topped mountain Albor Tholus rose up, its concave top whitened with dry-ice snow. Beyond it, the underlying uplift pedestal fell away in dark narrow rilles to the surrounding plain, charcoal-colored in the night. Away into the dark distance the plainlands stretched to a horizon just faintly hazed on their southwest edge with a thin line of silver light: the last remnant of sunset. Between Kit and that distant, shadowy edge of the world, craters dotted the ashy darkness, here and there shining pale at their bottoms with thin gleaming skins of starlit water ice or carbon dioxide frost.

It was clear tonight — a frigid pre-winter midnight in Mars's northern hemisphere, through which stars unimpeded by the thin atmosphere burned fierce and still. Kit shivered. Even with an aggressive force field and in a hemisphere where it was summer, Mars wasn't somewhere you wanted to spend much time at night. And in the winter — *Has to be a hundred below,* Kit thought. *Maybe a hundred fifty.* He glanced down around the low boulder where he sat, then bent over and picked up a little stone about the size of a golf ball.

Even though it had soaked up some considerable heat from the bubble of air his life-support spell was holding in place around him, the stone was still so cold it burned his hand. Kit had to juggle it to keep it from sticking to his skin. "How cold, fella?" he said in the Speech.

The rock took a moment about answering. Things made of stone tended not to understand the idea that cold and heat might be different: it was all just temperature to them. *A hundred and twenty-three point five degrees below zero Fahrenheit.*

Kit nodded and kept tossing the rock gently in his hand until it came up to a more bearable temperature. After a few moments he was able to hold on to it. He rubbed it gently between finger and thumb: charcoal-colored grit came off on his fingers as Kit looked south toward that acutely curved, silver-edged horizon. For a long time now, whenever he'd felt the need for a little quiet in his life, or a little mystery, he'd come here to sit and look out at this silent, uncommunicative terrain in perplexed wonder — for it was rare for a planet's landscape to have so little to say to a wizard. Wherever life had been for any length of time, the structure of the world tended to remember, and to be willing enough to "talk" about it. Here the ground seemed only to know its own strictly geological history. Yet there was also a strange sense of something being withheld: as if some dark tide of silence and secrecy had risen, submerging everything, and never receded. . . .

What about it? Kit said to the rock. In this starlit midnight, it was dark matte-gray, with here and there a fleck of mica embedded in its gritty sandstone. *What do you know about the world? Who's been here?*

No one but you and her, the rock said, *the other one. I know day, and night. Water snow and gas snow. That's about it.*

Kit nodded and put the rock down where he'd found it. As he did, the landscape around him lightened ever so slightly, a change he'd never have noticed on Earth: but here, now that his eyes were used to the dark, it made a difference. He looked up and saw the little moon Deimos rising, a planet-bright moving spark against the stars, about as bright as the International Space Station could have been at home when it went over. Deimos, though, moved quicker, almost imperceptibly changing the dark charcoal of the surrounding sands to a lighter shade as it climbed the sky, shifting the angle of the dim shadows in the craters below.

Kit stood up, dusted his pants off, and flipped his manual open to the Mars project précis. He ran one finger down the entry there, pinpointing the spot where he and Mamvish and the others had been earlier in the day, then tapped the page so the coordinates would load into the on-planet transit spell he already had bookmarked. Another flip of pages brought Kit to the transit spell, its characters glowing under the page and ready to go. He began to read.

Even in this empty silence, you could hear the universe leaning in around you to listen: and for some reason, the listening seemed to Kit unusually acute. He finished reading: the breath went out of his lungs again as things went totally black —

— then lightened again, but not much. Once again, starlight, a clear night, no dust in the upper atmosphere: two in the morning at Syrtis Major. Kit stood in the shadow of that towering black dune and shivered again, though not from the cold. The surroundings were noticing him, watching him . . . with what underlying reaction, Kit couldn't tell. All of a sudden Kit began to wish he hadn't come alone. The watchfulness of the surroundings was feeling increasingly creepy.

He grimaced. *Come on, what's the matter with me? I've been here in the dark before. Nothing's going to happen!* Yet he thought of the dust devil earlier. That had taken even Mamvish and Irina by surprise. There'd just been something about the way that whirlwind came straight at them —

He shrugged. *Just the planet noticing us, like Irina said. It does that all the time. In fact, it probably just noticed us harder because there was such a crowd there. Not to mention a Planetary . . .* Kit glanced around, determined to get down to business and shake the absurd feeling that he had stepped into an early scene of a monster movie.

He went closer to the dune. *This hasn't moved. At least I don't think it has —* The dune's face looked as it had the afternoon before: but as Kit glanced around, he saw with some disquiet that all the investigative party's footprints had disappeared — even Mamvish's. *Did somebody clean up?* But it seemed unlikely. On Mars, where the wind blew a lot of the time, tidying up evidence of your presence on the surface wasn't as vital as it was on the Moon, where there was neither wind nor erosion and your sneaker's footprint would last forever. *The wind did it. Or another dust devil . . .*

That moment at its heart had been astonishing. Yet now Kit found himself really unwilling to see another one of those bearing down on him. *Why do I keep letting myself get the creeps about it?* he thought. *Let's find that egg . . .*

He flipped through the manual again to the detector routine that Síle and Markus had designed. It was a longish spell and hadn't been set to execute automatically, but reading the whole thing would still take Kit less time than digging around in the dune in the hopes that the stony outcropping concealing the superegg would be easily found. *This dune might have moved, after all. Let's see.*

Kit read the spell through — four long sentences in the Speech — and stood gasping again with the exertion, waiting for the spell to take. Gradually a wireframe of glowing lines superimposed itself across one spot on the dune low down and to the right, describing the outcropping's humped-up appearance. Kit went over and checked the spell's glowing Speech-symbols to see how deeply the outcropping was buried. *Only a couple of feet. I was right; the dune hasn't moved —*

Yet still the uneasiness wouldn't leave him. Kit shook his head and hunkered down in front of the slope of near-black sand, whispering the syllables of the Mason's Word as he'd done the afternoon before. Then he reached in through the surface of the dune, the surface of the stone, until he felt the odd smooth coolness under his hands again. He made sure of his hold on it, and pulled.

This time there was less resistance. Seconds later the cold stars above Kit were gleaming on the superegg's dark surface, their reflections trembling in its mirrory sheen: and the tremor's source was Kit. He stood up with the superegg in his hands, shivering all over with the utter strangeness of where he was and what he held. *The age of this thing. Here it's been for five hundred thousand years . . . and not by accident. Who left you? Why won't you open up and let us find out what you're meant to tell us?*

He tried to stop his hands from shaking, and couldn't. Then after a few seconds, Kit realized that it wasn't just his hands that were shivering. It was the egg.

In the first shock of realization, he almost dropped it — but he stopped himself just in time. *Who knows what a hard bounce could do to it, even in this gravity?*

And if I break it, I'm going to be in so much trouble —
The memory of Mamvish's eye cocked at him flashed
before Kit as he tried to steady the vibrating superegg:
he thought of Irina's level gaze as she eyed him like
someone wondering if he was really as trustworthy as
she'd been told. *And I'm not. I shouldn't be doing this.*
Why *did I do this when I knew that I* — Whoa!

Kit braced the shaking superegg against his chest,
trying to steady it, but to no effect. Now it was lurching
from side to side in his grasp, more and more violently
every moment, until the thing actually vibrated right out
of his grip and into the air. Kit clutched at the egg and
just managed to get hold of it again before it gave one
shake more violent than anything that had preceded it —

And split in three. Kit tried to keep hold of all the
wedge-shaped pieces, but they struggled out of his
hands like live things desperate to escape, bobbling up
into the air in front of him. He made a grab at one,
caught it, and pinned it under his arm while reaching
for the second. But he couldn't get a good grip on that
wedge because of the way hugging the first one
between arm and body was limiting his movement.
The second wedge wrenched itself out of his one-
handed grip and into the air again. The third wedge
hit the ground, bounced in a puff of dark dust, and
rebounded into the second —

And stuck to it. Kit stared as the two adhering
wedges began, from the edges inward, to shred apart in
midair, shattering into shining fragments that thinned
to ribbons, then started tangling together like a nest of
snakes. The third wedge tore itself away from Kit,

leaped into the air, and shattered like its counterparts, then began stretching itself into ribbons and tangling itself up with the others. Seconds later they were melding together again, writhing and changing in a shimmer of consolidating metal —

The shrinking shape was still amorphous, like a bubble of water floating and wobbling in weightlessness. Then it put out projections, hurriedly, one after another — and fell. When it came down on the surface in another cloud of dust, it stretched itself out, long and sinuous, went flat like a steamrollered snake —

Now what?! Kit thought, panicked. The long, shining shape moved, twitched, and all at once sprouted from its sides what he initially mistook for long tufts of fur. The fur *moved*, though, waving, writhing—and the hair stood up all over Kit as the long, flat, blunt-ended shape stood up and slowly started moving toward him on entirely too many legs.

Kit backed away a step. Though he'd long since conquered his childhood nightmares about being attacked by giant bugs under his bed, he still wasn't wild about them, especially when he met them all alone in the dark on other planets. *It's not really a bug,* he thought, taking another step backward as the shining thing kept moving toward him. *It's not alive. It's some kind of machine. A weird, alien machine, yeah, but machines are a lot of what I do. I really should be able to —*

Kit lost the thought as little round, pebbly eyes suddenly bumped their way up out of the bug's blunt head. They were opaque, featureless . . . but they were all looking at *him.* And then the back end of the bug lengthened out, got long and sharp, and curved up over its back. *Oh, no. Not a bug.*

It was a scorpion.

At least it doesn't have claws yet, Kit thought, still backing up. And then the creature reared up, starlight sheening down it, and the many legs consolidated, getting thicker, sharper, more angular. Six legs, three and three, in the back: four legs, two and two, in the front, upraised, each of these splitting down the middle near the ends, the razory vee of newly created claws starting to scissor together. The clawed forelegs lifted, pointing at him as the claws worked against each other. Those eyes fixed on Kit more determinedly as the scorpion-thing came at him, faster now, on the point of breaking into a run —

Kit tried to gulp, and failed, dry-mouthed. *"I am on errantry, and I greet you!"* he said, probably a lot more loudly than he needed to. Still backing up, he reached behind him to zip open his otherspace pocket. He'd taken to keeping a little surprise in there if he ran into a situation like this —

Barely six feet away, the metal scorpion stopped short. The unsettling gaze of all those little eyes was still fixed on Kit, and it suddenly seemed as if the creature or machine was waiting for something specific from him, or not seeing something it expected. Kit, too, froze. *What does it want? What am I supposed to —?*

It lifted its claws. *Too late!* Kit thought, pushing his hand into the otherspace pocket and gripping the small, fizzing wizardry that lay there, ready and waiting —

The claws angled up and out, not at Kit, but in four different directions, and light burst up from them — not true beams of light, but curving arcs of a thin, pale blue-green radiance. They leaped into the air fluidly, like water from a fountain, curving in to twist together high above the motionless scorpion. There they knotted together, then separated and streaked toward the dark horizon, sending Kit's and the scorpion's shadows reeling and stretching across the dark sand. Kit spun around, trying to see where all the streaks of light were going.

He had only enough time to make out general directions before the streaks faded and were gone. The scorpion lowered its claws, folding them across its front in a strange gesture, almost formal. The eyes dissolved back into the creature's blunt head. It rolled up, the long, curved spine of the tail vanishing, the legs slipping into the body; the whole shape collapsed into itself, smoothed, solidified —

The superegg lay rocking gently on the sand, and finally came to rest on one end, perfectly still in the starlight.

Kit went over to the egg, knelt down beside it, almost scared to touch it. Finally he swore at his own nervousness, reached out and put one hand on the superegg. Nothing happened. The sense of latent energy within it was completely gone.

The sweat that had broken out on Kit was going cold: he hadn't been paying enough attention to his life-support spell, and his breath was smoking as the air around him chilled down. Kit more or less collapsed onto the dark sand and sat there trying to recover, staring at the egg. *Okay,* he thought, *I've broken it. And I'm now in the most trouble I've ever been in my life. But there's no point in freezing myself solid.*

Kit picked up his manual, flipped through it to check some spell syntax, and then spoke to the life-support spell's parameters, telling them to pull some energy from under the planet's crust, where a little residual heat lay stored. Then Kit rubbed his face, flinching at the grit, which as usual was getting every-place, and stared at the egg. *Those were signals. But to what, or who —?*

He flipped pages in the manual, turning to the place where local changes in the environment would have been logged. "What were those signals about?" he said to the manual. "Where were they headed?"

A long spill of characters in the Speech appeared all down the glowing page, filling it — the technical descrip-tion of what the scorpion had done. Kit read down it, turned the page, and found it filling up with description, too — a bewildering amount of it. "Whoa, whoa! Save that. And just give me a graphic for now, okay?"

The page dimmed the Speech-charactery down to near invisibility and drew him a simple outline map of the Martian surface in a cylindrical projection, a wide rectangle. Four glowing arcs drew themselves out-ward from Kit's location in Nili Patera, each a slightly different curve heading in a different direction: north-east, northwest, southeast, and much more deeply south. At each arc's end, the map labeled itself with the English-language names of the targeted features and their equivalents in the Speech.

"All craters," Kit said under his breath, noting their names: Stokes, Cassini, de Vaucouleurs, and Hutton. "Any response from anything there?"

The page blanked. Then a single character appeared, the Speech-symbol that could stand for either the number zero or a null response.

Kit let out a breath: his manual wasn't normally so terse. "Okay," he said. "Alert me if anything comes up . . ."

He closed the manual and put it aside, looking down at the superegg. "Might as well put you back . . ." Once more he hunkered down in front of the outcropping where it had been secreted. There was no point in leaving this out where one of the satellites orbiting Mars could see it.

What I'm really wishing, Kit thought as he put a hand out to the egg again, *is that there was some way to cover what I just did. Or some really good excuse for it.* But this wasn't one of those situations where you could just tell the local authority figure the equivalent of "the dog ate my homework" and expect to get away with it. And as he thought that, a small pain struck Kit somewhere in his midsection. *It's not like I can claim my dog is eating much of anything anymore . . .*

Kit made an unhappy face. His manual had been open and logging when this happened. Hiding anything of what had happened would be impossible. *I just wish I wasn't about to get yelled at for doing something wrong, and maybe get kicked off the whole project —*

It then occurred to Kit that telling just one aspect of the truth might be enough to keep him out of trouble. All he'd have to say would be that something had made him do this: some urge he couldn't resist had come over him. *And that was true,* Kit thought. *Or at least it kind of* feels *like it was true —*

But wait. Am I just talking myself into this because I don't want to look stupid? And no matter how thoroughly he talked himself into believing this irresistible-urge thing, one of the other wizards associated with this — Mamvish, Irina — might be able to tell him that the urge *hadn't* been all that overwhelming: that he could've resisted if he'd really wanted to. . . .

Then I wind up looking twice as dumb as I am already. And besides — The Speech, the most important part of wizardry, was about describing the universe as it really was. If you started taking liberties with that concept, you were doing the Lone Power's work for it. And when working with the Speech, trying to describe things the way they *weren't* could get very fatal.

Kit picked up the superegg, muttered the necessary syllables of the Mason's Word, and shoved the egg back into the stone. *Never mind. I'm gonna call Mamvish, come clean, and get the yelling over with.*

He stood up and flipped the manual open to the contacts section, put a finger on Mamvish's entry. He had to stop and try to swallow before he could speak: his mouth had gone dry again. "Page her," he said to his manual. "Ask if she's got a moment."

Mamvish's name dimmed, then blazed again. Under it a one-line phrase traced itself out in the curving characters of the Speech: *Unavailable: on intervention. No availability estimate at this time. If the matter is urgent, please leave a message.*

Kit stared at the words: somehow they were the last thing he'd expected. *Urgent. Is this urgent? How do I tell? And what if it's not, really?* "Uh," he said. "Mamvish, it's Kit. I'm on Mars. There's been a development. The egg went through, I don't know, some kind of metamorphosis, and it sent out signals. Nothing else has happened yet." He stopped, tried to think what else he should add that both he knew to be strictly true and wouldn't make him sound like an idiot. *No, just quit while you're ahead . . .* "Uh, that's all. I'll call you back later. *Dai stihó.*"

Mamvish's name flashed, confirmation that the message had been saved. A link to a copy of Kit's message, with a time stamp, appeared down the page.

Kit sighed and slapped the manual shut. The sudden feeling of reprieve was tremendous. . . . *And dumb, since I haven't gotten out of anything yet! Still . . . she'll know I tried to call her. That has to count for something.*

Kit became aware that his heart was pounding. He glanced around at the silent sands, the dark dune towering over him. Off to the northwest, Deimos was diving toward the horizon. *So now what?*

He stood watching Deimos's downward arc while his pulse slowed. *Well, now that you've got some new data out of this crazy thing you did, do something* useful *with it. Find out* why *those signals were sent to those spots! And this time, don't do it alone.*

Deimos twinkled through the atmosphere near the horizon while Kit wondered where *that* idea had come from. *Am I just trying to have someone around to share the blame with if something else goes wrong?* A depressing thought. *But company would be good for keeping me from screwing up again.*

That thought was nearly as depressing. *I'm going to go home and get some breakfast. Maybe Neets —*

But she'll still be asleep. And she said to wait till after lunch to call her ... Well, never mind! Who wants people getting the idea that you can't do anything without having her along? Or that you can't handle something unusual by yourself?

Kit glanced back at the outcropping. That strange feeling of the surroundings watching him was gone now. *It went away when the egg opened. But why wouldn't it do that before?*

Unless it was waiting for something. And, outrageously, the idea came to him:

It was waiting for me.

... After a moment Kit shook his head at the crazy idea. Mamvish had mentioned in the past that some of these "bottles" had timing wizardries attached, routines meant to give the wizardries time to see what conditions in the world around them were like before popping open. *Its timer probably just went off after it finished taking its readings. Then it started calling to its buddies. But why aren't they answering?*

In forlorn hope Kit flipped his manual open to the

page where those four craters were marked. But there was no sign of anything happening there: no movement, no heat, no unusual energy artifact.

Then again . . . it was how long before this egg hatched, after we took it out the first time? Eight hours? Maybe the other eggs, or whatever it was signaling to, have time delays set, too. The thought of another eight hours of waiting for something to happen seemed almost unbearable. *But wait. If there's going to be a delay, that's okay: it gives us time to put extra monitoring wizardries in place nearby.*

"Us." This time he felt better about the idea of someone else being there with him. *And a little weird, wasn't it, to be wanting to keep this all to myself? Where was that coming from?* Kit shrugged. Probably the suddenness of the egg's hatching had freaked him out.

He reached sideways, unzipped the air, and started to stick the manual into his otherspace pocket — then paused. *Better deactivate my last-defense gadget first.* With care Kit reached into the pocket, felt for the single thread of characters in the Speech hanging out of the compact little wizardry — its tripwire — and pinched it. The wizardry went inactive like a stick of cartoon dynamite that had had its burning fuse pinched out.

Kit tucked the manual into the pocket, zipped it closed, and glanced west, seeing Deimos's dimming spark vanish below the horizon: then looked the other way. Blue, bright, growing stronger and brighter by the moment, Earth rose in the east — Mars's northern-hemisphere morning star, this time of year, the herald of the dawn.

Kit's stomach growled. He grinned. *Home,* he thought, and vanished.

The next two hours were torture for Kit. He forced himself to have breakfast, though his insides were roiling with excitement and anxiety. But every minute that his manual didn't start flashing with an annoyed message from Mamvish, or worse, Irina, felt like a small triumph. Eventually, as the Sun started coming in the dining room windows around seven, Kit began feeling as if maybe he wasn't in incredible trouble after all.

His attention was presently divided evenly between two pages in the directory. He had a paper napkin stuck in each one, and he flipped back and forth between them about once every minute as the dining room filled with sunlight. What surprised him was on which one the gray print of unavailability first flashed dark.

Kit pushed his third bowl of cornflakes aside and pounced on the page. "How soon can you be ready to go out?"

There was a pause. *"Am I allowed to eat first?"* Darryl's voice said from the page.

Kit grinned. "No."

"You're cruel, man," Darryl said. *"Gonna stunt my growth. Don't you think I have enough developmental issues without you messing with my metabolism, too?"*

Kit snickered. The only thing wrong with Darryl's metabolism was that it seemed bent on getting ahead of everyone else's. The way he ate and drank, Kit routinely expected to see Darryl turn up at a meeting three feet taller than at the last one.

"I am going to sit right here for the next fifteen minutes and finish eating my chocolate-frosted sugar bombs," Darryl said. *"Part of my nutritious breakfast, and no, I'm not gonna go hyper on you. Don't think I can't just hear you thinking, so don't start! And then I'm going to put some clothes on, if that's okay with you. Not gonna go running around Mars in my bathrobe!"*

"Okay, okay!" Kit said. "As soon as you can."

"Fine. Thank you." There was a pause filled with noisy crunching. *"And what're you doing up so early? Thought I was the only one who liked this hour of the day."*

Kit wondered how to start explaining. He might as well have saved the effort. *"Uh-oh,"* Darryl said, *"I know, you were up there messing, weren't you? What did you do, Kit-boy? You* broke *something, didn't you?"*

Kit rolled his eyes. Darryl could be annoyingly acute, and could hear more about what was going on with you in a moment's silence than some people could hear in a whole paragraph. *"Man, you should be kept in a cage,"* Darryl said. *"Never mind, I'm not gonna make you all bad and wrong for whatever you did. At least not till I help you clean it up."*

"Thanks a heap," Kit said. "Finish being nutritious and then get your butt over here." He glanced down at the directory and saw another name go dark. "Aha. Later."

He touched Ronan's name; it glowed under his finger. "Hey," Kit said, "good morning."

"Oh, listen, Rodriguez attempts to score on irony,"

Ronan's voice came back. He yawned. *"But no! It bounces off the goalpost! What a shame . . ."*

"Why is it always sports with you?" Kit said. "Football, rugby, that thing with the weird sticks —"

"Hurling."

"Yeah, the only sport with a mandatory body count." Kit had seen the game played once and was glad he didn't go to school in Ireland: hurling came across like lacrosse on crack, but Ronan loved it and would blather about it for hours. "Forget the playing field for now, okay? We've got to go to Mars."

"Oh, really. What have you blown up now?"

Kit was tempted to bang his head on the table. "Nothing blew up!"

"You don't fool me," Ronan said. *"You went off to be with your friend the superegg in the middle of the night."* He laughed. *"The* Martian *night! You know, some day you may want to reproduce, but you're never gonna do it if you freeze off your —"*

"Ronan," Kit said. "I can either shoot you a précis from my manual, or you can force me to embarrass myself directly . . ."

"Always much more fun," Ronan said, and yawned. *"Go."*

Kit spent five minutes or so describing what had happened. Ronan stayed quiet during the explanation, then simply said, *"Creepy."*

"Yeah," Kit said. "But that thing's given its friends a shout. I don't think we're gonna have to wait for long before something happens up there."

"And when it does," Ronan said, *"it makes sense*

for there to be wizards there. Okay, sit tight and I'll have a word with my ride."

Kit's eyebrows went up. Irish wizards were restricted from casual long-distance transport due to the buildup of ancient spell residue on the island. Normally they had to go a considerable distance to get to a city-based rapid-transit worldgate, unless they were on active errantry and entitled to a personal transport dispensation. "What kind of ride?"

"Five minutes."

Ronan's listing in the manual faded down to gray again, while beside it an annotation came up: *In consultation; please wait.* Kit pushed his chair back and got up to take his bowl and spoon into the kitchen.

While he was putting them in the dishwasher, he heard someone coming down the stairs. Moments later Carmela wandered in, wearing one of her superlong striped nightshirts. She made for the refrigerator, stuck her head in, and just stood there yawning.

Kit shut the dishwasher and looked with mild interest at his sister, who was still contemplating the fridge's interior — morosely, he thought. "Looking for something?"

Carmela yawned again and straightened up. "I'm just thinking that this is the last morning for the next two weeks when I can be sure that if I leave a strawberry smoothie in here when I go to bed, it'll still be there the next morning."

Kit headed back for the dining room. "Why? I don't like your smoothies."

"I know," Carmela said. "But Helena does."

Kit stopped right where he was and stared at her.

"*Kit?*" said Ronan's voice from the dining room table. "*We're all set.*"

Carmela's head snapped around. "Is that who I *think* it is?" She pushed past Kit into the dining room.

"No, wait a minute! I mean, yeah —" Kit went after her. "Carmela, wait! What do you mean, 'Helena does'? She's not going to be here until next week!"

Carmela was leaning over his wizard's manual. "*Hiiiii,* Ronaaaaaan!"

There was a pause at the other end. "*Uh. Carmela, hi. Kit?*"

"Yeah, give me a minute! What did your ride say? When can you get here?"

"*Whenever you want. I'm in Baldwin now.*"

"What? Already?"

"*Yeah. Darryl fetched me over. How long do you need?*"

"Ten minutes."

"*Right. Cheers.*"

"Byeeeeeee!!" Carmela shouted at the manual as Kit slapped it shut. "Hey, that was rude. I wasn't done!"

"You can go all gooey over him when he gets here," Kit muttered, pushing past her to get his vest and jacket off one of the dining room chairs. "It was supposed to be Wednesday she was coming! When did everything get changed?"

"Last night," Carmela said. "You were asleep. Helena e-mailed Pop: the airline screwed up her flights. She had to either fly today or wait another week. She'll be here this afternoon."

Kit groaned as he zipped up his vest. "I do *not* need this right now ..."

Carmela leaned on the chair opposite. "Kit ... give her a chance. You've talked to her on the phone lately. You've heard her ... She's a lot mellower."

"You mean she no longer comes right out and *says* she thinks I sold my soul to the devil?" Kit said. He laughed. "Forgive me if I'm not convinced." He put on his jacket. "If I'm lucky, she'll be too busy running around socializing with her old friends to want to spend much time thinking about her weird little brother."

"Ooh, bitter ..."

Kit sighed and picked up the manual, eyeing Carmela's nightshirt. "You plan to be wearing that when Ronan shows up?"

Her eyes went wide. "Ohmigosh," Carmela said, and fled upstairs.

Kit leaned against the chair at the end of the table and sighed. When he'd realized he had to tell his mama and pop that he was a wizard, they hadn't had incredible trouble coping with the concept — at least after they got over the initial shock. Carmela had actually been delighted. But Helena had been horrified, and as upset by the rest of the family's relatively ready acceptance as by the idea that Kit could do wizardry in the first place. Though the whole family was churchgoing, Helena had always struck Kit as more religious than all the rest of them put together; and until she started getting used to the situation, Kit had been really annoyed by the scared or worried looks Helena gave him every time their paths crossed. When she finally went off to college and put some time and distance between herself and what her little brother had become, Helena had calmed down a little ... or so Kit had thought. *Oh, please, don't let her get all freaked out all over again,* he said to the universe in general. *The stuff that's going on right now is so important. It'd be a nuisance to have to sneak around and hide what's happening so she won't drive everyone crazy —*

Ronan appeared at the other end of the table in a muted *bang!* of displaced air that rattled the dining room's venetian blinds. *Like that kind of thing, for example,* Kit thought. *I was being* discreet *about wizardry when Helena was getting all nuts. What's she going to do when stuff like* this *happens out in the open?*

Ronan was all in black, as usual: though this morning the black was heavy black jeans and hiking boots, and a black parka better suited to January than June. He glanced around, then pulled a chair out and flopped down on it. "Where's the Mouth that Roared? Thought she'd be right here."

"She was. I told her to go put on some clothes."

"Thanks for that," Ronan said. He sounded actively grateful: but he gave Kit a peculiar look. "You okay? You look pale."

"I believe you." Kit laughed, rueful. "Just family stuff. My older sister's coming home for a few weeks. She's not so clear about who we work for."

"Uh-oh. Going to lie low? Or try to talk sense to her?"

"No idea. Depends on how she is."

"And you're not eager to find out."

Kit shook his head. "Don't get me wrong. As sisters go, she's okay. More than okay. But as soon as she found out about wizardry . . ." He shrugged a helpless shrug. "It's like . . . I don't know. Not just that she thought it was a bad thing: almost as if my being a wizard *embarrassed* her."

"Best reason to keep it quiet," Ronan said. "I feel for you. Glad I don't have to deal with that stuff."

"You never told your family?"

Ronan shook his head. "Tried it once or twice," he said. "It never felt right. Might have been something to do with the classified stuff the Champion was up to when he was stuck in my head. But now that he's gone, I'm not sure I want to rock the boat . . ."

Bang! Darryl appeared in the kitchen doorway, wearing khaki cargo pants and one of those many-pocketed vests favored by photographers. "Sorry I kept you waiting," he said. "I had to feed my turtle."

Ronan eyed him with amusement. "Looks more like you were feeding the lions. What, are we going on safari? I should get you a pith helmet and an elephant gun."

"Stop envying my style," Darryl said.

"Envying?" Ronan snorted. "It is to laugh."

"You're not fooling anybody." Darryl grinned at Kit, then looked around. "We all set? Where's Miss Neets?"

Despite how eager he was to see her, this kind of question from the others was beginning to grate on Kit's nerves. "Sleeping in," he said. "She had a long day dealing with her dad. And she was muttering about something she was doing with Carmela, probably some girl thing . . ."

Darryl's eyes went wide. "Oh, Kit, don't let her hear you say stuff like that! She'll pull your head right off and beat you over the shoulders with it."

Ronan rolled his eyes in agreement. "Miss Tough-Mouth Neets doing girly stuff?" he said. "Not usually on her program."

"Can we worry less about her program and more about ours?" Kit said.

"Right away, O mighty one," Darryl said, wandering over to the bowl of fruit off to one side and picking up an apple. "Hey, these look nice —" He glanced at Kit.

"Oh, go ahead. Why should a little errantry keep you from eating?"

"I assume you've got a plan ready," Ronan said.

Kit nodded. "Darryl, did he tell you about the signals to the other craters?"

Already three bites into the apple, Darryl paused long enough to give Kit a look. "I read your précis between the second and third bowls of sugar bombs," he said. "You want to keep up with me, Your Kitness, 'cause I might have been autistic, but I've never been dyslexic. You have a preferred target we should investigate first, or should we just flip for it?"

"If there's any flipping-for to be done," said a voice from the living room, "it's going to be by Ronan over *me.*"

All heads turned as Carmela walked in. She was wearing a short blue dress with a peach-colored tank top underneath it, leggings, and little high heels of the kind Kit had heard her call "kitten heels." The clothes were the same kind of thing you might see a lot of girls her age wearing somewhere casually, say to the mall. But there was nothing casual about the way Carmela wore any of her clothes anymore — not since last year, when she suddenly discovered she had a figure. The pigtails of ten minutes ago were gone. She had pulled her long hair off to one side, so that it flowed down in a raven sweep over one shoulder, and she carried herself with the gracious, queenly conde-scension of a supermodel who had descended for a time from her usual starry height to walk among the lowly *paparazzi*. What Kit found strange was that this lofty carriage didn't look preposterous on her. "Good morning, Darryl," Carmela said, smiling sweetly at him; then turned her head. "And Ronannnn . . ."

Kit could only roll his eyes as Carmela stalked over to Ronan with that smile turned right up. *It's got to be an act,* was all he could think. *She's just messing with him because he thinks he's such a hunk —!* For Kit had seen her pull this stunt with egotistical alien royalty in the past. After he worked out what was being done to him, the prince in question had eventu-ally recovered sufficiently to take nourishment and walk around. *For a while . . .*

"Carmela," Ronan said in what Kit was beginning to think of as the Tone of Great Forbearance, "don't you think I'm a little — *old* for you?"

His tone of voice suggested that Ronan expected no answer but "yes." Carmela, however, just looked at him brightly and said, "That's okay. In ten years you won't be."

Ronan opened his mouth and closed it again.

Kit didn't know whether to laugh or cry. But right now the laughter was threatening to win. "Ronan, don't we have places to be?"

"Oh," Ronan said, "uh, yes."

Carmela just smiled. "Nice save, Kit," she said, "but it's just temporary." She waved the fingers of one hand at them in a toodle-oo gesture as she wandered back into the living room.

Kit watched her go with slight relief. *Then again, why am I relieved? She's got a worldgate in her closet. The sooner we're out of here, the better.* "Let's go out back," Kit said. "It's shielded there; the neighbors won't see us."

They headed out the back door together. Under his breath, Ronan said, "Your sister —" He shook his head. "We have a word for her where I come from —"

"Maybe I don't want to hear it," Kit said. "She *is* my sister." Not that Kit wasn't finding it peculiar to suddenly be concerned about how Carmela dressed or acted around other people. He wasn't used to thinking about how girls looked in their clothes — *except what about Janie Lowell in chemistry the other day?* said one eager and interested part of his brain from the background. *That skirt she was wearing, it hardly even covered her —*

Kit made a face. Other girls were a different matter. But he wasn't sure he wanted to be seeing his sister that way, and he wasn't sure he wanted anybody else seeing her that way, either. *And just a few months ago, I wouldn't have cared one way or another. This is so weird . . .*

Ronan was shaking his head as they headed into the backyard. "Leaving words about *her* out of it," Darryl said to Ronan, "they have any words where you come from for the expression on your face when she said that?"

"Probably they do," Ronan said as they made their way down through the yard. "'Gobsmacked' would be one. Carmela" — Ronan shook his head — "is a whole bucket of gobsmack."

Kit grinned. "Cousin, I hear you *there!*"

"When's she going away to college?" said Darryl as they came to the weedy, tree-screened rear of Kit's backyard.

"Not a second too soon for me," Kit said. "No — that's not true. I don't know . . ." He and Carmela had always gotten along better than he and Helena did. And it wasn't just that Carmela hadn't completely blown a gasket when she found out he was a wizard, or that later she'd started to pick up the Speech. *There's something else going on. Maybe we're just closer in age . . .*

In among the trees, Kit had a spell circle laid into the ground under the carpet of leaf mold. "I need to make a couple of changes to this before we go," he said to the others. "I don't want her tracking us."

"We don't need that," Darryl said. "I'll transit us the way I brought Ronan in from Dublin. And I doubt she can track my kind of transit: it's real atypical."

"If you can go transatlantic on a personal transit without even breaking a sweat," Kit said, "I guess 'atypical' would be the word."

"It's to do with that bilocation stunt I stumbled

onto during my Ordeal," Darryl said. "Seems I don't need the usual spells to gate around in the neighborhood. I can go a long way without needing a spell, as long as I leave one of me on Earth and have coordinates to work with." He rolled his eyes. "Tom said he didn't understand it, and shoved me off on Carl. Carl gave me five different theories and then wound up saying he thinks I'm bypassing string-structure issues by selectively shredding the interstitial structure of local space-time." Darryl grinned. "Whatever that means! I don't think he understands it, either. Shredding —" He shrugged. "He wants to call it that, it's fine by me."

"Okay, shred-guy," Kit said. "Does the ground suit?" It was the question you asked another wizard when he or she was going to be responsible for a spell.

Darryl glanced around. "Yeah, it's fine. Where on Mars are we going, exactly?"

Kit flipped opened his manual. "A little crater called Stokes."

"Show me. Carl says I need to be careful about coordinates while I'm still getting the hang of this."

Kit nodded, thinking that Tom and Carl were wisely covering all the angles with Darryl. While they wanted him to be cautious about what he was doing, they also didn't want him thinking too hard about whether his ability to do it might be unusual. *Making it sound like something normal is smart . . .*

Kit found his marked map and tapped on it to bring it into higher definition, zooming in on the spot he wanted. "Right there —"

Darryl studied the map. "Okay. And about —

one second from now," he said. "They said I needed to specify temporal coordinates, too. Guess they're nervous I might overshoot."

"Probably something to do with you just being hot off your Ordeal," Ronan said. "You young super-powered hotshots, you want keeping an eye on until you settle down into more realistic power levels . . ."

Darryl nodded as he took a last look at the map. Kit shot Ronan a quick approving look over Darryl's head. Ronan raised an eyebrow in response, eyed the map in turn. "Not far from the north pole. We need to bring any extra heat with us?"

"No, I factored plenty into the spell," Kit said.

"Okay," Darryl said, "we're good to go. You guys ready? Life support's set? Don't make me come all the way back here for more air, now. It's fifty-four million miles to Mars . . ."

"We've got air for three people for four hours," Kit said, "and a heavy-duty force-field bubble."

Ronan suddenly got a wicked look on his face. "And since it's got to be dark there *somewhere* . . ." He pulled out a pair of black-lensed aviator sunglasses and put them on.

Darryl snickered. "Some of us," he said, "have been watching too many old movies."

"Old? That movie was young when I was!"

"So were the dinosaurs. Ready to shred?" And Darryl reached up and put a hand each on Kit's and Ronan's shoulders.

"Hit it," Ronan said.

Between one blink and the next, Earth went away.

Arsia Mons

NITA WAS STANDING near the edge of a gigantic lake, looking out across the still water, waiting for someone.

Where is he? she thought. *He's so late.*

The strange, many-legged creature sitting off to one side on the gravelly red ground at her feet looked up at her. *You've always known he might be someday,* it said.

Nita scowled. *Not that* way, she said in her mind. *Not funny . . .* She peered out across the lake, shading her eyes from the low sun and the pinkish glitter dancing on the water in the crater. *I don't like the way that looks,* she said as the speed of the ripples out on the water increased. *There has to be a lot more of that coming —*

The creature sitting next to her shrugged. *He won't notice it where he is,* it said. *The water would have to rise a lot higher to bother him there.*

The usual place? Nita said.

The creature nodded. *Up on his mountain.*

Nita turned and walked a few steps over to the transit circle she had left ready to go, blazing on the ground. *What about the other one you were supposed to be meeting here?* said the creature that still sat by the lake's edge, unmoving, gazing back at her with ironic golden eyes.

Can't wait, Nita said. *Come on, let's go.*

She stepped into the circle. It blazed up around her; the transit was instantaneous. Nita emerged barely a blink later from a flicker of darkness to a spot near the edge of the broad, dish-shaped depression on top of that ancient volcano. The view was amazing; she could understand why Kit loved this place so much. But she looked all around the crater and couldn't see him anywhere. There was no question of Kit being hidden behind anything. There were no big boulders, large objects, or outcroppings: just pebbles, sand, fist-sized stones, and cracks and crevasses caused by the contrast between the day's relative warmth and the night's ferocious cold.

Nita transited across the crater a couple more times, effortlessly, the way she'd seen Darryl do, but found no trace of Kit. The transits, though, were enjoyable for their own sake. *Pity this is a dream,* she thought. *It'd be great to be able to do this without having to do a spell and pay the price* ... The third time, she came out near the ridge at the crater's edge, where the dust and sand still held some trace of someone's sneaker prints. She dropped to one knee, touched one

print, then reached over beside it to pick up a little
stone that lay there. *What about it, guy?* she said. *Who's
been up here recently?*

Nobody, the stone said. *Just him, and her. The
other one.*

Nita blinked at that, confused. Well, rocks tended
to think of time in the geological sense; they could get
confused about shorter periods. *I haven't been up here,
though. This is the first time.*

No, the rock said. *But the last time you came, he
had been thinking of her; and he didn't want to stay.
He ran away. And so did you . . .*

Nita shook her head, uncertain what to make of
this. An odd feeling of dread was beginning to gather
at the back of her mind. Uncertain, she dropped the
stone gently to the sandy ground and climbed further
up the ridge.

There on the crater's edge, Nita paused, looking
out across the dusty red afternoon toward where the
low sun swung. At the edge of that sharply curved,
foreshortened horizon, something moved and glittered. *You did say you didn't like the look of that . . .*
said the creature crouching at her feet.

Oh, it can't possibly — Nita said. But then she
noticed that the silvery tremor out at the edge of
things was getting brighter. It actually seemed to be
humping up against the horizon — higher than the
hills of the Southern Highlands, impossible though
that was. Fear began to rise in Nita, growing more
pronounced as a thin, distant sound began to reach
her: the rush and roar of water. *There's no way I can*

hear that all this way up here, she thought. Her pulse began racing. She stared all around her in growing panic. Where was Kit? He was supposed to be here. But he *couldn't* be here. If he was here, and he didn't get away soon, he'd get caught in this —

All the southern horizon was awash now. Nita could see the foaming onrush of the initial waves, running northward toward her in a flood of ever-increasing speed, over the hills and down into the craters of the lowlands, splashing up around highland hills and making islands of them, rushing inexorably at the mountain where she stood. The new islands were swiftly drowned as the water raced toward Nita. She stood rooted in horror as the incoming wavefront, hundreds of feet higher in this gravity than an Earth-based tsunami could ever be, came plunging through the southern highlands and down over the edge of their plateau, pouring down into the vast cratery basin of the lowlands at her feet and rushing, uncheckable, toward the mountain where she stood. Within what seemed only moments, the water flowed around her on all sides, splashed up over the immense mesa on which the mountain stood, drowned it in a matter of a few breaths, began to climb the sides of the mountain —

Nita gulped with fear. She had to get away, fast, before the onrushing water changed the nature of the land where she was standing and made it impossible for her to use her already prepared spell to escape. Nita raised her hands, the summoning gesture for the transit spell she was carrying.

But no light erupted around her feet. The Speech-characters she was expecting didn't materialize. Nita began hurriedly speaking the words of an emergency transit spell — and then, shocked, stopped, realizing the words made no sense. *I don't understand! It has to work! It's a spell! A spell always works —*

I told you not to wait so long, said the creature crouching at her feet.

That's a lot of help now! Nita turned southward again, afraid of what she'd see. Between her and the pale, pinky sun, something rose up to filter and dim the sky. It was a wave, easily a hundred feet thick in this gravity, easily a mile high. Up and up it reared, now taller than the mountain, leaning over Nita, leaning farther out, the great sparkling arch of it stretching out over the top of the mountain-crater like a vast, downward-curving, smoked glass roof. The distant sun, caught in it, flickered and struggled to shine. It was no use. The thickness of the water was putting it out. And Nita couldn't transit. She was trapped, unless she found the right words to say, figured out what to do. But she was never going to figure it out. There wasn't going to be time. The wave arched, curved more deeply above her, then finally and immensely broke —

Nita had what felt like a lifetime's leisure to watch the water fall slowly toward her in a massive, incompressible, high-curved slab. Gravity or no gravity, when that wave came down on her, its mass would crush her just as flat as if it was stone and not water. *Too much mass at this speed,* some dry and terrified part of her brain said in the background, didactic to the end. *After all, g equals G times the mass of Mars over the square of the radius, so that would be at least three hundred seventy-two centimeters per second squared, and that means —*

The roaring and the blackness smashed down onto Nita.

The world ended.

Nita sat bolt upright in bed, gasping for breath.

It took a moment for her to register, as she stared around her, that everything was all right, that she was in her bedroom and all the usual safe, sane, familiar things were there. The posters on the wall, the library books piled up on the desk, the magazines stacked on her dresser, the shopping voucher plaques for the Crossings that Carmela had given her, saying, "I've only got about sixty of them; let me know when you need more . . ."

Nita worked on slowing her breathing down. After that, her first, somewhat panicked impulse was to try to completely forget what she'd just seen and try to go back to sleep. *What, and find myself back in that dream again? Not a chance!*

She got up, pulled down her nightdress, and went over to the desk, where she flipped her manual open. "Bobo," she said, "boy, have I got one for the dream journal today!"

The manual's pages riffled under her hands, laying themselves open to the section into which she dictated her dreams. *General theme?* said the voice in the back of her head.

Nita shook her head, sighed. "Water again."

You've been getting a lot of that lately.

Nita shrugged. "Probably something to do with the project at hand." But an echo of an old memory said, *Fear death by water . . .*

She shook her head. Picchu had just been quoting some poet at the time. And that had been such a long while ago. *Yet Peach's prophecies were always reliable. Who knows how long they might have been good for?*

Unfortunately, prophecy rarely came stamped with a sell-by date. Nita took the manual back to the bed, sat down cross-legged on top of the covers, and hurriedly dictated everything she could remember about the dream. ". . . And the wave," she said at last. "I can't believe I was standing there working out the acceleration of a falling mass on Mars." She laughed. "And that all mixed up with the water . . . Kit's thing is starting to get to me."

Well, after yesterday, possibly that's understandable.

"Might be right," Nita said. She stretched and glanced at the clock. "Where is he?"

Where do you think?

Nita laughed. "Don't know why I even bother asking." She got up, tossing the manual to one side. "Did he leave me any messages?"

Just a routine notification of where he was going.

She let out a breath and pulled a dresser drawer open, pulling out a big sweatshirt and a pair of jeans. These Nita held up against her, looking down to check the length, then paused: the act brought back that strange image of the transit circle that wouldn't flame to life. She let out a perplexed breath. *Wizardry,* she thought, *not working . . .*

That's something that's happened recently, the peridexis said.

She pulled the pants on. "Yeah... But I've dreamed that before." She considered as she finished dressing. "Maybe it's the wizard's version of those horrible dreams people have where you forgot to study and there's a test. Then you wake up in a cold sweat and find there's nothing to it..."

The peridexis offered no opinion. Nita shrugged and headed downstairs.

Her dad was sitting at the dining room table, staring at the screen of his cell phone. "Morning," Nita said, heading into the kitchen to make some tea.

"There's a fresh pot on the counter," her dad said.

"Thank you..." Nita poured a cup, got a spoon and the sugar bowl from the counter, and put what were probably too many sugars in the tea, then left it there while she went rooting through one of the cupboards over the counter for cereal. "You playing around with your address book again?"

"No," her dad said from the dining room, "it's Dairine's information coming through on the phone. The live feed of what she's doing today. What was it you called it? A spinoff?"

"Secondary spin," Nita said, reaching into the fridge for milk. "At least, that's what it's called when we're just excerpting nonwizardly stuff that's also in the manual. We might need to invent another word for this."

She brought in a bowl and a spoon and the cornflakes box, and sat down by her dad. "She's gone already?"

"Yup," her father said. He looked more resigned than annoyed. "She did her chores first, though."

"Good." Nita poured cereal into the bowl, reached for the milk, and then realized her tea was still in the kitchen. "Oops . . ."

She went back for it. When she came back, her dad was fiddling with the little joystick under the phone's screen. "What are you getting?" Nita said. "Text, or —" She looked over his shoulder. "Oh, no, there she is! Hey, that's pretty good."

The screen wasn't the best for this kind of work, but it showed clearly enough an image of the simulator hall in the palace at Wellakh, with Dairine standing in front of the slowly rotating Thahit-mirroring sunglobe. "Where are they, exactly?" her dad said.

Nita squinted at the screen. "See that icon over there on the left? If you hit that, it'll bring up subtitles. There you go. It's Roshaun's home planet, Daddy. About twenty-three thousand light-years from here."

Another figure moved into view on the phone's screen. "And that's — who? His dad?"

Nita nodded as she sat down and poured milk on her cereal. "Nelaid ke Seriv."

Her dad studied Nelaid for a moment. "Tall guy."

"Yeah, Wellakhit usually are. Their gravity's a little less than ours, so their bones grow longer . . ." Nita ate some cereal, then paused. "Oh, yeah — he wants to talk to you. At your convenience, he said. About Dairine."

Her dad glanced up. "She's not making some kind of trouble for him, is she?"

"Oh, no! I think —" Nita munched for a moment more. "I think he considers her a challenge. His family are big on that kind of thing . . ." She wondered how much of the political situation it would be safe to get into with her dad, then decided to leave that to Nelaid. "I think he just wants to talk dad-to-dad stuff with you. To let you know he's keeping an eye on her."

Her father looked concerned. "Is fatherhood on other planets really that much like fatherhood here?"

"Some places, no. But in this case, yeah. Hominid species tend to have a lot in common, depending on how their biologies work. There are always cultural variations, but —" Nita held out her hand for the phone, took it, and played briefly with the joystick, then handed the phone back. "Go through that section, and you can get a species-to-species and culture-to-culture values comparison. Have it generate you a matching-features chart."

"Like one of those compare-before-you-buy websites?"

Nita grinned. "Close. But let me know when you're ready to talk to Nelaid, and I'll send him word." She went back to her cereal, eating faster so it wouldn't have a chance to go soggy. "He was real gracious about this. Which he doesn't have to be: he's a king. He's used to having people jump when *he* says, not the other way around."

Her dad nodded, went back to watching Dairine and Nelaid while Nita finished her cereal. Shortly he said, "What exactly are they doing?"

"It's complicated," Nita said. "Nelaid's family are

responsible for keeping their planet's star from acting up. It's not the kind of wizardry it's easy to do from a distance. Sometimes you have to get in there under the hood and fix things . . ."

"'Get in'?" her dad said. "Into a *sun*?"

Nita nodded, eating the last of the cereal, then reaching for the mug of tea. "It's pretty specialized work. Roshaun did it for our Sun while he was here."

"And she was there for that?"

Nita nodded. "I think she had to be. I mean, it's *our* star. It wouldn't have mattered if Roshaun'd been a specialist at the galactic level: he still would've needed a local rep on hand to explain things to the star. A system's primary has a really deep connection with creatures born in its system. If an alien wizard tried to do anything significant to the Sun without an Earth-born wizard there, the star might think somebody was trying to tamper with it who didn't have permission." Nita shook her head. "Could've gotten real ugly."

Her father gave Nita a slightly cockeyed look. "The *star* might think?"

Nita sighed. "Daddy, I know how it sounds, but believe me, sometimes it's safer to treat inanimate things as if they were animate! Awareness levels in matter can be real situational. Anyway, I think Nelaid's teaching Dairine how to get into a relationship with stars besides her own. Seems like a good addition to her skill set. She always did like the high-powered stuff." *And the way her power levels have been dropping off, she may start needing finesse to keep doing that work. She's not going to have brute new-wizard strength to fall back on now . . .* Nita got up to put her bowl in the kitchen.

"So you're going off, too, now?" her dad said. "Whereabouts? Mars?"

"What, just because you think Kit's there?"

"Well, that'd be the normal assumption, wouldn't it?"

Nita had to laugh. Even her dad knew the score. "Yeah, I'd say . . ." She washed her bowl and put it in the dish drainer. "Well, guess what? Unlike just about every other wizard you know, I'm actually doing something close to home. Got to go to the beach and talk to S'reee. I had an idea last night before I went to sleep about something we've been talking about for a while." She came back into the dining room, bent down, and kissed her dad on the cheek. "You okay with this now?" She glanced at the phone.

"Yeah, I think so."

"Good. I'll be back later."

"Before you go to Mars, or afterwards?"

"Maybe before. It's not like he doesn't deserve his own private time up there."

"'Boys are from Mars,' huh?"

Nita snorted. "Believe me, I've been starting to wonder."

"Okay. Keep me posted."

Nita headed for the stairs again, smiling slightly. *This is working pretty well so far,* she thought. *If I'm real lucky, he won't get the bright idea that it'd be fun to watch* me *the same way he's watching Dairine.*

Well, you know, the peridexis said in the back of her mind, *if it came to that, you could always tell him I refused to do it.*

She snickered as she headed up the stairs. "Bobo," she said, "I know I can count on you. But let's not worry about it right now."

"You say something, sweetie?" her dad said from down in the dining room.

"Just talking to my invisible friend, Daddy . . ."

There was a pause. "Why do I even bother asking anymore?"

Nita laughed under her breath. She went into her room, threw some things into her backpack — a magazine or two, an extra sweater. Then she put out a hand and whistled for her wizard's manual.

You're really going to bring that with you? Such a crutch.

"We've had this discussion before, Bobo," Nita said, opening it and paging through to the messaging area to see what Kit might have left in response to her note of the previous day. "I kept my little blue babyblankie for a real long time, too . . ."

The peridexis fell silent, possibly confused. Nita grinned and looked at the messaging pages. The note she'd left Kit the previous day was grayed out: his response was underneath.

Headed out to check things out with Darryl and Ronan. Didn't want to bother you so early. Probably back around the middle of the afternoon. Take a look at my précis when you have a moment. K.

Nita raised her eyebrows as she closed the manual. *Kind of terse for him,* she thought. *Maybe he's realized how annoyed I was about him dumping me yesterday, and now he's feeling guilty? Good. But I'll take a look at the précis as soon as S'reee and I handle business, and then go see what he's up to. No point in making him suffer all day if he's learned his lesson.*

She shoved the manual into her backpack, then slipped one strap over her shoulder and pulled a pre-set transit circle out of her charm bracelet. Nita dropped it to the floor, where it came alive in the proper blaze of fiery characters in the Speech. Nita looked at it with unnecessary relief. *Just a dream, before,* Nita thought. *Just a dream . . .*

She stepped through the circle —

The boulder-built breakwater jetty that sticks out into the water on the east side of Jones Inlet once had a U.S. Coast Guard station associated with it. The station was gone now, the old low building at the jetty's landward end demolished: no structure remained but the tower at the bayside end that still held the light and horn. The horn was silent, since the morning was bright and clear. The light blinked as usual, making a faint *tink, tink, tink* noise that could be heard by anyone within twenty feet of the tower, even over the wash and rush of water where it ran up against the stones of the jetty's base.

Nita came out under eye level, from the landward point of view, on one of the big guano-streaked stones nearest to the end of the jetty. She had a low-energy visual shield-spell around her — a simple wizardly cloaking surface that redirected the images of objects behind her so that they appeared in front of her, making it seem as if she wasn't there. Nita held the slide-around cloaking spell in place while she glanced around to make sure no one in the area could see her. Fishing boats came in and out of the Inlet all the time, so this was something of an issue: but at this time of morning, the commercial boats were already out in the bay, and the small casual boats — charters that took parties of game fishermen out after sailfin and swordfish — were either well away or not yet ready to go to sea.

No person or craft was anywhere near enough to see her even with binoculars. Nita killed the shield-spell, then sat down on the stone and stared down into the murky water, where long, silky green weed attached to the big gray-black rocks swayed and rippled rhythmically as the water washed and splashed against the jetty. The image from her dream, that impossibly high wave with the pale struggling sun caught in it, rose before her mind's eye again. *Water, water everywhere,* Nita thought. *Why does it keep turning up in my dreams?* But not even the koi had any answers to that question. Sometimes Nita thought it had to do with the part she'd played way back when in the Song of the Twelve: the expression of some old pain or discomfort still undischarged after what had admittedly been a very trying experience for a wizard relatively new to wizardry and not entirely prepared for the dangers of the Art as it was practiced in the Sea. *But the problem doesn't have to be the past,* she thought. *It could as easily be something in the future.* Her specialty as a wizard was changing, or rather expanding:

the visionary gift had been making itself more obvious in her practice, which had meant that she'd had to start learning to handle it before — as Tom had said — it started handling her. *If that's not what it's doing already . . .*

The problem is, this predictive stuff — just isn't predictable! And something about that bothered Nita, even as the phrasing made her laugh. She preferred her spells straightforward and structured: she liked to do a spell and then get a result she'd known she could expect. But the dreams and visions she was now trying to learn to manage were maddeningly fluid — and Nita had to laugh again at her phrasing: the liquid imagery kept sneaking in. *I've got water on the brain . . .*

A hundred yards or so off the jetty, the water roiled, then sprayed upward in a noisy blast of spume that caught the Sun in rainbows. A few moments later a dark shape came looming up through the water into visibility, and the massive, gray-skinned, barnacle-spotted body of a humpback whale rose up to loll just under the surface. One eye broke surface to peer up at Nita, a lazy, interested look.

"*Dai stihó,* O Honored Senior for the Waters of Earth," Nita said.

S'reee rolled and blew spray at Nita, and Nita couldn't get any kind of force field up fast enough to ward it away: she got soaked. "No more of that, thank you very much!" S'reee said. "I've had it up to my dorsal with titles! And few I've been gladder to get rid of than that one, now that things have quieted down."

Nita snickered. "It just sounds good on you, that's all."

"I want nothing to do with it," the humpback muttered, slapping the water with her tail in annoyed emphasis. "All I want from the Powers is my own waters, my own name, with 'senior' added if anyone insists: that's more than enough honor for me." She blew again, resting the end of her long long chin on the breakwater's last stone, and looking up at Nita with one small bright eye. "What are you doing up so early in the day, hNii't? Isn't this supposed to be time off for you? Your learning-place work is almost done for this season, I thought: you were supposed to be relaxing —"

"I am," Nita said. "This *is* relaxing . . ."

S'reee back-finned and rolled over sideways in the water, the apparent smile of the long jaw reflected for the moment in the squeaks and clicks of her voice. "Oh, my, you've hit the bad phase of your wizardry already, where you can't stop working! Middle-aged so soon! I thought *I* was getting old before my time."

Nita laughed, for S'reee was younger in humpback terms than Nita was in human ones. "Oh, sure. You're a real ancient."

S'reee rolled right over on her back, partly in a gesture of agreement, partly to get a better view of the jetty. "And where's K!t today?" she said.

When are people going to stop asking me that? Especially when half the time they know the answer! "Where do you think?"

S'reee chuckled, a long string of squeaks and bubbling noises. "Don't give me that look! It's not my fault if he's predictable lately. And taking all this so seriously . . ."

"Yeah," Nita said. "Well, I'll catch up with him after we talk. But something occurred to me last night. Wait a sec, I'll come down —"

She clambered down off the rocks and carefully boosted herself down onto the surface of the water. There she stood fairly still until she got her balance, bobbing up and down while she reached around to one specific charm on her bracelet, shaped like a little glass bubble: the ready-made spell she used for underwater work when she wasn't up for a full shape-change. She pinched it between finger and thumb, whispering the last six words of the spell, the activating sequence.

Around Nita and under her feet, the transparent sphere of air went solid at its outer boundary, then sank. Nita leaned against the front of the bubble, indicating which way she wanted it to go: it began to glide along under the surface, while S'reee finned along beside her. "So what's it about?" S'reee said.

"Not what we've been working on. Something different."

"Oh?"

"The bombs."

"Oh, yes," S'reee said. After the end of World War II, the local authorities dumped a considerable number of out-of-date depth charges into the Great South Bay, along the main approach to the New York and New Jersey harbors. For some time wizards had been arguing about what to do with these, as they were becoming increasingly unstable and dangerous with age. "I do wonder sometimes what possessed your people to just dump those there," S'reee said. "They've been on my mind, too. This time of year, some of the trawlers get irresponsible and drop their nets where they might run into some of those charges if they got careless —"

"Well," Nita said, as they made their way into the green depths out past the shoreside reefs, "something came to me last night. I'd been doing some manual reading before bed, and when I was just falling asleep I got this image of a river flowing over stones, wearing them away —"

The water around the two of them darkened with depth as they made their way down toward the bottom of the Bay, the slope dropping off southward of the old oyster beds. "Well, all the rivers go to the Sea eventually," S'reee said, "but I'm not sure what that has to do with getting rid of the depth charges."

"This," Nita said. "We could dissolve them!"

S'reee looked surprised as they paused over a gravelly, barren spot where several large, lumpy shapes, encrusted with barnacles, lay half-buried in years of silt and sand. "Now, I've heard a lot of solutions to this problem suggested," she said, "but that one's novel."

"Well," Nita said, "the main problem with the depth charges right now is the instability of the explosives, right? Physically moving them would be dangerous for the wizards who get close enough to do an intervention — and if one exploded, the natural and artificial reefs around here would suffer. Years of growth gone in a second: we can't have that. But if we just dissolve off the casings —"

"How?" S'reee said.

Nita shrugged. "I was thinking we could just accelerate the rust. I mean, they're rusting pretty fast already. Look —"

She leaned against the wall of her air bubble, guiding it to float around the far side of the depth charge in a spot where there were no barnacles. The metal was deeply pockmarked, and Nita leaned close and pointed at one spot where the rust had clearly eaten right through. "No telling what the seawater's doing to the explosive," she said. "If we get the casings off, if something should blow, at least shrapnel won't get blasted into the reefs. Then we can dissolve the explosive and wash it away by increasing the current. Solve the problem from the inside out rather than the outside in . . ."

S'reee rolled in the water, considering. "Interesting concept. I'd need to check with our land-based Seniors, too, of course. But I like the sound of this, and it comes at a time when the problem's been preying on my mind more than usual. Time to do something about it."

"So when will you decide?" Nita said as the two of them turned and made their way back toward land.

"Over the next week or so. It shouldn't take more than that to do the necessary consulting and work out the actual process for dissolving the explosives. Nothing mechanical, though."

"Something chemical makes more sense. We can build a spell to neutralize the byproducts."

"And then the increased current takes those away, too? Makes sense." S'reee blew briefly, a cetacean chuckle. "It sounds like something Pellegrino would have thought of."

"I got the idea after I was reading about her," Nita said. Angelina Pellegrino had been a great wizard of the previous century, a specialist in working with water who had single-handedly designed a way to cleanse the western Mediterranean of that period's increasing pollution. That spell, the so-called Gibraltar Passthrough Intervention, was still reckoned by historians of wizardry as one of the greatest achievements of that period by any wizard working alone. "But this wouldn't have to be anything like that big."

"Which is good," S'reee said as they made for the surface, "as hydromages are few and far between, and to move a lot of water, you need a lot of power . . ."

They broke surface a few hundred yards out from the jetty: Nita kept her bubble level with the surface until they were close enough that she wouldn't be seen climbing out of the water. "You know, you should have a word with Arooon about her," S'reee said.

"What, our guy who sang the Blue in the Song of the Twelve?"

"The same. He told me once that his father knew Pellegrino. I seem to remember him saying that when she got started, she was just a human farm girl who noticed that water acted strangely around her. You know the saying, that wizards who have the earliest

Ordeals — and the latest ones — produce the biggest results. Angelina was one of those very late hatchers: almost out of latency when her Ordeal came along. She lived in the island down at the bottom of that long peninsula where the people lived who had that empire. You know the one, it was all around the edges of the Mediterranean —"

"The Romans. You mean Sicily?"

"That's the place. She went swimming on the evening she took the Oath, and the Lone One met her in some kind of demon shape and tried to drown her." S'reee snorted, a very wet blowhole-laugh that just missed drenching Nita again, though this time not on purpose. "Which was an error of judgment on Its part! The fight between them threw her straight into sync with the whole element of water, right across the Med. For something like the whole year after, every wizard on Earth who met the Lone One physically on Ordeal reported that It turned up dripping."

Nita snickered at the image. "She didn't just do the water stuff, though, did she? She got to be a Planetary for a while."

"So she did," S'reee said. "But something else was going on with her, too, which meant she spent less time as Planetary than she might have." S'reee rolled over, stretching those huge fins into the air. "In your reading, have you come across references to a manifestation of wizardry called infra-affinity?"

Nita considered. "Don't know. I might have."

"It's one of the so-called 'inner talents,'" S'reee said. "It's not a spell you design, or something you do, but something you *are.* Lots of wizards have affinities to one or more of the classic elements or states of matter. But *this* state implies such a profound connection to one state of matter or another that a wizard can go into complete union with it, then come out of the unified state without showing any ill effects. Infra-affinity tends to turn up in very new wizards as an Ordeal exploit, like the water mastery your friend Ronan manifested on his Ordeal. But it takes an incredible toll if you keep it up." S'reee looked thoughtful. "Arooon thought that Pellegrino's taking on the role of Planetary Wizard might have been why she died so young. A Planetary has to sync with the whole planet, and it's possible that the required affinities to earth and air and the Earth's interior fire started conflicting with Pellegrino's infra-affinity to water." S'reee let her tail fall over into the water in a sideways slap, a cetacean shrug. "No way to tell at this end of time . . ."

Nita sat thinking about that for a moment. "I wonder," she said. "About Dairine . . . you think she might have an elemental affinity? She was always big on fire when she was little. I can't think how many times Dad had to stop her from playing with the barbecue. She was always getting burned. And now here she is starting to play around with stars . . ."

"Plasma's a whole different element," S'reee said, "but you might be onto something there. It could explain the connection to your colleague Roshaun as well. Like does call to like sometimes . . ."

"I wonder," Nita said, "if I'm developing something like that for water."

S'reee waved a fin in agreement that this could be a possibility. "Could be. It might explain why you took to underwater wizardry so readily, and did so well in the Song. But it's a tendency, not a restriction. It doesn't have to dominate your practice."

Nita nodded and leaned against the rocks. "Something else to research . . ."

S'reee bubbled with laughter again. "The story of all our lives," she said. "Though I'd try to put the research aside for a little. We *do* have to make sure we have other things going on in our lives than just wizardry, or what good are we to the Powers?"

There was an amused quality to S'reee's voice, something almost secretive. Curious, Nita stretched out on the rock to get a better look at S'reee's eye on that side. "Oh, really? What's this all about?"

"Well, there are other reasons to go out singing than just errantry," S'reee said.

That was when Nita remembered that "out singing" had more than one meaning for a whale. "Whoa, wait a minute! 'Ree, are you *seeing* somebody? You are! You're finning around with someone!" Nita reached down and pounded S'reee on the flank in a congratulatory way. "Who's the lucky bull?"

"Someone I met out on errantry —"

"Hey, great! Another wizard?"

"Oh, no, not at all. We can't all date wizards, hNii't! I met Hwiii'sh a few weeks ago up by the

Grand Banks when I was on a meal break in the middle of a team wizardry. You know how it is, there are always tourists around who're all itchy to see wizards doing what they do . . ."

Nita smiled ironically, letting the "dating" reference go by. She was so used to hearing this kind of thing from kids at school that she'd stopped protesting, since it just made everybody sure they were right. *With luck, they'll stop eventually . . .* "Well, tourists aren't a problem I have all that much," Nita said. "So tell me all about him! What does he sing?" — that being what you generally asked whales instead of "What do you do?"

"He sings *aouih'hweioooiuh'hhaii!t.*"

Nita had to listen to the word in the Speech to make anything of it. "Am I getting that right? He's a *food critic?*"

"And very stuck up about it, too," S'reee said, blowing a big wet laugh. "You should hear him going on about Arctic krill, and South Cape squid, and all the rest of it! Fortunately he thinks it's a big deal that I'm a wizard, so I don't have trouble holding my own when his ego starts to run riot . . ."

Nita leaned against the jetty and relaxed while S'reee talked, enjoying the fact that for once she had time to kick back and laugh at the concept of a whale who did nothing but share news about the presence and quality of food with other whales. But then lately it seemed rare for Nita to have "quality time" like this — time without school or schoolwork hanging over her head, or some terrifyingly heavy piece of wizardry that needed her attention. *More of this, please, and enough saving the world for this year!* Nita said silently to the One. *Actually having the summer off, like a normal person, would be very, very nice!* Not that she could ever be precisely normal again: wizardry kind of precluded that. . . .

Up behind her on the jetty, Nita heard an odd sort of strangled pop. She scrambled around and peered up, one hand on her charm bracelet again, ready to wake up the light-diverting cloaking spell so she could pull it down over her and S'reee if need be. But there wasn't any need. Halfway down the jetty, Carmela had just walked out of the air and was heading toward them down the rough stony path on the jetty's top.

Nita let out a breath of mild exasperation. "'Mela," she said as Carmela got down near them, "you can *not* just go appearing out of nothing around here! People could notice."

"But they don't, mostly," Carmela said, clambering down among the rocks to perch on top of one of the biggest ones near the waterline, dangling her legs over the edge. "Isn't that one of the weird things about wizardry on Earth? Everybody says they want magic in their lives, and when it happens right in front of them, usually they don't believe it. 'Oh, she must have been there a moment before and I just didn't see her,' they're all probably saying." Then she paused and looked around. "Except, listen to me: *who's* all saying? There's nobody here. You're just being paranoid. Loosen up! Good morning, Miss S'reee . . ."

S'reee, half-submerged except for one big eye,

was bubbling in amusement. "And *dai stihó* to you, K!aarmii'lha. What brings you down here?"

"Well, my main project for the day is to go shopping," Carmela said, "and this time Nita is finally coming with me. *Aren't you, Miss Neets?*"

Carmela scowled a very overstated scowl at Nita. Nita laughed, glancing at S'reee. "She's the only one I know who can make a shopping trip sound like a death sentence . . ."

"Well, depending on where you shop at the Crossings, it could happen," S'reee said, rolling over in the water. "Some of the boutiques there are very species-specific: you'd have to watch what you bought. Sea's Name, even some of the restroom facilities there could be fatal if you walked in the wrong door . . ."

"S'reee, it's hardly about the toilets. We know all about which ones not to go into!" Carmela said.

"And if we didn't, we could always ask Dairine," Nita said under her breath, with a smile.

"Never mind the restrooms," Carmela said, "it's the stores that are interesting, S'reee. The clothes stores, especially. We've got to get Neets out of these floppy sweatshirts and jeans! I've asked her to come with me at least six times now." Carmela bent down toward the amused S'reee in a most confiding way. "But she just keeps handing me these lame excuses. Help me talk her out of this morning's one! Which I'm sure she will now provide for us." And Carmela turned expectantly to Nita.

A wave splashed higher than others had — the

tide was coming in — and Nita paused to wipe spray off her face. "I was going to go up to Mars first . . ."

Carmela covered her eyes theatrically. "I knew it, S'reee," she said. "It had to happen. She's finally come down with Kit's Mars bug!"

"Well," S'reee said, adopting a fairly diplomatic tone, "you have to admit, it *is* hard not to find it exciting —"

"Especially when he's up there with Ronan and Darryl," Nita said.

"I know," Carmela said. "That was going to be my first stop before I hit the Crossings. I was hoping Neets would come along with me so we could give them a good joint tease before moving on to more interesting things."

"No way, 'Mela!" Nita said. "*Not* a good idea! All the signs point to this being some obscure *boy* thing. The note Kit left me had 'Keep Out, Male-Bonding Road Trip' stamped all over it."

"All the more reason to crash the party!"

Nita began to sweat, realizing how much aggravation she was going to catch from Kit if she turned up on Mars with Carmela in tow. "No . . . seriously. You're right about how many times you've asked me to go. Why don't we let them get on with it and go shopping instead?"

"Too late, Neets," Carmela said, and stood up. "I'll go without you."

"To *Mars??*" Nita said, now becoming seriously concerned.

Carmela smiled slightly and reached into one deep pocket of her jumpsuit. From it she pulled not the curling-ironish laser dissociator that Nita was expecting but a TV remote. This she flipped expertly in the air and caught.

"I had a word with my closet," Carmela said. "Actually, I had a word with the TV remote that Kit did his magic tweaking on, and *it* had a word with my closet. And then, so I could have control of the worldgate in the closet when I'm away from home, the remote talked to Dairine's sweet little Spot, and cloned itself for me. Took no time at all." She smiled delightedly.

"Wait," S'reee said. "'Your closet'? Is that inside a house here?"

"Yup. It's in my bedroom."

S'reee looked puzzled. "You have a worldgate in your *house*? What does it run on? Besides wizardry, I mean. The necessary 'hard' power outlay would be considerable."

"I'm told I have a parasitic virtual catenary conduit from one of the nondenominated gates at the Crossings," Carmela said, and laughed. "Whatever *that* means! They've got it plugged into something or other; that's all that matters. My closet even has a Crossings gate number, though it's unlisted. Like a very classy Zip code." Carmela juggled the remote from hand to hand. "So now I don't need to bother anybody else to give me rides . . . and if I want to go to Mars, the boys can't stop me. Come to think of it" — and she grinned at Nita — "*you* can't stop me! Because you don't really want to. Do you?"

"Uh —"

"Oh, Juanita Louise, don't look so stricken —"

Nita clutched her head. "Carmela. *Do . . . not . . . say . . . the L word!*"

Carmela laughed. After a moment, to Nita's horror, so did S'reee. "hNii't," S'reee said, "I think she's got us both in the drift net at the moment. We may as well give in gracefully."

"'Us'? You want to go, too?"

"Well, why not? I'm not all that busy this morning. If *she's* supplying free transport —"

"Not free," Carmela said promptly. "This interspatial transport is supplied to you on a promotional basis courtesy of the Planetary Government of Rirhath B and Crossings Properties HyperIncorporated." She produced a very prim and proper expression. "Because I know that in wizardry there's no such thing as a free lunch." Then Carmela grinned. "But I can take as many people as I like whenever I like to, because Sker'ret said I could . . . and what the Stationmaster of Rirhath B says, goes."

Nita sighed. "She's got us there."

"So it's settled, then. Where exactly on Mars are we going?"

Nita pulled out her manual. "Wait a sec, 'cause I have no idea exactly what he's been up to —"

After a few moments Nita found the spot where Kit had filed his précis. "Uh-oh . . ."

"What?" S'reee and Carmela said in unison — Carmela with much more relish.

Nita tsked under her breath. "He just couldn't leave that egg alone," she said. "Looks like it hatched! And sent out some signals . . ."

S'reee, partially submerged again, listened to what the Sea had to tell her about this. "Odd. Four signals went out from the artifact. But I'm seeing *five* hot spots on Mars where wizardry is either working or waiting to start."

Carmela looked confused. "So where are the guys?"

Nita paged back to Kit's précis, found the map he'd labeled with the signal targets, and tapped the page: it updated. "Looks like the northernmost of the targets. Some crater called Stokes. Yeah, there are their life signs — S'reee, are you seeing this?"

S'reee's eyes were unfocused. "Yes. There's no missing Darryl's life sign, in particular; it's unique." She flipped a fin, looked up at Nita.

Nita nodded, not looking up from the manual: there was something strange about the diagram she was examining. Not knowing what to make of it, she flipped back to the messaging page and touched Kit's note to bring the contact up to live status. "Hey," she said in the Speech. "What's going on up there?" And she waited.

Nothing.

She looked up. Carmela was giving her an odd look. "Is there a delay?" she said. "Mars is a long way off."

Nita shook her head. "Lightspeed isn't an issue for the manuals." She turned back to the map on Kit's précis page, scrutinized it. "I don't like this. The manual says we can't go there."

"*What?*" S'reee said.

"The manual says the sites are 'Unavailable, blocked by previous declaration, investigation ongoing, comm functions blocked during evaluation.'"

"Whose previous declaration?" Carmela said, "and whose investigation? Blocked by who? And what —?" The rest of what she was saying got lost in the splash of S'reee submerging again.

"What?" Carmela said. "Did I say something wrong? What freaked her?"

Nita shook her head. "She's looking it up in detail. She gets her wizardry data from the Sea. She's more senior than me — she may be able to find out more."

In a few moments, S'reee surfaced and blew. "All I get is what you're getting," she said to Nita. "Definitely something to do with the superegg's transmission this morning — there are multiple delayed wizardries working. But don't ask me what they're doing, I can't get an analysis. Because what I'm getting makes no sense. The Sea can't give me enough context for a translation."

"Alien wizardry . . ." Nita said, getting more unnerved by the second. "Dangerous, you think?"

"No telling. But that fifth site isn't blocked. There's some kind of wizardry there that's alive and running, but not doing anything . . . just waiting."

"And transit's not prevented?" Carmela said.

Nita shook her head, showed Carmela the manual page. "There. Get the coordinates and do the honors. We can have a look at that hot spot: and when we're actually on the planet, we might be able to reach the guys. Or get a better idea of what's going on with them."

Carmela looked at the manual page and spent a moment tapping numbers into the remote. Nita was surprised to hear it make a little series of electronic beeps, at which Carmela's eyebrows went up. "Oh, you can do that?" she said in the Speech. "Sorry." She pointed the remote at the manual, pressed a button. The remote chirped; Carmela looked up at Nita. "It can take a scan. I didn't realize."

"hNii't," S'reee said, "you had a cloaking routine ready? Putting it up around us might be good. About a twenty-meter radius —"

Nita tucked the manual away, pulled the spell out of the charm bracelet, and said the words that kicked the spell into action. As she did, S'reee levitated gracefully out of the water, keeping just an inch-thick shell of it around her so her skin wouldn't dry out. "I've got all the air we'll need. K!aarmii'lha?"

Carmela raised the remote, hit what would normally be the channel-change button.

They vanished.

It was mid-afternoon on the red-brown southern slopes of the Martian volcano where two girls and a humpback whale appeared a second later. Away to the east, under the thin, filmy clouds of a windy day, the vast shadows and chasms of the westernmost end of Valles Marineris cut away from them in dust and haze toward the edge of the world, where a thin veil of pink-tinted sky hid the canyon's far end.

Carmela looked at the long, gentle slope of the worn old mountain behind them. "You know what you could build here? The universe's biggest ski jump. What's this place called, anyway?"

Nita had to smile as she and S'reee looked around. "Arsia Mons."

Carmela snickered. "Sounds like one of Ronan's rude Irish words . . ."

"Not this time," Nita said, pulling out her manual to cross-reference between the map and the down-slope terrain. "In the old days, people saw this was a bright spot that got dark sometimes. They couldn't see the cause — this big spiral of dust that updrafts from the volcano's side every winter." She looked up the long, shallow curve of the volcano's slope, where many dark-colored rocks were whitened on top by the last winter's dustfall. "But the astronomers back then thought maybe there were trees here, growing leaves and losing them again. So they called it Arsia Silva, the Arsine Forest, after someplace in Italy. Later when the telescopes were better they got rid of the word for forest and put in 'mons' for mountain, but they kept the 'Arsia.'"

Carmela stared at Nita. "Have you been secretly studying this stuff?"

Nita laughed. "I have been *not* so secretly listening to Kit's lectures on Martian stuff every five minutes! For months! So some of it I remember." She shook her head. "That pillar of dust is famous: it gets twenty miles high, sometimes. These, though . . . these got found later." They looked down at the side of the volcano, all spotted with deep black holes.

"They call them skylights," Nita said, bouncing down toward the closest of them. "Don't ask me why, but they gave them all girls' names. Dena, Chloe, Wendy, Annie, Nikki —" She stopped. "Can't remember the others . . ."

Abbey and Jeanne, said Bobo.

Nita nodded. "Seven of them, anyway."

"But there's another one," Carmela said. "Is that where we're going?"

Nita looked at the manual, looked at S'ree, nodded. "That's the one."

"I shall call it Louise," Carmela said, and bounced off that way as if everything was settled.

Nita made a strangled growling noise.

The more you do that, Bobo said, *the more she's going to keep saying it. I'd let it pass, if I were you.*

Nita went after Carmela. S'reee glided along beside her. "What's the problem with the name, hNii't?" she said.

Nita shook her head. "Long story . . ." She pulled the atmosphere spell out of her charm bracelet to make sure it would hold up under the extra distance that Carmela had bounced ahead.

"My air shell's much bigger than yours," S'reee said. "Don't worry; it'll cover us all."

They caught up with Carmela at the edge of the further skylight. All three paused to look down into the darkness. "Deep," S'reee said. "Thirty or forty of my lengths . . ."

"At least," Nita said. She unzipped her other-space pocket and pulled out one of the little wizard-lights she carried for such circumstances — just a long sentence in the Speech made virtually physical, then rolled up and compressed to about the size of a pea. She pinched it and said the trigger word. The spell came alive in her hand, a clear white light about as bright at the moment as a sixty-watt bulb. This she dropped down into the cave. It floated down about as fast as a large leaf might fall from a tree.

"Look at the top level of that," S'reee said, peering down into the darkness. "It's almost perfectly spherical."

"Like a bubble," Nita said. "You think that's what happened here? Some old volcanic eruption. The gases built up in the lava; a bubble formed real near the surface. Then cooled off really fast —"

"And then the top blew off it," Carmela said. She kicked gently at the stone at the very edge of the sky-light: a fragment flew off, fell gently down into the huge hole after the wizard-light. "Yeah. Look how thin that was. If you had a bubble half a mile wide . . ."

Nita nodded. She and Carmela stood, and S'reee hung, watching the light drift downward. "It looks a lot lighter down at the bottom," Carmela said after a few moments.

"That's dust, I think," Nita said as the light came to rest in a little halo of its own reflected glow, far down at the bottom of that huge empty space. "Let's go down. Ree, is it safe to spell inside your air bubble?"

"Absolutely — the spell structure's on the outside."

Nita spoke a few words to the air inside S'reee's bubble. From where she and Carmela stood, a near-transparent stairway of hardened air, like glass, built itself down into the darkness. Nita reached into her backpack for the latest in a long series of rowan wands. As she stepped down into the darkness, the wand began to glow with its charge of absorbed moonlight, lighting the stairway. "Just walk down behind me," Nita said to Carmela. "This'll build itself in front of us and unbuild behind."

"And if we need to run away in a hurry," Carmela said, sounding for the first time slightly nervous, "we're going to have to run upstairs??"

Nita snorted. "If we have to get out *that* fast, I won't waste time skywalking! And neither should you. If there's trouble just transport out."

They walked down to Nita's little light-spell. It was a long walk. Beside them, S'reee drifted down through the huge, dark, empty space, fins hanging motionless: but Nita noticed that there was a faint glow about them and about S'reee's tail, some wizardry in abeyance but ready to use in a hurry.

"I forgot to ask you," Carmela said, walking in sync with Nita. "Where's Dairine? I thought she'd be here, too. She was the one who was all hot for Mars, originally."

"Just on the first day of her Ordeal," Nita said. "This was a pit stop: she wanted to see Olympus Mons. Such a tourist destination." She smiled. "She headed for Wellakh first thing this morning. Our dad's watching her — he's got his own Dairine Cam."

Carmela's smile had a sad edge to it. "She's been out on the High Road a lot, hasn't she . . . ?" She used the Speech-word *allaire-nai* for the concept; it implied that the person being described wasn't just off-planet, but well away from one's usual mindset or psychology.

Nita nodded. "And treating the house like a bed-and-breakfast, my dad's been saying."

"But always looking for Roshaun . . ."

"Yeah."

Carmela nodded. "I can understand that. I may have given him a hard time, but I'd never want him to vanish forever."

"If anyone can find him," Nita said, "I'm betting she can."

At floor level, the last of Nita's hardened-air steps vanished behind her as she and Carmela came down to bounce on the slightly curved floor. Puffs of pale dust rose. Nita held the rowan wand up, and she and S'reee and Carmela looked around.

"There's another room through there," Carmela said, pointing off to their left. "Like another bubble bumped into this one —"

They moved forward. It was warmer down here than up on the surface, but still plenty cold enough. The next chamber was another bubble, smaller than the last: out of it opened numerous other circular portals, leading into more huge stone bubbles, each full of darkness.

"Look at that," Carmela said, peering away into the dark as they moved into yet another spherical chamber. "They just go on and on. Probably for miles ..."

"The whole volcano must be honeycombed with these," Nita said, listening nervously to the way her voice echoed in the present chamber, which was small enough for S'reee's air bubble to reach right to the edges. The cold, the dark around them were unnerving. Yet Nita found that she didn't feel precisely afraid or as if something was going to jump out of the shadows at her. There was just a growing sense of being —

"Not in the wrong place," she said aloud. "Just in a place no one was really expecting us to be —"

"Expecting," S'reee said. "You have a foresight about this, hNii't?"

Nita shook her head. "Even hindsight would make me happy right now," she said. "How much further in do you make the hot spot where the wizardry's live?"

"Maybe five of my lengths," S'reee said. "Not far —"

Carmela craned her neck back to try to see the ceiling of the next chamber they entered, a much larger one. "Honeycombed isn't the word," she said. "It's froth. A million bubbles, big ones, little ones, that all got stuck in the lava, way back when . . ."

They continued across that chamber, toward the dimly seen entrance to the next. "Neets," Carmela said, "the floor in here —"

For some reason she was whispering. "What?" Nita whispered back.

"There's nothing on it. But there was dust, back where we came in — stuff that must have come down through the skylight from the winter dust storm. Why wouldn't some be here? There should have been *some* air movement down here. Enough to blow at least some dust in, over the years —"

S'reee stopped her glide forward. Nita and Carmela looked at her.

"What?" Nita whispered.

When S'reee answered, she didn't do it vocally. *Did you hear that?*

Hear what? Nita said.

Something moved —

Something about S'reee's tone of thought left Nita more nervous than before. She held still, listening.

Carmela quietly reached into her jumpsuit pocket and came out with what could have been mistaken, by the uninitiated, for a curling iron. She glanced over at Nita.

Nita swallowed and held up the rowan wand, looking toward S'reee. The whale's attention was on something that moved and gleamed in the shadows of the doorway into the next chamber. As Nita followed

S'reee's glance, the thing she was watching moved into the light.

The wand's silver fire gleamed and slid down a skin that looked like green metal as the creature moved forward. It looked very like a scorpion: but it was almost the size of a Shetland pony. It had entirely too many legs and claws, and blank, cold polished-jade eyes. The scorpion moved slowly out of the darkness toward the three of them, the front two pairs of its claws lifted. Pouring along behind it out of the shadows came about fifty more like it, all their front claws scissoring together softly, making a grating, echoing whisper in the room of stone.

"We are on errantry," Nita said, trying to keep any tremor out of her voice, "and we greet you!"

The scorpions did not pause, did not slow: they came on, cold-eyed, claws working.

Nita lifted the wand . . .

Stokes

★

KIT, RONAN, AND DARRYL came out of transit to
find themselves standing at the dark far edge of a distant crimson dawn. In a gauzy wrapping of atmosphere just above the edge of the world, a small molten
Sun hung trapped as if in amber under a dome of
orange haze, not yet too bright to be dangerous to
look at. All around, under a sky only a few shades of
violet from black, lay the flat, dark rock-scattered surface of the little crater called Stokes. Away to the east,
the shadow of the crater's rim lay in a sharp black
crescent between the three of them and the morning;
and from every least rock and pebble, a pointed finger
of cold, dark shadow lay long against the ground.

First Darryl, then Ronan, stepped to the edge of
the force-field bubble that surrounded them and
gazed out, not speaking. Kit knew why. Full day on
Mars can seem matter-of-fact once you get used to it;
just another panorama full of red sand and rubble, just

another blue sky, sunlight seeming as dimmed by blowing sand as by a Sun that's fifty million miles farther away and twenty percent dimmer than it ought to be. But there was no making the same mistake at dawn or sunset. Then the surroundings became both bleak and beautiful in a way that was possible only here. That faint, thin hiss of wind, hardly to be heard; that sense of absolute, pristine barrenness, empty, but not in any of the usual ways — it all got under your skin, made you hold still and listen for some hint of the secret that was hiding from you, the real reason why this landscape seemed so studiedly unconcerned about your presence. It seemed to be saying, "This isn't your place: you have no business here. Do whatever you like. It doesn't matter." *But it does. It does. All we have to do now is find out* why . . .

Ronan turned away from the sunrise and looked toward the northwestern horizon, where the crater wall was closer and the cracks and ravines running down it glowed softly red in the fire of dawn. He glanced back at Kit, the sunglasses gleaming red. "Like it's whispering to itself about us," Ronan said. "Not so easy to hear when there are a lot of other people around —"

"Yeah," Kit said.

Ronan looked over at Darryl, who was still gazing at the dawn. "As for you, don't know how you're doing that."

Darryl looked at him. "What?"

"Being completely normal," Ronan said. Kit had to agree. Darryl might as well have still been standing in Kit's backyard for all the exertion the transit seemed to have cost him. "Every wizardry's supposed to have a price. And here you just hauled yourself and two other people fifty million miles without breaking a sweat! Seems like cheating."

"I am not cheating!" Darryl said, looking injured. "It's not a transport: it's a bilocation. Why should I pay some big price for going fifty million miles from Earth when I'm still there?" He brushed red dust off him. "You're just jealous because you can't pull the same stunt. Waste of time, if you ask me, because I may not be able to do this forever! So right now I plan to enjoy it. And so should you, because you're riding free."

"Okay, fine, I didn't mean to sound ungrateful..."

"Well, you do. But I forgive you, 'cause I'm nice that way." Darryl grinned, turned to Kit. "Where's the spot the first signal went to?"

"Over there." Kit pointed to the northeast. "A few hundred yards."

The three of them headed for the spot using the half-bounce, half-walk that worked best in this gravity. Ronan was humming under his breath as he bounced along, and after a few bounces, he started to fill in the lyrics. "Oh, the chances of anything coming from Mars ... are a million to one, he said ..."

"So how come you got up so late this morning?" Kit said.

Ronan threw him a sideways look. "Because I was out late last night, nosy boy." And he snickered. "While you're at it, *you* might look into trying some kind of social life for size! I had a date to go clubbing with my mates. Why would I dump them just because something admittedly exciting happened up here? You start acting that way all the time, pretty soon no one invites you out anymore." And Ronan turned his attention back to the landscape. "Oh, the chances of anything coming from Mars . . . are a million to one . . . but still they come . . . !"

"Okay, message received," Kit muttered after Ronan, "but you didn't have to jump down my throat about it."

"Yes, he did. Dirty job, but somebody has to do it," Darryl said, bouncing briefly higher to get a better view of where they were headed. "Everybody heard Miss Neets's reaction to how you just dumped her yesterday. When she's pissed off, her voice kind of carries —"

Kit flushed red. "I thought we said we were going to leave her out of this."

"Heh," Darryl said. He bounced high again. "How far now?"

Kit checked his manual. "A hundred yards —"

Darryl came down. "No outcroppings here. If there's another egg, it'll be underground."

"Yeah," Kit said. The crater wall was two miles away. The rest of the impact area was the usual rubble-strewn Martian landscape — sandy ground littered with rocks of all sizes, shattered by the summertime contrast between bitter cold and surprising warmth, and wind-worn afterward. Kit kept an eye on his manual, where the spot was highlighted on the map now showing their approach vector. Finally their path and the target's location converged. "Right here," Kit said, and stopped.

Darryl and Ronan stopped, too, staring at the ground under Kit's feet — just sand, a scatter of pebbles, a few fist-size rocks. "Okay," Darryl said, "dig we must. But not just on a hunch. We need ground radar."

"Now, it's funny you should mention that," Ronan said, and held his hands out in front of him, starting to speak softly in the Speech.

"Ooh, magic gestures," Darryl said, nudging Kit. "*This* should be cool."

Ronan threw Darryl a withering look. "It's to help me target, you plank," he said. "Now shut your tiny gob and watch an expert at work."

Kit and Darryl watched as Ronan started reciting his spell again. Within seconds, the ground faded to transparency under their feet. It was like standing on a bumpy glass floor, the "glass" apparently about a hundred feet thick beneath them, full of shadowy flaws and striations illuminated sourcelessly by the spell itself. "Look at that," Ronan said, sounding abstracted as the wizardry penetrated the surface more deeply and he peered down into it. "See how those layers are piled up? Looks like there was water here once."

"A lot of places," Kit said, as Ronan walked slowly around the spot where Darryl and Kit were standing. "There's enough water ice at the south pole to flood the whole planet thirty feet deep. But *how* it got down there, and when . . ." He shook his head.

"You need me to split this air bubble for you so you can walk further out?"

"Not yet," Ronan said. He kept walking. Everywhere he moved, for about ten feet in front of him and to the sides, the ground went transparent. The Sun rose higher as he went, and the light grew better as dawn shaded into proper morning; but there was nothing unusual to be seen under the ground. Finally Ronan paused. "How accurate was your tracking on the spot that signal targeted?"

"Within a meter," Kit said. "At least that's what the manual said."

"Might be something else going on," Ronan said. "Maybe something cloaking whatever's down there? I tweaked this scan so it includes the detection routine that Síle and Markus came up with. However —" He peered down into the unrevealing depths. "If whatever's here was alerted by the egg that the cloaking routine it was using had been broken —"

"Could be," Darryl said, pulling out his WizPod and touching it into manual function. "Let's see if any other wizardries are working around here. Maybe with different cloaking routines. I'll tell it" — he pulled a glowing page out of the body of the Pod, stretching it out on the air and writing on it in the Speech with one finger — "to look around for the material the egg was made of."

A few moments later Darryl stood back, leaving the Pod and its stretched-out manual page hanging in midair, and started whispering the words he'd written. The world went quiet around them as the spell "took" with unusual speed. *But he really is still pretty close to his Ordeal,* Kit thought. *His power levels are way above either of ours. And on top of that, he's an* abdal: *practically a living power conduit. No telling what he could do now if he wanted to. Assuming, like the rest of us, he can get enough of what he needs out of the manual to figure out* how —

Far down in that abnormal clarity of Martian soil, Kit could suddenly see a green light glowing. He gulped, recognizing the color. "Got some action here, all right!" Darryl said, as under their feet the glow rose and spread like a slowly rising tide of liquid light. "Something's awake! There are elements in this energy flow that're part of the transmission from the egg in Nili Patera —"

"Is this wizardry hooked to anything physical down there?" Kit said.

Darryl shook his head. "Nope. It's just linked to the terrain. Uh-oh —"

"Uh-oh" wasn't something Kit liked hearing another wizard say. He was about to ask what was wrong when that green light boiled up from the depths, bursting against the ground under their feet like blood under skin, and then flowed lightning-quick away from them in all directions. The rush of light left itself burning in every rock and pebble it passed as it flash-flooded out across the crater's bottom. Within seconds it washed up against the crater's rim, flooded up it on all sides, splashed over the ragged crest, and vanished over the side —

Kit and Ronan and Darryl stood looking across

the crater in three different directions. Darryl said, "Okay . . . now what?"

Ronan shook his head. "Maybe nothing. It's fading."

Kit looked around them. Right across the crater that light was already growing paler — not just because the Sun was higher in the sky and the sky was lightening into early morning's dark blue. "So what was that? Another signal? Or just some kind of acknowledgment that we followed up on the first one?"

Darryl was looking at the manual page he'd extracted from his WizPod. "It was a limited-run wizardry. It triggered right when Ronan did his see-into-the-ground routine. The triggered spell blew all its energy in one big spike. The energy's dropping right off the scale again." Darryl shook his head. "It was a *big* spike, though. And there was something funny about the time stamp —"

Kit looked across the crater for any sign of life or movement. There was nothing. "Analysis," he muttered. "Mamvish warned us we'd probably wind up doing a lot of it . . ." He pulled out his manual and opened it to the log pages for this trip. Among several charts showing what wizardries the three of them were carrying or utilizing, Kit saw the diagram that showed what wizardly energy was associated with this specific spot. Darryl hadn't been overstating the size of the spike associated with their arrival: the graph had stretched itself to the top of the manual page to accommodate it. "What was the problem with the time stamp on the spike?" Kit said. "It looks okay to me."

"Not the spike itself," Darryl said. "The indicator showing when the spell was actually installed here. It looked earlier than the egg's installation date —"

Then Darryl made a little hiss of annoyance as the indicator vanished from the page. Kit shook his head. "Can you get that back?"

"I'll let you know when I understand why it went away!" Darryl said. "Here —" But Kit was now distracted by his manual: its pages were flushing pink. He glanced up —

Atmospheric conditions could sometimes get very odd on Mars, but in all the times he'd been there, Kit had never seen anything like this. From where the three of them stood to the horizon, it was as if the Red Planet had suddenly taken the sobriquet personally and decided that this particular morning it was going to get really, *really* red: not just rusty-colored, but positively crimson. *Everything* was turning that color — the ground, the sky — as if Kit were wearing red glasses.

"This could give you a headache after a while," Ronan said. He sounded uneasy.

Darryl looked up and around. "Sky's clear. Not a dust storm, then —"

"This is that new wizardry working," Kit said. He started flipping through his manual to the defensive spells.

"But what's it doing?" Ronan said, taking the sunglasses off to stare at the horizon. "I mean, if something's going to . . ."

He trailed off. "What?" Darryl said.

Ronan pointed and shook his head. Maybe a

quarter mile away from them across the crimson sands, teetering unevenly along in their general direction, was something with four long legs and some kind of body hung in the middle.

They stared. "What *is* that?" Kit said. "A giant spider?"

Ronan squinted at it. "The legs look more, I don't know, crabby. Look, they've got webs or something between the joints." He paused. "I'm sorry, maybe I need to hit the optometrist when I get home. Does that look like it has the head of a *bat*?"

Kit shook his head. "I wasn't going to say anything. There's a tail, too. Like a rat tail . . ."

"One of the original inhabitants, maybe," Ronan said, "coming to say hello?"

Kit shook his head. The approaching thing unsettled him: it looked not just unlikely, but also somehow rickety and badly built. Kit flipped his manual to a bookmarked page where he'd set up a life-sign detector sensitive to all the kinds of life that wizards knew about — which were quite a few. But the display showed nothing in the area but three dots labeled with the twelve-character code in the Speech that meant Earth-human. "Not alive," Kit said.

The bat-rat-spider-crab came tottering toward them, only a few hundred yards away now. Ronan shook his head. "Illusion?"

"I wouldn't go that far," said Kit. "There's *something* physical there that wasn't there before —"

"A construct," Ronan said, frowning. "Great. If it's real enough to get physical, it's real enough to damage us. But since it's not alive, if that thing starts getting too cozy, I won't feel too bad about using *this.*" Ronan reached sideways into the air, grabbed something invisible, and pulled.

Something long, narrow, and blazingly bright came out of nowhere, following his pull. For a second Kit's memory flashed back to the Spear of Light that Ronan used to carry: but that was in other hands, or claws, these days. The object Ronan held though, was definitely "of light" — a cylindrical bar of burning golden radiance an inch wide and three feet long. Ronan lifted it up and laid it over his left arm, sighting on the bat-spider thing as it came spidering hugely along toward them.

Kit recognized what Ronan held as one of numerous deadly weapons that a wizard could construct from the universe's more basic energies. "You sure you want to do that?"

"Not at all sure," Ronan said, sighting carefully. "Entirely willing not to have to do it if that keeps its distance. But my mam didn't raise me to be bat chow, so you're going to have to forgive me if I —"

He broke off short as with a distinctive *crack!* a bullet flew over them. The head of the bat-rat-crab thing came up, reacting to something off to their right. It stared — then turned and enthusiastically ran off in a different direction entirely.

Confused, Ronan lowered the energy weapon and peered past the fleeing bat-rat-crab thing. "All right, now wait just a fecking minute," he said. "A rifle? Was that a *rifle??*"

Darryl started to laugh.

The sound made Kit realize that Darryl had been unusually quiet for the last few minutes. Now, though, he pointed out past where the bat-creature had been. "Will you get a load of *that?*"

Kit's eyes went wide as he looked where Darryl pointed. Running toward them across the crimson sand, under the carmine sky, were human beings. They wore space suits, but not modern ones: these looked like crude versions of a jet pilot's pressure suit. And bizarrely, they didn't seem to be affected by Mars's lighter gravity. They ran as if they were still on Earth.

Darryl was still laughing as the spacemen — there was no other way to think of beings so retro-looking — got closer. They slowed, took stance, and fired again, but not at the bat-rat-whatever: at the three astonished wizards. The bullets hit the force field holding in the wizardly air bubble and whined away.

Ronan had lowered his weapon, looking perplexed at Darryl's laughter. "I'm sorry," he said to Darryl, "but is there something funny I'm missing about this? Those are *bullets!*"

"Yeah," Darryl said, "but they're *movie* bullets!"

Kit stared at him. "*What?*"

"This is all out of a movie!" Darryl said. "First time I saw it was when I was really little. It completely freaked me out, because I didn't understand it was just a story. I thought it was the news from somewhere. Then I saw it again on one of the movie channels a few weeks ago, and when I recognized it, man, I couldn't stop laughing; it's so lame! It's called *The Angry Red Planet.*"

"Well, *somebody's* angry," Ronan said, as the barrage of bullets continued.

"Somebody's scared," Kit said. "Look, let's go talk to them."

"They're constructs!" Ronan said. "Barely a step up from illusions. You really think we're going to be able to communicate?"

Kit shrugged. "Do I look like an expert in what's happening here? But they're something to do with the superegg's signal. And we're wizards: communicating's what we do. Let's go see if we can find out what this is about."

"But why are they shooting at *us*?" Ronan said, glancing around him. "We didn't do anything!"

Darryl was looking over his shoulder. "Uh, Ronan? Could be they're shooting at *those.*"

Behind them Kit saw something moving, but the redness was bothering his eyes enough that he had to stop and rub them. Afterward he looked again, thinking he could make out large leaves and some waving tendrils, maybe a few hundred yards away . . . and getting closer. "There are — are those some kind of *plant*?"

Ronan squinted. "Only if plants have tentacles. And octopus faces."

Kit hadn't at first believed he was seeing those faces. Now he wished he still didn't believe it. "Carnivorous," Darryl said. "Wouldn't get too close."

"Seems to be what they have in mind," Kit said. "Those were in the movie, too?"

Darryl nodded, looking less amused. "Don't know if I'm wild about plants when they start walking around . . ."

Kit reached into his otherspace pocket and pulled out the piece of weaponry he'd almost used last night. Held in the hand, it looked like nothing more than a small, dark, shining globe, but it could be a lot more on demand. "You want to stay out of Nita's basement, then," Kit said as the plant creatures shambled closer.

"You kidding me? Those things aren't a bit like our friendly neighborhood walking Christmas tree," Ronan said, leveling his energy weapon again. "Our wee Filif could never give me the creeps like these. Will you look at the tentacles on them? I'd swear they have hinges! *That* can't be right . . ."

More bullets whined past them. "Come on," Kit said. "Those things won't get through our force field, hinges or not. Neither will anything the spacemen have."

"You sure about that?" Ronan said as one of the larger spacemen, getting within maybe a hundred yards, lifted a heavy-looking weapon and aimed it at one of the plant-octopi. A bright, hot stab of light leaped from it and hit the plant creature right between its bulbous eyes. After a few moments of theatrical thrashing and screaming, it fell to the scarlet dust. Its companions, seemingly oblivious, kept on advancing toward the spacemen.

Kit was now much more in a mood to pay attention to the weaponry of the approaching people. "Okay, they have lasers . . ." he said.

Ronan shrugged. "Your common-or-garden-variety ray gun," he said. "The beam didn't look all that coherent. It can't get through our shields."

"Oh, we *are* in a movie," Darryl said, and started laughing again. "Did you hear those things? Since when do energy weapons make a noise like that?!"

"Restrain yourself, laughing boy," Ronan said. "We're representing our species, here. If all this craziness is Mars trying to talk to us, don't make fun of it just because somebody underfunded its special-effects budget five hundred thousand years ago." He sighed and laid the long, bright rod of light over his shoulder. "Your idea's the best I've heard so far," Ronan said to Kit. "Let's go communicate."

The three of them headed toward the approaching spacemen, now only a few hundred feet away. "Maybe we should all hold up one hand," Darryl said. "That old 'we come in peace' gesture."

"Maybe I'd feel better about that if *they* hadn't started the unpeaceful part of this conversation," Ronan said under his breath. "And now that I think of it, look at their heads. Is there something wrong with their space suits?"

"You mean *besides* the fact that there's no glass in the helmets?" Kit said. "Wouldn't surprise me."

The two groups got within about fifty feet of each other, at which point the spacemen stopped, and four out of five of them pointed their rifles or ray guns at Darryl and Ronan and Kit. The three of them stopped, too. Kit cleared his throat.

"We're on errantry," Kit said in the Speech, "and we greet you."

All of the spacemen stared at them, the four weapons not moving an inch; and, piercingly, the fifth spaceman screamed.

Kit and Darryl and Ronan looked at one another. *And you're ragging me about* my *favorite movies being old?* Ronan said silently to Darryl. *At least in mine, woman astronauts are made of sterner stuff.* To the spacemen, Ronan said, "Please excuse us. We didn't mean to upset you. We're here to investigate the sites targeted by the messages that the superegg transmitter sent out. Are you here to speak to us on behalf of the planet, or some other instrumentality that's been operating here?"

The spacemen looked at one another nervously. "They look human," said one of them. "It's impossible! Humans can't survive in these conditions!"

Oh, yeah? We're not the ones wearing the helmets without faceplates, Darryl said silently.

"They must be illusions," said another of the spacemen.

"Or more monsters like *those* things —" said the single spacewoman, looking fearfully past them toward where the plant-octopi were still shambling closer.

"Please, believe me, we're human," Kit said. "We just have a force field protecting us. We're here looking for indications of past life on this planet, and we —"

"Those plant things are getting closer!" another of the men shouted. "I don't care how human these things look! This is a trap to keep us here while those plants surround us! We have to get back to the ship!"

Ship? Kit thought.

Darryl nodded off to one side. *That just appeared,* he said silently. *Wondered when it'd turn up.*

And indeed there it was, maybe a quarter mile away, gleaming metallically red in this weird lighting — a long cigar-shaped rocket ship very much in the old style, with a pointy nose and little fins down at the bottom. "Is that a *lake* over there?" Kit said, peering past the rocket.

"Looks like it," Ronan said. "This is getting weirder all the time . . ." He turned back to the space-men. "Come on, people," he said in the Speech, "would you ever just tell us what you're doing here on Mars? All we want to do is —"

"It's in my mind again!" the woman shrieked, and fainted. Kit winced: this lady had the screaming part of her performance honed to a fine edge.

Ronan shook his head. "Fainting," he said as one of the men hurriedly picked the woman up and carried her away. "You don't see a lot of that these days . . ." The other men started shooting at them again, ostensibly to cover their retreat. Bullets and ray-gun blasts splashed harmlessly off the force field as the spacemen hurried back toward their rocket ship.

"If there's a list of least effective first contacts in the manual," Darryl said as the spacemen fled, "I think we're on it now."

"Yeah," Ronan said. "As a definition of the phrase 'talking at cross-purposes,' this scenario works pretty well." He ran a hand through his longish dark hair, looking exasperated.

Darryl shoved his hands in his pockets and stood admiring that very retro spacecraft, while behind the three of them the man-eating plants bumped into their force field, tried to push through it, couldn't, and then blundered on around it in pursuit of their original prey. "Doesn't look real stable," Darryl said, watching the spacemen and once-more-conscious spacewoman clamber up the rocket's fragile-looking ladder in desperate haste. "Hard to believe those could even fly."

"That old V-2 design worked just fine in World War Two," Ronan said, looking grim. "Those things blew half of London to smithereens. But they're the granddaddy of every rocket since."

Darryl shrugged. "Well, okay, in atmosphere they worked. But they'd never have made it to Mars."

"The concept was right, though," Ronan said. "Thrust comes out the back end, pushes the rest of the craft forward: got us to the Moon, didn't it? Granted, this thing wouldn't have made it forty million miles, but —"

"Guys?" Kit said. "Something *else* that I wouldn't have thought could make it to Mars?"

They looked at him.

"The giant amoeba??" Kit said, pointing.

Darryl and Ronan both looked shocked. But there was no arguing the presence of the gigantic green blob that had appeared from nowhere in particular and was now oozing its way up the side of the rocket . . . and, incidentally, out toward them as well.

Ronan looked annoyed. "Oh, come on, that's never an amoeba! Lookit there, it's got a couple effing great eyes stuck in the middle of it!"

"Three," Kit said, peering at it. "Might be more . . ."

"Okay, give me a break, so it's a *space* amoeba," Darryl said. "They could have eyes, maybe . . ."

"*People of Earth!*" a gigantic voice shouted from somewhere or other.

They all jumped. "Okay," Ronan said, unlimbering his weapon again. "Here we go . . ."

"*Do not return to Mars!*" the great voice cried. "*We can and will destroy you if you do not heed our warning!*"

"Not just a space amoeba, but a *cranky* space amoeba," Kit said, hurriedly flipping his manual open, as boosting the force field surrounding their air bubble struck him as a good idea.

From across the crater came a roar and shudder, and the ground under their feet shook as the rocket ship took off. Or, rather, it tried to. The space amoeba was hanging on to it as tenaciously as a baby unwilling to let go of a favorite toy. In a great cloud of smoke, slowly and with difficulty the rocket pulled up out of the amoeba's grip — then blasted free, leaping away from the surface in a great flare of fire. The giant amoeba slumped back to the surface to lie in a sulky, gelatinous heap.

"Is *that* thing going to come after us now?" Ronan muttered.

"I'd be more concerned about the green leafy octopi . . ." Darryl said.

"Wait," Kit said, glancing around. All around, the color was draining out of the landscape. It took some moments for Kit to realize that the vista around them had actually resumed its proper colors, which now looked bizarrely pallid in contrast with the previous unnatural redness. The carnivorous octopus-plants disappeared, along with the giant space amoeba, the bat-rat-crab-spider thing, and everything else that had pertained to that other and much more peculiar Mars.

Darryl was standing there blinking. "Everything's green," he said.

"It's what your eyes do after staring at red for too long," Ronan said. "It'll go away." He sat down on a nearby rock, gazing up into the Martian sky, now sedate and empty of anything but some passing clouds. "So is it just me . . . or was that unusual?"

Kit laughed. "Not just you, no."

"But no question," Darryl said, "the planet was trying to communicate with us!"

"If that's true," said Ronan, "then the planet needs its head felt!"

"Seriously!" Darryl said. "It was trying to get through to us. It took something from inside our heads —"

"*Your* head maybe," Ronan said. "Got better things going on inside *mine* than bat-rat-crab puppety thingies where you can still see the strings hanging off them! Not to mention man-eating broccoli with tentacles." He rolled his eyes. "Tentacles held together with eyelets and wire!"

"I can't help the details," Darryl said. "*I* didn't make the movie! Which I said was dire! But something here felt it — or got into my head and saw it — and tried using it to get through to us."

"And say what?" Ronan said. "'Bugger off'?"

"Language, guy," Darryl said. "But yeah. And it'd make sense for them to be trying to scare casual visitors off! If Mamvish is right — if the people who lived here managed to store some way to wake them up — then they don't want it trashed. They want to make sure anybody who comes poking around isn't just going to run away, and knows what they're doing. If they can scare you away, so much the better for them and you."

Kit and Ronan sat thinking about that for a moment. "Yeah," Kit said. "I mean, if you were a normal astronaut and you landed here and found these bat-rat-crab things running around and giant amoebas sliming all over the place, what would you do?"

"Seek professional help," Ronan said.

"*On Earth,*" said Darryl. "In a hurry! And not come back any time soon."

"But if you're *not* scared off," Kit said, "that means you can see through the illusion. Which also means you're probably a wizard, and you'll be able to figure out what the planet's trying to tell you."

"And it's going crazy doing that right now because you broke that egg," Ronan said.

Kit glared at him. "No, you dummy," Ronan said,

"not broke as in 'caused to stop functioning.' Broke as in 'you have to break a few to make an omelet.' You don't leave a message-capsule wizardry around for nothing, right? You *want* it broken. And maybe it's not about *just* messaging."

"Maybe it's a test?" Darryl said.

Ronan shrugged. "Makes sense. And the same forces that busted loose out of the egg, and made this weirdness happen, are watching to see what we do."

"Well, great," Kit said, "but if this was a test, how do we know if we passed or failed?"

The other two shook their heads. "Keep going, I guess," Darryl said. "Visit the other places where the signal went. Maybe one thing being tested is whether we give up when nothing seems to happen."

Kit nodded. "And also nobody gives you a test if they don't care what result you produce! If we finally pass, then something should pop up and tell us what all this has been about."

"You hope," Ronan said. He sighed and stood up again, dusting the omnipresent beige-y dust off him. "At least we can see all right again. Why did everything go that weird shade of red?"

"That was in the movie," Darryl said. "Some effect they put in to make the puppets and the cheap background paintings look less cheap."

"Well, cheap or not," Ronan said, looking back toward the crater, "I wouldn't have liked to meet those things without a force field."

"No argument," Darryl said. "Now, while we're all feeling good about how competent we are, I have a question." He turned to Kit. "And since you are, as our overly tall cousin here says, Mars Uber-Geek Boy, you should have the answer. How many satellites are in orbit around Mars right now, and when's the next one due over?"

Kit's eyes went wide. He started paging hurriedly through his manual.

"And if one's been over already," Ronan said, "did it see anything? And if it did, what? And how can we keep the imagery from getting back to Earth? Because I think that the poor guys at NASA are going to have big trouble with the giant amoebas."

"*Space* amoebas —" Darryl said.

"And finny rocket ships and bat-rat-crab things," Ronan said, "and wizards shooting at them . . ."

"We've got two satellites right now," Kit said. "Odyssey and Mars Express. Here are the orbits —" He held out the manual, touched the open pages: they produced a double-page spread of sine curves spreading themselves across the rectangular whole-planet map. He studied the diagram, then let loose the breath he'd been holding. "We got lucky," Kit said. "Odyssey's on the other side of the planet: Express is a third of the way around. Both out of range." He glanced out at where the giant amoeba and the rocket had been.

"Any residual heat from that, you think?" Ronan said.

Darryl was pulling another page out of his Wiz-Pod and examining it: over a map of the area, a few nested blobs of various colors were displaying. "Some," he said. "The heat was real. Those constructs were able to affect their surroundings, even though themselves they were only temporary."

"We'd better go cool down the places where they were, then," Ronan said.

"Don't think we'll need to," Kit said. He looked over Darryl's shoulder at the notations under the graph showing the heat readings. They were already sinking toward baseline. "The crust here doesn't hold heat real well: that's why the surface erosion's so aggressive. By the time the satellites come around again, the heat'll be gone. It's not a big worry right now."

Darryl looked alarmed. "Got something worse?"

"Kind of a worry," Kit said. "What if we didn't just trigger this one site by turning up here? What if we triggered the others, too, and they're doing something right now? Something important that we shouldn't miss?"

"You're not going to suggest that we split up to investigate them separately, I hope!" Ronan said.

Kit rolled his eyes. "A recipe for trouble," he said. "In weird other-planet horror movies, or out of them."

Darryl shoved his WizPod into a pocket. "*I* could split up," he said.

Kit and Ronan exchanged a glance, and Ronan looked at Darryl with some concern. "You sure that's a good idea? You're here twice already. I mean, here *and* on Earth, so that's twice —"

"I think I could do three," Darryl said, "one after another. I did three at once back home, last week. Wouldn't want to push it much further, though — all of me kept walking into things. Too much data to process, or else my brain doesn't like working in triplicate." Darryl glanced around. "So let's get busy. Where do you want me?"

Kit showed him his manual. "These three spots. They're all near largish craters. De Vaucouleurs — Cassini — Hutton."

"What are the names for? Famous people or something?"

"Yeah, or places on Earth."

"Okay. Which is closest?"

"This one." Kit pointed at de Vaucouleurs. "A couple of hundred miles south, right by Wahoo."

Ronan gave Kit an incredulous look. "You're just yanking our chains. There's never any crater called Wahoo!"

Kit scowled, pointed at the map. "Right here, next to Yuty."

"You didn't even need to *look* at the map just then," Ronan said in wonder. "I'll decide whether to be impressed or horrified later. Darryl?"

"On my way," Darryl said. And he flickered.

There was no other way to describe it. Darryl was still there: there had been none of the usual air movement that was so hard to avoid when doing a physical transit. "You set that spell up wrong or something?" Kit said.

"Oh, no, it worked fine," Darryl said. "For that one of me." He swallowed hard.

"You okay?"

"Yeah, fine. Just a little more effort than usual to offset the fact that I wasn't all here to start with. Cassini next —"

The flicker happened again. Darryl was still standing there, and this time he looked pale, and his eyes seemed unfocused.

"Darryl?" Ronan said.

"Don't joggle my elbow, Ro," Darryl said: and his voice was strange. It sounded as if there were several of him, even though there seemed to be only one standing there. He flickered around the edges again, once, twice —

— and crumpled straight down to sit crookedly on the dusty red ground, holding his head. Ronan caught him on the way down, easing the collapse, and started patting his face. "Darryl, hey, look up! Come on —"

"Will you stop whacking me, man, do I look like I need the smelling salts?" Darryl pushed Ronan's hand away. "I'm fine. Let me breathe."

Kit hunkered down in front of Darryl. "What happened out there?"

Darryl shook his head, rubbed his face for a moment. "Nothing," he said. "It's harder to do that stunt here than on Earth, that's all. Or I need more practice. Important thing, though, is that nothing's happening at two of the other sites. *Yet,* anyway. But your friend over by Wahoo, de-whatchamacallit —"

"Vaucouleurs," Kit said.

"Right. It's warming up: I could feel the wizardry getting ready to execute. We'd better get over there."

Kit and Ronan got up: Darryl did, too, without help. "Better," he said. "See, I just needed a second. You guys gotta stop treating me like I'm Fragile Boy." He reached up to put a hand on each of their shoulders. "You ready?"

Ronan picked up his long rod of light and laid it over his shoulder: it blazed, then died down, subdued but ready. Kit glanced at him, reached for his little silvery sphere and juggled it in one hand.

"Hit it," he said.

They vanished.

Shamask-Eilith

IN THE GREAT DARK DOME under Arsia Mons, Nita watched the giant green metal scorpions pour toward her, claws uplifted. On one side, S'reee drifted closer, a hard-to-see fire dancing about her fins; on the other, Carmela moved in until she was touching shoulders with Nita, her "hot curler" ready. "What are they?" Carmela said. "Are they alive?"

S'reee cocked an ear, listening to the distant whisper of another planet's Sea. "No. Not the way we think of life, anyway. They're recordings, reconstructions of something that was alive before."

Nita gulped as they kept coming. The foremost of the scorpions were only ten feet away now, and right back to the dark doorway the whole space was filling with more and more. *Where are they all coming from? Even if we start blowing them up, we won't be able to deal with them all before they deal with us —*

Nita stopped, blinked, suddenly blind in the darkness. Or not blind. As if it was happening to someone else, she saw herself step hesitantly forward, go down on one knee, look into the head scorpion's cold, dark eyes. And the scorpion just looked back at her, and then after a moment walked around her, passed her by.

But the image flickered. Once again she walked up to the scorpion, went down on one knee. And the claws flashed out —

Nita shook her head. The tide of scorpions was scurrying closer. *I have to do something!* But there was nothing to choose between the two moments she'd glimpsed, no way to tell how to make one happen or keep the other from happening —

Except that one of them turned out okay, she thought. *I've got at least two chances that I've seen. If I just stand here, something different is going to happen that I won't have had* time *to see —*

She stepped forward.

"Neets?!" Carmela whispered in shock. Behind Nita, S'reee started to surge forward. With her free hand, Nita waved her back, went down on one knee as the foremost scorpion came up to meet her. It stopped. Stared up into her eyes —

The strangest sensation followed, like little tickly feet walking around on the surface of her brain. Nita shivered one big shiver all over, but didn't move otherwise.

And the scorpion swung its eyes and its body away from Nita — walked around her and then off past Carmela. Carmela swiveled with a panicky expression as the scorpions headed after their leader, back the way she and Nita and S'reee had come.

S'reee turned in the air, watching the scorpions pour past. "Now, what was that?" she said. "hNii't? Did you speak to them? Or they to you?"

Nita was still down on one knee as the scorpions kept pouring past her and into the chamber previous to the one they were in now. "They might have listened to me somehow. But I didn't say anything."

"You did," Carmela said. "You got down on their level. That's saying 'hi.' Actually, you said 'hi' first."

Nita slowly stood up, pausing to rub her knee: it was sore. "Maybe. But I just saw myself doing that, and it seemed like the thing to do." *Better than the other thing, anyway —*

"You've been doing envisioning work with T'hom, haven't you?" S'reee said, turning all the way around to watch the last of the scorpions vanish into the next chamber. "I'd say it's paying off."

"I don't know. What if there was something else I was supposed to do?"

"Like what?" Carmela said.

Nita shook her head. She was sweating, but feeling less panic-stricken as the last scorpions passed out of the chamber, the sound of metallic feet tapping on the stone now ticking away into silence. "Ree, where are they going?"

S'reee drifted up to the door, peered through. "That I can't tell you," she said, "because they're gone. Vanished."

Carmela turned and went to the doorway to join S'reee. "Just passing through?"

"I don't think so," Nita said, lifting her wand again and heading toward the next chamber. "They were guarding something. And they decided we were okay. That was their whole job, and when it was done, they went away . . ." She looked over her shoulder at the other two. "S'reee, can you feel it? That hot-spot wizardry's shut down."

S'reee turned, finned back through the air toward Nita and Carmela. "You're right," she sang. "And if they were guarding something . . ."

Nita was heading toward the next chamber, holding the wand high. The rowan wood, soaked in moonlight from fifty million miles away, made a sphere of silver radiance around her as she stepped through the wide, round portal into the next chamber.

For several seconds she saw nothing at all in the darkness. Nita turned leftward to see what was inside the chamber near the left edge of the portal. At first it seemed to be a straight wall. She went to it, holding up the wand for a better view. On closer inspection, she found that the wall wasn't straight after all, but curved like all the others. The curve was just very, very slight, because this was by far the biggest room they had come to as yet. And as far as the halo of light from the rowan wand spread, from side to side and high up into where the light was lost in the gloom, nearly every inch of the wall was covered with writing.

Nita reached out and touched the wall. The writing was engraved in long, thin columns in the stone, not very deeply, the characters just a few shades paler than the darker, redder surface. "It's warm," Nita said. "How can it be warm? The volcano here hasn't been live for thousands of years . . ."

Nita turned to look out across the chamber. It was massive, easily a thousand feet across. S'reee and Carmela came in behind her, Carmela with a flashlight and S'reee bringing her own wizard-light with her — several sources of it hovering around her like a little school of pilot fish. They gazed across the huge space.

"One about us," S'reee sang softly, waving her fins gently to turn and look at the vast expanse of the dome, "*what* have we found here? This must fill the whole mountain." She tilted all of herself back at an angle, gazing up into the dark; her wizard-lights swam up through the dark above as if through water, looking for something like a surface and for a long time not finding it. It was many moments before their radiance made several small diffuse circles against the uppermost curve of that immense bubble.

"I don't think this is natural," Nita said, walking along the wall. "It might have started out as a bubble in the stone once. But this —" She touched the writing again. It was nothing like the graceful curvatures and ligatures of the Speech, but angular and sharp, line after line of strung-together structures like little trees with branches growing out of them at strange angles. "This has all been smoothed down. And isn't this weird —"

She moved on, puzzled, for she wasn't able to make anything of the writing. "What?" Carmela said, leaning over Nita's shoulder to gaze at the engraved characters.

"They were running up and down before. Now they're going side to side."

Carmela reached out past Nita to touch the letters, the light of the rowan wand catching in her eyes. "Look, the characters flip. Mirror images." She peered at them more closely. "Boustrophedon . . ."

It wasn't a word in the Speech. "What?"

"Boustrophedon," Carmela said, tracing the characters with one finger. "When the words in a sentence go in one direction to the end of the line, and then the next line goes back in the direction it came from. You read from right to left, then left to right. Or up to down, then down to up." Carmela walked along to the next section of writing. There were panels of it, separated by thin engraved borders or sometimes just by empty space. "People used to plow their fields that way . . ."

Nita went after her, looking across the dome. "More light?" she said to the rowan wand.

It brightened until it was as blinding as an arc light, and Nita winced from the brilliance, looking away from it and across the great floor as she held the wand up. It took that much light to enable her to see all the way across the chamber and to be sure that there were no more visible entrances or exits: the portal they'd come in by, the one the scorpions had guarded, was the only way in. "This must have been important," Nita said. "Could this be a history? Mars's history?"

"Or the Martians'," S'reee said. She drifted closer to one wall, peered at it. "No way to tell. I can't make fin or fluke of it. You?"

Nita shook her head. "I don't get it," she said. "Usually knowing the Speech lets you understand any writing you see —"

"Not always," S'reee said, drifting down the wall to look at another patch of writing. "That condition obtains when the manual can find live members of the species to contribute the underlying context from which content can be understood. But when a race has died out, you may only get content with no context, which isn't a lot of use. And there are recensions of the Speech that have been completely lost over time, because all other information about the species for which they were intended has also been lost . . ."

"Even for the manual? Is that possible?" Nita said.

"Entropy's running," S'reee said. "And the medium it runs in is time. Even the manual's subject to that, in its merely physical manifestations." She let out a long, hissing breath.

"Neets," Carmela said, "S'reee, look. Pictures —"

They came over to look at part of the wall in front of which Carmela stood, deeper into the chamber. Here, arranged in a column stretching up the curve toward the ceiling, there were images, mostly geometric shapes, precisely scribed into the dark red stone, but it was hard to be sure what their relationship was: some of them seemed to run into one another. Nita reached up to touch one — a series of concentric circles with a single small circle inside them. She took a long breath. "Is that supposed to be the Sun?"

S'reee, looking over Nita's shoulder, leaned in very close, until her nose almost touched the stone.

"If it is, we may have a problem," she sang softly. "Because we've got a couple of extra planets."

Nita, too, leaned in, looking closely at the diagram. Four smallish worlds, and then a slightly larger one, and beyond that, four great worlds, and five tiny planets out in the farthest orbits.

"It can't be," Nita said to herself. "*Can't* be . . ."

Carmela was shaking her head as she peered at the smallest markings, furthest from the engraved Sun. "They keep finding these little bitty ones way out at the edge. I can never keep track of how many there are."

"Dwarf planets," Nita said. "Pluto, Haumea, Makemake, and Eris."

Carmela glanced at Nita, picking up on something in her voice. "What's the matter with them?"

Nita made a face. "Pluto's still a planet to me," she said. "Call me stubborn. But there's another problem. Look at that fifth one. It's further out than the others, and not in line. Like it doesn't belong here . . ."

"There's another diagram over here, in this next column," Carmela said. "This one's got twelve."

Nita went over to look at the second diagram. This one showed an empty place where the fifth world's orbit had been: a gap. "So that's where the asteroid belt would be?" Carmela said.

"It looks like this gap would match their orbit . . ." Nita said.

"And the furthest worldlet is missing," S'reee said. "A captured world that got lost again, perhaps?"

"It happens," Nita said. "That far out in the

system, the Sun's gravity's not so big a deal as it is closer in . . ." But her main attention was on the empty space between Mars and Jupiter.

Carmela was looking at that, too. "So the asteroids are actually from this fifth planet blowing up?"

Nita shook her head. "'Mela, a lot of people have had that idea, but it doesn't work, because all the stuff in the asteroid belt put together isn't enough to make a planet, even a small one. Definitely not enough to make a planet the size of the one in that picture."

Carmela glanced over to the right of the second image, where there was another column full of writing. After a second she shrugged and started to walk away — then paused and turned back, giving the column a strange look. "That was weird. Just out of the corner of my eye, I saw something." She put up a hand to touch the characters, squinting.

"More light?" Nita said, lifting the wand.

Carmela waved her away. "Less might be better."

Nita shook the rowan wand down to a fainter light. "Yeah," Carmela said. She tilted her head to one side, looking at the characters. "Something — went, went to the —" She paused again. "It found the — something or other. I don't know what that is. Then — but the sword —" Carmela grimaced in annoyance. "Dammit, it won't hold still —"

"Can you actually read this stuff?" Nita said.

Carmela's annoyance was fading into perplexity. "Some of it. Most of it looks like nonsense marks." She shook her head. "Until it jumps, somehow, and parts make sense. I don't get it."

"I wonder," S'reee said, drifting over to peer over Carmela's shoulder. "K!aarmii'lha, you came to understand the Speech pretty quickly, didn't you, for someone who's not a wizard? Were you studying other languages first?"

"Yeah," Carmela said, looking over her shoulder at her. "I did German in school, and then I started picking up Japanese, for manga and anime. And Italian, and some French. And when I started hearing Kit using the Speech, I started seeing it on the alien cable channels, and I don't know, I just" — she shrugged — "started picking it up."

"You know," S'reee said, "you may have some version of the steganographic gift."

Nita glanced over at S'reee. "Is that good?"

"Possibly good for us," S'reee said as Carmela worked her way down the graven wall, her lips moving as she traced the symbols with one finger. "Other linguistic gifts can come with it. But mostly it implies the ability to pull context out of writings when the writers' culture has left no other trace. It's an intuition rather than a skill. K!aarmii'lha, do you mind donating what you see to the manual system?"

"Huh?" She was peering more closely at some of the characters. "No, sure. What do I need to do?"

"Nothing," S'reee said. "I'll have a word with the Sea —"

Tell her there's no need, the peridexis said in Nita's head. *I'll have the data assumed into the system as she works.*

"Bobo's on it, S'reee," Nita said. "He'll handle it

the same way the manuals pull in data off TV and the Web on demand." She went over to stand by Carmela, reaching out to the incised characters again: but they had nothing to say to her.

"What do you see, K!aarmii'lha?" S'reee said.

"Weird stuff . . ."

S'reee made a long, bubbling moan of laughter. "More detail, please?"

Carmela stood with hands on hips, staring at the wall. "This part is something about food," she said. "For all I know, I'm looking at somebody's shopping list." She turned away. "This thing needs an index. Or a table of contents. If I were an index . . . where would I be?"

"By the door?" Nita said.

Carmela headed back to the doorway, where she began studying its edges. After a moment, she said, "Nope. If there *is* an index, they're not thinking about it the way we do . . ."

"Let me go topside and see if there's anything different from what's here," S'reee said. She angled her body up and swam upward through the darkness toward the zenith of the bubble-dome, her little school of lightfish darting upward with her.

Carmela leaned against the wall, gazing into the darkness, thinking. "Maybe they wouldn't put an index out at the edges," she said, "but in the middle?"

"Makes sense to run with your hunches on this one," Nita said. Together they walked across the great expanse of dark floor. Nita pulled out her manual,

holding the wand underneath it to light the floor
where they were walking, and started paging through
the book in search of "steganography." Carmela craned
her neck up to see where S'reee was headed. "How
high do you think that is?"

Nita paused, glanced up. "Two hundred feet?
Three?"

"Might be . . ."

Nita shook her head and kept walking, her attention on the manual. "Well," Carmela said, "I guess the
shopping can wait a while longer."

Nita snickered. "You sure? Don't let us keep you.
We've only stumbled into some kind of alien library
thousands of years old. You *really* sure you wouldn't
rather be trying on designer exoskeletons or something at the Crossings?"

"Oh, Juanita *Louise* . . ." Carmela said, shaking
her head as they made their way through the darkness.
"You are mean to tease me . . ."

"Carmela, you just keep on saying that word!"

"Yup. And I'll say it again unless you appease
me," Carmela said, peering through the dimness at the
floor ahead of them.

Nita rolled her eyes. "Okay, fine. Every time you
say my middle name, I'll say *yours!*"

"Like I care!" Carmela laughed, glancing around
them. "Go on! I'll help you. *Emeda!* Emeda, Emeda,
Emeda!"

Nita shook her head, the irritation passing; it was
hard to think petty, mundane thoughts for long when

surrounded by such massive and ancient strangeness. "Mine's just a pain, but yours is *weird*," Nita said. "Why did they hang that on you?"

"It's my aunts' and uncle's fault," Carmela said. "Mama said they were fighting so much over which one was going to be my middle name, she took all their initials and made a new name out of them."

Nita cracked up. "I bet that shut them up . . ."

"Nope," Carmela said. "Auntie Emma and Tante Elle are still arguing over which of them is the first E. And I won't tell them, because it's too much fun listening to them fight . . ." She paused, looking ahead. "Neets, you see that?"

"What?"

"Look at the floor over there. Is something shining?"

Nita looked where Carmela pointed. "Something green," she said. "Come on —"

They broke into a trot, heading for the center of the huge floor space. It took a while to get there, but as they drew closer, the glint of green grew stronger and stronger in the light of Nita's upheld wand, spreading more widely across the floor. By the time they were still a hundred feet or so away, they could see that they were heading into a circle of green designs nearly that wide — a tangle of broad curves or ribbons of verdant color against the paler stone. Some of these green ribbons arced away from the central design, ending in sharp points: some of them seemed to twist back on themselves, narrowing, broadening out again, dividing and sharpening to points again.

At the edge of the design they stopped, Nita holding her wand out over it. The color wasn't flat: it gleamed, metallic. And there were subtle changes in its color and in the way it reflected the light when Nita moved the wand slightly. "'Mela," she said, "it's not solid."

They both got down on their knees to look at one of the broad strokes of the design. "It's all inlaid," Nita said. "Little thin pieces of metal . . ." They bent over it together. It was surprising to Nita how closely she had to look to see the separate elements in the delicate tangle of inlaid metal. "How in the worlds did they do this?"

"Wizardry?" Carmela said. "Are there wizards who're artists?"

"Sure. And if a wizard did this, no question, he or she or it was an artist." Nita looked more closely at the end of the nearest ribbon, a sharp point. "But look how this line starts, and then it starts weaving back and forth in the main design . . . It's like the letters on the walls."

"But curved, not straight," Carmela said, putting out a finger to touch one long, curving letter or character. "A different font. Don't know if it's more formal or less. But this is soooo detailed . . ." She bent close, squinting at the long, delicate thin-and-thick strokes of the alien lettering as they tangled among many others, all making their way like twining plant fronds toward the center of the design. "This part is — I think it's just names. Nouns, but no verbs . . ."

After a moment Carmela shook her head, got up, and stood with her hands on her hips, looking over the design. Nita realized that Carmela was trying to get to grips with the whole pattern. But it was hard, from way over at one side like this: and if you ventured into the design, it made even less sense, or you got caught up in the fine detail —

Hmm, Nita thought. *Bobo?*

You rang?

Got the stair-making routine on tap?

Right here.

Nita watched the air beside her harden into an almost invisible flight of steps up over the design. She felt for the first one, found it, made sure of the width and the depth of the treads, and then trotted steadily up about two storeys into the air. Carmela watched her go.

This high enough? the peridexis said.

Just fine, Nita said, looking down at the great design. From up here, her sudden suspicion was instantly confirmed. The design wasn't random. Up here you could see the larger shapes — the four uplifted claws, the six rear legs, the long tail with its fierce spine. *Is it really a sting, or something else?* But the whole creature had been designed as if in calligraphic pen strokes, thicks and thins, and was bent back on itself almost into a spiral: the head and foremost claws in the middle of the design, the rear legs and finally the tail defining the outside of a circle or disc. "'Mela," Nita said, "it's one of our scorpion guards. The design's stylized, but you couldn't miss it."

"Okay. Where's the head, and where's the tail?"

"The head's near the middle. No, more to your right. The tail's at the edge, on your left."

Carmela headed for the center of the design.

From above, more light came dropping slowly down in S'reee's wake, her near eye glinting in the silver light of Nita's wand. "Nothing different," S'reee said. "More words that I can't read, all the way up." She cocked that eye down at what lay below her and Nita. "But you two seem to have found something."

Together they made their way down to floor level. Carmela had come to the scorpion's head and was kneeling on the densely inlaid metal. As Nita walked over, Carmela looked up with an expression of absolute excitement. "This is it!" she said.

"What?" Nita said.

"Where it starts," Carmela said. "Not an index. It's the start of a story. The words are simpler here. I can see them like I couldn't right away on the walls —"

Nita went down on one knee again and touched the green metal of the design. From within it she got a faint, faint sense of some power stirring. "It may be helping you," she said.

"I can use some help," Carmela said, without looking up. "This isn't easy . . ." She put a finger on a spot that was a shade of green darker than the rest of the design, in the right position to be an eye.

"'First there is the Old World,'" Carmela read. She leaned in to look more closely at the long, twisting line of alien charactery. "The tenses in this are all present tense, as if it's happening *now* for them. Does that make sense?"

Nita shrugged. S'reee flipped her tail. "There are any number of species who see the present and past as one. Go on."

Carmela squinted at the writing, tracing it with a finger, occasionally shuffling along a little way on her knees to pick up the next part. "'And the Old World has swung in its — old orbit?' — mmm, no, it's more formal: make that 'its ancient round' — 'since the First People awoke in the heart of the worlds.' No — 'in the centermost of the Circles.'" Carmela paused, then went on with increased certainty. "'So that when the World awoke, life and thought at last — were company for? — companioned with the star which for long had burned alone in the night at the Circles' heart.'" Carmela scooted along as the sentence stretched away from the scorpion's head, then picked up the thread again as it twisted and coiled among many others. "'Yet' — Wait a minute. No, I see it. 'Yet with the new life came the promise of a death that should come out of the darkness, as the light and life had done.'" She paused, and scowled at the next sentence for a moment as if perplexed, before translating it: "'And the First People swore that it might be so for others, but should not be so for them.'"

"Huh," Nita said. "Is that a species having its Choice, or fighting it? Or just refusing it?"

"No telling." Carmela scooted farther along in the diagram on her knees, then sat back on her heels for a moment as she looked down at it. "But I think maybe they had different ideas about how to keep this death from happening." She bent down to look more closely at the long, inlaid sentences, seeming to read them more quickly now. "Let me just paraphrase; the straight translating is tough to do fast. The people here — or the countries? Maybe the cities. It doesn't say anything about how many people we're talking about — Anyway, it looks like they split up in a lot of different ways . . ." Carmela paused, frowned. "It might mean in terms of distance, or mentally. Or both. But it looks like the biggest and strongest groups swallowed up the smaller ones, or stamped them out. Finally there were only two big groups left. All the clans or cities ended up either in one camp or the other . . ."

As Carmela spoke, Nita felt herself coming up in goosebumps. A twitch, a tingle that wouldn't go away along the skin and the nerves: the feeling of little feet scurrying, scurrying over her brain. And out at the edge of things, a sense of darkness leaning in from those walls, the world going quiet to listen. . . .

"hNii't," S'reee sang very softly. "Look —"

The darkness of the space out past the edge of the scorpion pattern was becoming less complete. Shadowy shapes were forming between them and the distant walls: transparent shadows on the dark air, almost impossible to see. "It's such an old wizardry, I hardly felt it start," S'reee said. "Whatever was set to power it is very weak now."

"And this is part of the hot-spot wizardry that brought the scorpions in?" Nita said.

"Probably," S'reee said. "If the scorpions were the defensive part of the wizardry, they might have been activated often enough to siphon a lot of power away from this part of the spell. Now it's using whatever other power it can find to do its job. And even our sensitivity to the fact that there's a story here could be helping." She glanced around at the almost-unseen, multitudinous engravings in the distant walls. "The Speech isn't the only language with power. If a story hasn't been heard in a long time, much power can lie in it, tightly compressed until it's told again . . ."

Nita nodded. *Bobo,* she said silently, *this might be important. Can you add some power to the equation?*

Some, the peridexis said. *But this wizardry is fragile. I'm limited in how much I can help without interfering, maybe even destroying what it's trying to do. Also, the power must be paid for.*

That was no surprise. *Okay, let's do what we can —* "'Mela," she said, sitting down, "Bobo and I will try to stick a little juice into this."

Carmela nodded, absorbed. Nita closed her eyes and started a little exercise that Tom had taught her: concentrating on her breathing, and then imagining herself breathing a little of her power as a wizard out into the spell around her with every outward breath. It was one of many ways a wizard could manage the way he or she paid the energy price for a spell — a gradual, steady outflow of intention, rather than a single unmanaged moment of payment that left you limp. Nita imagined that she could see it, a hazy cloud of light surrounding her, more visible with each breath. Shortly it seemed that out at the edges, that cloud was thinning, being drawn away. *We getting some uptake?* she said to Bobo.

Some. It's slow. Take a break for a moment; don't feed it too fast . . .

Nita opened her eyes again, feeling faintly fatigued, the normal result of this kind of power outlay. Out past the edges of the pattern, those shadows in the dark air were more substantial. She tried to see more detail. There were spiky shapes, jagged, rearing up against deeper darkness. "Mountains?" Nita said.

Carmela didn't look up, just nodded. "Neets, whatever you did is just helping. I'm getting a lot more of this now . . ."

"Great. What kind of people were they? Much further out from the Sun and you'd expect something that wasn't based on carbon."

"There's not much about that here," Carmela said, standing up to move along down the pattern, as around them the shadowy landscape became less obscure. The mountains becoming visible all around them seemed to cover all of a vast landscape stretching away in all directions. It was as if the pattern-disc was at the top of some peak supereminent above the others. All around, in endless shades of navy and sky blue and violet, the narrow, spearlike mountains cast long fingers of indigo shadow away behind them in the light of a Sun that made Nita blink, for — considering the distance they were discussing — it shouldn't have been so bright.

"Not a friendly-looking place," S'reee said, "to our eyes, at least . . ."

Nita had to agree. In this vista, at least, there didn't seem to be any flat land: it was all ups and downs. A haze of atmosphere was visible, hanging low, completely covering some peaks, reaching only partway up others. On those lower peaks, Nita could make out the glitter of lights, scattered down from the pinnacles like snow. On some of the nearer mountains, she thought she could make out buildings partially mimicking the structure of the peaks to which they clung — upward-jutting crowns of stony thorns, artificial spires spearing up from the passes or saddles between peaks. Here and there, dartlike shapes soared or arrowed between the city-mountains, but it was impossible at this distance to tell whether the moving shapes were creatures or machines.

In the imagery surrounding the pattern-circle, time sped up, fled by. The world changed with the passage of thousands of years. Mountains eroded and crumbled, pinnacles shattered and fractured to sharper points; on those heights where the Sun reached best, low-domed cities now clung to the ancient cliffs. Like glassy nodules of some exotic gemstone, by night the cities gleamed and glowed from within; by day the Sun glanced from them, blinding. "It's brighter than it should be," Nita said.

"The Sun's much younger," S'reee said. "And it did have a variable period early in its history. This is a long, long time ago . . ."

The machines that rode the violet-dark sky grew, changing shape, as more cities budded from the peaks their view included. "Those people were there for a long time," Carmela said, looking over more of the writing. "And they got really technologically advanced. Antigravity, ion tech, a lot of fancy stuff. But no worldgates." She left the long curve of pattern she'd been reading and stepped to another. "Isn't that strange?"

"Not always," S'reee said. "The technology's not universal, as Mamvish could tell you. There are worlds that can't conceive of other planets or dimensions, or even other ways of life: yet they still have wizardry."

"'Mela, you see anything about what they called this planet?" Nita said.

Carmela shook her head. "I'm not sure," she said. "There were lots of names for it, at the beginning. Probably as many names as we have for Earth. But then they start to get fewer. In all this later stuff, there are just two left, and I don't know which one to use. One of the two groups that dominated the planet called it Shamask. The other called it Eilith."

"What do the words mean?" S'reee said.

Carmela looked up then, and her expression was grim. "'Ours,'" she said.

Nita and S'reee exchanged a glance.

"They don't seem to have liked each other a whole lot, the Shamaska and the Eilitt," Carmela said, getting down on her knees to look at the writing embedded in that part of the pattern. "All along here, it's descriptions of things that one side did, or the other side did —" She shook her head. "I don't understand most of it. But the tone's never friendly. Then it gets angry. Then —"

Nita started in surprise, and so did S'reee, as the first flashes and impacts of energy weapons erupted among the spires of the First World. Mountains fell and buildings crumbled in a newer and deadlier sort of erosion. "Surprised it took that long," Carmela said, getting up again to head farther down that stroke of the pattern. "Their first really big war . . ."

"Why were they fighting?" Nita said.

Carmela stood where she was and looked all along that stroke of the scorpion pattern with her hands on her hips, hunting an answer. "I'm not sure," she said. "There are so many reasons and excuses here. A lot of them don't make sense. I think each side thought the other had cheated them out of something, or stolen something, that they needed to survive." She shook her head, annoyed. "So they started having wars. This one went on for —" She hunkered down to trace out, with one finger, a specific sequence of the long, curved characters. "Twelve or thirteen thousand years."

Nita and S'reee exchanged a glance. *"This one??"* Nita said.

S'reee blew out an unhappy breath. "There are species," she said, "that are very advanced at science and technology . . . but the technologies of being in harmony with one another elude them somehow. They tend to have more wizards than most."

"You'd think species like that would blow themselves up quicker," Nita said.

S'reee flipped a fin, resigned. "In such cases, the Lone One can have Itself a long, ugly playtime. Often It tries to keep the combatants from ever destroying each other completely, so the 'fun' can go on for as long as possible."

"I'd believe that was happening here," Carmela said, getting up to walk along another long, tangled chain of symbols buried in the design. "You'd have trouble finding any time when these guys *weren't* fighting. Though here they seem to have taken a breather..."

Carmela straightened up. Nita could feel that slight draining sensation that said the wizardry needed more power. She sat down where she was and closed her eyes, concentrating on breathing more power into it.

But even with her eyes closed, she could sense a cooling and darkening around her. "That would be why," S'reee sang, sounding somewhat troubled. "The Sun is dimming. And how quickly..."

Bobo, Nita said, *will this much power hold the spell for now?*

Yes. But it won't run much longer. If there's anything to be learned, better do it with your eyes open —

She opened them, stood up, staggered. "hNii't," S'reee said, "are you all right?"

"Yeah," Nita said, looking toward the Sun. No wonder that S'reee had been taken aback: it was getting fainter by the second, as if someone was turning down a dimmer. The elapsed time was passing by at thousands of years per second, but the speed of the Sun's fading still seemed uncomfortably swift. In the precipitous valleys between the needle-sharp peaks, the atmosphere was freezing out, dusting itself down as dry ice and oxygen snow....

"They started doming their cities over," Carmela said, "and trying to change their climate. But the Sun just cooled too fast. All the changes they made weren't enough."

Nita watched the Sun's light keep on fading. It had struck her hard, some time back, how dim the Martian day seemed compared to Earth's, even at such a small increase in the distance from the Sun. And Shamask-Eilith would have been maybe sixty or eighty million miles farther out, getting even less light and heat than Mars. *A cold world, getting colder...* she thought, as she watched the Sun far off in the deeps of space slowly settling into what would be its future normal magnitude.

"And still their wars went on," S'reee said, turning gently in the air to watch yet another swath of nuclear explosions and massive energy-weapon fire scorch its way across the planet's increasingly ravaged surface.

"Oh, yeah," Carmela said, sounding resigned. "They weren't going to stop fighting just because of a little thing like the Sun going cool..."

"You'd think if they had a technology like this, they'd have considered moving everybody to a warmer world," Nita said. "There weren't all that many Shamaska or Eilitt by then. They'd already killed so many of each other..."

S'reee swung her tail in agreement. "The Sun's behavior could even have been a hint," S'reee said. "The Powers That Be have been known to make Their suggestions indirectly — usually with some hope that the peoples involved will come to some greater good that way than just by being told right out what to do. Or maybe this was just an attempt to break their cycle of destruction when other hints had failed."

"'Those who will, the Powers lead,'" Nita said,

quoting a line from the manual, "'and those who won't, They drag ...'"

"If you guys are right," Carmela said, "this might be where the dragging started." She gazed down at the floor in a slightly unfocused way as she walked around, pausing at one particular spot. "Listen to this," Carmela said. "'Then from the darkness ... came the fate and the death which had long been promised. And all the folk looked up into the night and cried out in rage and fear that all their striving against each other was wasted —'"

They looked toward Shamask-Eilith's spiny curvature and saw, distant but enhanced by the wizardry, the incoming shadow of "the death long promised." From high above the plane of the ecliptic — the orbital zone in which all the other worlds of the Solar System except Pluto rode — a dark rogue planet, ensnared by the Sun's gravity who-knew-how many years before, was diving slowly and inexorably into the system. There could have been no possible error about its path, which was taking it straight toward where Shamask-Eilith would be in its orbit in only a matter of decades.

"I don't suppose this possibly means that they saw sense and stopped fighting with each other?" Nita said.

From the look S'reee gave Nita, she had her doubts. "I wonder, how quickly did they see it?" S'reee said.

"Pretty quickly," Carmela said, walking along and looking down at the pattern. "The scientists on both sides worked out that it wouldn't hit them. But it *would* come close enough to destroy their world, even if it didn't actually hit. Just the tidal forces of the bigger body as it passed by would break the First World up. So they started making plans to save as many of their own people and life forms as they could, and make their way to the next planet in. But it looks like both sides did it secretly."

"What?" Nita said. "Why? Are you trying to tell me —?"

Carmela looked at Nita and S'reee with an expression both annoyed and completely unsurprised. "You got it," she said. "Each side figured that if it didn't tell the other one, their enemies might not have enough time to evacuate their populations. Then the ones who escaped successfully would have the whole new world to themselves."

S'reee blew softly, a sound of sorrow and disgust.

"And when it all came out in the open and both sides started accusing each other of attempted genocide," Nita said, "gee, I wonder what happened then?"

Carmela merely raised her eyebrows as the image of those ancient jagged mountains erupted in unprecedented violence. "They all got right to work reducing the number of people their enemies would be moving off the planet . . ."

Nita scowled. "And these were the first intelligent life forms in our solar system? *Theoretically* intelligent, more like! They're embarrassing me."

"Hard to believe they wasted precious time on more slaughter," S'reee said sadly. "And their wizardly talent probably didn't have power enough to move the planet. Or maybe there were too few of them . . ."

"It says here they did try to push the incoming planet off course," Carmela said, walking along and reading more of the inlay of the central pattern. "But they failed. A whole lot of their wizards died trying. Finally some people on each side realized that whether they liked it or not, they had to help each other get out and resettle closer to the Sun. They'd also have to change themselves physically to fit into whatever world they wound up on. So . . ."

Glints of movement above the dark peaks caught all their eyes: small shapes, leaping upward. One glittering round shape came closer to their point of view, closer yet, swelled until it seemed to fill half the huge dome: then flashed past them, gone. But it didn't move so quickly that they couldn't see the glitter of interior lights stellated all over some more complex shape, spiky, angular. "Cities," Nita said. "They got a few whole cities off the world —"

But very few of those tiny desperate city-seeds escaped as the terrible wanderer from outside the Solar System plunged in, growing in the First World's sky, a terrible pale shadow. As it filled the sky, the upward-jutting needles and precipices of the ancient mountains trembled as the two planets' interacting tidal forces strove together, and the First World started to shatter —

They saw only a few moments of that massive destruction. The incoming rogue planet, so much bigger and more massive than Shamask-Eilith, stayed in one piece. But Shamask-Eilith simply tore itself apart in the intruder's gravitational field. Vast yawning crevasses stitched themselves along Shamask's surface, ripping open the crust. The planet's molten mantle burst outward through the tears in all directions, fountaining countless millions of tons of magma into space. The suddenly exposed planetary core plunged away through the no-longer-confining mass of the rest of the planet like a bullet through flesh, tumbling into the darkness of space as the planet disintegrated —

In the dome, the shadows faded, the imagery failed; the dome dimmed down again. *The wizardry failed,* Bobo said in the back of Nita's mind. *It couldn't cope with the extra power feed from outside.*

Carmela and Nita and S'reee were gazing at one another in silent horror. After a moment, Carmela said, "You know, I was watching some documentary about the Moon the other day. It said a lot of scientists think the Moon was formed by some big piece of a planet or something hitting the Earth while it was still molten and splashing a lot of stuff out. Was this it, I wonder? Did the rogue planet do it? Or maybe Shamask's core . . ."

Nita considered. "That was a real long time ago that happened, 'Mela. Four *billion* years and change." She looked around. "And however old this place is . . . it's not anything like billions of years."

Carmela sighed. "I take it the playback's broken?"

"Yeah. My manual will have a copy of what we saw, though."

"And I've kept a copy in the Telling," S'reee said. "We may want to compare them later for perceptual differences."

Nita nodded. "But for the moment," she said to Carmela, "looks like you've got a lot of reading ahead of you."

"Well, yeah, because what happened next?" Carmela said, waving her arms. "Where were they going to go? Not Mercury: it was way too hot. And not Venus or Earth, if they were still molten. Nobody could change themselves enough to cope with *that*—"

"With wizardry," S'reee said, "maybe they could have, if everyone involved in the change was sufficiently committed. But that kind of complete agreement is rare. That's one of the reasons the Troptic Stipulation is in the Oath — the part about not changing a creature that doesn't desire the change. The rule goes double, triple, for a whole species."

"Then it has to be Mars," Carmela said. "Why else would all this be here for us to find?" She waved an arm at the dome full of writing around them. "I really doubt anybody said, 'Oh, let's spend weeks and months writing the whole history of our species in here, and then go off somewhere else . . . !' So where *are* they?"

Nita shook her head. Carmela was plainly fascinated by the mystery of where the inhabitants of the lost planet had gone: but Nita was thinking, *And what if this is the species that Kit and his team are so excited about waking up? These people, who went thousands of years without having any time they* weren't *having a war, might wind up being our new next-door neighbors?*

Oh, boy.

"'Mela," Nita said after a moment, "you saw how they were with each other on their original world. Maybe the ones who made it here didn't learn the lesson. Maybe they finally wiped each other out . . . and this is all that's left." But as soon as she said it, Nita somehow knew right down in her bones that this was not the case, and the situation wasn't going to be anything like that simple. She frowned. *I hate feelings like this,* Nita thought. *Even though they're going to be useful later . . .*

"There's something else that strikes me as strange," S'reee said. "All through that — we never saw an image of what *they* looked like, the people of the First World." She swung her tail. "It's true enough that there are species that don't or won't make images of themselves. But they're in the minority." Her voice went wry. "Most species can't get enough of looking at themselves . . ."

Carmela shook her head. "Maybe they were making a clean break?" she said. "If they did actually change themselves to suit another planet — this planet — maybe they didn't want to be reminded of what they had to abandon? Seems like they thought it was a failure to have to change at all . . ."

She stood there with her hands on her hips, looking around her at the dome, at all that unread writing. Then Carmela turned back to Nita and S'reee.

"I've got to work on this," she said. "It's going to

drive me nuts. I need to go get a notebook. Do you want me to give you guys a lift back home?"

"You might take me back with you," S'reee said. "But does this mean that you're not going shopping?"

"It can wait." Carmela turned back to gaze around the dome with an odd look on her face. "There's something going on here."

Another one gets bit by the bug! Nita thought. She glanced at S'reee. "You just may have heard history in the making," she said, "whatever kind's recorded here. Carmela said she was *not* going shopping somewhere."

S'reee whistled with laughter. Carmela ignored them both as she looked down at the design under their feet, following one long, tangled thread of writing. She pointed at it. "That bit," Carmela said, "that's a poem. Can you see it?"

Nita and S'reee looked at each other. "No," they said in unison.

"Well, I can. And I want to see what it says!"

Nita sighed. *So much for getting her safely out of here and off to the Crossings!* "I'm not sure I'm wild about you being by yourself up here . . ."

Carmela gave Nita a look. "Even Mamvish said there was no reason I should be excluded from this stuff. What're you worried about — our little scorpion buddies? They let me alone before when they came through. If they were interested in chewing on me, they'd have done it then. And they haven't been back —"

"As far as I can tell," S'reee said, glancing around

the vast round chamber, "that wizardry's now defunct. A one-time assessment, I think."

"See that?" Carmela said. "Neets, when I come back, I'll have the remote. And I've got my 'curling iron.' If anything jumps out at me, it's not going to get anything for its trouble but a real big hole straight through it, and I'll be gone before it can do anything else."

Nita looked over at S'reee. S'reee just shrugged her tail. "Recent events suggest that K!aarmii'lha can take care of herself. She's armed, she can get away quickly if she must, and if she has a cell phone, she can call you for help if she needs it, yes?"

"Yeah," Nita said. *Bobo, is the wizardry here really done running?*

Yes. I doubt it could be reactivated now no matter how we tried.

"Okay," Nita said. "I'm gonna try again to get at that spot where Kit and the guys are working . . . at least, find out why we couldn't transport there."

Carmela pulled out her remote and got busy punching its buttons. "And you, cousin?" S'reee said. "Are you sure you'll be all right without backup?"

Nita nodded. Unsettling as her experience with the scorpions had been, it had left her with a sense that she had been examined and found nonthreatening: she was safe enough on Mars. *Until some new weird thing happens . . .* But the moment of foresight Nita had had, and correctly read, now left her feeling less concerned about coming up against something completely unexpected. *As long as the universe keeps those helpful hints coming . . .*

"Go on," Nita said, patting S'reee's side and pulling out her manual again. She flipped it to the page describing wizardries ongoing in the area, glanced down it to the description of the life-support spell that S'reee was running, and laid a finger on the written version: it glowed as Nita took over its management. "I'll be in touch if I find anything."

She looked past S'reee to Carmela. 'Mela waved the remote at her, punched a button. She and S'reee vanished: the air inside the support spell imploded in a brief, sharp breeze toward where they'd been, then settled again.

Nita stood there in the silence, the rowan wand in her free hand now the only light. "Okay, Bobo," she said. "You have Kit's first set of coordinates? This crater —" She peered at the manual. "Stokes —"

Got them.

"Are they still blocked?"

Not precisely. Conditions there are . . . peculiar.

It wasn't the most reassuring thing to hear wizardry itself saying to you. Nevertheless, Nita shrugged. "Let's go find out how peculiar," she said.

The transit circle laid itself out glowing around her. *Transiting now.*

Around Nita, the world went dark again.

Gusev

PALE PEACH-COLORED DUST fluffed away in the gust of wind that accompanied the three human forms who appeared atop the low, rounded ridge. It wasn't a particularly sharp or edgy piece of terrain — just a rough escarpment of beige and cream-colored rock, with dust and sand spilling down in little rills, almost like water, from cracks in the low cliff's edge. To the south and west spread a vast, shallow, circular depression, itself dimpled and cratered with the remnants of newer, lesser impacts. Level with the old crater's rim, the surrounding landscape to the north and east, more brown than red, was strewn with nondescript boulders well into the distance. "Here we are," Kit said, glancing around to get his bearings.

"Wahoo," Darryl said, ironic.

"Nope. De Vaucouleurs."

"Pedant," said Ronan, looking around with the

expression of someone eager not to see any more giant bat-crab-spider creatures.

Kit rolled his eyes. "We're in the right spot, anyway. There's Kayne, over that way —" He pointed: another crater's low rim was just visible, looking like a low line of hills maybe ten miles away. "And Shawnee . . . Bok . . ." He peered further away to the south. "Hamelin —"

"I take back what I said before," Ronan said, concerned. "You don't need a social life later. You need one *now*. How long have you been staying home nights memorizing crater names? They're holes in the ground, Kit! There's nothing but rocks in them! Set yourself free! *Life's too short!*"

Kit turned to Darryl. "Doesn't seem to be much going on here at the moment. What've we got?"

Darryl brought out his WizPod and pulled out a wide, semitransparent page that he studied for a moment. He shook his head, holding it up for Ronan and Kit to see. "Okay, look. The wizardry you triggered is getting ready to spike here in a few minutes. But before it goes off, you can still see some indications of how old it is and where it came from. Look quick —" He pointed at one long line of symbols. "See that? The power to fuel this wizardry wasn't locally sourced."

Kit shook his head. "What?"

"The energy didn't come from this planet, originally! It came from —" Darryl looked up, pointed. "Somewhere up there."

Kit and Ronan looked up into the empty Martian sky. "Nearby?" Ronan said. "One of the moons, maybe?"

"Don't think so," Darryl said, studying his read-out. ". . . Nope. Much further. Maybe thirty million miles. Actually, make that fifty."

Ronan and Kit stared at each other. "What's out that far?" Ronan said.

"The asteroids?" Kit said. "I mean, I'm not sure about the distances . . ."

Darryl was still looking at the wide page of manual that he'd pulled out of the WizPod. He shook his head, looking perplexed. "There's something wrong with the timing, too," he said. "I can't get a clean read on it. But, look, if the wizardry's running and about to go off, it'd make more sense for us to deal with what it's about to do right now than get too hung up about who emplaced it and when . . ."

"Yeah. Meanwhile," Ronan said, glancing around him, "what's the satellite situation? That last jump was biggish, to judge by how high the Sun's up now." He had a point: Kit glanced up and saw that it was almost noon. "The schedule has to be pretty different here. And where exactly is this wizardry going to go off? Not right underneath us this time, I hope —"

"No way," Darryl said. "I factored in a nice big offset. Off that way —" He looked east and south. "In the middle of the next big crater over. About fifty miles, as the wizard jumps."

"Uh," Ronan said softly, "maybe time to jump, then —"

They looked where he was looking. Kit gulped.

From beyond the low crater rim to the east, a pale green glow was rising.

Darryl grabbed them each by an arm. "I'll put us down on the far side," he said. "The view'll be better." He took a deep breath.

As the momentary darkness of a bilocation transit shut down around him, Kit was trying to visualize the orbit of the *Mars Express* orbiter in his head. But something else was niggling at him. The name of the crater they'd come down on the edge of meant something besides being just the site of one of the active wizardries. *De Vaucouleurs,* he thought. *De Vaucouleurs. There was something special about that area, I could have* sworn —

The darkness gave way to daylit Martian landscape again. They were standing on the rim of yet another crater, but this rim was much higher and better defined than the last, and the crater seemed far bigger: the two arms of it ran straight to the foreshortened horizon and vanished. *For it to look this big, it'd have to be about a hundred miles across,* Kit thought. *And the surface down there is maybe two miles deep* — Or so it seemed where it wasn't being rapidly overrun by the green glow of a working alien wizardry. That emerald light was flooding outward from a spot off to their right and about halfway across the visible portion of the crater, making the whole area look bizarrely like a reverse-action film of water going down a drain.

"If the action this time's going to be anything like it was back at Stokes," Ronan said, "I think I prefer the view from up here." He looked down at the outward-spreading light. "Look at it go —" He shook his head. "What about the satellites?"

"Yeah," Darryl said. "If something comes over now, it's not just going to see our infrared signatures. At night the guys back at NASA or ESA might think we were just a transient hot spot, a meteorite impact or some such. But in the daytime, when they have something overhead that can see us in visible light, too? And not just us. *That* —"

Kit was going through his manual in a hurry. "Obviously we can spoof them," Ronan said. "Mess with their machinery somehow."

"If it can figure out the right way!" Kit said. "Spoof 'em, sure, it's easy to say. But how do you do it so the rocket-science guys don't *notice*? They're not dumb! Take one of the satellite's cameras out of commission? Sure, but how? Make a piece of the machinery fail? Better make sure you're not failing out something you can't fix right away when you don't need the fault anymore. And you've got to pick something to interfere with that'll seem to make sense when it stops working *and* when it just starts up again for no good reason —"

"You'll figure something out!" Darryl said. "This is your specialty. You haven't done anything but think about this stuff for weeks now —"

Kit held his manual up right in front of Darryl's face to show him the orbital diagram he'd been looking for. "But not *this* exact situation! Here comes the *Mars Express* orbiter. Eighteen minutes and ten seconds from now. Either we stop *that*" — and Kit pointed at the spreading green glow — "or the *Express* sees a lot more than just our own hot spots. Those we can hide — put a stealth shell over us that mimics the local temperature. But what about *that?*" He nodded at the oncoming tide of green light. "No way they're going to believe that's a dust storm! We can't let them see it; it'll screw up their science! And we don't have enough power to hide it even at the size it is now. If it spreads much further —"

Darryl glanced up from his WizPod to peer down into the crater. "Uh-oh," he said. "Got some kind of secondary locus popping up."

"Where?" Kit said, trying to see what Darryl was looking at.

"Crap, it's gone —" Then Darryl pointed. "No, there it is again. See it? No, more to the right. Maybe five miles to the right of the green zone. It flashed. There it goes again —"

They all peered down at the spark of fire Darryl had spotted. It was a small, hard, bright light, faintly pinkish. And as Kit looked at it, it moved just slightly, a tiny jitter —

And he realized what it was. He looked over his shoulder to judge the Sun's angle, and then back down at the little sharp light. "That's not the wizardry!" Kit said.

Ronan stared at him. "What?"

"It's a reflection!"

"From what??"

"Solar panels!"

Now it was Darryl's turn to stare. "What would there be to — oh, my god!"

Kit nodded, sweat popping out on him. "I never come at it from this side," he said. "Or from all the way up here on the edge! I always just transit straight in. That's why the name de Vaucouleurs didn't remind me of anything in particular at first. But now it does. It's the next crater over from *Gusev!*"

Ronan's eyes went wide. "What, you mean that's one of the wee rovers down there? *Opportunity?*"

"No," Kit said. *"Spirit!"*

Ronan said something in Irish that didn't sound like a compliment. "Could this get any fecking worse?" he said. "It can't see us, can it?"

"Not at this range," Kit said. "It's what else she might see that worries me now. If the same kind of stuff starts happening here as happened back at Stokes —"

"NASA'll start seeing things they shouldn't," Darryl said. "Come on, we've gotta get down there and protect the rover. Blind it somehow, block its vision —"

"Vision won't be enough," Kit said. "It's got other sensors. Either way, we can't sit this one out up here ..."

Ronan said something else in very annoyed Irish. Darryl grabbed his arm. "How close do you want us?" he said to Kit.

"Not in the green," Kit said. "We need a few minutes to work something out. A hundred yards away or so —"

Darryl grabbed Kit's upper arm. Things went black —

— then went beige. Kit took a long breath: though he knew Darryl was careful about making sure their air and spells came with them all when they jumped, there was always the chance that some day he might get overexcited and slip —

"You know," Darryl said as they came out in the middle of more beige, rubbly ground, "I can just hear you thinking sometimes, your Kitness. I like breathing, too, you know? I'm real used to it. So cut me some slack. Where's your little friend?" He stared around him. "And I keep meaning to ask: why isn't this place red when it always looks that way in the pictures?"

Ronan snickered. "They adjust the images," he said, while Kit tried to get his bearings. "People don't like the Red Planet being beige. Gotta give the public what it wants . . ."

Kit glanced around, getting his bearings. The spot where Darryl had landed them wasn't so far from his own usual transit spot: as he looked around, the landmarks started falling into place one by one. The *Apollo 1* hills off northward, the *Columbia* hills to the west told him that they were standing on the elevated ground called Home Plate, with its many eclectically named pits and rocks and rises — Missoula, Palanque, Lutefisk, Clovis, Larry's Lookout, McCool Hill. And not far from McCool, still close to the north-facing crater wall where she'd spent the last winter —

"There," Kit said. He headed straight off across the rocky landscape at the bounce. Even without the high angle of a few moments ago to give the Sun something to reflect from, there was no mistaking the small, angular shape hunkered down against the rising ground in the near distance, its little camera pole sticking up. *Good thing she's too small to be carrying seismic sensors,* Kit thought as Ronan and Darryl came hurrying along in his wake. *Otherwise there's no telling what they'd think was going on up here . . .*

As Kit got closer, he slowed: there was no use kicking up more dust on the hardworking little machine — it had more than enough trouble with what the winter dust storms left layered on its solar panels. The scientists at NASA had for the past couple of years been surprised and pleased that the *Spirit* and *Opportunity* rovers had managed to keep working for so long: mostly, they theorized, because of passing dust devils that blew the accumulated storm dust off them. The wizards who came up here every now and then with cans of compressed air and puffer brushes while the probes were asleep were delighted to let the scientists think that — and careful not to remove enough dust at any one time as to make them suspicious.

Kit, having occasionally done this duty when there was the "excuse" of dust devils in the neighborhood, waved at the others to drop back and wait where they were. He looked carefully to make sure that the main camera hadn't moved while they were approaching it. Then Kit hunkered down quietly on *Spirit's* blind side and put his manual on the ground, paging along to a two-page spread that showed him a list of the rover's diagnostics.

After glancing down it to see what was working and what wasn't, he waved at Ronan and Darryl; they came quietly up to join him. Ronan raised his eyebrows, tapped one ear: *Can it hear?*

Kit shook his head. "Look at all the dust and dents," Darryl said. "Poor beat-up baby."

Kit nodded. "She's had a bad time. The front right wheel got stuck two years ago, so they had to drive her backwards after that, dragging the bad wheel. Then the dust storms came. She almost died altogether: they had to shut her down, wait out the dark time for a few months . . . Things kept breaking. She got stuck in the dirt for a few weeks. The dust started scouring off the protective coating on the solar panels. They got covered so often that her batteries started draining too fast and her software started glitching. One instrument had to be shut down, it got so much dust in it. But she just wouldn't stop working. Tough girl . . ."

He reached out a hand, then stopped; there were too many things he might break or mess up. "Not to cut short a touching moment," Ronan said, "but the green's getting close. You're the machine specialist: just tell her to close down for a little while."

Kit shook his head. "It's not that easy."

"Why not? She's full of computers. Should be fairly smart as machines go."

"That's the problem," Kit said, looking at the oncoming flow of green. "The more complex a machine gets, the harder it is to persuade to do something unusual. It's not like you're trying to talk, say, an electric can opener into doing stuff. A can opener's life isn't long on excitement, so it's glad to do something strange! But a machine with a lot of complex programming grows a sense of purpose. Even loyalty." Kit frowned. "And when you try to get it to do some-

thing weird all of a sudden, it wants reasons. Especially if it's got much security built into it. Machines
can get suspicious of your motives, whether they
understand what wizardry's about or not . . ."

"I don't think we're gonna have any time for a
prolonged conversation," Darryl said, looking east.
The tide of green light was running toward them fast.

Ronan looked up from his manual. "That stealth
shell you were talking about?" he said. "I'd say this is
the moment. We can't hide the whole crater from
space. But we can hide it from the rover if we put the
shell over it —"

"Better hope they don't decide to move the rover
while the shell's over it," Darryl said. "Even anchor-
ing the spell to it won't help if what the shell's 'seeing'
doesn't move when *Spirit* does —"

Kit shook his head: there was nothing they could
do about that at the moment — the green light was
only a hundred or so feet away now, and there was
still the *Mars Orbiter* satellite to think about. "We'll
have to finesse that in a few minutes," Kit said, picking up his manual and getting up. "But right now —"

He pulled out his antenna-wand, thought about
the wizardry he needed. *Just a quick wheel-freeze.
The rovers have had that happen sometimes if there's
been a temperature fluctuation —* "Half a sec," Kit
said, pointing the wand at *Spirit*'s left front wheel. It
took only a few words' worth of the Speech to heat
the joint up so that it swelled a few microns thicker
than usual, locking the wheel in place. Kit backed
away. "Okay, go —"

Ronan began reading hurriedly in the Speech. Seconds later a shimmering hemispherical dome-shell about three meters wide appeared over *Spirit*, swirling with a soap-bubble light of working wizardry. "Okay," Ronan said, wiping sweat off his brow and breathing hard as he finished the spell. "While that lasts, it won't see or sense anything it hasn't seen for the last few minutes."

"Good," Kit said, turning to face what approached. "Because here comes trouble —"

The green light washed over them, turning everything as verdant now as it had been red in Stokes. Then darkness fell.

But not complete darkness. It was more a dusk light, the last embers of local sunset burning at the bottom of it, and the surroundings were beyond peculiar, bearing in mind what "local" should have been. Kit and Darryl and Ronan were now standing, not amid Martian rocks and dirt, but on a sidewalk next to what looked like a somewhat rural street with a double yellow stripe painted down the middle of it, and down the length of the road, streetlights were coming on, burning yellow against the oncoming evening.

Kit stared around him. The dusk slowly falling around them was earthly, not Martian. Scattered down their side of the street were some very normal and suburban-looking houses; across the road were more of the same. Nearby, a smaller street met this one. A street sign stood at the corner.

Ronan looked around him suspiciously, then made his way over to the sign, looked up at it. "Cranbury Road?" he said. "I'm no cooking expert, but don't you usually spell that with an *e* and two *r*'s?"

Darryl was meanwhile turning slowly around, examining the houses and front yards and driveways of the surroundings with an expression of utter astonishment. Then he stopped, staring at the biggest of the nearby structures. It was a red clapboard building with white-painted windows and a side door of the kind you might see on a barn, painted white on the doorsills and crossbars, red on the main panels. At one end of the building, among various enameled-metal signs advertising the makers of farm equipment and power tools, was a set of concrete stairs leading up to a door. Over the door hung a sign that said:

GROVERS MILL CO.

At the sight of the sign, Darryl's eyes went wide. Then he burst out laughing and turned back to Ronan. "*Now* I get it!" he said. "I am *impressed* with you!"

Startled, Ronan looked around, as if expecting the person Darryl was really addressing to be standing behind him. "Why me?!"

"Because this is *your* fault!"

"*What?*"

"You were the one who was singing the If-any-thing-was-going-to-come-from-Mars music!"

Ronan suddenly looked very defensive. "But — well, why shouldn't I? It's good music, and anyway, it's famous. Anybody might have thought about it when they came to Mars! Besides, how was I supposed to know this would happen —?"

"Too late for excuses now!" Laughing, Darryl salaamed before Ronan, though with a total lack of respect. "Seriously, we are not worthy to hang out with an adept like you! You are the wizard's wizard, man! *You have turned Mars into New Jersey!*"

Even in the general alarm of the moment, Kit had to snicker. Ronan stood there looking as cool as usual, but something in his eyes betrayed the fact that he wasn't sure he was being complimented. "Could have been worse," Ronan said under his breath as he looked around. "I could have done it the other way round."

"This is the place where that old radio version of *War of the Worlds* happened, isn't it?" Kit said. "The one they did on Halloween way back whenever it was, and they pretended it was happening in New Jersey somewhere, instead of England."

"And it's not even the *right* New Jersey!" Darryl said. "It's New Jersey *now!* Look over there —" He pointed. Off to their right, across the street, was a big handsome blue building with a long, peaked roof. On the opposite side of the road in front of it stood a pole with road signs that said ROUTE 629 and TO NJ TURN-PIKE. Farther down the pole were posted a laser-printed ad for an Internet café and a faded picture of somebody's lost dog.

Darryl was looking at the big blue building. "Bet you that was the mill once," Darryl said. "Look, I was right! There's the old millstones. They've got 'em sunk into the ground so cars won't ruin their lawn when they turn the corner. There's where the water came out past the mill. *But no Martians!*" He started laughing again.

"I wouldn't be too sure about that," Ronan said, very quietly.

There was something about the way he said it that stopped Darryl's laughter. He and Kit both looked up at where Ronan was pointing among the trees behind the old mill building. Half-obscured by a stand of big old trees that surrounded it stood what looked like some kind of elderly, jury-rigged water tower. The part that had held the water, like an upended bucket, was suspended between four narrow iron uprights, all rusty with time.

Darryl peered at the vessel, which had individual wooden staves like an old bucket, held together with rusty iron hoops. "Are those *bullet holes* in that?" Darryl said, still amused: but now there was some unease to the amusement. "Can't you just see it? People around here were listening to that radio broadcast, the night before Halloween, and some of them really bought into it, and they ran outside with their guns when they heard that Martian war machines were landing in *their town*, and some of them saw that thing in the dark, looking all tripod-y, and they shot it up —"

"Darryl," Kit said.

With a long, low moan of bending metal, the water tower *moved*.

"Bad," Ronan said, sounding utterly conversational, "this is very bad. We had TV shows like this back home on Saturday afternoons when I was little. This is the part where I always hid behind the couch."

Against the cold, hard stars of the Martian sky, among the trees of a suburban New Jersey that had no business being where it was, the water tower lurched to one side, then lurched the other way, hard. It shook itself like a creature trying to rid itself of some kind of impediment: and the fourth upright fell away, leaving it on three. The water tower shook itself again, picked up one of those legs and jerked it back and around somehow until it was balanced evenly on all three of them. Then the water tower started getting taller against that blackness, rearing up past the tops of the highest trees. Up near its top, a red glow started to develop into an eye that Kit felt was looking right at him.

"Anybody got an idea that doesn't involve us all bailing out of here and completely disgracing ourselves as wizards?" Kit said.

"Uh . . ." Darryl's head tilted back as that red glow slowly grew a stalk that raised it higher and higher above the trees, and those legs got longer and thicker, and the water vessel started to develop itself into something far more massive. "Who was it said 'discretion is the better part of valor'?"

"Doesn't matter, 'cause we've got no time for it now," Ronan said, and pulled out his light-rod weapon. Kit heard the soft singing sound it started to make. "Running won't help. What about *Spirit*? Poor beastie's gonna get stomped if we don't stick around and do something. And what'll NASA think if that happens?"

"Or Irina," Darryl said.

Kit's sweat went cold on him at the thought. "You carrying?" Ronan said to Darryl as he lifted the light-rod.

"Don't be hasty! Got a couple of things handy," Darryl said. He pulled the WizPod out. "Need to concentrate on this, guys, so if someone wants to buy us a moment —"

Ronan leveled his light-weapon, fired. A narrow line of blinding yellow-white light ravened out of it and struck the still-forming war machine in its underbody —

The stalk on which that red light had formed was now stretching toward them entirely too flexibly, and the light was going a far deeper and deadlier red. "No, you dope," Darryl shouted, "I meant something *passive*, like a force field!"

"Leave it with me," Ronan said, and held up one hand. The air above them shimmered as the force field went into effect. Kit was relieved to see it, as away above the force field, the Martian war machine took its completely realized form: gleaming in the rusty light, the bronzy body hoisted high over them on its cabled tripod legs, metal groaning ominously as the great mass paused, the roving eye deadly red at the end of a long, gooseneck stalk as it sought them out, focused on them —

"Here it comes!" Ronan shouted. Above them, the sunset was washed out by a wall of fire as the heat ray hit the force field and splashed away like water. By that awful light Darryl pulled out a page from his

WizPod, muttered under his breath, threw it glowing to the ground, and pulled out another one —

The ray stopped: the war machine above them wailed, an earsplitting howl of rage and frustration. Out beyond it, over the suburban New Jersey rooftops, a second red eye appeared, and then a third.

"You want to hurry up with that!" Ronan shouted at Darryl. "The force field was already start-ing to give just then —"

"What, do we need to kick the power up?" Kit said, reaching into memory for a different force-field spell of his own. He hurriedly recited the words in the Speech that brought it shimmering into operation above the three of them, then stood there panting for a moment with the reaction.

"No!" Ronan yelled as a second war machine started to move toward them. "Whatever's making these things appear is learning from what we do. I could feel the war-machine spell solving the shield while I was holding it —"

Another furiously concentrated line of fire came splashing down from the first machine and its ap-proaching compatriot. Kit, looking up, saw Ronan's shield fail while his own held: but now he, too, could feel what Ronan had described, that sense of his own wizardry being frayed at, pulled apart, with dreadful energy and persistence. "He's right!" Kit shouted at Darryl. "What have you got?"

"Gonna trip this closest one," Darryl said. "Watch out for which way it falls —"

"One is what you're gonna get," Kit said, feeling his force field continuing to fray. "Dammit! Ronan?"

"Might not be able to trip one," Ronan said, pulling his light wand out to full length, almost five feet. "But chop one down, yeah —"

"Save it for a moment!" Kit said.

Darryl was muttering under his breath in the Speech. Then he made a huge, expansive gesture with both arms, and from them sprang what at first looked like a jet of white mist. It wrapped itself around the legs of the closest war machine as it was rearing that flexible neck back for another attack on the force field. Then with another groan of metal the mist knotted itself tight, yanking the legs together at their "knees." The first machine leaned, tottered, and fell even as it fired. The bolt it shot went high over their heads, but as it went down, Kit felt his force field fail.

The second machine targeting them strode closer. Darryl threw another jet of mist at it, but this time as it knotted tight, the machine broke through it and strode on. "Bad, bad, bad . . ." Kit muttered, reaching into his otherspace pocket and pulling out the little shining sphere he'd been hoping he wouldn't have to use, especially as once he used it, no second one would work. "Darryl?"

He was backing away, along with Kit and Ronan. "This is getting us nowhere!" he said. "Stay close if we have to jump out of here —"

"Don't want to jump!" Ronan said. "If we do, we'll fail this test!"

"Yeah, well, how do we ace it?" Darryl said. "What kills these things?"

"Germs!" Kit said.

"Took a while in the original!" Ronan said, backing up and looking thoughtfully up at the legs of the walker that was stalking closer by the moment. "Couple of weeks, wasn't it?"

"I think what we've got is a couple of minutes," Darryl said. "And to buy us a little time —?"

He pulled another page out of his WizPod and started reading hurriedly. Kit kept backing up, in tandem with Ronan, as above them the walker peered around, looking for its prey. Darryl stood right where he was and kept on reading. Then, in what seemed mid-sentence, he stopped, took a deep breath, and shouted one last word, making a sweeping downward gesture with one hand.

Then he paused, looked behind him. *Hold still!* Darryl said silently. *Don't move!!*

Above them, the walker loomed up, stepped down toward them. Kit saw the great trilobed metallic foot come down at them, right on top of them — and then *through* them, past them. Fleetingly he saw the interior of the foot, the biocabling and mechanisms of its interior, as they slid down past his eyes like too-solid ghosts and stopped against the ground.

Ronan and Kit stared. *What was* that, *exactly?* Kit said silently as the great foot lifted again, and the creature stalked away.

Micro-bilocation, Darryl said. *I might not be able*

*to move us away from here, but I could stay here and
bilocate it. I just let it slip through the empty spaces in
our atoms. It thinks it stomped us, so keep quiet!*

They watched the walker stalk away across the
suburban darkness, toward the green-scummed pond.
"And *this*," Ronan whispered to Kit, looking at Darryl approvingly, "is why it's fun to play with the little
kids every now and then. You never know *what*
they're going to pull."

"Oh," Darryl said, very soft, "so all of a sudden
I'm not the superpowered brat anymore?" He chuck-
led. "Well, good, because I'm gonna yell at you now.
If *you* hadn't lost it and started shooting —"

"Yeah, well if you'd just tell people when you —"

"*If you two would please just shut up?*" Kit
whispered.

Astonished, Darryl and Ronan both fell silent.

"This is not the moment," Kit said. "Okay?"
Because yet another war machine was now coming
toward them, and in the distance Kit could see yet
another. "Brute force and random wizardries aren't
gonna solve this! We have to do this by the book. Lit-
erally." He pulled out his manual, looking up nervously at the machines approaching.

"Which book?"

"The one they came from," Kit said, starting to
flip through his manual. "So there's only one thing we
can do. Mess around with time."

"What? A timeslide? Have you gone *spare*?"
Ronan shouted, for mind-talk plainly wasn't going to
fool the machines now bearing down on them: they

were already being targeted. "We can't do that! We'd need ten million kinds of authorization —"

"Not for this!" Kit said, frantically hunting the page he needed. "I'm not talking about a slide! This isn't about going backwards! What we want is a local acceleration, *forwards.* Not changing what's going to happen, just making it happen a whole lot faster. There's no way to damage previous causality, so you don't need an authorization —"

Finally he found the page. "How long have you had *this* one under your hat?" Ronan said.

"Found it when I was doing some research a few months ago," Kit said. "I was going to use it to age some metal under Martian conditions to see what kind of remains I'd be looking for from stuff left over from ancient times. But it was all long-duration aging. Didn't occur to me it might be useful for this until you and the Squirt here reminded me." He glanced at Darryl. "'Took a few weeks in the original?' It won't take anything like that this time!"

Kit reached into his manual page and pulled the spell template out of it, a long elastic ellipse which he dropped to the dusty ground in front of them. "Hurry up, get in here," he said, stepping into the center of it. "Stick your personal info into the empty circles! There — and there —"

Darryl and Ronan both jumped into the interior ellipse and got to work inserting their personal information into the vacant templates in the spell circle. "This'll keep the altered flow clear of us," Kit said, watching the machines as they slowly stalked toward them, howling. "Now all we have to do is wait for them to get close enough —"

Darryl had his eye on the war machines. "Uh, your Kitness — just how close is close?"

"This is gonna take a lot of energy," Kit said. "Can't kick the outer circle out too far. But once they're inside, we'll be good. They've been breathing the same air we have, and *we've* been breathing out lots of lovely germs and viruses —"

The secondary circle laid itself out as Kit spoke, maybe a few hundred yards distant all around them, glowing against the ground. "Is this safe?" Ronan said, sounding nervous. "If something slips and our personal space-time gets deranged somehow because these things stumble into the circle —"

"We'll be fine!" Kit said. "The spell puts a stasis on everything in the area but the 'forward arrow' of time itself —"

"You sure physics lets you do that?" Darryl said, sounding twitchy, too.

"The manual says so," Kit said, glancing up at the war machines, which were now unsettlingly close, "and I think so does Stephen Hawking. That's good enough for me —"

He ran down the manual page and found the words he needed to recite. "You two ready?" Kit said. "Dar, better grab hold of us. The spell won't mind, and if we do have to jump —"

Darryl reached out to Ronan and Kit, grabbed one shoulder of each. "All set —"

The war machines lowered over them, stepping

into the outer circle. Their long necks reached down. As Kit began to read in the Speech, fire spat from the two terrible eyes —

— slowed in midair, slid to a halt, and hung there right above them, frozen in place.

The machines froze, too, held still by the spell. All around them, kicked-up dust in the air was holding its position: smoke, billowing from where the machines had burned trees or buildings while heading toward Kit and Darryl and Ronan, lay unmoving on the air as if painted there. Inside the shell of space around the war machines, though, Kit could feel time speeding up, faster and faster: could hear its rising whine inside his head, scaling up, nearly unbearable, as the spell circle inevitably passed back to him the neural side effects of the abuse he was inflicting on the time trapped inside the circle. All Kit could do was finish reading, squeeze his eyes shut, and try to bear up under the screech of pain of the space itself, miserable at having to endure being pushed into the future faster than the normally mandated one second per second —

The spell ran out: the circle went dark. Dust started to move again; smoke started to drift. "That way," Kit said to Darryl, *"quick!!"*

The world blacked out, went bright again as the war machines' beams hit the ground where they had all been standing until a moment ago. But then, slowly, one of the machines started to sag forward, the other one sideways toward them —

They scattered as the machines fell with a tremendous crash — one of them onto a frame house nearby, a second right onto the hapless Grover's Mill Company building, which flew up in a little storm of timber and roof shingles as the machine crashed into it. Both machines cracked open as they came down, and the smell that poured from them afterward was truly impressive.

The three of them drew together again, breathing hard. "Wow," Ronan said. Kit bent half over, trying to get his breath back: the spell was still taking its toll on him. Around them, though, the New Jersey suburbs were already fading away, leaving the cratered Martian landscape again. Last to go were the shattered war machines, dead from the microorganisms for which their inhabitants were no more prepared on this planet than they would have been on Earth.

"Now *that*," Darryl said, "was great thinking."

"Thank you," Ronan said.

"I meant Kit," Darryl said, as Kit managed to straighten up enough to look around.

"Oh, really. If you remember, he said that I —"

"Some more of the shutting up, please?!" Kit yelled at them. "Because we have another problem now!"

Darryl and Ronan stared at him again. "What? *Spirit*?" Ronan said. "What now? I thought you said you could —"

Kit pointed across the crater, not at *Spirit*. Boiling up out of the sand all around them were what looked like streamers and ribbons of green metal.

Darryl's eyes widened. "Those are the exact same color as —"

"The superegg," Kit said. "Yes, they are. And if they do what the superegg did —"

"Uh-oh," Darryl said.

"You'd better pull out some more wizardries you haven't used yet," Kit said as the ribbons of metal started writhing and knotting together. "Because I don't think you're gonna be able to do your micro-bilocation trick again."

Darryl frowned. "I could try —"

"If it doesn't work," Ronan said, "we're going to find out about that just as something new stomps us flat! So don't bother! We need something else —"

Low shadowy shapes were starting to form all around them, out in the dust and sand, surrounding them in a triple ring. They hurriedly placed themselves back to back. "What about the rover?" Ronan said.

"She can't see this," Darryl said.

"I wish *I* couldn't," Kit muttered as the metallic shapes twined and conjoined into their final shapes, gleaming in the dull sunlight.

"Bloody 'ell," Ronan said, disgusted. "Giant robot scorpions. Why is it always giant robot scorpions?"

Kit rolled his eyes. "You sure they're not alive?" he said to Darryl.

"Not even slightly." Darryl raised his hands and said one quick sentence in the Speech.

Four or five of the nearest scorpions blew up. "Don't let them get near the rover!" Kit shouted to Ronan as the fighting heated up. "We don't have time to spend repairing her right now if something happens!"

"Got that," Ronan said. He threw his bar of light into the air, spinning: as it came down, he caught it by one end and waded into the scorpions, using the dissociator like a sword.

But he wasn't able to cut down more than a few of them. Within a few strokes, his light-rod was simply bouncing off them, and though Darryl threw another destructive bolt at another gaggle of the scorpions, it had no effect. Ronan was backing up, and as he did one of the scorpions got behind him: he tripped over it, went down —

The dome of wizardry over *Spirit* wavered and went down at the same moment. *Oh, no,* Kit thought. *He started holding the wizardry in place by direct intent, from moment to moment!* It was one of a number of ways a wizard could save energy when doing a spell, but it required you to have your attention on it to keep the spell running. *Falling over was one thing too many —*

"Darryl," Kit yelled, "grab him, we're gonna jump!" He turned his back on *Spirit*. *Sorry, baby, we'll brainwash you or something later, but right this minute —*

"But if we fail the test —"

"We won't. We're not jumping that far! We need to get them away from the rover, draw them off —"

"Using what?" Darryl said as he helped Ronan back onto his feet and the three of them backed away from the scorpions now advancing with raised claws.

"Us!" Kit said. "It's us they're attracted to . . ."

Darryl and Ronan exchanged a glance. "Got a point there," Ronan said. "Where'd you have in mind for our heroic last stand?"

"Don't say 'last'!" Darryl said.

Kit pointed. "The far wall of the crater, on the south side. The rover's been there already: even if NASA makes it look back there, it won't see the fine detail of what's going to happen to the rocks. I'll freeze the rotor gear on the camera pod for the next few minutes. That won't raise any red flags back at CalTech — they're always having these little movement glitches."

"Let's go," Ronan said.

Kit pulled his wand out and froze *Spirit's* gear. "Okay," he said to Darryl, "jump us over there —"

Darryl grabbed him and Ronan: things went dark, then late-daylight dim again. Within seconds the scorpions were already boiling up out of the ground around them again, closing in —

Kit pulled out the little spherical wizardry he'd been hoarding and put it down at his feet. Very carefully he said the sixteen words that armed it. "Dar," he said, "wait till the last minute. We need to take them all out."

"I hate this!" Darryl said as the scorpions poured toward them.

"Wouldn't be a big fan myself," Kit said under his breath. "Just hang on . . ."

Ronan's hands were clenching on his light-rod. "Now, yeah?"

"No," Kit said as the scorpions ran closer. The

foremost ones were scissoring their claws together in a way he found really upsetting, but he didn't dare take his eyes off them.

"Now?" Darryl said, twitching. "Come on, your Kitship, how sure do you have to be?"

"Really sure," Kit said. "Put us down on the other side of *Spirit*, okay? About the same distance. No, *not yet!!* Just be ready to —"

"I don't want to look," Ronan groaned.

"Don't," Kit said. "But I'm gonna rag you about it forever if you close your eyes."

Eyes were foremost in Kit's thoughts at the moment: the hard, cold glint of the Martian day on the eyes of the approaching scorpions was unnerving. They were twenty feet away — ten — six —

"Go!" Kit said to Darryl. And as things went dark, he said the word that set the exception grenade off.

When things went bright again, Kit turned to look back the way they had come. Many, many tiny sparkling bits of metal were turning and glittering high in the air, and the ground was completely obscured by a huge cloud of red dust, from which shot more shards and fragments of scorpion every second. And more, and more, as the explosion seemed to go on forever in the light gravity.

Ronan was staring at the results of the detonation of Kit's toy. "Janey mack," he said, "*what* did you make that out of?"

"A pinhead's worth of strange matter," Kit gasped, doubling over as the completed spell finished pulling its energy price out of him. "And three syllables of the Denaturation Fraction."

"*Whoa,*" Darryl said.

"Can we sit down for a moment?" Ronan didn't wait, just picked a nearby boulder. "I have to get my breath . . ."

Kit needed to get his, too, and for a moment couldn't find any and just shook his head. Finally he managed to say, "Can't wait. Got one more problem —"

The other two stared at him: unbelieving in Darryl's case, slightly wounded in Ronan's. "You're really enjoying being the bad-news boy today, aren't you?" Darryl said. "What *now?*"

Kit pointed up into the sky, still gasping.

"What?" Darryl said. "You said there weren't any satellites due —"

Kit pointed at *Spirit,* shaking his head.

Ronan stared at it, then at Kit. "What? What's the problem?"

After another moment or so, Kit was able to straighten up again. "Everything that happened here just now," Kit said, and took a long breath, "everything visible, everything that made a vibration, is being transmitted back to Earth!"

Ronan looked at him in bemusement. "But if there aren't any satellites —"

"You don't get it. When *Spirit* realized it couldn't make contact with either of the satellites, it would've sent a data burst back to Earth directly!"

"Okay," Ronan said, rubbing his eyes. "Let's just mess with the antennas back on Earth or something —"

Kit shook his head. "Won't work. There are three Deep Space Network antennas spaced around the planet, and we'd have to waste time figuring out which one's aimed this way. Our best bet's probably to interfere with the transmission while it's on its way. It takes about fifteen minutes for a signal to get to the DSN from Mars." He looked at Darryl. "If you can jump back to, say, the Moon, and catch the wavefront on the way in, scatter it —?"

"Then it'd just look like there'd been a hole in transmission," Darryl said. "Got it. How big a hole do you need?"

Kit turned to Ronan. "When did this start?"

Ronan cocked an eye at the sky. "About twenty minutes ago?" he said.

"Okay," Kit said, and turned to Darryl. "You can just beat the wavefront back."

Darryl nodded and vanished.

"Now sit down," Ronan said to Kit, "before you fall down!" He glanced around him, plainly not convinced that the excitement was over. "I'll keep an eye on things . . ."

Kit sat down and tried to breathe more easily. It was tough: the grenade spell had not been cheap as wizardries went. "Thanks."

"And that really was smart of you, the speeding-up-time bit," Ronan said in a low voice. "Had to fight with Dar about that: he expects it."

Kit laughed under his breath. "You two should

do standup," he said. "Only thing that's bothering me now —"

Darryl reappeared a few yards away from them, moseyed over to them. "Done," he said. "I caught the whole last fifteen minutes' worth of transmissions and dissolved them to white noise." He sat down on the rock and looked with concern at Kit. "So what were you bothered about?"

"Why Mars is playing back our imageries like this," Kit said. "We need to find out. Because if this is going to keep happening every time a human being shows up on the planet from now on, it's going to have repercussions back on Earth!"

"And not just with NASA or ESA," Darryl said. "Mamvish'll be beyond cranky."

"Forget Mamvish," Kit said. "And even forget Irina —"

"*I* wouldn't," Ronan said.

Kit rolled his eyes at Ronan. "What I'm trying to say is that the *Powers That Be* aren't going to take it kindly if we've made one of the planets in our solar system uninhabitable! Humans may need Mars for something one of these days. And even if we don't, it has a right to be an empty planet at peace! Not one where another species' weird fantasies are playing themselves out all over it every time a living thing sets foot or tentacle or whatever here!"

"May be too late for that now," Darryl said.

"Gee, that never occurred to me — thanks for the helpful comment," Kit said, and looked over at *Spirit*. Very slowly its camera pod was starting to move, a hesitant inch-by-inch rotation toward them. "But as for this test, I think we've passed. We didn't run away from the machines and the scorpions. We stayed here and defended our little buddy."

"So what's the next move?" Ronan said.

"We go on to the next site," Kit said. "Or I do."

Ronan and Darryl looked strangely at him. "What?" said Ronan.

Kit stood up, dusted the usual rusty grit off his pants. "Think about it. Each time, we saw a Mars that one of us brought with him. First time, Darryl's crazy, scary Mars movie. Second time, Ronan's rock-opera Orson Welles war machines. We aced both those scenarios —"

"You mean they just barely didn't kill us," Ronan said.

"Whatever," Kit said. "But I think the trouble was that we overloaded the scenarios that the old buried spells were producing. Each of them was based on one wizard's imagery. But when three wizards responded — or more than three there, for a moment" — and he gave Darryl an amused look — "something went wrong and everything got all hostile. The spells read it as an attack, maybe, instead of a test."

Kit glanced over at *Spirit,* sitting sedate in its crater. "Logically," he said, "the next scenario that comes real should be mine. So let's try it differently this time. I'll do this next jump by myself."

"Whoa, now," Darryl said, "a while ago you were all about us not splitting up!"

"If I can't come up with a new plan when the old one starts looking dumb," Kit said, "I don't think I'll last long in this business." He pulled his wand out of his belt. "Look, you can eavesdrop on me. No problem with that. But let me go investigate this one by myself for just a few minutes. If I need help, believe me, I'll yell for it fast."

Ronan looked at Kit dubiously. "Another hunch?"

Kit thought about that. "Yeah," he said. "Let's see how it goes. If things go okay, you two can follow me in a few minutes."

He pulled out his manual, paged through to the spot where his beam-me-up spell was written down, and added the fourth set of coordinates to which the superegg had sent its signal. It was down near the south pole, at about longitude 240. There was a long, high scarp there, Thyles Rupes, angling northeast to southwest, and around it a scatter of craters named after notable science-fiction people who had worked with Mars: Heinlein, Weinbaum, Campbell. Hutton, the target crater, was west of them.

"Let's go," he said to the manual.

The brief night of an on-planet transit spell fell around him.

And then, suddenly, unexpectedly, *day* —

Hutton was a big crater, something like a hundred kilometers across. Kit had known that its walls wouldn't be visible from where he was planning to come out in the midst of the crater proper. What was visible, and caught him by surprise for a few seconds, was the thick haze lying low all around on the horizon as he turned and took in his surroundings.

"Yeah," Kit said softly. "I should have expected this . . ." For the crater was full of air: not the normal thin and freezing-cold Martian atmosphere, but thicker air, as full of oxygen as Earth's, and no colder than an average spring day. A soft haze overlay the horizon near the crater walls. And near the center of the crater, where he stood —

— lay a city. The center of it bristled with spires that shone in a summer sunlight that would last, unbroken, for some months: for this close to either Martian pole would be midnight-sun country. The high towers of polished metal glinted green, and chief among them, more than a mile high, a tower armored in brilliant metallic scarlet speared up against the rusty-red landscape. Nor was this the desolate red-brown stone and dirt vista of the Mars from which Kit had just jumped. Spread out all around the high city walls were thousands of smaller buildings, metallic and gleaming like the greater ones. Beyond them stretched dark blotches against the ground — some kind of wiry, rugged plant. *Forestry,* Kit thought. And above the landscape, the air was alive with airships darting here and there about their business, glinting when the high pink sun caught them. An uneducated observer might have thought he was looking at a Mars of the future, a terraformed place, especially when they caught sight of the slender streams of liquid water meandering here and there across the rugged countryside.

ne clothes on . . . though calling a few wisps and
fts of something like blue smoke "clothes" might
stretching the point. Kit started wondering whether
e inaccuracy was due to the power running this illu-
on, or some backstage piece of his mind chickening
t on him. But then the thought went out of his head
the girl approaching him got close enough to see his
ce clearly.

Her whole face changed. Her expression had
een merely hopeful before: now it became one of
nalloyed joy. She hurried to him, exerting such per-
ct control over her movements in the light gravity
nat she came to an effortless, bounceless halt right in
ront of Kit, close enough to reach out and take his
and — which she did.

Kit blushed all over. *What* is *this?* said one part of
his mind: while the rest of him, mind and body
ogether, said *Wow, look at her, she's — just* wow . . . *!*
That was when she spoke, in a soft, small voice that
was almost inaudible with astonishment. "You are
here at last!" the girl said. "I cannot believe it. You're
here at last."

She stood there holding Kit's hand as if she never
wanted to let go of it, gazing into his eyes, and put up
her other hand to touch his face.

"Welcome home, my warrior," she said. "Oh,
welcome home!"

But Kit knew the ancient Barsoomian city of
Greater Helium when he saw it — even if no such
place had ever existed. A long while back, it seemed
now, he'd been drawing it in his notebook at school.
Now here it was, no smudgy pencil rendering, but the
city he'd seen in his imagination, his dreams. *I was
right,* Kit thought. *We've each brought our own
favorite Mars with us. The real one, whatever it is, is
underneath what we're seeing.*

*All we have to do is break through . . . if we can.
And can I? This one's tailored to me. Whatever's running these scenarios has been in my head and knows
it's one I won't want to break.*

Kit frowned. Cool as this was, it was only a substitute or stand-in for the truth that underlay it — the
Mars that Kit had been looking for all these months.
That lost history was calling out to him now in this
peculiar idiom, and Kit shivered all over at the sense
of ancient secrecy looming over the scene before him.
It was what Mr. Mack had warned him about: *You'll
want to get into their heads, into their lives, and you
won't be able to get enough of it* . . . Kit gulped with
the excitement of it. *Someone, or something, is using
this to try to tell me something important. So let's find
out what that is.*

He started walking, or rather bouncing, toward the
gates of the city. They were huge slabs of sheer green-
tinged metal, like the city's outer walls and as tall as they
were: even from his starting point, maybe a half mile
away, the gates were impressive. *A hundred feet high?
Maybe higher* — Kit had the Scarlet Tower to judge by,

so he started doing simple fractions in his head as he got closer, passing among the lesser buildings. As he went, tall and handsome red-skinned humanoid people wearing beautifully wrought, art deco–looking ornaments of silver and gold and green — and very little clothing — looked curiously at him. *Let's say a hundred and fifty feet high. Think of the machinery it takes to move those —*

So what?? Darryl said in his head.

"I'm fine," Kit said under his breath as he made his way onto a broad white-paved roadway that led toward the city gates.

And nobody's shooting at you? Ronan said.

"No!" Kit said. "You just want an excuse to start shooting somebody up yourself. Can you just chill for a little and let me see what's going on here?"

It took them a while to get started with the shooting last time . . . Ronan said.

Kit rolled his eyes as he got closer to the gates. "You are genuinely a hopeless case," he said. "Having the One's Champion in your head has taught you all kinds of bad habits! Always looking to pick a fight with somebody —"

Kit paused, then, bouncing in place for a moment in the midst of the wide boulevard. The shining, unbroken expanse of the huge gates before him had suddenly developed a dark seam. *They're opening —*

He headed toward the gates again, picking up the pace. Ahead of him the gates continued to open, revealing an interior at first shadowed by the walls, then glinting in the sunlight that the opening was let-

ting in, so that Kit got a slowly broadeni[ng] the massive bases of the towers inside.

Down at ground level, tiny against t[he] single form slipped out through the wideni[ng] and made its way toward him. It was boun[d] as Kit was, but so gracefully that the motion[?] like a dance. Something dark was wav[ing] behind it. *What* is *that, some kind of veil —*[?]

But as the two of them drew closer Kit realized that what he was seeing was l[ong?] dark hair, rippling as easily as water or smo[ke?] morning breeze and the lighter gravity. Th[e] approaching him was just slightly taller than coppery-skinned like everyone else here, and the same kind of handsome ornaments aroun[d] and wrists and ankles and waist, flashing bli[nding] pink-white where the clear sunlight caught the[m]

She slowed down as she got closer. Kit aware that he was staring . . . and he didn't car[e] was someone who'd also been a drawing in th[e mar]gin of his notebook, and once again this unex[pected] and stunningly fleshed-out reality far surpass[ed] uncertain, much-corrected sketch.

She couldn't have been more than a cou[ple of] years older than he was. Wide, dark eyes; a [heart-] shaped face; long, *long,* slender legs — and besid[e the] gorgeous jewelry, she wasn't wearing a whole lot[. This] is *definitely* not *exactly Edgar Rice Burroughs's [Mars,]* Kit thought, wavering between embarrassment a[nd] slightly hungry fascination, *because she's actually*

Burroughs

NITA APPEARED IN A PUFF of red dust and came down on the ground with a slight jar. She glanced around the stony red landscape, taking it all in; the little *Spirit* rover off to one side, and the still-settling smoke from what appeared to be a recent explosion. *What the heck have they been* doing *here?* she thought. "Kit?"

"You just missed him," said a voice from behind her. She turned. Sitting there on a rock were Ronan and Darryl, looking at her with amusement. Darryl turned to Ronan. "You owe me a fiver," he said.

Ronan rolled his eyes, dug around in his pocket for a moment, and came up with a bill, which he stuffed into Darryl's held-out hand. Darryl accepted it with a smirk, then stared at it as he unrolled it. "Oh, man," Darryl said, annoyed, "this isn't even from *Earth!*"

"So stop whinging," Ronan said, "and go get it

changed!" He gave Nita an ironical look. "You'd think he couldn't even get off the planet, the way he carries on."

Nita gave them a look and stepped away for a moment, as they were plainly in one of those boy moods that involved being as unhelpful as possible. The rover was sitting quietly by itself, for all the world as if it was having a perfectly ordinary day; whatever had been going on around here, it seemed unaffected. "Where'd he go?"

"A crater called Hutton," Ronan said. "About five minutes ago."

"He was okay when we talked to him last," Darryl said.

Nita turned back toward them. "*Was* okay?" she said. "You mean you're not in touch with him now?"

Ronan stood up and dusted himself off. "No," he said. "We've been trying to reach him since just before you turned up."

She stared at them in concern and surprise. "Well, if you can't reach him," Nita said, "why the heck haven't you gone over there to find out what's going on?"

"Because we can't," Ronan said, sounding annoyed. "The site's blocked for transit."

Nita let out a long breath as annoyed as Ronan's. "Dammit," she said, "this keeps happening . . ." And she didn't like the sound of it. "Okay," she said under her breath, "we'll see about that. Bobo?"

But that was when her phone went off, loudly starting to sing "Girls Just Want to Have Fun" from deep in her jeans pocket. "*Now* what?" Nita muttered, pulling the phone out and hitting the "answer" button. "Yeah?"

"Neets?" Carmela's voice said. "I dropped S'reee off in Great South Bay, and I'm back home now. But I find that we have a little situation going on here . . ."

"Here, too," Nita said. "You tell me yours and I'll tell you mine."

"Three words," Carmela said. "Helena's home early."

"Uh-oh," Nita said.

"I've been trying to get through to Kit," Carmela said, "but I can't reach his phone. Neither can Mama or Pop. I tried using the closet to get over there, but it won't let me: keeps blathering about some kind of local limitation. And the Aged Parents are going to throw some kind of non-tasteful fit if he doesn't turn up pretty soon, because we're supposed to be having a big happy family reunion right about now, and we are, as you might say, missing an element. You have any luck reaching him yet?"

"Working on that right now," Nita said. "Give me ten or fifteen minutes."

"Okay," Carmela said. "Just tell him this is not negotiable, and he needs to hurry."

"Gotcha," Nita said. She hung up and stuffed the phone in her pocket, then turned to Darryl and Ronan. "You two coming?" she said.

Darryl jumped up, dusting himself off. "Now, where were we?" Nita said.

You were about to let me do what I do best, Bobo said. *Handle the fiddly stuff for you.*

Nita briefly made a wry face at the concept of wizardry itself wanting her to view it as a laborsaving device. "Okay," she said, "get handling. But what's going on over there? Why's that site blocked?"

The wizardry running over there is personality-keyed, Bobo said after a moment. *It has been built to exclude intrusions until it has run its course.*

"Oh, great," Nita said.

"Problem?" Darryl said.

"Yeah," Nita said. "You might say that. Bobo, do you mind allowing these two to hear you as well? Just so they'll stop staring at me as if I've gone insane."

Ronan and Darryl suddenly acquired extremely innocent expressions. *That's not a problem,* the peridexis said in a pleasant tenor, like that of a very high-end television announcer.

"Good," Nita said. "Bobo, we need to get over there, anyway — check out the ground; see what we can find out about what's going on. Because Kit has business on Earth."

I should be able to inject you three into the space where the wizardry is running, Bobo said. But it sounded dubious.

"I know that tone," Nita said. "Are you suggesting that doing this might be dangerous for Kit?"

I have insufficient data for such a suggestion. But the wizardry running in the vicinity of Hutton crater is already under some strain. There's a possibility that it might fail completely if too much stress is put on it — which attempting to inject you into the structure of the wizardry itself might cause. And should it fail, it is difficult to predict what the effects would be on Kit, as the spell presently running is doing so under a structure cloak.

That made Nita stop and think. Such cloaks were used by wizards who were working spells in a competitive environment — one where they were concerned about other wizards discovering and possibly appropriating parts of their spells. It was not a mode that Earth wizards usually found themselves working in these days; wizardry as practiced on the planet in this day and age was routinely seen as a cooperative effort. But it had not always been this way, and Nita knew that on many other planets it still wasn't so, for various cultural or psychological reasons.

Ronan was frowning. "So even you can't see the details of what the spell is that's working inside the cloak," he said.

No, the peridexis said. And Nita shook her head. "A spell always works," she said. "Even wizardry itself can't stop a spell that's running, or break the rules it's running under." And she got a sly look. "But if we can change the conditions of the area where it's running —"

By simply forcing the issue and presenting the spell with your transit into that area as a fait accompli *could cause the spell to lapse without actually failing. Normally the structure of wizardry itself would not allow such a transit.* And Bobo sounded momentarily smug. *But since I* am *wizardry —*

Darryl was looking confused. "You said that spell was personality-keyed?" he said. "To *Kit?*"

There is another personality named in the key as well, Bobo said. *But I cannot determine anything further about it due to the cloak.*

Nita shook her head. "Don't know what to make of that. We can ask Kit after we get him out of there. Meanwhile" — she grinned — "let's get down there, find out what the rules of the game are — and change 'em. You two ready?"

Ronan and Darryl nodded.

They all vanished.

In front of the gates of the mythical Barsoomian city of Helium, Kit was looking with amazement into the eyes of the girl who was holding his hand.

"Uh," he said, ". . . hi!"

She burst out laughing at him, caught his free hand in her other one, and squeezed them both. The laughter was so delighted and overjoyed that Kit wasn't made at all uncomfortable by it. What threw him, though, was the look in the stranger's eyes. It was absolute certainty, comfortable recognition, and a strange sort of unspoken relief at his presence — a sense that now that he was here, everything would be okay. Kit stood there gazing at her and trying to figure out where he normally saw a look like that. Then he realized: Nita looked at him that way.

But Nita wasn't here . . . and this was somebody Kit had never met.

She was laughing again. "Oh, Khretef," she said, "what's this strange look you're wearing? You'd think you had never stood here before!" But then she paused, looking at him more closely. "Is there something I'm missing? A long time you've been gone, yes, a long journey, but maybe something else needs saying between us?"

Uh — how about 'Who the heck are you and what's going on here?' Kit thought. But aloud he said, "Well, just that I'm on errantry, and I greet you —"

Her eyes didn't leave his: but some of the joy ebbed out of her expression, and Kit found himself very sorry to see it go. "Well, of course," she said, her voice trying hard to keep its certainty, "of course you're a wizard, Khretef; how else could we be here? How else would you have won me? And my father is waiting for you, he'll have no choice now but to admit that you were right! But what's the matter? Has something happened on the way —?"

Kit blinked. This was not at all like being shot at by war machines or rubber-suited spacemen: and as those pretty dark eyes searched his for some clue as to what was wrong with him, Kit started wondering whether he preferred the more impersonal style of interaction with these scenarios. He had to work hard to remember the superegg, to keep reminding himself that what was happening here was a key to what had really happened on Mars in the ancient days — something he had to be as tough in handling as he had been with the metal scorpion-beasts.

"My name's not Khretef," he said finally, trying not to say it in a way that would hurt her. "It's Kit."

She looked actively confused. "Is this some quest name you've taken along the way?" she said softly. "Something wizardly? Of course I don't understand all the things you have to do in your art, not the way my father would —"

"No," Kit said. "It's just my name." He paused: she knew him and there was no way he was going to be able to ask her this without hurting her, so he just said it. "What's yours?"

She took a long breath. All this while her eyes had never left his; now at last they glanced away toward the distant, hazy horizon, as if for a moment she couldn't bear what was happening. But then she steeled herself, looked back at him. She dropped his hands, straightened up, tilted her chin up.

"Perhaps I see," she said. "This is some matter of spelling that you're forbidden to describe to me: forbidden even to hint at. Well enough. It won't be said that Iskard's daughter is less able for the challenge than the warrior-wizard who went out to save us and now returns." And without warning, that smile came back to her face and her eyes: though this time there was a little edge of wry challenge on it, something that said, *When you're finished with this game, I'm going to take it out of your hide!*

She tossed her head, and that wonderful hair rippled lightly around her. "Aurilelde I am," she said, and suddenly she seemed significantly taller than Kit, and unquestionably far more regal. "Iskard Tawan Shamaska is my father: the en-Tawa Shamaska are my people, and this is our city Prevek." She glanced over *some clothes on* ... though calling a few wisps and drifts of something like blue smoke "clothes" might be stretching the point. Kit started wondering whether the inaccuracy was due to the power running this illusion, or some backstage piece of his mind chickening out on him. But then the thought went out of his head as the girl approaching him got close enough to see his face clearly.

Her whole face changed. Her expression had been merely hopeful before: now it became one of unalloyed joy. She hurried to him, exerting such perfect control over her movements in the light gravity that she came to an effortless, bounceless halt right in front of Kit, close enough to reach out and take his hand — which she did.

Kit blushed all over. *What* is *this?* said one part of his mind: while the rest of him, mind and body together, said *Wow, look at her, she's — just* wow ... ! That was when she spoke, in a soft, small voice that was almost inaudible with astonishment. "You are here at last!" the girl said. "I cannot believe it. You're here at last."

She stood there holding Kit's hand as if she never wanted to let go of it, gazing into his eyes, and put up her other hand to touch his face.

"Welcome home, my warrior," she said. "Oh, welcome home!"

ting in, so that Kit got a slowly broadening view of the massive bases of the towers inside.

Down at ground level, tiny against the gates, a single form slipped out through the widening opening and made its way toward him. It was bouncing along as Kit was, but so gracefully that the motion was more like a dance. Something dark was waving along behind it. *What* is *that, some kind of veil —?*

But as the two of them drew closer together, Kit realized that what he was seeing was long, long dark hair, rippling as easily as water or smoke in the morning breeze and the lighter gravity. The figure approaching him was just slightly taller than he was, coppery-skinned like everyone else here, and wearing the same kind of handsome ornaments around throat and wrists and ankles and waist, flashing blindingly pink-white where the clear sunlight caught them —

She slowed down as she got closer. Kit became aware that he was staring . . . and he didn't care. Here was someone who'd also been a drawing in the margin of his notebook, and once again this unexpected and stunningly fleshed-out reality far surpassed the uncertain, much-corrected sketch.

She couldn't have been more than a couple of years older than he was. Wide, dark eyes; a heart-shaped face; long, *long,* slender legs — and besides the gorgeous jewelry, she wasn't wearing a whole lot. *This is definitely* not *exactly Edgar Rice Burroughs's Mars,* Kit thought, wavering between embarrassment and a slightly hungry fascination, *because she's actually got* so he started doing simple fractions in his head as he got closer, passing among the lesser buildings. As he went, tall and handsome red-skinned humanoid people wearing beautifully wrought, art deco–looking ornaments of silver and gold and green — and very little clothing — looked curiously at him. *Let's say a hundred and fifty feet high. Think of the machinery it takes to move those —*

So what?? Darryl said in his head.

"I'm fine," Kit said under his breath as he made his way onto a broad white-paved roadway that led toward the city gates.

And nobody's shooting at you? Ronan said.

"No!" Kit said. "You just want an excuse to start shooting somebody up yourself. Can you just chill for a little and let me see what's going on here?"

It took them a while to get started with the shooting last time . . . Ronan said.

Kit rolled his eyes as he got closer to the gates. "You are genuinely a hopeless case," he said. "Having the One's Champion in your head has taught you all kinds of bad habits! Always looking to pick a fight with somebody —"

Kit paused, then, bouncing in place for a moment in the midst of the wide boulevard. The shining, unbroken expanse of the huge gates before him had suddenly developed a dark seam. *They're opening —*

He headed toward the gates again, picking up the pace. Ahead of him the gates continued to open, revealing an interior at first shadowed by the walls, then glinting in the sunlight that the opening was let-

But Kit knew the ancient Barsoomian city of Greater Helium when he saw it — even if no such place had ever existed. A long while back, it seemed now, he'd been drawing it in his notebook at school. Now here it was, no smudgy pencil rendering, but the city he'd seen in his imagination, his dreams. *I was right*, Kit thought. *We've each brought our own favorite Mars with us. The real one, whatever it is, is underneath what we're seeing.*

All we have to do is break through . . . if we can. And can I? This one's tailored to me. Whatever's running these scenarios has been in my head and knows it's one I won't want to break.

Kit frowned. Cool as this was, it was only a substitute or stand-in for the truth that underlay it — the Mars that Kit had been looking for all these months. That lost history was calling out to him now in this peculiar idiom, and Kit shivered all over at the sense of ancient secrecy looming over the scene before him. It was what Mr. Mack had warned him about: *You'll want to get into their heads, into their lives, and you won't be able to get enough of it . . .* Kit gulped with the excitement of it. *Someone, or something, is using this to try to tell me something important. So let's find out what that is.*

He started walking, or rather bouncing, toward the gates of the city. They were huge slabs of sheer green-tinged metal, like the city's outer walls and as tall as they were: even from his starting point, maybe a half mile away, the gates were impressive. *A hundred feet high? Maybe higher* — Kit had the Scarlet Tower to judge by, her shoulder at the walls and the towers, then back to Kit. "And you," she said, that glint of challenge catching fire in her eye again, "are Khretef Radrahla Eilithen, son of the Ardat Eilittri, whose name is not spoken —" Then she grinned at him. "But Kit we'll call you, since you say that's who you are today."

Kit had to smile back. The difference between this encounter with another Mars and the previous two was getting more pronounced all the time: he had half expected Aurilelde to name herself after a princess of Mars, or rather of Burroughs's Mars, old Barsoom. But the reconstruction seemed not to be going quite that far this time. "Aurilelde," he said.

"Kit," she said. She gave him a level look. "Well, we'll go see my father, since you've returned," she said. "Let's go in. But Father will wonder if we've fallen out, when he sees your face and mine. And so much rides on this. Can you tell me nothing about why you won't avouch your right name?"

Kit was wondering where to go from here: but since he was inside this scenario, and it wasn't trying to kill him, it seemed smartest to play along. "I can't," he said as they turned toward the city gates. "Maybe it would be simplest just to say that there's a lot I don't remember —"

"Well," Aurilelde said, "what would be so different about that?" They passed in through the gates together, and as they did, Aurilelde threw Kit an amused look. "You've been forgetting things since we met. Though perhaps that's not something I'd say in front of my father . . ."

Her expression was still serene enough, but there was a sound to her voice as if Aurilelde was thinking of some old trouble that she didn't want to revive. *Now, what's that about?* Kit thought as they came out into the wide plaza inside the gates. *This is so weird. She really thinks she knows me. Where do I go with this? What's Mars trying to use all this stuff to tell me? Nothing I can do but keep my eyes open, try to pick up on the message, see what the imagery has to tell me —*

Kit craned his neck up to look at the spearing towers and the little bronze-and-gilt airships veering and darting among them. Seen close up, their design looked handsomely retro, with spiky fins and a surprising number of rivets. *Late Marillan,* something whispered in his ear. *The last of the technology to be preserved from the Great Flight. And there will be no more —*

Kit blinked. Aurilelde followed his glance. "Yes, it's busy, isn't it?" she said as they crossed the plaza. "People have been coming in from the lesser cities all morning." She laughed, and for the first time that laughter was uneasy: from the sound of it, Kit thought there was something at the back of her mind that Aurilelde didn't care to be thinking of right now. "Very many thought that someone else would come to the gates first this morning —"

The nervousness in her voice came through much more clearly just then, and as Kit looked over at her, Aurilelde fell silent. The two of them continued across the plaza, and Kit became aware that the two of them were becoming the focus of attention for the many other people there, men and women dressed as

Aurilelde was — *Somewhat dressed!* Kit thought — who watched them pass. Many of those people bowed as Aurilelde and Kit went by, though in some cases those who bowed were wearing slightly dubious expressions, and looked at their neighbors as if unsure what their opinions might be of the two who walked through the middle of it all.

They were making for a high archway across the plaza, one that apparently led into the bottom levels of the Scarlet Tower. Aurilelde, catching Kit's glance at the bowing people of the city, said softly, "The usual doubts. Rorsik's party in the Chambers has been stirring up what trouble it can, though they've suspected that he'd never be able to find the prize you set out to bring us."

He wouldn't have had the courage to find it on his own, anyway, the back of Kit's brain whispered to him. Kit blinked again: but then he realized that this was what he had been half hoping would happen — that the spell itself would clue him in as to what was going on here, what tack he should take. *I wanted it to tell me what was going on. So let's have it,* Kit said silently to the magic. *Who's Rorsik? What's going on here? Are these people the original Martians? And what happened to them? Tell me!*

The archway before them was guarded by men in leather crossbelts and more utilitarian-looking clothing than Kit had seen so far — loincloths of some shimmering metallic material. The guards blocked the way with long, crossed lances that appeared to be tipped with something like diamond. *Not Barsoomian weapons,* Kit thought. *Something else is seeping through the spell's appearance now, the way Aurilelde's name did.*

"Aurilelde —" Kit said as they made for the archway, and the guards there, seeing them, came to attention and pulled the weapons out of their way, raising them to the salute. "What exactly is your father going to be expecting me to do?"

She shot him a slightly surprised look as they entered the Scarlet Tower. "Well, of course you've brought the Nascence —"

Kit didn't say anything for a moment, having been thrown off slightly by the discovery that the metal of the Scarlet Tower was transparent: the Sun falling on its outer surface poured straight through and splashed to the white floor like blood. He paused, seeing that they had stepped into the heart of a great atrium. All around the inner skin of the Tower, platforms and floors reached up for more than three-quarters of a mile, ceasing only in one final floor near the one-mile mark that took the Tower's whole width at that height.

Aurilelde had kept on walking for a moment: now, though, she paused, looking over her shoulder, surprised that he hadn't answered her. "Kit," she said, very quietly, like someone saying a strange word and fearing to be overheard saying it. "The Nascence. You *do* have it, don't you?"

Kit looked at her and felt a sudden terrible wash of embarrassment and fear. "No," he said. "But I know where it is."

Then he blinked again. *I do?*

But the whisper inside Kit's head was coaching him now, and things were starting to come back into focus — slowly, as if he'd been waking up from a long sleep, these last few minutes. It was like that time when he'd been away with the family on vacation, and they'd changed motels three or four nights in a row. The fourth morning he'd awakened and stared at the ceiling, unable to work out where he was or how he'd gotten there. Now once again he'd been seeing everything around him with that same traveler's confusion, uncertain where or when he was —

Aurilelde retraced her steps to him, reached out to him, and took him by the arms. It was an urgent gesture, a frightened one. "If you don't have it," she whispered, "why did you come? You know what they'll do! Rorsik especially! He'll claim forfeiture — he'll say you've proven unable to defend the city from its enemies, to free us to take our rightful place in this world. He'll accuse you of treason — you *know* he's always wanted an excuse to do that! And if my father agrees —"

"He won't." The whisper in his head was certain now. "Rorsik is the only man in the New Lands that your father wants in the Tower even less than he wants me."

Aurilelde's face went pained at that, and she opened her mouth to say something. But then from across the huge interior of the Tower, a crazy, yodeling yelling went up. Aurilelde turned, and so did Kit —

Running at them from one of many doors right

across the atrium came a glinting green shape, many-
legged, claws clacking on the polished floor as it came
howling toward them. Kit saw the two raised pairs of
claws in front, realized what he was seeing, and
snatched the wand out of his belt and got it ready —

Aurilelde grabbed his arm. "Khr — Kit!" she
said. "No, don't —"

But there was no need. One second Kit had
believed himself to be looking at a monster, another
example of the things that had just attacked him. *Just?*
said the voice in his head. Now it seemed a month
ago, a year. And the horrible thing running toward
him was suddenly harmless, even funny, as the hind
claws scrabbled for purchase on the floor, as it hurled
itself toward him. "Takaf!" he said, and started laughing: he couldn't help it. He got down on one knee.

The *sathak* flung itself at him, howling in inane
greeting. Kit shoved the wand back into his belt and
batted the claws away in the usual way. Then he
grabbed the bizarre body, flipped it onto its back, and
started rubbing the soft underbelly plating in all the
right places, while Takaf squirmed and waved his
claws around and made the usual idiot of himself.
Some other part of Kit stared at the strange thing on
the floor, obsessed by a dream-memory of glinting
green claws and deadly, empty metal eyes. But his
waking mind now knew that the cold-hearted mechanical *mav-sathakti* were just imitations of the *sathak*,
the few remaining companion-creatures from the
First World to have survived here: and Takaf was

probably the friendliest, most faithful, and dimmest of them all.

It took some minutes before Takaf had had enough reassurance that his master had returned for him to stop howling his relief and delight to the uttermost heights of the Tower. Then Kit stood up and looked over at Aurilelde, smiling slightly.

"I couldn't go up there without him," he said. "Last time it was the three of us. This time it had to be the three of us again."

Aurilelde looked at him, and a small, relieved smile started to creep across her face. "You are you again," she whispered. "It's truly you, come back as you promised. Even from so far, from so long! You had me frightened there for a while —"

Kit shook his head. "Let's go up," he said. "Let Rorsik bring on anything he likes. When we're together, we can take on anything he's got. Even the Darkness and the Doom —"

Aurilelde shivered. But she took Kit's arm, and they headed across the Tower together to the transit cluster at the heart of the ground floor, with Takaf scuttling along behind.

The centermost pad in the cluster was empty. The three of them stepped on it together, and under them the circle of white stone lifted and began levitating into the Tower space, heading for the topmost floor and the tiny opening in it. "How many of them are up there, do you think?" Kit said.

Aurilelde shook her head. "Hundreds," she said as

they rose upward more and more quickly. "Rorsik has been whispering in a lot of ears that he'd take Father's place if you don't prove his trust in you to be wise. No one dares to be absent: everyone wants to prove they're on the right side when the trouble starts . . ."

Kit swallowed, hearing that. But at the back of his mind, something odd was going on. The stranger-soul, the one who had been looking through his eyes and finding everything so weird and frightening, was now settling itself into a peculiar armed readiness, alert and waiting to see what would happen next. It was ready to intervene. Its heart was a wizard's heart, and it seemed to be saying to him, *I've come up against the Darkness every now and then, and It hasn't done all that well. Let's see what It's got this time —*

The pad of stone was drawing near the upper level now, and the aperture that would admit it was growing bigger and bigger above them. "'Lelde," Kit said, while Takaf stood staring up at the many eyes gazing down at them through the nearing, glassy floor, "are you ready?"

"By myself?" She shivered. "But if you are — then I can be ready with you."

He hugged Aurilelde's arm to his side for a moment, then stood free of her as they ascended through the floor, concentrating on standing straight and tall beside her, trying to match a Daughter's proud dignity with his own. As the pad locked into place, he heard the rustle and mutter of the crowd about them, felt the pressure of the hundreds of eyes on them: the fear, the unease, and in some cases the hate, bizarrely paired with hope. *They hate it that they need an enemy to save them,* Kit thought. *They wish it could be any other way —*

The two of them stepped out onto the ruby floor and headed for the Throne. Takaf came clacking along behind them, glancing nervously from side to side, for he could feel the threat as clearly as the two in front of him. Here, at the top of the Tower, the metal had been altered to let the clear light of day pour in; and under it, alone on that plain red sandstone bench, Iskard sat awaiting them, arrayed in the robes of the Master of the City, with a short lightgoad in his hand.

As they approached, he rose. Kit looked up at him — a man big and tall even for a Shamaska; the red-skinned face cold, set, and chiseled; the dark eyes cold, too. Only on his daughter did those eyes rest with any affection, and even then only for a moment — there were other influences in the room that mattered more. Coming closer, Kit tried to keep his face set, too, trying not to betray any response that might upset what was happening. It had taken Iskard long enough to come to some kind of interior accommodation as regarded the relationship between the Daughter of the Shamaska and the son of the man who would have been the Eilith Master had their ancient rivalry followed the normal course. But no courses were normal anymore, nor could they be until both sides were freed to follow their separate fates in the New World —

They came to a halt before the Throne, and Takaf crouched behind them. "Welcome, young Khretef —"

Kit bowed. Aurilelde stood straight. "The Son of

the Eilitt has returned," she said, "bringing with him news of the prize the Master of the City requires."

"News?" came a harsh voice from the crowd, and within a moment there was movement there, the expected shape forcing itself out into the open.

"My daughter always said you would return," said Iskard, ignoring the interruption. "Many others had given you up for lost, Khretef. When you ventured out into lands filled with the creatures loosed on us by our ancient enemies, we feared you lost forever. Some there were" — and he looked toward the source of the interruption — "who even said you had betrayed us. But the Daughter spoke for you, and Aurilelde has always been wiser than fear: one who's been able to see what others couldn't, a seeress of the Old Light as well as one who sees into the Dark left behind us."

The people gathered around the Throne rustled and muttered approval, some laying fists to chests and bowing in Aurilelde's direction. She smiled at her father, and at the reaction of her people, but the expression had an absent-minded quality to it: it was Kit she was watching.

"She has seen nothing," said the Shamaska man who was now approaching the Throne, "if this child of traitors and murderers has not brought back the Nascence with him! But he has nothing. Otherwise the City would not now still be trapped behind walls that cannot be broken, hemmed in by command of its enemies!"

Kit looked over at the owner of the angry voice

now approaching them. He wore robes that were meant to recall the ones worn by the Master of the City, and he carried a lightgoad like the Master's — through prudently unkindled: the city guards and warriors in the room would not have taken kindly to such a gesture, an overt challenge to the Master's power. For his own part, Kit, now aware that his own clothes had somewhere along the line transformed themselves to a warrior's proper harness, simply touched the firesword hanging at his belt and was reassured to hear the metal speak back to him in his mind as usual. That at least was normal, in this time when nothing else was —

"Rorsik," said Aurilelde's father in a dreadfully level and quiet voice, "be still. Your time to speak will come all too soon, I fear." He turned to Kit. "So, Son of Eilitt: where *is* the Nascence, then?"

"Found, Master of the City," Kit said, "in the green dunes halfway around the planet, where the enemies of Shamask once hid it."

"And you should know, traitor, son of traitors," cried Rorsik, "for it was your people who —"

"Rorsik," said Iskard, and the lightgoad blazed up in his hand.

Rorsik fell silent.

"You have not brought it, however," said Iskard.

"No, Master of the City," Kit said.

The people gathered around muttered in distress.

"Then your life is forfeit," said Rorsik, and his face twisted up in a dreadful smile.

"I can't produce it," said Kit, "because it's been sealed against us. Wizardries greater than ours have been used to render it dormant. It can't be used to free us until the New World's soul is found and mated to it. And this we cannot do without the help of the wizards of the Blue Star."

A mutter of concern went among all those who were gathered to listen. But Rorsik only laughed. "This is *mythology!*" he shouted. "Just more tales of mysterious unknown magics from one who has everything to gain from spinning out his time among you until you actually start to believe his stories. What else would you expect from a child of the other side, one of those who watched the Darkness and the Doom come down on us, and laughed to see it come, and plotted to leave us to die as our world tore itself apart —"

"The wizards are here *now!*" Aurilelde said, and every eye in that great room turned to her. "They've found the Nascence in the dunes; they released its power; they triggered the tests, even the one that called for the manipulation of time. One has even invoked the Kinship upon himself! Soon we'll be able to go among them and show them what we need. Then they'll help us as I foretold, and there'll be peace at last —"

Rorsik laughed again. "We all know why you want peace, Master's Daughter! You and your traitor lover. You will sell us all to the Eilitt and destroy your own people. You are nothing but a tool of the ancient Power that sent the Darkness and the Doom upon us to begin with —"

A growl of anger started to go up from around the room. In the back of Kit's mind, something said, quite clearly, *Uh-oh — here we go! I was wondering when* that *name would come up —*

He shivered at the sudden clarity of that voice, and Aurilelde, almost as if she'd heard something, too, glanced at him, worried. Undeterred by the anger of the crowd, Rorsik was shouting, "We can do nothing to make ourselves safe until the Dark Ones are destroyed — until their cities are dust, and the New World is cleansed of them! Only then can we spread safely through this world, make it our own, and resume our place in the light of the Sun as the First Ones, untroubled, in mastery over our world and our system again! And until the Nascence is ours, and the Dark Ones' cities are revived and wiped out, none of us can be safe —"

Our *worlds and* our *system?* There was something about the phrasing that got the uneasy attention of the stranger-soul at the back of Kit's mind. And something else was happening as well. The hair was standing up on the back of his neck. At his feet, Takaf was hissing, glancing about him with all his eyes, uncertain.

Above them, the sunlight was wavering, looking suddenly strangely faint. Almost everybody standing in that great assemblage under the Tower's peak stared upward, even Iskard and Rorsik. But Aurilelde did not. She turned to Kit.

"It's breaking," she whispered. "It's breaking too soon. There's someone else here —!"

Kit blinked — and suddenly he was Kit again, not Khretef with Kit watching from the background. It was strange, though, that now he could look at Aurilelde and see her as Khretef did. "It's all right," he said. "If it's breaking, I can guess why. My friends have followed me — the other wizards. No, don't be afraid! They're really smart. They can help you! It's what we came for, to help you —"

But Aurilelde was shaking her head, and her expression was frightened. "One of them is here already," she said, gazing up into the sky, then looking nervously around her as if she was expecting something sudden to happen. "You can't stay —"

"It's okay," Kit said, "they're nice guys; you should meet them! One of them in particular is kind of special. Actually, they both are, but I should warn you about this one —"

"I know," Aurilelde said, looking more alarmed by the moment. Her expression began to darken. "That one cannot come here. It would be dangerous — the City's protection will break prematurely. You have to go!"

"Huh?"

"Khretef, listen to me. I don't want you to go but you must!" She was staring around her now in real fright, and Kit started to get frightened himself, besides wanting to calm her down. "If the spell breaks before the right safeguards are in place and there's enough power present to back them up, everything will be ruined. I won't be able to stay. *You* won't be able to stay! Please, Khr — Kit; I'm sorry, Kit; you have to go before anyone else comes. Please *go!*"

"All right," Kit said. "But you have to try to let us help you, and if we can't come here, how're we supposed to —"

"I can't tell you now. Later, later I'll tell you, but this is a bad time, the wrong time!" Aurilelde was looking pale and scared. "It's like it was before — when all the times were bad times, when it went cold and the Darkness was coming. We can't let it come again — not after so long, not after all the time we waited!" She looked like she was about to burst into tears. "Please, Khretef; please go before the spell breaks!"

And now she was actually pushing Kit away, pushing him back toward the pad that had brought them up into the great throne room.

"Okay," Kit said, backing away, "sure, no problem —" He glanced down and noticed that his clothes had shifted back to jeans and shirt and down vest: the sword that had been hanging at his side was a wand stuck in his belt again. And then as he looked at Aurilelde, he saw that her shape was wavering, too, and the long dark hair vanished and came back again, the beautiful face flickered and went smooth and gray, then came back; the eyes went pale, went dark —

Around him, the sunlight went weak; the Tower itself started to waver, to shimmer —

— was gone. Kit fell. Just for a second he had a glimpse of the bare red ground, far far beneath. *Skywalk!* was his first thought, and he felt around in his head with desperate haste for the spell that would make the air go solid under him —

WHAM!

Kit came down on his face much too soon, as if he'd only fallen a few feet. All the same, the impact jarred the breath right out of him. He lay there gasping.

"Whoa," he heard Darryl say. "Kit, you okay?"

Kit groaned and rolled over.

"If he can make *that* noise," said a voice he wasn't expecting, "he's fine."

He opened his eyes. There was a girl looking down at him: dark-haired, but the hair was strangely short. It was odd how much she reminded him of Aurilelde —

He blinked. Nita was looking down at him. Of course it was Nita.

"Where've you been?" she said, reaching down to help him up.

Kit staggered as he got to his feet. "Uh," he said, "in the middle of a *really* strange experience."

"Stranger than what we've *been* having?" Ronan said as Kit looked around him. They were near the edge of Hutton crater, and Kit looked southeastward from the crater's edge to glimpse the edge of the next one over. Then Kit grinned a small crooked grin, for that crater's name was Burroughs.

"You have no idea," Kit said. "Come on and I'll tell you —"

"You'll tell us later," Nita said. "You have to go home."

"What? Why?"

"Helena's back."

For a second the name meant absolutely nothing to him . . . but only for a second. "Oh, no," Kit said. "Better get it over with . . ."

"Like you have a choice," Nita said. "Darryl, can

you do the honors? We can all meet up tonight or something and go over the details of what just happened here."

"Sounds like a plan," Kit thought. But privately it occurred to him, as Darryl laid a hand on his shoulder, that the details might take considerably longer to sort out.

And as he and Ronan and Darryl all vanished, it seemed to Kit that there was somebody else inside his head who was agreeing with him. . . .

Olympus Mons

NITA STOOD THERE looking out across the crater called Hutton. It was late in the sol, and the light here would start failing in a while. But a glow of residual wizardry lay over the whole crater, sheening the surface with a thin skin of greenish light, as if with water.

In the midst of it all, Nita could still glimpse something that wasn't really there anymore. A memory of gleaming towers and spires towered up into the Martian afternoon, the red tower at the heart of it all glancing back light at the setting Sun like a beacon.

She shook her head. Nita didn't know the planet's satellite schedule the way Kit did, but she knew that every inch of its surface got covered sooner or later. "Bobo," she said under her breath, "we'd better stick a shield-spell over this until it fades out. It's going to have to cover a lot of real estate . . ."

For how long? Bobo said.

Nita shook her head. There was no telling how

long this effect might linger: the wizardry that had initially fueled it had surprising staying power. "Maybe a couple of hours?" she said, but it was a guess at best. "Can you get any sense of how much oomph is left in the original spell?"

A fair amount, the peridexis said. *You could parasitize it, if you wanted to.*

"You mean tell the illusion to hide itself?"

Yes. That will save you having to make the energy outlay for the shield yourself. And it'll run the spell down faster.

"I'm all for that," Nita said. "Let's do it."

A moment later the heat-shimmer of the simplest kind of visual shield came alive in the air above the city and spread itself downward toward her in an expanding dome. Seconds later, nothing was visible but a duplication of the rock-tumble and cratery landscape directly beyond the city's limits. "Okay," Nita said under her breath, "that should keep the neighbors from getting too crazy ..." For there were already enough people on Earth who got all overexcited about rock formations that they insisted as seeing as faces and pyramids and whatnot — people who also insisted these "carvings" were proof that the doings of alien civilizations were being covered up by one government or another. *Sometimes I wish wizards could just come out and tell them how hard it's been to find out anything on the subject, even when you're right down here walking around on the planet!*

But that wasn't likely to happen for a long time. Nita glanced around, seeing nothing outside the shield but the usual scatter of reddish stones and sand. "Everything behaving itself at the other spell sites?" she said.

Yes; those wizardries have run their course. Just as well — they were potentially quite dangerous, especially the second one.

Nita blinked as the peridexis showed her a few glimpses of the previous visitations. "Yeah," she said, and shivered: she'd never been wild about the whole war-machine concept.

But certainly elegant in that the wizardries were built with the expectation that each triggering wizard would set the parameters of his own test . . . and then be required to understand the trigger in order to defuse the attack.

Nita stood looking southward for a moment. "Sounds almost like you approve, Bobo . . ."

I can hardly fail to appreciate good workmanship in a spell, that's all, Bobo said, sounding a little hurt.

She snickered a little as she turned, looking southeastward toward Burroughs crater. "Well," Nita said, "maybe it's just as well I wasn't on site when one of those other spells was live. No telling what might have turned up . . ."

She turned back toward were the city was hidden and abruptly realized that something was standing between her and the slight waver of the force field. It was a small red-suited alien creature wearing what looked like oversize white sneakers, white gloves, a green metal tutu, and a shiny green helmet that appeared to have a scrub brush attached to the top of it. Out of a dark and otherwise featureless face, large oval eyes regarded Nita with mild alarm.

"What happened to the kaboom?" the creature said. "There was supposed to be an earth-shattering kaboom!" And he scuttled through the force field and vanished.

Nita just stood there for a second. "Bobo . . . ?!"

Just a flicker of residual spell artifact, Bobo said, unconcerned. *Nothing to worry about.*

Oh yeah? Not sure I want to know what this says about my *relationship with Mars* . . . "Do me a favor?" Nita said as she headed for the force field herself.

Speak, demand: I'll answer.

"If there's a spell against the use of an Illudium Q-36 Explosive Space Modulator, get it ready. Just in case . . ."

Nita stepped through the shield, looking cautiously around her. To her relief, there was no further sign of her own brief Martian moment. But the city was there: a handsome place, futuristic-looking in a charming and retro way — doubtless accurately reflecting Kit's take on the Burroughs Martian books. Nita had read them years previously, but for some reason their vision hadn't really appealed to her. She had too much trouble syncing the writer's ideas about the Martian climate and terrain with what people now knew to be true about the place — and the concept of egg-laying humanoids and green-skinned, multi-armed tusky guys riding ten-legged lizard creatures all over the landscape and shooting at one another with radium guns simply struck her as funny.

He likes it, though, Nita thought. *Just what makes it so interesting for him?* The whole place lay still and quiet now, the wizardry running down. *But . . . I wonder. I should still be able to see what he saw, if I work at it. It's just the recent past, after all, and the imagery was wizardry-based to begin with. I might be able to use the visionary talent a little to patch into it . . .*

It would be like the viewing she'd been doing in the library cavern a while ago, though she would have to power it herself. Nita closed her eyes. *Let's see* —

The proper state of mind took a few minutes to achieve. As she'd been discovering more and more often lately, this kind of vision was usually more about letting go than about staring at something and willing yourself to see the reality behind it. Realities were shy, Nita was discovering. To get a good look at them up close, you had to tempt them out by holding still and letting them get curious about you — the way a nonwizardly person might pique the curiosity of a wild bird by standing still for a long time with an outstretched handful of birdseed.

When she started getting that sense that things outside were becoming curious about her, she opened her eyes and looked around casually. The city was alive now, as Kit had seen it. Little ships were streaking around among the towers, and Nita noted that some of them looked a lot like those she'd seen as part of the exodus from Shamask-Eilith. *Interesting . . .* And then she caught sight of the gates of the city starting to open.

Hmm, she thought. *Let's have a look at that.*

Instantly Nita was down there, standing on the wide white roadway outside the gates. So was Kit — or the Kit of a while ago. And as the gates opened, out came something that Nita hadn't quite been expecting . . .

Would you get a load of that, Nita thought. *A genuine Martian princess. Well, sort of genuine . . .*

Nita walked around them, observing, as Kit and the stranger met. *God,* Nita thought, *she's really pretty. Though did Kit even notice, the way she's dressed? Or not dressed . . .*

Her smile was more wistful than annoyed. There was nothing wrong with Nita's figure: it was average for her age. But she couldn't help but feel scrawny and non-toned next to this interplanetary pinup girl. And the way the princess moved, and the way her hair floated in the air, made Nita feel clumsy and inelegant. *But this isn't about elegance,* Nita thought. *There's something else going on here.*

Specifically — that spell was personality-locked. Whoever designed this piece of work wasn't looking for just anybody. They were looking for Kit.

But why?

Nita watched that beautiful shape come close to Kit, taking his hand, looking into his eyes with real emotion. But as she watched, she caught a glimpse of something else under the red-Martian illusion. Something dark —

Now what the — But the glimpse was gone, and she was looking at the beautiful girl and Kit again.

Nita frowned, then let out a long breath and shut her eyes again. *Don't try to force it,* she thought. Doitsu and the other koi had said it often enough. *Vision comes in its own time. Pushing won't help. But intention will. Be patient: wait. But wait with purpose.*

She stood quiet and waited, thinking of the sun on the water on the koi pond in back of Tom's house: the ripple and the flicker of it, coexisting with what lay under the surface, only hiding what was under there when you looked at it from the wrong angle. There was no rush: what she needed to see wanted to be seen, would be waiting for her when . . .

. . . she opened her eyes again. Standing in front of Kit was a tall, slender young girl, not red-skinned, but gray — as gray as polished stone. Around her head, smooth as a sculpture's, clung and wavered a long rippling cloud of hair that was more like smoke than anything else and was a deep twilight blue. Her clothing did not change, and under its light veiling and the glint of her ornaments, her body merely hinted at female contours without showing the anatomical details that would have been normal for humans on Earth.

So, Nita thought, *this is what the people of the First World made themselves into after they came. This is someone from Shamask-Eilith . . . and now, by location anyway, a Martian.*

The eyes looking into Kit's were pupilless and solid, and their depths were that same vivid dark blue, almost black: but they were expressive — hopeful and, yes, overjoyed, but also frightened. *It's as if who-*

ever lives behind those eyes is scared this can't be true,
Nita thought. *As if she sees something else happening:*
something much worse than this —

For just a second those indigo eyes glanced in
Nita's direction. Then immediately they looked away
again, disturbed and afraid. A sense of déjà vu
promptly caught hold of Nita, disturbing and dissolving the vision — but not before she remembered what
it had reminded her of. That glimpse in the mirror the
other morning: instead of seeing herself, seeing this
stranger, with the strange implication that they were
somehow connected. Somehow the same —

"Bobo," Nita said.

At your command, imperious leader.

Nita began to wonder whether Bobo had been
spending too much data-grab time slumming on
the local nostalgia-TV cable channels. "That name-
development and analysis utility I was using on
Carmela?"

What about it?

"Run it on Kit's welcoming committee. Save the
analysis for me. I'll look at it later."

Running. Power deduction will be deferred until
the end of the run.

"Fine."

Nita scowled as the more accessible illusion of
the Martian princess re-manifested itself — copper-
skinned, doe-eyed, the perfect humanoid alien, physically gorgeous: a genuine fantasy heroine and a teenage
boy's dream. *But younger than she is in the books,* Nita
thought, walking around the Martian princess figure

and Kit as they looked into each other's eyes and spoke words she couldn't hear. *Someone's designed this particular apparition just for Kit. How? And why?*

She stopped, folded her arms, and stood there for a few moments, thinking — and trying hard to think straight and not be thrown off by her own feelings, especially when she had no information to go on. Yet suddenly it came back to Nita what that stone had said to her up on top of Elysium Mons. *No one's been here. Just him, and her. The other one.*

The other one.

Nita scowled. *What's going on between them?* she thought. It wasn't like she was jealous or anything. But she knew Kit . . . and this sudden out-of-nowhere relationship made no sense to her. Also, there was no missing the sexy-looking component to this meeting. It was being used on Kit as some kind of way of getting at him, she was sure.

Nita frowned harder. Though she'd occasionally been curious about it, Kit's fantasy life wasn't her business. But someone else, someone or something associated with the Shamask-Eilith presence here on Mars, was not above exploiting it for its own purposes. And that was worrying Nita.

. . . Especially now that she thought she knew why Mars had so long been associated with war in human thought. Nita knew from her reading in the manual that all living thought was connected — though the connections could take strange twists and turnings through space-time. Whatever the mechanism, some distant whisper of the ancient conflicts obsessing those who fled here from the First World had over the millennia filtered through into the dreams and imaginings of the beings on the next planet over. *We've always known,* Nita thought, *maybe since we started writing things down. Maybe even longer.*

Kit had come here looking for the romance and mystery of lost ancient life, and the possibility of resurrecting it, making contact with it, learning its secrets, helping an empty world find its life again. She wondered what he'd think when he found out that the Martians weren't indigenous, but immigrants. And based on the past behavior of the species that, it now seemed, had lain hidden on Mars for so long — assuming that the history that she and Carmela and S'reee had read or experienced in the cavern was true — the thought of having any close dealings with the Shamaska-Eilitt was making Nita nervous. *To these guys,* Nita thought, *all was fair in war. But what about love?*

She let out a long breath. The information in the Cavern of Writings had been short on details about the personal lives of the Shamaska-Eilitt. *They might be very nice people, for all I know.* But their behavior as a species made her think otherwise.

Still. Nita let out a breath. *It's too soon to judge. And what Kit's been interacting with here is basically a recording: a wizardry set up to talk to someone who triggers it, and then get them to do . . .*

. . . what?

Nita watched Kit and the princess start toward the gates together. *Let's just go have a look . . .* she thought, and started to follow them.

But as she did, the whole scene started to go hazy. *Uh-oh!* she thought. *Bobo, wait, we need to pump some energy into this thing! Shift the payout to me. I don't mind —*

But it was too late. The whole view — city, Kit, princess, and all — faded away to bare Martian landscape in a matter of just a few seconds.

Sorry, Bobo said. *There wasn't time: the illusion's power reserve exhausted itself in something of a rush.*

Nita made a face. *Almost as if somebody didn't want me to see something. No, that's just paranoid...* "Never mind: I can get the details from Kit."

Of course.

"Do you have that persona analysis for me?"

A pause. *Unfortunately, no. The outer spell ran out of power before the full analysis could complete.*

Nita let out an annoyed breath. "Can you keep working on whatever you got before the playback went down?"

Of course. Just note that it may take some time to extrapolate the missing data.

"Go for it."

She turned away and looked toward the Sun. Down low, near the horizon, she could see that little spark of blue-white fire twinkling slightly in the troubled air. "Dust storm coming up," she said under her breath. "Well, I want some lunch, and I can catch up with Kit afterwards. Let's get back . . ."

✳

The Rodriguez household was not exactly in an uproar when he got back, but a sense of disruption was clear when Kit came in the back door. There were suitcases in the back hall and in the kitchen, and voices in the living room, laughing and talking very fast: Kit's mama — the deeper of the two voices, more of a contralto — and Helena's soprano.

Kit swallowed and headed into the living room. His mama was in scrubs, having apparently come from work over her lunch hour. Carmela was there, too, sprawled on the couch. And in the midst of everything, sitting on the floor and going through the contents of another suitcase and dividing them between two piles destined for the laundry, was Helena.

Kit had always considered her as more or less a larger version of Carmela: a little taller, a little longer-faced, with darker, bigger eyes; broader across the shoulders and in the chest, definitely bigger in the hips. But Helena had dropped some weight since she'd gone away in September, which surprised him — and the new haircut, level with her jawline but short in back, left Kit wondering whether Helena had decided that she wanted to look as little like her little sister as possible. Whatever the case, here she was, sitting in the middle of the living room, talking a mile a minute and dominating everything, the way she liked to do. "And I told him that he wasn't going to take me by surprise like that," she was saying to Kit's mama, "and he said to me, 'Oh, really? Well, we'll see how you do on the exam.' And I just laughed at him! I mean, he never —"

Kit leaned over the chair nearest the dining room, and Helena caught the motion: her head turned, and she took him in. "Kit!" she said. "My god, Kit, look at you!"

She jumped up and practically leaped on him to hug him. Then she held him away from her. "You are *six inches taller!*"

"Seven," Kit said. "I'm making up for lost time."

She laughed and mussed his hair, then let him go and collapsed into the middle of the floor again. Kit tried to put his hair in order without making too much of an issue out of it, as there were few things he hated more than this particular gesture of sisterly affection. "How've you been doing?" Helena said. "You done with school yet?"

"On Tuesday."

"That's so great!" Helena said. And she glanced around. "Hey, where's —" Then she stopped herself, and her face fell. "Oh, I am so sorry," she said. "I was going to ask you where Ponch was."

"It's okay," Kit said.

"I'm so sorry about him," Helena said, the laundry she was sorting momentarily forgotten in her hands. "It's like he was here forever. It's so weird with him gone . . ."

"I know," Kit said. His mother hadn't given Helena all the details, simply telling her that Ponch had "been in an accident," which was true as far as it went.

"How are you doing?" Helena looked into his eyes as if that would be enough to tell her what she wanted to know.

Kit flashed briefly on the princess's eyes, then

turned his mind purposefully away from that subject. "I'm okay. Getting ready to kick back a little over the summertime."

"Yeah . . ." Helena said, and paused, as if there was something else she could have said but was having second thoughts about. "So am I. You heard about the craziness, I guess . . ."

"'Mela told me a little."

Helena sighed. "Yeah," she said, "so much for my poor broken heart." But to Kit it didn't sound all that broken. "Back to playing the field."

"Shouldn't be a problem," Carmela said, "considering the twelve million phone calls you've had this morning . . ."

"Oh, you know how it is," Helena said. "Everybody wants to be in touch all of a sudden when they hear you've been dumped! It's nice of them, but they're all 'Oh, my god, why aren't you crushed?' And I just have to keep saying, 'It's all right; I saw it coming; it's not like I've been run over by a truck! There are a million other fish in the sea, yada yada yada . . .'"

Kit's mama glanced at him with a resigned expression as Helena kept talking. There had been some joking in the family when mama had complained about the house getting "too quiet" when Helena went off to school. *It's not that 'Mela's not talkative,* Kit thought. *But at least when she talks, she says something . . .*

"Let me get rid of these before they pile up," Kit's mama said, coming into the middle of the room to pick up some of the laundry. "You want me to start these up?"

"Sure, mama. *On delicate!*" Helena shouted after her as she left the room.

"Delicate, sure . . ."

"You ever do any laundry at school?" Kit said. "Or have you been saving it up till you got back?"

Helena sniffed, that specific sound of scorn that made Kit realize suddenly how long it had been since he'd heard it. "Huh," Helena said, amused. She craned her neck, looking up and past him, hearing the sound of Kit's mama going downstairs to put the laundry in the washer.

"Look," she said, in a lower tone. "While you're here, there's just something I wanted to clear up."

Kit swung around and sat down in the chair he'd been leaning on. He thought he knew what was coming and was now wondering whether it would be smarter to just cut and run. But this was his sister, not some monster from another world. *Theoretically . . .*

"When I was home last, I was giving you a hard time about, you know . . ." Helena winced. "The weird things you were doing."

Kit wasn't sure where she was going with this and didn't want to accidentally help her in the wrong direction. "And?"

"Well." She straightened up, let go of the present piece of laundry, and sat there with her hands clasped in her lap, staring down at them as if they were unusually interesting. "For a while, before I went off to school, I was really worried about you, Kit. Seriously worried. I thought you were . . . you know."

The Spawn of Satan? Kit thought. *In league with*

the Forces of Darkness? But he said nothing out loud. If Helena was finally seeing sense, he wasn't going to derail her.

"But I spent a while thinking about it, and finally I started to understand. I can't believe it took me as long as it did, but you know how it can be, you hit something that you can't really get to grips with, and you back away and dance all around it . . . till you realize that maybe you misunderstood the situation from the very beginning. And once I understood that you weren't doing anything, you know, evil, then it was all right. I just didn't understand. I do now."

And Helena looked at him with an expression of not just understanding, but bizarrely, pity. "Why didn't you just *tell* me that you're a mutant?"

Kit sat perfectly still.

That . . . I'm . . . a what??

He turned slowly to Carmela, who was still sprawled on the couch, though she'd now propped herself up on one elbow to observe the proceedings. "Please tell her I am not a mutant," Kit said, a lot more calmly than he needed to.

Carmela's eyes glittered with mischief. "I don't know," she said. "It *would* explain a lot . . ."

It was more than Kit could bear, as it always had been when his sisters ganged up on him. There was something intrinsically unfair in having *two* of them who were older and more in control than he was. He still had the photo of the time when he was four and they'd all been playing soldiers, and Carmela had stuck a saucepan on his head, telling him it was a helmet. Then Helena had snuck up on them to take the photo, one Kit's mom thought was incredibly cute and refused to get rid of. No one seemed to care that Kit winced every time he saw the thing, and the thought of some friend from school somehow seeing it occasionally kept him up at night. Unfortunately, even with extensive usage of wizardry, he had never been able to locate the negative.

And now here again was one of his sisters trying to perpetrate him with another image that was going to stick for years if he didn't do something now. "I," Kit said, "am *not . . .* a *mutant!!*"

"But you *would* say that, wouldn't you?" Helena said with some compassion as she grabbed an armload of the laundry scattered around her and stood up. "It's all right: I understand now." As she headed out of the room, Helena paused by the chair, looking down at him affectionately, and mussed his hair again. "I can cope with you being a mutant," Helena said. "Actually, it's kind of cool. So don't worry: I'll keep your secret."

And she went after their mama. "Mama? Did you start it yet? *Don't start it yet! . . .*"

Kit stood staring after her, openmouthed and fuming. Then he rounded on Carmela. "Are you going to let her get away with that?"

"Are *you?*" Carmela said.

Kit let out a long breath, thinking. Infuriating as Helena's new attitude was, it was possibly preferable to the way she'd been acting when she thought that Kit's wizardry meant he'd sold his soul to the devil. He shook his head. "But it's not *true!*"

"The more you tell her so," Carmela said, "the more she's going to think you're in denial. And she's just going to feel more sorry for you. She might even start worrying again."

Kit rolled his eyes. If worrying were an Olympic event, Helena would have effortlessly qualified for any U.S. team. "You've told her the truth now," Carmela said. "Isn't that enough? Isn't honor satisfied?"

"Yeah, but —"

"Kit," Carmela said. "Let her be. Let her think her life's actually the way she wishes it was. Don't make her follow you places she's just not built to go." His sister's voice was suddenly full of not only disappointment, but a pity entirely different from Helena's.

"But *you're* going to follow me there —?" Kit said.

Carmela raised her eyebrows. "'Follow'?" she said, and grinned. "Like *I* follow people! 'Chase,' maybe." She stretched, then got up off the couch and started picking up more of the scattered laundry.

"Yeah," Kit said quietly. "Okay."

He got up, too, and started helping her, and a few moments later the two of them followed Helena downstairs.

Having spell-transited into the shielded part of her backyard from Mars, Nita came into the house and realized that she was itching all over. *Mars dust!* she thought, trying to brush it off herself, and failing as usual: the stuff was aggressively static-charged due to the dryness up there. *I need to change . . .* She started heading upstairs to her room to do that but was distracted by finding her dad sitting in his lounger in the living room, looking at his phone.

"Lunch hour?" she said to him as she passed.

"Yeah," her dad said. "It's quiet in town today . . . I'm taking an extra half-hour." But he looked distracted and didn't glance up as he spoke.

Nita could guess what he was looking at: Dairine. "What's she up to?" she said, pausing at the bottom of the stairs.

"They're playing around with some kind of artificial sun," her dad said. "She keeps getting in and out of it."

"Yeah," Nita said, "I saw her doing that. It's a simulator."

"Something else weird about this —"

He pointed at the screen. Nita went to look over his shoulder. Her dad was indicating a text window on the little screen. Inside it, text — initially in the Speech, but translating itself on the fly — was rolling downward at considerable speed. She squinted at it. *Don't know what to do about this — oh, wait, now I see — no, that's all wrong. I wish he wouldn't stare like that. I can't concentrate when he's looking at me all the time; don't want him to think I'm not in control here! What was that reading? No, back off —*

"Wow," Nita said. "That's Dairine *thinking*." She smiled slightly. "Streaming consciousness . . ."

Her dad chuckled at the pun. But then he shook his head and put the phone down. "I don't know," he said. "Nita, when you said I might get more information than I wanted? I didn't think that was likely. But now —" Her dad glanced at the phone's screen. "I don't know that this is the kind of thing I want to be seeing, no matter *how* concerned I am about her. I feel like I've been going through her diary. Worse than that."

Nita stepped back behind her dad to lean against the nearby breakfront dresser, attempting to hide the fact that she was blushing red-hot with guilt. There had been a time, years before she'd become a wizard, when after a fight with her sister, Nita had found out where Dairine's diary was hidden. Still furious enough that she didn't care what Dairine or anyone else would think about what she was doing, Nita stole the diary and read it cover to cover. There hadn't been anything in the diary that had been all that interesting . . . which at the time had made Nita even angrier. Understanding that this new anger wasn't at Dairine, but at herself, had taken Nita a while. And then the anger had turned to shame. She could now never think of that horrible episode — hunkered down in the corner of her bedroom before Dairine got home from school, turning the pages of the little pink-plastic-covered Barbie-splashed book — without feeling a hard, hot stab of shame and disgust with herself. And now she was stuck in it again.

But her dad didn't notice. He was staring at the phone. "I had no idea what the inside of her head was like," he said. "I wasn't expecting something that was both so — adult — and so —" He stopped, shook his head. "So, I don't know, *fierce*. And so absolutely focused. I keep thinking, have I just forgotten how it is to be eleven? How immediate everything seems, how life-or-death? Or is it that Dairine's just different? The inside of my brain was never anything like that, as far as I can remember. The only kind of eleven-year-old I've ever been was a boy. Eleven-year-old *girls* —" He shook his head again. "When you're a dad, you see them one way. Your baby daughter. But when I was twelve, if I thought about them at all, I thought maybe they were some other kind of species. They didn't do the things I did, act the way I did. They were a nuisance, mostly. Good for getting me in trouble."

"Who, your sisters?"

Her dad smiled. "Them and their friends," he said. "Funny how you never think about such things when you're older. Like when your aunt Annie fell out of the tree when she was six, and told your grandpa I pushed her."

Nita was still recovering from her own embarrassment, and wasn't able to give this all the attention she would have at some less unnerved moment. "She didn't?"

Her dad laughed, rueful. "She was the one with the Superman towel around her neck, not me! Grandpa was sure I did it, but your Gran made him see reason. Always her specialty."

He sighed, looking back at the phone. "But . . . I don't know. I don't want to be seeing the inside of Dairine's head. That's just wrong. You need to find a way to turn that off."

"I'll have a word with Bobo," Nita said. "He and Spot set it up. They can filter it."

"And I've been seeing how Nelaid is with her," her father said. "He's stern. Maybe better at 'stern' than I am. I might be able to pick up a trick or two from him."

Nita didn't say anything, though inside she felt like smiling. It was not the kind of admission you usually expected to hear from your dad, and was all the more sweet because of it. "Aw, you do good stern!" Nita said. "Don't knock yourself." And she reached around to scratch her back. The Mars dust was getting to her again. *I don't just need to change: I need a shower.*

"I wonder if that's true," her dad said, looking vague for a moment. "I wonder if I've done too much of the wrong kind of stern in the past, and now she's looking for the right kind. Because . . ." He trailed off for a moment, then looked up at Nita again. "Sweetie, she's away *all the time.*"

"But you know why," Nita said. "She's looking for Roshaun."

"And about that," her father said, looking actively troubled now. "There is — let's just say there's a certain age difference between them. I know what you're going to say: he's from another planet, there are cultural differences —"

Nita waved a hand. "Daddy, you're reading too much into it. Sometimes a girl can have a best friend who's a boy."

Her father's eyes dwelt on her, thoughtful. Nita started to sweat, but decided that it was too late to stop now. "Okay, I know what you're thinking. But besides that —"

"And that you're both wizards —"

Nita laughed one helpless laugh at a dad who

could both tease her and be serious at the same time. "Besides that — she's not *like* me."

"Somehow," her father said, "over the years, I've picked up on that."

"And she's never going to be. She's not that much like you or Mom, either. And she doesn't fit any of the family stereotypes. Sometimes it's like she's from another planet —"

There Nita stopped, astonished at what had fallen out of her mouth.

"It is, isn't it?" her dad said.

Though Nita heard what he said, she didn't really have time to react to it, because of the completely bizarre idea suddenly occupying her entire mind.

Did she take a wrong turn?

From a casual conversation with Carl and some follow-up reading in the manual, Nita knew that there were always a certain number of wizards who cropped up on one world and seemed to spend their whole lives yearning for, and dealing with, some other one. The Powers That Be were notably silent on such subjects: privacy issues were a big deal with Them, and They didn't go into detail on what made a wizard uniquely him- or herself. But there was an unspoken understanding among those out on errantry that some wizards who were born in one place but mostly lived and worked in another were meant to be bridge builders . . . or, more simply, to *themselves* be the bridges, with a foothold in each world, bearing a most unusual burden — sometimes consciously. There was an abbreviated word-phrase in the Speech for this kind of profound involvement with another place and people: *taraenshlev'*. It didn't translate well, like many words in the Speech: but there were curious and uncomfortable resonances with English words like *expatriate* and *exile*. "Took a wrong turn" was one shorthand phrase that attempted to express the tension: as if someone originally "supposed" to be born in one place had hung a left instead of a right and wound up somewhere else.

Nita stood up straight, aware that her dad was looking curiously at her. *Kit,* she was thinking. *I never thought about him this way. But I never had reason to.*

Could it be that this is more than just some thing with Mars? Could it be that Mars *has a thing with* him?

And why *in the world . . . ?*

"What?" her dad said.

". . . I don't know," Nita said. "Thinking. Maybe thinking dumb things."

Her dad gave her a dismissive look. "Whatever my daughters do," he said, "and whatever planet they do it on, they do *not* think dumb things." And then he regarded her with concern. "Have you had lunch?"

"No," Nita said. "Gonna have that now. But I need a shower first. Jeez, Dad, when you go to Mars, wear a coat or something, because if you don't the dust gets everywhere!"

"Okay," he said, as she started up the stairs. "So when am I going?"

Nita paused. "Where?"

"To Mars!" He laughed. "What's the point of being a wizard's dad if I don't get some perks out of it?"

"Uh —" She laughed. "I'll set it up. Maybe in the next few days, okay?"

"Fine," her dad said.

And Nita went up the stairs with something itching at her mind that was more than Mars dust.

To Kit, dinner seemed to take forever. It wasn't that he didn't enjoy it — he was starving — and the conversation over dinner had been innocuous, even fun: it only became boring when Helena started telling stories about the now-history boyfriend who'd dumped her.

But even during the more interesting parts of the conversation, Kit had trouble concentrating. The things he'd experienced on Mars today kept coming back to haunt him. And something else was bothering him that seemed to have gotten stronger since he'd come home: a sense of someone whispering in his ear, words he couldn't quite make out against the ongoing conversation.

It wasn't a new sensation. He'd noticed it a few times over the past couple of months. He'd even mentioned it to Nita once, and had then been surprised when she got a panicked look and said, *"Tell me you're not hearing Bobo!"*

He'd been glad to tell her that whatever else was going on, no, he wasn't hearing Bobo. Nita had looked bizarrely relieved. Kit had wondered about that at the time, and wondered again now. *Did she think Bobo was going to start telling me Secret Girl Stuff?*

Now, though, Kit found himself repeatedly straining to hear the voice that seemed to be whispering in reaction to things it heard other people say — or trying to get his attention during the silences. The experience made for a peculiar dinner, and Kit was relieved to get home and back to his room where he could shut the door and relax.

He checked his manual for anything from Nita, but she'd left no notes for him. On inquiring about her location, the listing next to her name merely said, *Sunplace, Wellakh: transport flagged as family business: please do not contact except in emergency.*

Dairine again, Kit thought. *Never mind, I'll catch up with Neets in the morning... I'm bushed.* But he had reason to be. Spending the better part of a day being chased around Mars by various peculiar wildlife, not to mention visiting the ancient city of Helium, could kind of take it out of you.

He wrote Nita a note about getting together to exchange notes after the family got back from church in the morning, and then nervously took a look to see if there was any answer to his previous message from Mamvish. But there was none. He felt strangely relieved. *Okay,* Kit thought. *Either she read what I sent her and it wasn't a big enough deal to get right back to me, or she's really busy and hasn't had time to answer at all. Whatever. I'll check again in the morning.*

He stretched out on his bed and lay looking for a while at the twin discs of the Mars map hanging on the wall. Full with a good dinner, tired, he never really realized when he fell asleep.

What took him by surprise was to find himself sitting in the Scarlet Tower, side by side with

Aurilelde on the red sandstone bench at the center of it all.

"You saved us before," she said. "And then you saved us again. You'll do it a third time now: I see it." She looked at him with a slight smile. "And anyway," she said, "you promised you would — and that you would come back for me. And you always kept your promises."

Kit looked around, somewhat in panic. But they were alone, and Aurilelde's father was nowhere to be seen. As for Aurilelde — as she turned to Kit, he got something of a shock. The Martian princess he had seen was gone. Now he found himself looking at a slender young female figure, still not much older than him or Nita, but all gray; a handsome, polished-steel gray like stone come to life. Her eyes were dark — that much persisted at least from the previous vision. But the hair, the beautiful flowing dark hair, was hair no longer. It was a waist-length flow of deep sapphire-blue smoke. Kit thought for a moment of the filmy draperies she'd worn before and smiled.

She had been watching him with concern. Now, seeing his smile, Aurilelde smiled back. It was altogether like having a statue smile at you — but a vital one, with life in the eyes, and on the smooth features a look of intense life — made still more intense by an edge of fear.

"You've changed," Kit said.

She gave him an amused look. "Of course I had to change. We all changed. We had no choice. The new world wasn't going to suit our old bodies . . ."

Something else was different now: the light. Kit got up from that bench and walked over toward the side of the Tower, where he could get a clearer view of what was outside. It took no more than a few steps for him to realize that the city was no longer sitting in a flatland crater but under a mighty shadow. Looking out through the walls of the Tower, he looked a long way up indeed before he could see the top of the vast shape shutting away that whole side of the sky. The city was sitting on the shoulder of the highest mountain in the Solar System. The wide flat rust-colored cone of Olympus Mons loomed behind the spire of the Scarlet Tower, utterly dwarfing it.

Kit gazed at this in amazement . . . then made his way back to Aurilelde and sat down again. "Maybe you want to start from the beginning," Kit said. "And tell me about this as if I don't know anything. Because I don't —"

She looked at him thoughtfully. "No," she said, "I understand that. A lot of us had trouble remembering, when we woke up from the long sleep —" She shook her head. "It was a hard time. Everyone was afraid. Everyone was horrified, and in grief. Nobody wants to see their planet destroyed . . ." She reached out to his face: then paused. "May I?"

Kit looked at her, perplexed. "May you what?"

"I can't let you see what I see without asking leave first. I may not be a wizard" — and her eyes glinted at him, amused — "but that much I know is the law. The mind is the outer fastness of the soul, and access to another's mind must be requested."

Kit nodded. Aurilelde reached out, simply touched the side of his head, then looked away.

All around them the view of the Tower washed out in a wave of dark. *We lived on the first world for a long time,* Aurilelde said as they looked down on a distant world in Earth's solar system. *We were all alone in this system. That aloneness gave some of us — ideas. And those ideas were possibly fed by the one you know, the one all wizards know — the one who lies in the darkness, waiting.*

The Lone Power.

Yes, Aurilelde said. *Because we were the first ones to come to life in this system, at the bottom of all our lives, and all our joys, there was always a shadow of fear. We knew we would bear the weight of the Dark-ness's enmity: it would come for us and try to destroy us. Even the* Red Rede *spoke of it.*

The Red Rede?

One of my ancestors wrote it, Aurilelde said. Then she laughed. *Or I did! Some people say we're all the same person, the Seers in the Dark. They say we come back, again and again, to get it right — to stop making the mistakes we made the last time. So after our world was destroyed, it was hard to know how that could still happen — how the Darkness might return and attempt to destroy us once more. You'd have thought once would be enough . . .*

Kit saw it as she saw it. Out in the darkness, locking away the stars, the shadow grew. *We could not divert the planet,* Aurilelde said sadly. *All our wizards tried. It was a mighty effort, in which many died. Even then they could only deflect it enough to avoid a direct impact.* Through her vision, Kit saw the rogue planet approach. *And in retrospect,* she said, *there are those who said it might have been wiser if we hadn't — if we'd just let the Doom out of the Darkness end everything, there and then.*

Together, they watched the rogue world come plunging in through the system. Kit was horrified. *You couldn't just sit there and let all your people be doomed!* he said.

But look what happened, said Aurilelde, as the last-ditch forces crafted by the planet's wizards lashed out. Shamask-Eilith shattered; the rogue world's course, perturbed by the forces applied to it by the wizards and by Shamask-Eilith's fragmented mass, now shifted, heading for the inner worlds. A second later, Kit saw it plunging in toward a new world much closer to the Sun, a world where the surface was still molten. As he watched, the rogue planet struck the edge of that new young world, and a vast gout of magma and barely solidified stone splashed outward in its wake as the rogue planet blundered on. Behind it, the Earth shuddered, nearly disintegrated, and then slowly, painfully began to reform itself.

See what we almost did to your world? Aurilelde said. *Because of the blow the rogue planet struck yours, the silicon-based life that had just arisen there was all but wiped out. Life found another way, but —* She sounded sad. *It might have been better if we'd left well enough alone.*

But you couldn't have known that, Kit said. *You were trying to save yourselves!*

She looked at him sadly. *That's what you said the last time,* she said. *You were always the pragmatist.*

Kit looked at her and shook his head. *Aurilelde,* he said, *you can't be sure it was me. I don't remember any of that! Of being — what's-his-name, Khretef —*

I am sure, she said. And she looked at him sadly. *I understand. You've been a long time in your present life; the old one must seem like a dream, if that.* She fell silent. Kit, watching the young Earth slowly coalesce, and watching the splashed-out rock gradually form itself into the Moon, shook his head at himself. *How come I never used the manual to take a look at this moment in time myself?* he wondered. *How come I had to wait for someone else to show it to me?* Considering how much Kit liked the Moon, it seemed like a missed opportunity. But then again, in recent months, Mars had come to occupy the forefront of his mind —

Kit let out a breath, looked over at Aurilelde again. *How come you showed yourself to me that other way first?* he said. *This way is prettier —*

Even as Kit spoke, he was surprised that something like that had come out of his mouth. But it was true. This shape had a fitness about it that the sultry look of the previous Aurilelde had not. She just looked at him, though, and smiled sadly. *It was the way best suited to you right then,* she said. *I knew that as soon as you were ready, you would want to see me as I was again. You were never one for false seemings.* She smiled, again sadly. *When we were ready to settle in the New World, you were the first one to come and tell me that you liked my new form even better than my old one.* And Aurilelde smiled. *Even my father didn't think to do that.*

She sighed, looking at the scattering fragments of the First World as the ships and the two surviving cities, one from Shamask, one from Eilith, fled it. *But there was so much ambivalence about having to change our shape, our way of living. Many of us said that if we changed our form, it would change our minds, the way we thought: we would no longer be the people we were. Others said* — she looked down — *that maybe that would be a good thing. That since our people awakened in the First World, we had done nothing but cause each other grief. And truly, we were never a peaceful species. Some people said that was because we were in the wrong shape: that when we took the new one, things would settle down — we would find the way of life the One had always meant for us.*

She shook her head. *But no one wanted to decide on the new forms right away, so soon after the disaster, and not without careful assessment of which other world in the system would be best for us. The refuge-cities and the ships were built so that all the survivors could sleep for many years, allowing the system to settle after the disaster. For none of us wanted to leave the system: this was our home! We were the First Life here, and we dared not abandon the place.*

Aurilelde looked sorrowful, as if at a memory that still hurt. *The Sun* — *even at this distance, the Sun cried out to us, 'Don't go!' And we couldn't. But there were no other worlds ready. The other solid ones were too close to the Sun, not yet settled out of the molten state. The outer ones were places where not even we could have lived — and our old forms were used to the cold. So our last wizards swept all but the least fragments of Shamask-Eilith into a nullspace portal to ensure that the new inner worlds, our homes to be, would take no harm from them . . .*

Aurilelde shrugged. *And then we slept. A long time, out in the darkness, the ships and the cities slid in long slow orbits far from the Sun, waiting. How many years —* She shook her head. *If I ever knew the actual count,* Aurilelde said, *I've forgotten. But eventually we woke. The city-ships knew, because the wizardry and science built into them told them, that the system was ready for us again. And so we woke, and looked about us. We saw the beginnings of your kind of life on your world —* She looked at Kit with a strange, affectionate expression, almost the way someone might look at a pet, some life form not quite up to your standard. And for a second Kit saw the Earth for a moment as she and her people saw it: a small, new, green world, where the native bipedal life had just begun to look up into the sky and wonder about the little bright lights it saw there and the two great ones. *That looked like a good shape for a life form,* she said, *the one that rose on the surface of your world. And so we thought,* Why not? *And for a while there was discussion about whether we too might settle there. But others looked at the further one — the red one in the next orbit out. It was empty. Water it had, and air it had —*

Kit saw the young Mars as Aurilelde and her people had seen it: a Mars with huge icecaps and half-blue with seas. He gulped in wonder, for the oceans were of much wider expanse than even the most ambitious Earth scientists' theories had yet suggested. *And so we adapted ourselves into bipedal form like yours,* Aurilelde said, *but hardier, tailored to that world's temperatures, ready to make it our own.*

Through her eyes he saw the last two great cities settle onto the Martian surface, a very long way from one another — one near Olympus Mons, even then one of the greatest shield volcanoes ever seen on any planet in this galaxy: the other at the far end of Valles Marineris, then a vast channel being carved out by fierce young rivers running down to the sea, untrammeled by the heavy gravity of a world like Earth, and eroding the ancient sandstones mightily. *There we settled, and there we lived: and for a while it seemed as if everything would go well...*

Aurilelde shook her head sadly. *But then we found that the Darkness and the Doom had other plans for us. Our new home's atmosphere had never been thick. The Sun flared many times over several centuries and stripped much of the red world's air away. And worse, its orbit seemed to be shifting. We feared it would edge out into the great dark again, perhaps even drift too close to the great banded world in the next orbit out and be torn apart by its tidal forces. Our birth system was beginning to look like a trap. We would be forced to move from world to world and never find a home we could depend on —*

Aurilelde looked sadly at the floor of the Throne room. *And so many of our wizards had died,* she said.

There were not enough left to change what was happening to us. Khretef was one of the last great wizards among the Eilitt; my father was one of the last among the Shamaska. Of course, there were some others, from the other city — the ones who disagreed with us . . .

Your enemies, Kit said.

Yes, Aurilelde said. *They offered to work together with us to save our whole species.* She laughed bitterly. *But we didn't trust them: they had tried to betray us before. And they didn't trust us, either, certain that we would do the same to them. Even back in the First World, there had always been voices in the City of the Eilitt calling for us to be stamped out — for the world to be cleansed of us so that our race could begin again, have a fresh start.* She shook her head. *Again and again my father and others from our city came to me, saying, 'See the future for us! Tell us what to do; show us how to find peace, stability, an end to the danger and the death!'* She looked into Kit's eyes, troubled. *But I could never see that. You cannot compel vision . . .*

Kit nodded. He'd heard this often enough from Nita, lately. *So what did you do?*

We feared we would have to sleep again, she said, *as the New World grew colder around us, as the oceans dried and froze and the air fled. We tried to change the world, to preserve the air, the water —* Aurilelde shook her head, suddenly looking miserable. *We could not. Nor could we take the cities out to space again: there was not enough of their motive substance to power them — and where once wizardry alone could've driven them, we no longer had enough wizards. So we buried*

*the cities and greatly against our will we slept again, set-
ting protections about us that would warn us when
someone came to disturb that sleep. Whoever came
would be set tests that would assess whether they had the
skills to wake us in a world that was stable at last.*

She looked proudly at Kit. *And you have the
skills,* she said. *You've proved it. Now is the time.
Break the spell: let us out into the new life! We're
ready! We've been in prison for so long, children of
misfortune, the species that has tried and tried again to
get its start in the right way, and been foiled again and
again by circumstance and the ill will of the Power
that walked behind the Darkness, and waits still to be
our Doom.*

Kit shook his head. *I can't just do that!* he said.
*It's not up to me. I haven't been a wizard very long: I
don't have the authority to take a decision like this
into my own hands!*

Aurilelde looked at him incredulously, took his
hands again, and gripped them. *Your power gives you
the authority!* she said. *That you've come this far, that
you've done this much, says that this is the will of the
One! It's our time to be awakened! You can't deny
us this —*

And she reached up to touch his face again. *Especially not you,* Aurilelde said. *Long ago when you went
into the last danger to try to save our world, you said
to me, 'If worse comes to worst, I'll weave my last
wizardry in such a way that you will be the one to
whom I return. One way or another, you and I will be
the ones to free our people —'*

She shook her head again, turning her face away. *What's the matter?* Kit said.

Aurilelde seemed once again to be fighting back some emotion that ran deeper than tears — if her species could even shed them. *He said to me, 'The Third World seems the most likely to bring forth civilizations, and wizardry. So I will die so that I may return with a foothold in a soul of that world. I'll come to you as a wizard of the Third World and help you awaken the children of the First One.'* And then Aurilelde laughed sorrowfully. *He said to me, 'Don't be afraid! I may look strange and alien to you when I come again, but it will still be me, your Khretef. I'll set you free, and we'll be together again, together the way we were always meant to be . . . but were never able to because the world went wrong . . .'*

She turned away from Kit. *The vision came on me then,* she said, *and I looked forward and saw that it was true: that it was even written in the* Rede, *and I had never realized it before —*

Something came into Kit's head. *'The one departed is the one who returns,'* he said, *'From the straitened circle and the shortened night . . .'*

Then he looked up at her, surprised. *How did I know that?*

Because you are Khretef, Aurilelde said, smiling. *You have come back to me, as you promised . . . and you always keep your promises.*

And Kit sat bolt upright in bed, staring in sudden morning light at the map of Mars . . .

Tharsis Montes

NITA WAS UP EARLY on Sunday morning. She'd gone to Wellakh the previous evening to have a word with Spot, even though Bobo reassured her that he could make the necessary adjustments to Dairine's "brainfeed" without her doing the extra mileage. But she'd also wanted a chance to see firsthand how Dairine was getting along with Nelaid, for she was starting to have a feeling that things were about to get busy at home.

Dairine had been so busy working with the Thahit simulator that she'd barely had time to even look at Nita. When she did, Dairine just sort of frowned absently at her sister as if not sure what the heck she was doing there. Nita found this entirely acceptable, especially when she stepped aside to talk to Nelaid, who was watching from one side of the simulator hall.

"She has reached that point in the study where

the mind starts to catch fire with it," Nelaid said softly to her. "I hadn't hoped to see her in this state quite so soon: it is a good sign, though I will admit it may seem slightly disconcerting to you —"

Nita shook her head. "I get this way sometimes. It's a family thing. Should I tell my dad she might wind up staying here some nights?"

"No need for that, I think," Nelaid said. "I think she will sleep better on her own couch —"

"Bed, we say."

"Her own bed — and your father will be relieved to see her do so. He and I will consult at his leisure as to what to do if she wishes her study to become more intense by virtue of having to travel less."

Nita had nodded and taken herself back home. She'd picked up the note Kit left her late that night and gone happily to bed, grateful that an already busy day had presented her with nothing more challenging. Now, in early light in the quiet of the dining room — for Dairine had once again left very early — Nita was browsing through the Martian section of her manual, surprised to find that there was already a new section about the Cavern of Writings (as the manual was now calling it), and an early Shamaska-Eilitt syllabary. *This is so cool!* she thought, turning the pages and looking over some early diagrams and annotations. And there was also imagery from the Cavern, and a replay of the memory spell that had played out for them there.

It had surprised Nita to learn that the manual didn't have all the answers. *But then,* she thought, *it never claimed to. I just assumed* . . . It turned out, however, that a surprising amount of the information in it came from wizards themselves — as Nita had started discovering during some of her more recent studies, especially just before her mother died, when she had been seeking desperately for ways to save her mom's life. There were many strange sources of power out there, not least among them the manual itself, which kept the secrets of the universe, new and old, structured and updated so that wizards could find them. But the strangest and most unpredictable power might very well be wizards themselves — bending the universe to their will, finding solutions where no one had found them before, driven by their own needs. Wizards were making it up as they went along — just as, in Their own time, the Powers That Be had done. *And they're looking to us for the answers as much as we are to them,* Nita thought. *We're all helping each other out here, trying to make sense of the universe, trying to make things work.* The thought left her feeling both very intimidated and, strangely, much less powerless. *What we write in the manual is as important as what we find there already . . .*

Nita flipped back to the general Mars pages, glancing at the maps that were showing the hot spots in the last day's activity. That side of Mars featured some very striking terrain, and one feature, or set of features, now caught her eye as it had once or twice before. Olympus Mons, of course, was famous, both on Earth and elsewhere among inhabited worlds: as one of the biggest volcanoes anywhere, it drew a fair number of tourists, both Earth-based and alien. But not far from it were three other volcanoes strung along in a line, labeled collectively as Tharsis Montes, the Tharsis Mountains. The features taken all together always reminded Nita of the end-knob of a sword and the sword's hilt or crosspiece.

There ought to be something marking the point, she thought, letting her gaze run along the line of where the blade would be. It led across the Martian equator, missing the vast irregular crevasse of Mariner Valley, then passing through highland country and ending in a huge low-lying circular splat of a basin — some ancient impact crater that had once filled up with lava, and then probably later with water. *Argyre Planitia,* said the label on the map.

Should really have been another volcano, Nita thought. She yawned and flipped back to the messaging area in the manual. Kit's listing there was dark now: he was awake. Nita tapped on his name. "What's going on over there?" she said.

There was a pause before she got an answer back. "Nothing much," Kit said. "Just got up. Gotta go to church . . ."

Nita smiled at that. "I bet. How was Helena?"

There was a short laugh at the other end. "Not as bad as she might have been," he said. "Just as well . . . I couldn't have taken much more excitement yesterday."

"I hear you there," Nita said. "But today's another day. There's a ton of new stuff in the manual."

"Yeah, I saw some of that."

Nita was slightly taken aback at how bored he sounded about it. "So when are you going back?"

"Well, there's church first. I kind of have to do

that to keep Helena calm. Though I may have a different problem with her now."

"Oh? What?"

"She thinks I'm a mutant."

Nita's mouth dropped open. Then she laughed. "Oh, come on, she has to have been joking!"

"Nope."

She got control of herself. "Denial is such a wonderful thing," she said. "Well, never mind. What time's Mamvish getting in? She has to want to have a look at what's been happening."

"I don't know. Haven't heard anything from her."

That made Nita blink. "Huh. Well, she's busy, I guess. But you'll be going over, won't you?"

"Sometime in the afternoon, maybe," Kit said. "I haven't decided yet."

There was something in his tone of voice, even in this disembodied form, that made Nita think Kit either wasn't particularly excited about going to Mars today — which was insane — or wasn't particularly interested in having Nita with him. That by itself wouldn't normally have rung any alarm bells for her. But today was different, in that Nita had seen exactly who Kit had been talking to in the lost city before heading back to Earth with Darryl and Ronan. She was instantly suspicious, and instantly annoyed with herself for feeling suspicious. *It's not me he wants to be seeing,* said that suspicion. *It's her —*

"Okay," Nita said, trying to sound casual. "Well, let me know when you make up your mind. We could save some energy by going together."

"Yeah," Kit said, but he sounded noticeably unenthusiastic. "Look, they're getting ready to head out. I have to go —"

"Sure," Nita said. "Call me later —"

"Right," Kit said: and his name grayed out. *Unavailable* —

Nita felt a small, tight frown forming between her eyebrows. She sat back in her chair, staring at her manual.

This is what I was warning Carmela about, she thought. *Did I get so busy warning her that it didn't occur to me I might be messing up, too? Did I maybe do wrong by going up there at all and horning in on their male-bonding trip?*

It was always possible. Nita swore under her breath. *Are boys another species?* she wondered. *And if they are, why do I have so much trouble figuring out what's going on in their brains? Because I sure don't have this kind of trouble with the other alien species I deal with, and they have all kinds of legs and tentacles and things...* Nita leaned forward again and put her head down on her arms, the frown deepening at the thought of her beautiful rival. *None of this would be bothering me the way it is if it wasn't for* her. *What is going* on *with her? And why's she coming after my* —

There Nita stopped. From what seemed about a thousand years ago came the memory of Dairine's voice: *Nita's got a boyfriend! Nita's got a boyfriend!* At the time it had been an annoyance, like being accused of having a large and unusually noticeable pimple — especially since there had been much more interesting things going on. Now, though, as she'd occasionally done over the last year or so, Nita held the word up against her and looked at it, the way she might have looked at a new skirt she was thinking about buying. *Boyfriend . . . Is it really that bad?*

She tried to consider the word dispassionately. *It's not as if he's not good-looking. Especially since he hit that growth spurt and got so tall.* This in particular had been turning some of the girls' heads at school, as Kit's early stockiness had shaken down into a leaner look. *And he's funny. And smart.* And *he's a wizard.*

Interesting how for a change, instead of coming first, that idea came last. . . . Once again Nita wondered whether the B-word was something she might safely say out loud, one of these days when the moment seemed right. It was a word she'd heard other girls at school use about Kit where Nita was concerned, though some of them meant it mockingly, in the "nerds of a feather flock together" mode. But that thought immediately cast a long shadow of fear across the whole train of thought: the idea that Kit might hear the word . . . *and not agree.* Where would Nita be then? *Everything would be ruined.* Was it worth chucking years of shared wizardry, a partnership that until now had pretty much worked fine, over a word?

She sighed and mentally put the word back on the rack. Then Nita went back to listlessly flipping pages in the manual. Finally she shut the manual and got up, wandering into the kitchen to find herself a banana. *I'll give him a couple of hours,* Nita thought, *and try him again later. There's always the explosive thing that S'reee and I were discussing: she needs some more data on how fast we could dissolve them . . .*

And this she dutifully did, researching seawater chemistry until well after noon, and finding out more than she ever wanted to about the unstable nitrates involved in solid explosives. Then she stuffed her manual into her backpack, let her dad know she was going out, and headed over to Kit's.

The Rodriguezes had not yet returned from church, but Carmela was home: Nita found her and numerous cushions and notebooks strewn all over the living room. "I thought you'd have gone with them!" Nita said, unslinging her backpack.

"No," Carmela said, "I don't always go. Today was all about placating Helena, anyway." She smiled slightly. "I wasn't needed for that."

"They having a special service or something today?" Nita said. "Seems like a long time."

"Oh, no," Carmela said, "church is over. Mama and Pop and Helena are having brunch at the pancake place. Kit ditched brunch: he hates that place."

Nita blinked at that. "So he's been back here?"

"Sure," Carmela said. "You missed him by about an hour. And you'll *never* guess where he's gone!"

Nita rolled her eyes, exasperated. "So much for splitting the energy costs of getting up there today," she said. "I'm starting to think we should install some kind of commuter worldgate in the area. You think you can work out a bulk discount for me with the Crossings?"

Carmela waved her hand, a gesture suggesting that this was no problem at all. "Neets, come on, you didn't push the Crossings management for a tenth of the perks you could have had for getting rid of the aliens there —"

"I was on errantry," Nita said, frowning. "Wizards don't charge for that. I found a problem; I helped solve it."

"Who said anything about charging? You should just have let them be a little more grateful to you." Carmela waggled her eyebrows. "I know for a fact that the Stationmaster would give you at *least* a transit discount for jumps from here to Mars. You wouldn't even need to hub through the Crossings: Mars is right next door by their standards. The power outlay would be minimal. But meantime, don't sweat yourself about it — you need your wizardry for other stuff. *Mi* closet, *su* closet."

"Thanks," Nita said. "Want to set me up? I'll go see him —"

"Unless it's something very Mars-based, don't bother," Carmela said. "He'll be back here at six. He has to: we have a Big-Deal Family Dinner tonight at seven, and we're going out someplace serious, with tablecloths and everything. Besides, I want you to look at something —"

She picked up the remote. Nita looked around, concerned. "Is that smart at the moment?" she said in an undertone. "What if Helena comes back all of a sudden?"

Carmela shrugged. "The question's more like, will she even notice? She hasn't been here all that much since she arrived. She keeps going out with all these friends who keep turning up — I never knew she had so many." And she grinned. "Maybe because she didn't want to invite them over before, when she thought anybody who got involved with Kit might wind up going to hell."

Nita had to snicker at that. "You mean they finally got things sorted out? *This* I have to hear about. He said she thought he was a mutant."

"Yeah, well, I don't know about sorted," Carmela said. "Might still be a few issues. Mutancy being one of them. But I'd say the worst is over. Meanwhile, take a look at this. I've been working on it since we got back."

Nita had half noticed Carmela rubbing her eyes, and now looked at her with some concern. "What?? You slept, right?"

"Huh? Yeah, a little. But this thing was making me crazy. I got up early to take another run at it."

Nita shook her head. "'Mela," she said, "school's out, nearly! Cut yourself some slack!"

"But this isn't school," Carmela said, looking up at Nita, and Nita noticed that there were actually circles under her eyes. "And slack's not what we need right now, is it? My little brother's acting slightly weird, and this has something to do with it . . ."

Nita made a sideways smile — not at Carmela's concern for Kit, which was always there: but for the sudden memory of S'reee saying to her, *Oh, hNii't, middle-aged so soon! You've hit the part of your wizardry where you can't stop working!* — and of what Nelaid had said about Dairine. It hadn't occurred to Nita that something similar might happen to Carmela: falling in love with the serious part of wizardry, as you realized this wasn't anything like a lot of the stuff they gave you to do in school — well-meant busywork that had nothing to do with what your life was going to be about. This was important work, work on reality — stuff you had to get right. And when you first realized that, it was hard to do anything else for a while.

"Okay," Nita said. "Let's see what you've got. But what's been taking you so long with this?"

Carmela made a fake-pouting face. "Oh, Juanita L —"

"Don't say it!" Nita said. Then she grinned. "I'm teasing! You know I'd never rush you. But you were cruising right along there when we were in the library cavern."

"Yeah," Carmela said, "I know." She slumped back among the cushions she'd been lying on. "The wizardry was helping me. Now I'm running slower. Still, something started coming up. You know how it is when you're reading something, and you can see that whoever wrote it has been really picking the words so that you'll feel the way they want you to feel about something? Whether that's the right way or not."

Nita nodded, remembering one morning when one of her English teachers, Mr. Neary, had gone on about this at length. "Loading the adjectives?"

"That's part of it." Carmela scowled at her notebooks, and the TV, and the world in general. "When I was looking at most of the stuff written there — and I've been back a couple of times to check this, just to make sure that the invasion of the giant scorpion guys hadn't messed up how I was seeing things right afterwards — a lot of it was like that. All loaded. 'We are right; they were wrong; they started it; we had no choice!' And that was making me suspicious. But then I found this thing. Stumbled on it, really. It was off by itself with some stuff I couldn't read at all."

Carmela dropped the remote, then flipped through the notepad to the symbols she had copied out there in red ink, and handed the pad to Nita. "This was the only material I could find there that *wasn't* loaded like everything else. It was very — I don't know — very *dry*. Very matter-of-fact. Not like the other stuff, where they want you to think the way they were thinking. It wants you to figure out what it means by yourself." She scowled down at it. "I think it's important. But don't ask me why."

"You have to follow your hunches," Nita said. "And the sooner you figure it out — "

"Believe me," Carmela said, "you'll be the first to know."

"Not Kit?" Nita said.

Carmela gave her an amused, sideways look. "Don't know if he's listening to me at the moment. I gave him some advice yesterday that he might have had trouble taking."

"Oh," Nita said. "Helena . . ."

"Yeah. Anyway, I've got about half of it now," Carmela said, flipping through the notepad's pages. Nita could see that they were completely covered with a combination of blocky or scrawly Shamaska-Eilitt characters, notes in English and the Speech, and the aimless arrow-ended curlicues that she'd previously seen Carmela make all over a page when she was trying to figure something out. But finally Carmela came to one page that had a neat block of the Shamaska characters on it in red ink: and underneath it, also in red, a number of lines in English. She handed the pad to Nita.

She gazed down at what Carmela had written. "It has a meter," Carmela said, "though it's a weird one: real short lines. You can see where I broke them. The rhyme is there most of the time in the original, so I kept it. It's weird, too: they don't rhyme the way we do . . ."

Nita nodded and read.

> *The one departed | is the one who returns*
> *From the straitened circle | and the shortened night,*
> *When the blue star rises | and the water burns:*
> *Then the word long-lost | comes again to light*
> *To be spoke by the watcher | who silent yearns*
> *For the lost one found.*

Carmela fell silent, scowling at the page. Nita looked at her. "And?"

"That's all I've got so far," Carmela said. "There are some weird verbs in the rest that I don't understand yet. This —" She pointed at one line near the end of the Shamaska block. "That's the word for the First World. And there's 'departed' again." She indicated the last line. "But the rest of it I don't get yet." Carmela looked uncharacteristically annoyed.

"You shouldn't be so tough on yourself," Nita said. "This is more than I could ever have gotten out of what we saw . . ."

"Yeah, well." Carmela was frowning. "It's just that . . . this is something important; I know it is." She leaned back among the pillows again, staring at the pad. "You know how everything looked in there? Green, green, green?"

"Yeah —"

"This was all by itself, in red. Completely different from all the other stuff. Even the font looks more serious somehow."

Nita shook her head, uncertain how a font could be serious: but Carmela was much more attuned to that kind of thing than she was, and it was probably smart to take her word for it. She turned her attention back to the verse. "Did you misspell 'straightened' here?"

Carmela shook her head. "Nope. Different word. The Shamaska word means something that's been made narrower or smaller . . ."

"Oh." Nita looked at the rest of the verse. "A smaller circle . . . A shortened night." She let out a breath. "Could that have something to do with Mars's orbit? It's a lot narrower than Shamask-Eilith's would have been."

"Might be. But what's 'the blue star'? And since when does water burn?"

Nita shook her head. "There are a lot of bluish stars that would stand out if you saw them from Mars. Sirius, Rigel, Deneb . . . And water burning? That can happen, when the conditions are right. It did that down by Caryn Peak during the Song of the Twelve: under enough pressure, when the heat's high enough, it doesn't have a choice — it just catches fire."

"Weird," Carmela said. She was still frowning at the pad as Nita handed it back to her. "But I don't think we're gonna be able to make any real sense of this till I get the rest of it figured out."

"Well, do what you can," Nita said. "Meanwhile —"

"You want to go up there?" Carmela said. "I'll set the gate up for you. Take the remote, if you want."

"No, it's okay," Nita said. "You might need it for something. I can come back home with a spell: I've got one on my charm bracelet."

"Fine," Carmela said. "But seriously, next week when school's really finished, let's go up to the Crossings and have Sker'ret do you a favor. It's not like he doesn't want to! It probably just didn't occur to him. He's so used to having unlimited worldgating available that he forgets other people don't have it. Anyway, where do you want me to drop you off?"

Nita thought about that for a moment. In her mind's eye she suddenly saw the map she'd been looking at earlier.

"Argyre Planitia," she said.

"You got it," Carmela said. "Come on."

They headed upstairs.

Fifty million miles away, Kit was sitting out on the vast southwestern shoulder of Olympus Mons, where Aurilelde's city had stood in his dream, staring into the distance and wondering what exactly he was waiting for. From where he sat to the edge of the southern horizon, where the shoulder of the mountain dropped away and out of sight, the fine dust of carbon dioxide snow lay over everything, lightening a vista that normally would have been much darker in the predawn twilight.

He felt strange. For one thing, he'd found it peculiar to come here and not find Aurilelde's city still standing where he'd seen it last. That was impossible, of course: logically Kit knew that. Logically he knew that his dream, and the image he'd seen during the wizardry at Hutton yesterday, were of things that had happened in the deep past. Yet the feeling that they should be happening here and now was something he couldn't get rid of — especially since his presence in those visions had seemed to alter them. There was a sense that the landscape of the present that he had moved through coming here was a thin veil over something far stronger, deeper, more real. All it would take would be the right action, the right words, to sweep the veil aside right across the planet and bring the old Mars alive.

Air it had . . . water it had. Aurilelde's remembered words brought the hair up on the back of Kit's neck. That living Mars, awash with oceans and the promise of life, was the Mars he wanted to see more than anything: and Aurilelde had all but promised that he could see it again. All he had to do was finish the task that had been his, that had been Khretef's, before Aurilelde's people buried their cities on Mars and immersed themselves in their long sleep again, waiting for the help they needed to come from outside.

The only thing that would stop it would be inter- ference from people who didn't understand. Kit was half afraid what he might hear from Mamvish when she finally finished with whatever business was keep- ing her away from here. *She has to see what needs to be done,* Kit thought. *She has to understand!* She was, after all, the Powers' own Species Archivist. Here was a species that had survived incredible adversity, that had archived itself! Now all they needed was some help getting reestablished. *Sure, it'll be tough, when they have a planet next door that doesn't believe in aliens yet, a planet covered with telescopes. But it can be done. The right wizardries, the right implementa- tions of power, and you could have another species liv- ing here right under the noses of all the nonwizardly observers on Earth.*

Misunderstanding, though . . . that was going to be the great enemy. Even Nita, who normally got the sense of what was going on without too much trou- ble, seemed to be having trouble understanding why Kit needed to be let alone to work out what to do up here. *Why was she insisting so hard that she wanted to go with me?* Kit thought. *Unless she saw something —*

Kit sat there wondering about that for a moment. Nita was working very hard, lately, on the visionary specialty that she'd been developing. There were times when she turned to Kit and finished a sentence for him, or described something that was at the back of his mind that he'd meant to tell her about and had then forgotten. *What kind of things is she seeing that she's not telling me about?* he'd wondered before. And now he was wondering about it harder than usual.

What if she *had* seen Aurilelde somehow? Or knew something about her that Kit didn't? There was no way to be sure she hadn't. Trouble was, Nita's visions weren't always right. He'd heard her himself complaining that sometimes they turned up too late to do her any good: or that they emphasized something that turned out not to be all that important later. All it would take would be for her to get some wrong idea about Aurilelde into her head . . . and then there would be trouble.

Better to keep her away from Aurilelde and her issues entirely. 'Lelde had told him candidly enough about what her own fears and hopes were like. And as for Khretef —

Kit let out a long, uncertain breath. There was definitely some connection between them, though he didn't understand how or why. Early this morning, soon after he woke up, he'd started to consider some of the similarities between Khretef's and Aurilelde's life, and his and Nita's. *Two wizards, one a visionary — or getting to be that way — one good with machines. And another pair, one a wizard, good with machines and concrete things, the other one not a wizard, but a visionary, definitely . . .*

Am I what I am because I really am Khretef come back?

He sat there considering that for a while. The manual, as on some other vital subjects, was silent on the subject of reincarnation. There were hints that it could happen under some circumstances, but it seemed to be an elective issue, not necessarily enforced or enforceable. Apparently the One felt you were competent to decide when you were ready to come back, or how long a respite you needed from the business of errantry and life.

It doesn't matter, Kit thought at last. *They're alive, her people. Or waiting to be alive again. But there's something she needs to make it happen, so that they can settle themselves down on Mars and get back to living their lives again. Khretef went to find this thing that Aurilelde needs . . . whatever it was.*

And died —

Kit hunched forward on his stone again, thinking about that, scuffing with one foot at the snow lying at his feet. There had been no mistaking the word she'd been using; Aurilelde's language was one that came through perfectly clearly when you listened to it with a basic knowledge of the Speech —

A breath of cold wind went past Kit's ear, raising the hair on his neck again. *I need to see to this force field,* he thought. *What's going on? Is it leaking a little?*

He pulled out his manual and checked the status on the spell that was managing his air and temperature control. It was fine. Kit sighed, shut the manual, put it down, and ran his hands through his hair, finally hiding his face in them. He let out a breath —

And saw something. Darkness: and in it, a tiny faint light, distant, shining. The light was a deep, vivid blue-violet.

That's it, said the voice in his ear. *The thing that's needed.* And it was his own voice —

Kit shivered, opened his eyes.

Everything was as it should be: the mountain, the snow, the falling night. "This is really creepy . . ." Kit said aloud.

Possibly because you're too hung up on the connotations of the word 'dead,' said the voice in his ear. *You're a wizard! You know other species don't necessarily handle 'dead' the way your species does.*

Kit swallowed. "Okay," he said, "I'll grant you that. But you get to explain how this is happening."

He could feel that the owner of the voice was grinning at him — a strange amusement born of seeing how like itself Kit was. *The whole planet is awash in newly released wizardry now,* it said, *hunting for an outlet or a purpose the way lightning looks for something tall to strike. But you caused that. You broke open the Nascence.*

"The superegg," Kit said.

That's right. You've turned loose a series of events like the series I set free long ago. That was when enemies of Aurilelde's city, the Shamaska City, stole something she and her father needed to master the planet. A tool . . . a weapon. Or a key to both. The Eilitt City stole it, and hid it, and I went to find it. The Nascence held the wizardry that would show the location of what was stolen, and it did reveal that to me. But when I went looking . . .

"You got killed," Kit said.

The voice sighed. *It was kind of unavoidable,* he said. *Our enemies knew me too well. They laid enough traps that sooner or later I was likely to fall afoul of one of them. And eventually I did. But this time, when you set out to complete the task, you have an advantage.*

Kit looked out toward the sunset. "That being?"

Me. I know where the traps are. There's no need for me — for us — to fall into them this time. We can go straight to the place where the Shard is hidden, find it, escape with it, and put it in Aurilelde's hands. After that . . . everything changes.

Kit swallowed. "That's what's needed to make it possible to wake the Martians up?"

If this is Mars, said Khretef, *and we are the Martians . . . then yes.*

Kit hesitated . . . then stood up and got out his wand. "Let's go," he said.

Some four thousand miles away, Nita stood in the basin of Argyre Planitia and looked around her. A phrase that had crossed her mind many times recently in terms of the landscapes of the Solar System now came up for consideration again: *magnificent desolation.*

It was well past midnight, local time: morning would be coming along in a while, but not soon. Snow had fallen here recently, but after that had come a dust storm, and snow and dust had been all whipped up together. Now a combination of powder-fine dry ice and pale gritty dust lay drifted between a foot and two feet deep over everything, glowing faintly with starlight.

Through this pallid emptiness Nita slowly made her way, her force field brushing the dust and snow aside as she passed. *How beautiful this is,* she thought. *But not a place where you'd ever really want to live.*

She breathed out then, annoyed at her Earth-centric viewpoint. In its ancient state, this wilderness had looked like an untouched paradise to the people from Shamask-Eilith when they arrived: close to the sun, better provided with atmosphere at that point — that much the manual had confirmed, suggesting an overactive, younger Sun had later on torn much of a too-light atmosphere away — and flowing with liquid surface water. This spot, for example: the manual had said that a lot of the stone fragments scattered around were sedimentary. *So there were rivers here: maybe even a lake . . .* This place must have seemed energy-rich and hospitable to the Shamaska and Eilitt, especially once they had finished tailoring their new bodies to the world that would be their home.

But then things went wrong for them, Nita thought, stopping and looking out across the pale, rippling dunes of dust and snow. *And after coming such a long way . . .*

We had such high hopes for the new world, she heard a faraway voice saying. *We changed our bodies. We changed our minds. We thought that surely we had now left the old troubles behind and could have peace. And for a while it seemed so. But we couldn't change our souls. And so it turned out that not only were the same old troubles with us, but now they were even worse . . .*

Nita paused, listening as the voice faded away. Her visionary tendencies were taking unusual forms in this environment: normally she saw things rather than hearing them. "Bobo," she said, feeling unnerved, "is this going to get to be a habit?"

It was a moment before she got an answer back. *There is a lot of wizardry loose on this planet at the moment,* he said. *When Kit broke the superegg open, the first effect of the breakage was to send out those signals to the various sites around Mars. But since then, levels of available power — unfocused, unassigned power, which any running wizardry might access — have been slowly rising all over the planet. It's as if the wizards who came with the Shamaska and the Eilitt stored great reservoirs of power in the fabric of the planet itself, ready to be used when that resource was broken open. And now it's welling up. You want to be careful about any wizardry you start under these conditions . . .*

Nita shivered inadvertently. "It'd be like dropping a match in gasoline . . ." she said.

It could be. You must take care.

She started walking on slowly again. "They must have had some really big wizardry in mind," Nita said, "to lay in that much power."

That would seem like a reasonable assessment.

"Great," Nita muttered. "Terraforming, maybe?"

Possibly.

Nita shook her head and walked on. Despite the difference and strangeness of this landscape, that reminded her strongly of the rest of Mars in feeling not just empty, but sad: not just like a deserted house, but like one where all the furniture's been moved out and no one ever intends to live there again. *The other kind of desolation,* Nita thought. *Not just physically empty, but empty of soul.* Maybe that was why she'd never been as keen on Mars as Kit was.

Nostalgia seemed to be part of the appeal for Kit, and for some of the wizards working with him on the greater Martian project: that wistful longing for a time when water ran here and the air had been dense enough for the sky to be really blue. It would never have been a warm place by Earth's standards — its orbit was all wrong for that — but Mars would nonetheless have had a chance to come by its own kind of life eventually. That had all gone wrong, though. Nothing was left but this sad emptiness, this hollowness.

It's the missing kernel, of course. Probably its absence was so much more noticeable now because she was here alone, instead of in the company of Kit and his Mars-team buddies, as she'd often been in the past. Nita stood there considering the bizarre lack all over again, wondering what could have caused it.

When she'd still been desperately trying to find ways to save her mother's life by manipulating her body's kernel, Nita had worked closely with all kinds of kernels, even planetary ones and wizards expert at handling them. A wizard with the right training and enough power could manipulate a world's kernel into doing all kinds of amazing things — offsetting climate change, shifting the planet's interior structure, even changing elements of its orbit if they knew what they were doing. *Which is always the problem,* Nita thought. *You have to be absolutely sure you* do *know what you're doing.* Kernels were so sensitive and risky to work with that there was a whole practice universe equipped with test kernels where you were sent to train before you ever touched a real one.

Nita had never bothered looking into the issue of Mars's kernel herself. Seniors and Planetaries hadn't found it over many years of looking, and she'd had her own projects to think about; but now her curiosity was getting the better of her. Where exactly *was* Mars's kernel? What had happened to it? Kernels didn't just get lost or fall off into space. And no wizard in his or her or its right mind would have considered removing one from where it belonged. The whole structure of the planet could have been deranged. *But maybe it was hidden? Somebody went to a lot of trouble to hide the superegg. And on some planets, wizards do hide kernels to keep them from being tampered with . . .*

Standing in the midst of that snowy, dusty wilderness, Nita got out her manual and paged through it to one prominently bookmarked section, a line of light in the closed pages: the Kernel Tactics and Management section for which she'd been cleared for access months ago. The page that itemized local kernel presences confirmed that no planetary kernel was present anywhere in the areosphere, though there certainly had been one here once. In the distant past, the kernel had even been present right here in Argyre Planitia for a while. *No*

big surprise, Nita thought: unsupervised planetary kernels had a tendency to wander around freely in the
bodies they inhabited. Only if a planet had a resident
wizard operating actively as a Planetary did a kernel
tend to stay in one place, mostly because the wizard
working with it wanted to be able to get his, her, or its
hands, fins, or tentacles on it quickly in an emergency.
But there hasn't been a kernel here for . . . She frowned
as she deciphered the Speech-character suffix after the
number she was looking at. *Half a million years . . .*

Nita shook her head. The manual confirmed that
no other Planetary in the system had interfered with
Mars's kernel. *So where'd it go? What happened to
it?* She looked again at the page for Mars. It showed
the date of the original establishment of the kernel,
shortly after the coalescence of the planet — a date
coordinate with a negative powers-of-ten suffix far,
far bigger than the first one — and after that came a
long, long period of uneventful tenancy during which
Mars's kernel oscillated gently about inside the planet's
bulk in the normal way, until half a million years ago.
And after that — nothing. Nita scanned up the page
again, and after the word *STATUS* there appeared
only the notation: *Indeterminate.*

Nita put her manual away and looked around at
the silent, frigid night in complete bemusement.
"Bobo," she said after a moment, "what the heck does
'indeterminate' mean?"

*It means that the kernel disappeared with no doc-
umented cause,* said the peridexis after a moment.

"How come you don't know where it went?"

The peridexis sounded almost embarrassed now. *I may be wizardry,* it said, *but that doesn't necessarily mean I have access to all the universe's knowledge. And data, or even just the ability to understand it, can be lost over time, as you saw in the Cavern: or misplaced.*

Nita frowned. ". . . Or hidden," she said.

Redacted, yes. Sometimes by the Powers, of course, or those acting for Them —

"And the Lone Power?" Nita said.

There was a longish silence. *It cannot interfere with manual content directly,* the peridexis said. *But it remains one of the Powers, and has enough strength to range about interfering with matter and spirit — out of sight, as it were. At which point the manual will find no data to store or relay.*

Nita was beginning to wonder if what she was starting to think of as the Case of the Purloined Kernel was going to reveal, lurking at the bottom of it, every wizard's oldest adversary. *But why? It doesn't make sense. Right next door to Mars you've got a planet full of nosy wizards. There's much too much chance that one of them would notice . . . even though, all right, none of them did. But they* could *have. And anyway, why* would *the Lone One come sneaking in here and run off with Mars's kernel?*

Nita stood there for some moments, running various scenarios in her head. Finally she stopped. "Bobo," she said, "it's not good for a planet not to have a kernel. They get run down . . . like a house that's not maintained when it's empty. And the matter gets lonely."

It would, yes.

Nita shoved her manual into her otherspace pocket.

"Somebody needs to look into this again," she said. "But first things first. Where's Kit?"

There was a long pause.

Indeterminate . . . said Bobo.

Kit stood there on the shoulder of Olympus Mons and looked out into the falling night. "So listen," he said, glancing around him and wishing there was something to fix his attention on: this talking to the empty air was extremely hard to get used to. "Before I start running around just doing errands for you, I need some questions answered."

That makes sense, his voice said to him.

"What exactly is it we need to do next?" Kit said. "Where do we need to go?" He paused. "And would you please explain why I should be helping you in the first place?! You're trying to take over my mind! Or my life. Or something."

It's nothing to do with taking anything over, Khretef said. *We're the same. I'm you . . . just earlier.* And Kit could feel his shrug.

He couldn't do much but shake his head at that. "Assuming that that's true," Kit said, "there's something really wrong with you being here now. I mean, I'm no expert, but as far as I understood it, one soul should only be in one place at one time. Sure, there are some exceptions —"

You mean like the wizard who was here with you before? Khretef said. *True, he'd be a special case. We had wizards like him once: but ours died.* And Khretef shook his head sadly and sat down on one of the stones of the cavern.

Kit looked around him in alarm at the discovery that they were suddenly underground and that he wasn't talking to empty air anymore, but to someone of the same species as Aurilelde — apparently about his own weight, though taller. Khretef had the same smooth, gray, stony skin, though a shade darker than Aurilelde's, and he was dressed in the harness of metals and silks and leatherlike material that he'd seen on other Shamaska-Eilitt males, with a long, slim sword at his side. Khretef's smoke-hair was much shorter than Aurilelde's, just a film of darkness around the top of his head, like a buzzcut made of haze. Aside from the slight difference in the hair, Kit realized that the being he was looking at really did look a lot like him — or the way he'd look if he'd been born into that species.

"Now, how'd you do that?" Kit said. And then he just had to laugh, if uncomfortably, for Khretef was studying Kit with the same look of uneasy recognition. "And how do you keep pulling these fast ones on me? Not very polite to the new wizard on the block."

"I don't care for it much, either," Khretef said, looking up at Kit with an expression that suggested he really meant it. "But maybe not wasting time is a smart thing, because we don't have a lot to waste right now. Entropy's running. And for me, the time that's running is also running out." He shook his head. "We really should get going, because they're going to be here soon."

"They?" Kit said.

"Can't you hear them?" said Khretef.

Kit held still. Distant, somewhere down deeper in the caves, he could hear the gravel and ratchet of claws on stone. "Don't tell me," he said. "It's more of those scorpion things! What *is* it with those?"

"They're just constructs," Khretef said. "They recall an animal that was once our great companion in the First World, from way back in time. Very few survived the move to this world: they were too bound to the First One. Some of us got an idea that it would be good to build new ones. But they were never quite the same. You saw mine —"

Khretef sounded wistful. Kit looked at him with sudden understanding. "The one in the tower . . . he was your — your dog."

"That's right," Khretef said. "I had him since I was a child. Or he had me. You could never really tell, my mother used to say. He was always underfoot, or under my couch, or just *under*." Khretef sighed. "He made it here, but he didn't last long. Though it wasn't the usual wasting away. He" — Khretef frowned — "he had an accident."

A little chill ran down Kit's back as he remembered how his mama had told Helena that that was what had happened to Ponch: "an accident." The chill got worse a second later as Kit started to hear more clearly those claws-on-stone sounds from somewhere farther down in the caves. "I think we'd better get moving. What exactly is it that we're looking for?"

"Something Aurilelde's father said was vital to his ability to make this world livable for us," Khretef said, getting up. "When we knew we were coming here, we used wizardry and science together to build ourselves new bodies to suit the local environment. But you can only do that so many times. Too many changes, and you're not the species you were anymore." He slipped the sword he was carrying out of his belt, glancing around him in the dark. "So if our species was going to survive here, it'd be the world that had to change. Aurilelde's father was one of the last of our senior wizards who survived the journey, and one of the most powerful: so much so that he became Master of the City after we first came. He used his power to find the Heart of the planet, the Soul Bundle —"

Kit understood that Khretef was using both the Shamaska and Eilitt words for a single word in the Speech: *tevet.* "Mars's kernel," Kit said. "I know about those. My partner works with them —"

Khretef looked at Kit very strangely indeed. "Does he, now?"

"She," Kit said.

Khretef's dark eyes widened. "This is beyond strange," he said softly. "Her, too?"

From down in the darkness came another roar. "We should go," Khretef said. "If we stay here they'll catch us where we won't have any advantage."

Kit nodded and pulled out his antenna-wand.

Khretef snapped his fingers, and a small constellation of wizard-lights sparked to life in the air and drifted ahead of the two of them as they started picking their way downslope across the rough floor of the cave. By the glow of the wizard-lights, he caught a gleam off the surface of Kit's wand. "Noon-forged?" Khretef said.

Kit nodded. "Present from a friend."

"Best kind," Khretef said, hefting the sword. "So was this."

They walked downhill together in a silence that was both companionable and uneasy. "Anyway," Khretef said, "the kernel. Iskard found it, but spies for the City of Eilith discovered where it was being held in the Shamaska City, and their wizards stole it. What they didn't know was Iskard had suspected something like this could happen, and before the kernel was stolen, he'd managed to fragment out a part of its power core. The kernel couldn't be used without the missing fragment: so what the spies and wizards stole was useless. Later, after a great battle between the Cities, the kernel was recovered by Iskard. But even as that was happening, the fragment — the Shard, as Iskard called it — was taken and delivered to the Eilitt by a Shamaska turned traitor. Here they hid it, right under the Shamaska City, to taunt Iskard — for it was so surrounded with deadfalls and wizardly weapons and barriers that no one could reach it alive."

"Booby-trapped," Kit said.

Khretef nodded. "A good word. And as the final mockery, a great wizardry was locked around the Shard itself that would kill any Shamaska who touched it. But they forgot something." Khretef's mouth stretched in his people's version of a grin. "I am not Shamaska."

Kit blinked. "You're not?"

"No. I am Eilitt by birth. My mother was a Co-Chief of the City of Eilith."

"Then how come you're working for their side?"

Khretef gave him a wry look. "Aurilelde," he said. Then he held up his hand for a moment, listening. "Not this way," he said. "A side access instead. Follow me."

He turned and headed toward another opening off to one side of the cavern. "I don't get it, though," Kit said. "If all your people needed to have this happen, and Aurilelde's dad found the planet's kernel and was about to make it happen — why did the Eilitt stop him?"

"They were afraid he secretly intended to destroy the City of Eilith," Khretef said. "And even if he didn't want to do that — which the rulers of the Eilitt didn't believe — they didn't want Iskard to have the kernel. They wanted for themselves the power that would come with control over the planet. They would have preferred both Eilitt and Shamaska to die together rather than suffer the shame and humiliation of being saved by a Shamaska."

Kit shook his head, disgusted. When he had been studying Earth history — and especially during the last month or so, when North Korea had come up in his history unit — he'd found himself hoping that only human beings went so far out of their way to rabidly distrust one another, and to teach their innocent children to do the same. "Nut cases!" he said.

"I hear you," Khretef said, "whatever a nut is."

Together he and Kit paused in the huge opening to another gallery. Khretef glanced from side to side, then up at the huge chandelier-mass of stalactites hanging down from the high ceiling. Kit, looking at them too, shook his head in wonder. "Think of how much water," he said. "And how many years . . ."

Khretef nodded. "Not long now," he said, and led Kit onward through the cavern and downward again.

"Am I right," Kit said, "to say that your two cities have been fighting all the time since you settled here?"

"Oh, yes," Khretef said. "A constant state of — what was the term for it? Armed engagement." Khretef laughed. "Both cities were constantly exchanging diplomats and deputations to try to talk things over, solve our grievances —" He shook his head. "But it was never about that. It was always about finding a new way to stab the other side in the back . . . or finding out what they were *really* up to and then looking for ways to stop it. That was, after all, the way things had always been . . ."

Khretef sighed as they made their way across the cavern, toward another dark exit. "There came a time, after I passed my Ordeal and became a wizard, that my mother decided I should go on one of these deputations. So I went."

Kit got a sudden flash of Khretef's memory of that first trip: and of a moment of astonishment on the way there — of his party being overtaken by a sudden wonder; one of the Martian dust-devils. Again Kit saw the view of the circle of sky far up that whirling tunnel, and now understood his rush of déjà vu. *This* was the connection —"I was ready for it. I knew the Shamaska would all be looking for ways to trick or betray me because I was new and young — trying to turn me into a tool they could use against my own people. I was on my guard. Then I went to the Shamaska City, and —"

He laughed, bitter. "I discovered that the terrible Shamaska, our ancient enemies, were just people like us! It seemed like the worst kind of betrayal. Either I was completely confused, and they were pulling one over on me — or this had always been true, and we were the deluded ones. Like us, the Shamaska were scared of the other side, trying to keep themselves safe, but unsure how to do it when the others were so determined to wipe them out. Watch out where you put your feet here —" The surface underneath them was changing to rough, stony ropes of pillow lava, all crusted with the pale leached minerals of millennia. "Anyway, I kept my mouth shut and went through with my duties in the deputation, and waited for it to be time for us to go home, for I didn't like what I was seeing, and I didn't want to do any more of this work, where it was impossible to ignore how our own leaders had been lying to us. And then, at a function just before I was to return home to Eilith, I met Aurilelde."

As they paused before negotiating another long gallery leading to a third cavern, Khretef's face changed subtly, and even by the now-subdued wizard-light, Kit could see the change. When Khretef looked over at Kit, his uncertain expression suggested that he wasn't sure Kit understood what he was saying. "I thought she was going to be just another of these cold, proud Shamaska I'd spent twenty days meeting: someone who'd be hating me but polite to my face. Then we looked at each other, and there was something different about her. I still don't know what it was. We started talking . . . ."

Khretef glanced around again, then pointed. "Down there. See that opening? That's what we want. — Oh, we were so careful to try to look like nothing different was happening. We knew everyone was watching us. But finally we realized that we liked each other. Aurilelde was interested in meeting a wizard her own age. I was interested in her talents as a Seer: it's a gift that's rare among the Eilitt —"

Kit felt that chill again, thinking of Nita's growing visionary specialty. Khretef shrugged. "I went home, eventually. But soon I told my mother that I wanted to go on the next deputation, that more experience would be good for the son of a Chief of the City. And I went, and Aurilelde and I met again. And again, the next time. After that we kept meeting privately. We were terrified, but we knew we had to find a way to be together that wouldn't be misunderstood."

From ahead of them, from below, Kit heard a subdued roar. "But they misunderstood, anyway," he said, "so you left."

Khretef nodded. "I fled to her city," he said. "My

people declared me a traitor, to be killed on sight. My mother disowned me. And though I'd come over to the Shamaska side, they never trusted me. Rorsik — one of Aurilelde's father's counselors — claimed that the only reason I'd sought refuge in the city was to seek ways to betray the Shamaska to the Eilitt. He claimed I'd seduced the Daughter of the City in order to render her visions friendlier to the Eilitt side. I think possibly Rorsik wanted her for himself, and saw me as a rival." Khretef snorted, a sound so like one that Kit's friend Raoul would make that Kit couldn't help laughing. "He didn't see how she loathed him, the idiot! But even her own people were starting to distrust her because of me. They thought that she was lying about her visions to forward my agenda. We thought they'd understand that we just wanted to be together, but . . ." He shook his head.

Kit frowned. "We have stories like that where I come from," he said, thinking of his last year's long English unit on Shakespeare. "Mostly the star-crossed lovers wind up dead."

Khretef gave him an ironic look. "Well, I did, anyway —" he said.

That was when they heard the huge roar away ahead of them. Kit froze where he was. "We're too alike as it is," he said, "and if it's all the same to you, I'd sooner stop before we get *that* alike!" He shook his antenna-wand, and a reassuring jolt of red fire ran down it, vanished. Its charge was running full. "That really didn't sound like your usual scorpion —"

"No," Khretef said, "they weren't. Down this way —"

They walked a short way along to the entrance to a narrow gallery, like a hallway, leading down into a wider space. There Khretef paused, uneasy. "This is where I got killed the last time . . ." he said.

The hair went up on the back of Kit's neck. "Yeah, about that," Kit said. "If you're dead, how come you aren't in Timeheart?"

"I wasn't finished," Khretef said. "You know how it is sometimes. People hang on, even though there's usually no hope of doing what they've left undone. Usually after a while they move on. But I couldn't leave. So many lives depended on what I'd failed to do — so many futures. My people. Aurilelde's people. Aurilelde . . . I couldn't leave. And when they had to go back into stasis, which they had so much been trying not to do — then even more, I had to stay."

The dread in his voice surprised Kit. "What was the matter with the stasis?"

"There were not enough wizards left, not enough power, to rebuild the spells correctly. The stasis wasn't true dreamless sleep any more, but a half-life full of repetitions and endless dreams without resolution, a journey with no end. The souls of those in stasis were being damaged, their personalities corrupted. Once more we could endure it without being destroyed as a species, Shamaska and Eilitt together. But not again."

Khretef shivered all over with the memory. "So for so many years I waited in this not-life, not-death while they slept, all the time fearing what they were going through would destroy them before help came.

But then, just now, something happened." And he looked at Kit, his eyes alight with an excitement he had plainly been fighting to keep under control. "*You* got here. You cracked open the Nascence. You let loose the wizardry to fuel the awakening of the unfinished past. And you're me. Or a version of me, one rooted in the present and with access to its power. How could I *not* come find you? Now it can all be finished. Now we can remake the world; now the last problem can be solved. And Aurilelde and I can be together . . ."

Kit wasn't so sure about that, but for the time being the subject was better left alone. "Just so we don't wind up repeating past events, you should probably dump the light now," he said softly. "You know the spell for seeing by heat?"

That took Khretef by surprise. "I know the theory," he said. "But it's not something I'd have thought of. In our old bodies, in the cold of the First World, almost any heat would be blinding. Degrees of it didn't seem to be much use —"

"How do you get your spells?" Kit said. "Our species has several methods, but a lot of us read ours from a book or a portable device —" He pulled out his manual, showed it to Khretef.

He peered at it. "How unusual. We call ours the Dark Speaking: we hear it in the silence —"

Kit found the spell, flagged it. "Here," he said.

Khretef stood listening. "Ah," he said. "Not too complex. Let's see —"

Kit, meanwhile, very quietly spoke the Speech-words for the spell. A second later his vision had changed, and he could see Khretef as a Shamaska-shaped light in the darkness. All around him the cavern gallery glowed faintly — more brightly nearer the floor, more dimly up above where the stone was losing heat to the Martian night. "How's that?" he said.

Khretef was looking around him, then down at his arms and the sword he held. "That works very well —"

"And the scorpions are metallic, mostly?" Kit said. "How are they powered?"

"Cold power cells," Khretef said. "They would be far below your ambient temperature or mine."

"We'll be seeing dark blots as we come up with them, then," Kit said. "Can they see in the heat wavelengths?"

"I wouldn't be sure," Khretef said. "I never had one of the substitutes: I much preferred the real creatures."

They walked on cautiously together. "Yeah," Kit said. "I saw your guy. I could see why you'd prefer the real thing —"

He stopped still as Khretef held out the hand with the sword, a gesture of alarm. *Silence would probably be better than speech now,* Khretef said. *They're in the next chamber. Though they're expecting us to come in through another entrance, we'll have little time to deal with them.*

They can't hear thought, though?

No. That only the original creatures could manage, and not always.

Good. Kit looked up ahead toward the glow of

warmth that came from the archway before them. *Warmer . . . Does the ground drop off in there?*

There's a deep pit. The Shard is down at the bottom of it, protected by the final spell-shield, the one proof against any Shamaska.

Kit thought. *Okay,* he said. *Are these like the ones up on the surface? Do they learn from past experience?*

They do. That's what killed me. It was a development I hadn't been expecting, and when I used the fire-sword the second time, it was ineffective. It should only have taken a second to bring up another spell, but in that second —

He went silent. Kit could feel him wincing from the memory. *Right,* Kit said. *I think I have something useful.*

He reached out beside him, opened his otherspace pocket, and felt around in it, bringing out a device that Khretef looked at curiously: a smooth metal rod about a foot and a half long, with what looked like white ceramic striping down the side of it, a half-sheath of more ceramic down its length, and a thick handle with various controls. Kit touched one of the controls. At the butt end of the device, a tiny blue light came on.

What is it? Khretef said.

Something never used on this planet before, Kit said. *Should take them by surprise. Come on.*

Silently they made their way down the length of the gallery, toward the glow of heat. *Tell me something,* Kit said. *When you got here from the First*

World, did you find any signs of any species having been here before you?

None, said Khretef. *There was no evidence of any life more advanced than simple one-celled or multi-celled organisms.*

Kit sighed. *Pity,* he said.

As they drew near to the entrance to the next chamber, Khretef held up the sword in warning again, then waved Kit to one side of the narrow gallery and flattened himself against the other. Together they inched toward the entrance, peered through.

Beyond the archway, a crowd of green metal scorpions was moving about a near-circular cave, almost obscuring the floor except in one spot — the center, where the circular pit Khretef had mentioned fell sheerly away. Kit looked the situation over. *Nasty,* he said. *Fight them and they take you down before you're anywhere near the Shard. Try to avoid them by jumping into the pit, and they all just pile on top of you.*

Khretef nodded. *Fortunately there is no need to take them all on.* He pointed at the largest one, the scorpion that Kit had earlier heard roaring and that let out another uneasy roar even as they watched. *They're all linked,* he said. *It handles their processing. Take out that largest one, and they'll all go together.*

Kit nodded. *I did that by accident before,* he said. *Good to know. Got a self-defense shield? Good. Put it up —*

He glanced around one last time, then spoke the words in the Speech that activated his own shield, thumbed the setting on Carmela's portable dissociator up to "overkill," and stepped out of the gallery.

Instantly the scorpions all raised their claws and turned toward him, and the biggest one crouched down. But Kit was already shouting the Mason's Word, the version with the additional syllables for the Martian ecology, and was running up the hardened air. It was squishier than usual because of the thinness of the atmosphere, but he didn't let that stop him — he just ran up the air high enough to get a clear shot at the biggest scorpion.

It tried to leap into the pit as its lesser associates rushed Kit's skywalk: but it had no time. The dissociator field hit it and tore it into thousands of microscopic fragments, all of which promptly flashed into plasma and sizzled away to nothing, leaving behind only a blinding flare of heat. All the remaining scorpions promptly crashed to the stony floor in a metallic clamor of collapsing claws and joints.

Kit looked over his shoulder and saw Khretef emerging from the gallery. "You all right?" he said.

"Much more so than the last time," Khretef said drily, but with a grin. "That was nicely done!"

"Yeah," Kit said, shoving the dissociator back into his otherspace pocket. "I'm gonna get it from my sister when she finds out I borrowed this without asking, but I'll make it up to her later . . ."

He said a few more words of the Speech under his breath, changed the angle of his skywalking steps so that they led down into the pit, and walked down into it. There at the bottom, the Shard shone as he'd seen it in his earlier vision. It looked like nothing but a little round, red sandstone pebble, but it burned with an intense blue-violet fire. Around it was a shell of paler, bluer brilliance, sparking with hot green lights. "Is that the anti-Shamaska wizardry?" Kit said.

Khretef nodded. "Since you're not Shamaska, either," he said, "it can do you no harm."

Kit could already feel as much. He reached down, picked up the pebble, and jumped at the jolt of power that ran through him from it. "Wow. Aurilelde's dad packed a whole lot of the kernel into that . . ." he said. He stood up, wobbling slightly.

"And more than just the kernel," Khretef said. "One other thing as well. *Me.*"

Kit's eyes widened. But it was too late. His consciousness whited out: and a moment later, when vision returned, there was only one of him standing there — Khretef.

He looked down at the little shining thing in his hand with a great rush of excitement . . . but also fear. *Now to get this back to her,* he thought, *and put everything right. Finally, finally we'll be free!*

And he vanished.

Oceanidum Mons

"*INDETERMINATE?*" Nita said to the peridexis. "What's *that* supposed to mean?"

The peridexis paused for a moment. *No,* it said, *that was an error: sorry. He's now showing in the neighborhood of Olympus Mons. There was a momentary difficulty in reading his status.*

"Not usual for you," Nita said. "Well, everything else has been crazy here . . ." She let out a long breath, which actually froze out of the air and started drifting down as tiny flakes of snow.

You want to be paying more attention to your life support, Bobo said.

Nita rolled her eyes. "You're always saying you want to handle that for me," she said. "You deal with it."

Immediately she started feeling the air warming up around her, and started to smell the odd gunpowdery smell of Mars dust. "Thanks," she said. *Kit?* she said inside her head.

No answer.

Once again she started to wonder if he was annoyed with her for breaking in on his boy-trip the day before. Nita pulled out her manual, flipped it open to the messaging section. There on her contacts list his name appeared as usual. *Location: Olympus Mons* — and a set of coordinates. *Mission status: independent investigation; occupied; please do not disturb.*

"Well, fine," she said under her breath, starting to feel annoyed. "Messaging, please?"

The space under Kit's name cleared. "Kit," she said to the manual, "sorry about yesterday. Give me a call or drop me a note when you're done." She tapped the page: the message inserted itself and began to flash bright and dark, with the notation appearing beside it, *Holding for delivery.*

Nita shut the manual and put it away. *No point in getting all cranky about this. He wants to be too busy for me? Fine.* "Okay," she said, "might as well head home. Want to handle the gating?"

No problem. Off to one side, dust and snow whirled away from a flat place among the stones; a circle of light appeared there. Nita stepped through —

— and came out in her bedroom as usual. She sighed and tossed her manual onto the desk while she pulled off her outdoor clothes, then grabbed it again and headed downstairs.

Her dad was in the living room, reading the Sunday paper. Dairine was actually in the same room with him, stretched out on the floor and paging through the travel section, while Spot looked over her shoulder with stalked eyes. All of them glanced up as Nita came in. "You hungry?" her dad said. "I'll make you something."

"No, it's okay," Nita said. She dropped her manual on the dining room table and wandered into the kitchen, glancing at the clock. *Two thirty. Okay, I'll give him till five. He has to be back then, anyway, Carmela says. And I want lunch.*

She rummaged around in the fridge for the makings of a chicken sandwich, put the kettle on, assembled the sandwich — all except the mustard she wanted, which Dairine had apparently finished, so that Nita had to make do with mayonnaise — and then wandered back into the dining room and sat down, staring morosely at the manual while she ate half the sandwich. *What is it with him?* she thought.

But Nita had her suspicions. Right there as if in front of her, she could just see the Martian princess. *It's not fair,* she thought. *She was pretty. She was stacked.* Nita squirmed uneasily in the chair. *She had* nothing on. *Almost. And it looked* good *on her!*

"Dammit!" Nita said under her breath.

She scowled at the rest of her sandwich, then picked it up and ate it, annoyed. *How am I supposed to compete with that?*

Are you crazy? You're not in a competition, said some part of her brain that was taking desperate refuge in rationality. *She was a hallucination. She was a character in a book that the wizardry used to communicate with him . . .*

Yeah, and I know just what she was communicating!

answered back another part of Nita's mind, one that had no intention of being thrown off the track by logic, especially as logic when used on boys lately seemed to produce only indifferent results. *You saw him looking at Janie Lowell the other morning. Her and that alleged skirt.*

Nita dropped the rest of the sandwich on the plate and put her head in her hands. *This is dumb. I don't want to wear that kind of skirt, anyway. If "skirt" is the word we're looking for, and not "belt"! I just want —* She groaned. *I don't know what I want. Kit, you're an idiot!*

And this statement embarrassed Nita profoundly, since it both flowed naturally from what she was feeling right now and made no sense whatsoever.

"Aaaaaagh," she said under her breath after a moment, which also made no sense, but at least discharged some tension. Nita picked up the rest of the sandwich, ate it while glowering at the table, and then noticed that the kettle was screaming for her attention.

"Sorry, sorry," she said, and scrambled up to turn off the stove and get the kettle off the hot ring and find herself a tea bag. "Sorry . . ."

The kettle regarded her with mute accusation. She picked it up and poured hot water onto the tea bag in her mug. "Maybe I'm the idiot," she muttered, putting the kettle down.

It didn't respond. She immediately felt somehow inadequate, as Kit always got immediate responses out of the household appliances: they were very forthcoming with him. "Never mind," she said, and patted it on the handle as she went out. "Different wizards, different specialties . . ." But she still felt it watching her as she went out.

Nita sighed and went back into the dining room, where she sat down at the end of the table and drank the tea. Finally she reached out to her manual again and opened it, going back to the Mars data for the previous day. In particular, the reports on the meetings with the scorpion creatures were now in there, both the encounter in the Cavern and those that had happened out in the Martian terrain, and Nita read them both over with interest. *So weird, though,* she thought. *The encounters were so different.*

Across the table, Dairine had left a pad and a few pens from something else she'd been doing. On impulse Nita reached out and pulled them over as she looked over the details of power levels and personnel, topography and coordinates. *What a crowd of us,* she thought. *But our two groups got such different results. Did one group have a higher aggregate power level or something?* But the groups' power levels weren't really all that different, when you averaged things out. *Okay, Carmela's not a wizard. But she has her own specialties. And S'reee and I were there: a more senior talent and a lesser one. And on the other side there were Kit and Ronan, and Darryl, who's not an older talent, but in his own way as powerful as a Senior: maybe more so —*

She picked up the pen and started making a list on the top page of the pad, comparing power levels and matching them off against one another: Kit, Nita, Ronan, Carmela, Darryl, S'reee. Nita shook her head and tapped the names idly with her pen, looking for some other factor that could be operating: ages, origins, wizardly specialties. *Newer wizard, older one. Younger person, older one. Boy, girl, boy, girl, boy . . .*

Nita stopped. She stared at the lists.

Our team was all girls. Theirs was all guys.

Her first thought was that this was just a coincidence. *But the scorpions walked right past us! And we didn't get what the guys got — this weird re-creation of somebody else's Mars. We got what had actually been left there. We identified ourselves as wizards and they let us right in. Almost ignored us, even.*

Whereas the guys had all these hoops to jump through. Something to prove.

Nita stared at the manual page, shaking her head. *Why? Just because they were guys? It doesn't make sense. There has to be something else going on.*

She sat back in the chair. *Even the guys were clear they were being tested for something. At the very least, that they were wizards. But maybe something else, too. Possibly to see whose mindview was closest to the Martians'?*

Nita picked up her tea mug and had a swig. She couldn't get rid of the feeling that there was something about this situation that Kit was hiding specifically from her. The hurt this was creating in her at the moment was all out of proportion to any real reason for it, but that didn't make it easier for Nita to bear.

And she kept trying to reason his behavior away, and failing.

We've been through a lot together. All kinds of crap. But we've never gone out of our way to hide stuff from each other.

There could be something bad going on with him and this connection to Miss Martian Princess, Nita thought. *Some bad influence. It's happened before. Sometimes it's taken some work to get him out of trouble. Big deal! He's done the same for me.*

But why doesn't it feel like that's what's happening this time? It's something else. I can feel it. Something he doesn't want me to know about.

And what could it be?! She banged her mug down on the table, and tea splashed out of it. Nita didn't care, just sat staring at the splashed droplets.

Crap! Crap, crap, crap!

"You drop something?" her dad said from the living room.

"Huh? Oh no, sorry . . ."

Nita scowled. If only there was some way to get at what he was really thinking. Something like the live stuff coming out of Dairine's manual, the "streaming consciousness . . ."

And then she stopped as the idea came into her head.

If it worked on Dairine's manual, she thought, *it would work on Kit's.*

She held still for some moments longer. Then she said, "Bobo?"

You rang?

"You say something, honey?"

"Just talking to Bobo, Daddy."

"Oh, okay . . ."

Nita took another drink of her tea. "The thing you did to Spot," she said. "Or to his manual functions —"

She stopped again.

Yes?

"Could you do that to Kit's manual?"

It was some moments before Bobo said anything.

Spot gave consent.

Nita swallowed. That was the point, of course. And Bobo hadn't actually answered her question.

"But you *could* do it."

If a wizard feels that a wizardry is not in contravention of the Oath, Bobo said, *or is certain beyond any reasonable doubt that a given spell is required to fulfill the conditions of the Oath, then that wizardry can be implemented and will execute.*

Nita sat there and just thought for a minute, then two.

She found that she was trembling.

Certain beyond any reasonable doubt.

The problem was that doubt was all she had at the moment. *It is impossible to serve the Lone Power directly:* that was one of the most basic tenets of wizardry. The power itself would refuse to be used in such ways. But there were lots of ways the Lone One could get you to do Its will *indirectly.* In fact, It preferred those. It liked, whenever It could, to get wizards into situations where they felt that the only way to do right was by doing something that would later turn out to be wrong.

Am I sure I'm really wanting to do this because it's right? And not just because I'm scared that she's really the one that he — that Kit and I — that I have to know if he —

She swallowed. "It's all about the situation you're in, isn't it?" Nita said under her breath. "It all comes down to how it looks to *you*." She took a long breath. "Free will . . ."

The Worlds are based on it, Bobo said. *The One has no interest in inhabiting a universe full of puppets.*

"Even though we get it wrong a whole lot?"

Apparently the benefits are felt to offset the dangers, the peridexis said. *Or counterbalance them.*

"Doesn't make me feel any better," Nita muttered. "Because I'm not sure which side I'm coming down on."

Yet she did know. It was wrong, *wrong* to tamper with the private insides of someone's brain. This was why the psychotropic wizardries tended to backlash so violently on the user. And this would be only a step away from that. It was like stealing Dairine's diary and reading it that time.

But I can't get rid of the feeling that if I don't stop him from what he's doing, bad things are going to happen. I think he's in danger somehow. And I don't know if it's just me thinking that because I want to think that . . . or because it's real.

Nita hid her face in her hands. *If this is what adult*

wizardry is going to be like, she thought, *I prefer the kid kind. More clean-cut. More obvious.*

But she had the horrible feeling that her preferences weren't at all the issue here. And worse, the fact that Bobo still hadn't clearly answered her question told Nita something she didn't want to know: that if she told him to bug Kit's manual — or his brain — and she was convinced that this was the right thing to do, *then Bobo would do it.*

Nita's mouth was dry. It suddenly seemed to her that, from the time she took the Oath until now, she had been using some kind of wizardry that had kiddie-gates installed at the top of the stairs. But now she had a way to get the gate off. Now it was entirely up to her what she did with the power. *All I have to do is convince myself that what I'm doing is right.*

And it would be so easy to do that. Too easy.

Nita put her head down on the table and was tempted to moan, except that in the living room they might have heard her. In there she could hear her dad quietly talking to Dairine: actually talking to her, not angrily, just a normal conversation, despite the uncomfortable way things had been going just a few days ago. *And that's because of what I did to her manual.*

Or is it because of what Dad saw there, and it bothered him so much that he didn't want to see any more?

Oh, I don't know what to do about any *of this!!*

But she did. Right now, at least, Nita was sure that what she was considering was wrong. *If it sounds like something the Lone Power would suggest . . . if it walks like the Lone Power, and quacks like the Lone Power . . .*

And she was suddenly caught completely off guard by the image of the Lone One as an evil duck — a black duck in a shiny black helmet, and maybe even a cape, waddling along to ominous movie music. Nita burst out laughing at the image. She could just hear the noise Its breathing would make, a dreadful asthmatic *snerk*ing —

She burst out laughing. "Bobo being funny in there?" her dad said.

Nita couldn't stop laughing to answer him.

"Stress," Dairine said, sounding dry. "She's got that hysterical sound."

This was possibly true, but Nita was still laughing so hard she could barely breathe. Finally she choked herself back into some kind of control, wiping her eyes. *Yeah,* she thought. *I'll have to watch out . . . keep an eye on how I'm thinking. This is a really big deal we're involved in here, and It'll move in the first second It catches somebody getting careless.* Nonetheless, the thought of ultimate Evil coming after her in the shape of a duck was strangely reassuring. *Lone One or not, a duck I could handle.*

Nita caught the laughter trying to start again, and stopped it. *But what a way to get up the Lone One's nose,* she thought. . . . *Or beak.* She allowed herself a last giggle. *It's so hung up on being taken dead seriously. Pull that line on It, and who knows, It might do that cartoon thing: get so mad, It'll make a mistake . . .*

Finally Nita sighed and got up to get a sponge so that she could clean the tea off the table before it dried sticky. She picked up the mug and wiped up wet tea from underneath it, and put the mug down again, and then froze as the room abruptly blanked out around her. Behind her eyes, Nita saw some city's streets full of screaming, plunging crowds. She saw Mars, Mars, Mars, a hundred times, on a hundred TV screens. There was something wrong with that Mars: it was turning blue. She saw Kit skywalking precariously over a pit of giant green metal scorpions. She saw a line of fierce light stretching from dawn into darkness, pulling and pulling at something with great force, singing like a plucked string with unbearable tension. And she saw a huge wave that was slowly, slowly leaning up over her. The Sun was caught in it, faint, pale, fluttering weakly in the water like a drowning bug.

Then she found herself looking at the tea mug again.

What was that?!

She was breathing hard. The images had come fast but were entirely clear ... and they scared her.

... *Okay,* she thought. "Bobo? Did you see those?"

It would have been difficult to avoid *seeing them.*

"Take notes!"

Consider it done.

Nita stared at the mug, then went back into the kitchen for more tea. As she turned on the heat under the kettle again, she had a sudden thought. She dug around in her pocket for her phone, pulled it out, and dialed.

"*Hola* Nita!" said the voice on the other end. "Hey, you're back already. I thought you'd still be up there."

"Nope," Nita said. "Got bored, came home."

"What, didn't you find Kit?"

"Oh, he's up there all right," Nita said, "with a big Do Not Disturb sign hung around his neck."

Carmela snorted. "Counting craters again," she said. "Never mind. He'll be back here pretty soon for dinner. I'll tell him you called."

"Oh, I wasn't calling for him! Thought you might have something else on your poem."

"Turns out it has a name!" Carmela said. "It's called the Red Rede."

"So it is a big deal, then," Nita said.

"I think so. Anyway, I think I've got that last verse translated. Though it's vague."

"Par for the course at the moment, isn't it?" Nita said. "Shoot."

"Here's the whole thing," Carmela said. And she recited:

> *"The one departed | is the one who returns*
> *From the straitened circle | and the shortened night,*
> *When the blue star rises | and the water burns:*
> *Then the word long-lost | comes again to light*
> *To be spoke by the watcher | who silent yearns*
> *For the lost one found. Yet to wreak aright,*

> *She must slay her rival | and the First World spurn*
> *Lest the one departed | no more return."*

Nita sat there for a moment and felt again, in full force, that sense of impending doom that had taken her by the throat during those strange moments when the imageries of crowds and water and scorpions and Kit had flickered behind her eyes, like shots from an unusually eclectic movie trailer. Now, as Carmela spoke the words, Nita heard the rhythm of them behind the images like a drumbeat, slow, threatening, and she could almost feel a physical pressure building up in her head as the beat went on. *When the blue star rises.* She saw Mars lowering overhead, in TV screens, in views from telescopes, going suddenly and scarily blue. *When the water burns.* She saw the struggling Sun caught in that bizarre wave, dimmed down and out after a moment by dirt in the water, then lost in a greater shadow that came crashing down. *The lost one found.* She saw the princess come dancing up to Kit and take his hand with a look on her face that said she'd been waiting for him for a long time. *She must slay her rival.* Nita seemed to be hanging high above a vista of cloud-streaked terrain, glinting with water, and somewhere between her and the Sun, blocking away its light, a dark and furious female shape with near-invisible energies flowing about its hands —

"Neets?"

"Uh, yeah," Nita said. "Yeah."

"What do you think?"

"I'm not sure. Are you pretty clear about the translation?"

"Oh, yeah," Carmela said. "I took my time. You have any ideas about this?"

The kettle started whistling softly. Nita pulled it off the heat and got herself another tea bag out of the canister. "Some," she said. "I need to touch base with Kit first."

"Okay. Well, I'll tell him to call you."

"Yeah. Thanks! And hey, you did a great job."

"I hope so. Let me know."

"Yeah," Nita said. "Later." She hung up and found herself staring out the kitchen window, where the morning glories that climbed up the chimney every year were as usual making a bid to climb in through the screen. They suddenly struck Nita as looking bizarre and alien, and the color of them made her think immediately of the too-blue Mars.

Kit, she thought, *get your butt home. Because we need to talk!*

Kit straightened up from where he'd been hunched over on the rock at the top of Olympus Mons. For a second or so he just let his eyes rest in that astonishing view . . . and then slowly realized that something was wrong with the view. *It should be much darker. Why's it so light?*

And then he realized that out there, at the edge of things, the Sun was about to come up.

What?? It was — where was — what time is it?!

He stared at his watch. *Oh, my god, it's five thirty; dinner's at six!*

Kit frantically paged through his manual to the bookmarked area, where he kept his pre-prepared spells, pulled the transit spell off his page, dropped it to the icy dirt, and jumped through. A second later he was in his bedroom, and he could hear a lot of voices talking underneath him in the living room. He ran down the stairs.

The whole family was standing in there, dressed up and ready to go. Now they turned to Kit and looked at him with a broad assortment of expressions — annoyance, confusion, resignation, curiosity.

"Kit," his papa said. Pop was the one doing annoyance. Kit immediately panicked. "I'm sorry," he said, "I'm really sorry, I — I — just sort of lost track of the time. I'll be dressed in five minutes —"

"We'll go wait in the car," said his mama, who was handling the resignation end of things. Kit fled up the stairs before Helena would have a chance to get really started on the curiosity, now that she had a reason to think it was safe to be curious.

Kit plunged around in his room getting undressed and redressed, hearing people head out the back door, hearing the car start. *What happened? How did I do that? Why did I do that? Since when do I fall asleep on Mars? What if my wizardry had failed?* But he didn't have answers for any of those questions. *This is so bizarre . . .*

Dressed in cords and a shirt and the really nice jacket his mama had gotten him — which he hated but which he was hoping would confuse her out of being annoyed with him for the evening — Kit paused just long enough to return Carmela's hot-curler weapon to its usual place. Then he pounded down the stairs and was just heading out of the living room when the front doorbell rang. "I'll get it!" he yelled, and ran to the door. *Probably one of Helena's crowd. Who knew there would be so many of them?* He unlocked the door, pulled it open —

— to find himself looking at Tom Swale. "Kit," Tom said. "We need to have a word."

He looked grim. Sweat burst out all over Kit. "Uh, sure," he said, and went outside, pulling the front door closed behind him.

"I was really expecting you to get in touch with me," Tom said, "or at least with Mamvish —"

Kit flushed hot, then cold. "I left her a message. At least, I tried to. Her manual wasn't taking messages —"

Tom stuffed his hands in his jeans pockets and looked at Kit with an expression of disappointment. "And then you went ahead," he said, "and called Ronan and Darryl, and went off to Mars. And there —" He shook his head. "I don't know if I can specifically characterize what you did as damage: it's too soon to tell. But you got involved with things that you actively should *not* have gotten involved with. At the very least, not without expert assistance! The *minute* that superegg sent out signals to those four other sites, you should have backed off and called for backup. You know that this has been a team effort from the start! There's too much riding on this for any one wizard to go off in some novel direction, no matter how good an idea he thinks it is, without consulting everyone else."

He fell silent. Kit couldn't do anything but stand there in terrible embarrassment and wonder what he was going to hear next.

"It's true what Irina told you the other day," Tom said. "Mostly, in the past, you've been able to depend on the sheer power of a relatively new wizard, and a certain talent for riding unfolding events, to get you out of Dutch. But this time, unfortunately, you've gone a little bit too far. The power that was let loose on Mars last night went right off the scale. And unfortunately, you and Ronan and Darryl don't seem to be good influences on each other as regards, well, exercising restraint in team situations. You're all too far into the loner column for that kind of thing to be easy for you."

Tom rubbed his eyes. "Now locally, when small-scale personal wizardries are involved — all right, we can find ways to make exceptions for when circumstances allow. But when I have my supervisory levels come down on me and inquire why I'm allowing new wizards to plunge around unsupervised in an off-planet wizardry that could theoretically affect the viability of an entire species, I'm afraid I have to pass some of the pain around."

He looked at Kit with a mixture of annoyance and disappointment. "I hate having to be in this position," he said, "but for the time being I'm going to have to ground you. I'm pulling your ability to transit off the planet. And I've specifically instructed Darryl not to assist you in this matter. When you're under supervision, when you come up with other more senior members of the team, that'll be a different issue. Your sympathy for the planet, your resonance with it, are unquestionably valuable to the project. And they'll make a big difference in the way we handle the situation as it unfolds. But for the time being, you're not going to be allowed up there alone."

Kit couldn't do anything but nod glumly. "I understand," he whispered. But he didn't, really. An unrepentant something in the rear of his mind was shouting, *Not fair! It's just not fair!*

"I have a lot on my plate today," Tom said, "so let's call this discussion complete for the moment. Just —" He looked hard at Kit. "Use this upcoming time to think, all right? I'm not suggesting that you go stand in the corner. You have other things to do here on Earth, and you can get into your manual and annotate the précis we got back of the events of yesterday. Will you do that?"

"Yeah," Kit said. "I'll do it when we get back."

"Right," Tom said. "I'll see you later." And he walked off down the street, vanishing into the early dusk.

Kit stood there, staring down the street after him and burning with embarrassment. The restriction would show up in the manual next to his name: he could just imagine what Nita would think when she saw it. *And she doesn't understand,* he thought. *Not the way that Aurilelde would —*

Then he stopped. *What?* Kit thought. *What's going on in my head?*

There was no way to find out. The answer was on Mars . . . and he couldn't get there. Even trying would be hopeless. Kit remembered how hard Dairine had tried to break her ban, the time she'd been restricted to staying inside the Solar System for misbehavior. She'd come back furious, describing it "like hitting your head on a stone wall again and again. Except not just your head: all of you." And then she'd gone off to sulk.

Kit was tempted to do the same, except there was no time: in the driveway, his dad was beeping for him to hurry up. After locking the front door, Kit headed around the side of the house to close the side door, then got into the car. His dad pulled out of the driveway, and everybody rode to the restaurant in that tight-faced fake good humor that means the whole family's trying to avoid taking out their annoyance on a single transgressor.

The mood had broken by the time they got to the restaurant, but Kit found that he couldn't enjoy the evening. His mama had picked a place by the water in Bay Shore that had been in the same location for nearly a hundred years. The food was terrific, and the conversation loosened up and became positively fun, and Kit strained hard to not bring the others down by letting them notice how he was feeling at the moment. At this he succeeded pretty well. But all the time he kept imagining how his name was going to look in the manual with the notation *DISCIPLI-NARY TRAVEL RESTRICTION* against it, and then he would blush with fury and embarrassment and have to work at covering it up all over again.

Finally it was over and they went home, and Kit found that he was developing a case of indigestion. It was a big relief to get back up to his room and change out of his dinner clothes into some sweats. As he headed downstairs to see if there was Alka-Seltzer in the downstairs bathroom, Kit passed Carmela heading downstairs for something, too. She had her earphones in and was bopping to something inaudible on her iPod. As she met up with Kit, she paused and said, more loudly than he liked, "What's the matter? You look like somebody just stole your wand."

"You have no idea," Kit said as he headed down the stairs. For some reason, Carmela's good mood infuriated him. He made and drank the Alka-Seltzer, then stomped back to his room, didn't quite slam the door shut behind him, and threw himself down on the bed.

That was when the idea hit him, complete from beginning to end. Kit got up again, opened his door very softly, and made his way as quickly and silently as he could down the hall to Carmela's room.

It wasn't someplace he usually ventured — not so much because of privacy issues as because it was his sister's room and therefore usually void of interest for him. However, there was something in there that, though he normally tended to ignore it, was now very much of interest indeed.

The room was very tidy. This was yet another relatively recent development which Kit found peculiar; teenage girls' rooms were supposed to be a morass of clutter. But Carmela had become compulsive about putting everything in its drawer or on its hanger or shelf without fail. Sometimes he made fun of her for this. But today, just this once, it was useful.

He crossed softly to the closet and opened it. It was full of clothes — much fuller than it had used to be: Carmela had caught the clothes bug only recently. Everything here was on its hanger, all perfectly neat. But there was also something else in this closet.

Kit reached over to the bookshelf next to the closet and found there what he'd known would be there: a clone of the downstairs TV remote. At least it had begun its life that way, but now it had a lot more buttons on it than the original remote had. Kit knew what every one was for, as he had programmed them himself. Now he studied the various buttons, chose one, pointed at the back of Carmela's closet, and punched the remote.

The back of the closet instantly went black, then flickered into light again — the random rainbowy moiré pattern of a commercial worldgate not yet patent but ready to be activated. At the forefront of the carrier pattern was the identifying brand of the Crossings' worldgate system, its famous logo of linked gate hexes prominently displayed with the notation in the Speech and several other languages, CROSSINGS INTERCONTINUAL WORLDGATING FACILITY, RIRHATH B — DESTINATION ONE. Kit grinned and began punching coordinates into the remote.

He knew what he was planning would fly in the face of the spirit of the ban Tom had imposed on him. *But he'll have to see,* Kit thought. *When I show him, when he understands what's at stake — he'll have to see why I can't leave this to anybody else. Nobody else has my perspective —*

He punched the button again. The Crossings logo vanished, replaced by a long spill of coordinates. Under them appeared a single word in the Speech: *Confirm?*

Kit punched the "go" button on the remote. The gate went patent. A second later he found himself looking at red-brown soil again, the cratered landscape, the hazy pink horizon, and, silhouetted against it, in the light of local sunset, a city of spires and gleaming metal.

All right, Kit thought. He punched another set of buttons on the remote, locking the coordinates in storage for later. Then he hit the remote's off button.

The gate flickered out, leaving nothing but the back of a closet full of clothes. Kit quietly put the remote back on the shelf, slipped out of the room, and shut the door.

Later that evening, Nita was lying upstairs in bed with a throw over her, trying to relax and get some reading done, but finding it impossible. She had Mars on her mind.

For about the twelfth time that evening, she pulled her manual over to her and had a look at her messaging section, but there was no answer yet to the note she'd sent Kit. *What is going on with him?* she thought. Idly she flipped back to the previous page of the messaging section, and her glance fell on Darryl's listing there.

I wonder, she thought. She reached out and touched Darryl's listing: it blinked.

"Yeah?" his voice said from the page. *"Oh, it's you, Neets! Hi."*

"Hey, Darryl. How're you doing?"

"Pooped," Darryl said. *"And bruised. What a day."*

"Bruised? What, did you take a spill up there while you were running away from the movie monsters?"

His laugh was rueful. *"Wish I had,"* Darryl said. *"It might ache less. I had a little visit from Tom a while ago."*

Nita blinked. "What?"

"Yeah," Darryl said. *"Looks like he and Mamvish and some of the Upper Ups weren't real pleased with what we were doing up there. I guess I can understand why, after the fact. But he was really steamed. I don't get to go up there again without other team members along, he says. Neither does Ronan. And he grounded Kit."*

Nita's mouth fell open. "No way!"

"Oh, yeah," Darryl said. *"Escorted visits only, and no other travel off the planet for the moment —"*

But Nita was already paging through the manual to Kit's listing, and sure enough, there was the red no-travel access flag. She was shocked. "Wow! He must be crushed —"

"I wouldn't be surprised," Darryl said. *"I sure feel like an idiot. I can't believe I didn't think it through while we were up there. Though there didn't seem to be a lot of time to think; everything kept happening so fast . . ."*

Nita was still shaking her head in disbelief. "Have you talked to him? How is he?"

"*No, he wasn't home. Didn't he have to go out or something?*"

"Yeah. They must still be out —" She rubbed her eyes. "Poor Kit! This is gonna make him crazy."

"*Yeah.*" Darryl sighed. "*Look, Neets, I'm having some trouble with my own peeps. They're still uncertain about me going to Mars all by myself. I should get off —*"

"Sure," Nita said. "Darryl, thanks for letting me know. I hadn't even noticed."

"*Knowing Kit, he might be grateful for that . . . Don't beat him up too much, Miss Neets.*"

"I won't. Talk to you later —"

"*Yeah,*" Darryl said. And his listing grayed out.

Nita closed the manual. *Wow,* she thought. She closed her eyes for a moment. *Kit?*

It was several moments before the answer came back. *What?*

Her insides clenched. He sounded sullen and hugely hurt, and there was something else hanging over the back of his mind that Nita couldn't read and wasn't sure she wanted to — a strange sense of mingled frustration and fear.

Listen, I heard —

Of course you did, he said. *The entire planet has to have heard. Other planets, too. Every wizard who can read, anyway.*

His anger was simply sizzling under his skin. *Look,* Nita said, *try not to take it so hard! You've been in situations like this before and you've come out okay —*

Oh, really? When have I ever been banned? Kit nearly shouted. *And this is the worst time, the* worst *possible time. We didn't hurt anything. Nothing bad happened. I don't get why I have to be banned now!*

Kit, look —

Yeah, but I'm sure you've *got some good reason. Why don't you enlighten me?*

Nita blinked at the nasty tone. *Kit,* she said, *I don't have any reasons. I don't know that much about what happened up there. You're the one who knows —*

Oh, yeah? You know about some *stuff, all right. You know about Aurilelde. I saw you looking. I could feel it —*

She had half been afraid of that: but she couldn't let herself be ashamed of what she'd done. *Kit, I was just worried about you. I had to make sure that you —*

Weren't in some kind of trouble I couldn't get myself out of, is that the excuse? Well, I wasn't! I was fine! But I can't do anything by myself without you getting involved, can I? Watchdogging me all the time. Spying on me! Like you're jealous!

Nita's mouth dropped open. *Kit,* she said, *no way I would spy on you, I just —*

It just sort of turned out that way, huh? Sure, I believe that. You just can't cope with the idea that there might be somebody else in my life, somebody who's not a wizard, somebody you can't control —

She took a long breath, and another long breath, before saying anything further. But Kit said, *So just do me a favor and butt out, all right? Now that I'm nice and safe and grounded on Earth, you won't have to worry about me getting myself in trouble and needing to be rescued! So take a break, all right? Just let me alone!*

And he cut the connection.

Nita stared at the manual in complete astonishment.

What . . . was . . . that? *It almost didn't even sound like Kit there in the middle. . . . Well,* like *him, yeah . . .*

. . . but not like him saying it. Not really *him.*

She lay there for some time, in shock. Other thoughts were roiling in her head: ideas that she'd previously dismissed as bad ones were starting to look not only good but necessary.

Yet if I do this, it will be exactly what he's accusing me of. I'll be spying on him.

Nita lay there for some moments more. After a while, almost reluctantly, the peridexis said, *I have the results of that persona analysis of Kit's experience with Aurilelde.*

Nita raised her eyebrows. "Took you long enough!"

I warned you it would take some while. Even now some of the extrapolation is dubious.

Nita sighed. "Never mind. Show me what you've got." She closed her eyes.

In the dark behind her eyelids, the analysis displayed, laid out like a sector of a spell diagram — not the full circle, but the chord and arc that expressed and described the important physical, mental, and spiritual aspects of the subject of the analysis. It was the person's wizardly signature, expressed in the Speech so that a spell into which it was inserted would include that person properly. Normally working this out could take quite a while: the utility was handy for last-minute work.

Nita looked the signature over. The curved ribbon of it was spotted with dark empty patches, but the main structure was plain enough to read. As she looked it over, Nita felt some puzzlement. "This looks familiar . . ." she said. "Why does this look so familiar?"

She peered more closely at the particular structure she thought she recognized, an intricately knotted string of Speech-characters. *Look at that, it looks just like —*

— just like the one in my *signature —*

Nita stared. The longer she looked, the more obvious it became that there were a *lot* of parts to this signature that looked like hers.

I would say perhaps forty percent, the peridexis said.

Nita opened her eyes and sat up. "How does that happen?" she whispered.

And the thought came into her head: *Somebody's using things they found out about me to trap Kit.*

"Bobo," Nita said after a few moments, "I hate this."

That, the peridexis said, *closely reflects the sound of all wizards everywhere when making difficult but closely considered ethical choices.*

"But I don't see that I *have* a choice," Nita said.

"Too many lives depend on it. People on Earth, wizards who might get involved . . . even the Shamaska-Eilitt! If this goes wrong somehow, they're all in danger. At the very least there's going to be a lot of disruption on Earth. There could be riots. People could get hurt or killed. And there could be other effects I can't foresee."

You do have a choice, Bobo said, *and you're about to tell me what it is.*

Nita took a deep breath. "Bug him," she said. "Put a spinoff on Kit's manual's log like the one on Dairine's. I want the same kind of readout on his thought processes that Spot was giving Dad — the streaming consciousness."

There was a silence. *I am required to remind you that there will be a 'final reckoning' payment when you decommission this wizardry, and the payment may be personally damaging if oversight determines the wizardry was not successful, or successful in the wrong ways.*

"I understand," Nita said. And she swallowed. "Do it."

Done, the peridexis said.

She looked at the manual, ready to pick it up right away and see what it revealed. But she just couldn't bring herself to do it. *Tomorrow,* she thought. *Tomorrow morning. Wait for some content to build up and I'll look at it then.*

But she knew that she wouldn't be eager to look at it in the morning, either. . . .

It was two thirty-three in the morning when Kit finally worked up the courage to open his bedroom door and sneak down the hall toward Carmela's room. He knew it was two thirty-three because every minute, from about half past midnight on, he had been looking at the digital clock over on his desk and thinking, *Now. Now I'm going to do it. No, I'll wait a few minutes more — somebody might hear me . . .*

Kit was heartsore. He was angry at Nita and knew that it was wrong for him to be angry at her, but he didn't want to stop. His guilt at what he was about to do was also terrible, though he hadn't done it yet. But stronger by far than either of these feelings was the sense that he had to get back to Mars: that if he didn't, terrible things were going to happen: that the fate of a people rested on what he did or didn't do. And even more important than that was the expectation of what he would do to a single heart up there, the imploring look in those eyes. *I can't let her down. I can't fail her. Not after all this time —*

Nonetheless, sweat was trickling down Kit's back as he made his way down the hall to Carmela's bedroom door. *I am going to get in so much trouble for this,* he thought. But there was simply too great a compulsion to go through with this, to get back up to Mars and find out. . . .

. . . What, exactly? *Well, among other things, where did three hours of my life just go!?* He could remember the brief battle with the scorpions under the mountain, all right. The only thing Kit regretted about that was that he wouldn't be able to use the "curling iron" at any later date: the scorpions would be armored against it. Then he'd gone down into the pit and picked up the Shard, and then — what? He had awakened by himself on the cold mountainside, with a strange feeling that somewhere else, in a world or a time more real than this one, something more important than anything else was going on. But even as he regarded that, he got a sense that there were parts of Khretef's story, or their joint one, that Khretef hadn't been telling him. Something he was having trouble with — something he didn't want to come to grips with. And it was important —

Maybe something to do with him dying, Kit thought, as he crept cautiously step by step down the hall. *Well, that would make me nervous, too.* But there was something else going on, he was sure. Part of it had to do with the Nascence, as Khretef had called it. The Nascence was part of the key to this world. With it properly awakened and energized, the City could make itself safe. And once they were safe, they could turn this world into a paradise —

Kit stopped at that point in the hallway and stepped close to the wall between the door of Carmela's room and the bathroom. There was a board here that, if you stepped on it, would go off like a gunshot as soon as you lifted your weight off it again. Kit was intent on missing it. Carefully he edged down the hall, trying not to bear his weight too heavily on the floor. Once he was past the dangerous spot, Kit put a hand on Carmela's bedroom doorknob and very slowly and softly turned it.

It wasn't locked, but then it wasn't usually. Kit eased the door open, just a crack, and peered inside, letting his eyes get used to the slightly darker conditions in her bedroom. He knew its layout quite well. The foot of her bed was near the door, which swung open to the left. All he had to do was edge in and close the door, then very softly move over to the closet door, feel just to his left for the shelf where the remote was, open the closet door, step in, and close it. Then he could use the remote to wake up the worldgate, and be gone.

Kit slipped in through the door, then quickly and quietly closed it behind him so the light from the night-light out in the hall wouldn't disturb Carmela. Once again he stood still, making sure he knew where he was and where everything else was. He looked toward Carmela's bed. From somewhere in the tangled lump of covers on top of it, a tiny snore emerged. Kit was suddenly, bizarrely reminded of Ponch . . . and he couldn't keep himself from letting out a soft sigh. *This would be so much simpler if he was still here,* Kit thought. *All I'd have to do is put his leash on, say 'Ponch? Let's go to Mars!' And three steps later, we'd be there . . .* But that couldn't happen now. Kit shook his head and silently tiptoed over to the bedroom closet.

He put his hand up to the shelf on the left, felt around . . . and froze.

Where's the remote?!

From the bed came a rustle of someone turning over, covers moving and shifting. *Oh, please don't wake up right now!!* Kit thought. But it was easily thirty seconds before the rustling stopped coming from the bed, and the little snore resumed.

Kit breathed again, though with difficulty. Once more he put his hand up to the shelf, felt around more carefully. Then he let out another breath, of relief this time, as he felt the cool plastic of the remote under his hand. *She just moved it further down the shelf, that's all . . .* He grabbed it, held it close to him, and reached for the closet door.

It took him a moment to find the doorknob. Very softly Kit turned it and opened the closet door, slipped in, and eased the closet door closed behind him. It was a matter of a few seconds to wake the remote up, punch in the macro settings he'd laid into it earlier, and wake up the gateway to Mars.

A few seconds later he was looking through the back of the closet at the gleaming city standing in the midst of that red-brown desolation. Just the sight of it suddenly left him feeling less like Kit. Suddenly he felt as if he was in a strange, closed-in place, being kept away from the one place that mattered to him most in the world, because Aurilelde was there.

Hang on, guy, Kit thought, *don't get all fired up just yet. We'll have you there in a moment. And then you can start explaining to me what the heck is going on up there!* And he stepped into the gate —

And found that he was still standing in front of it. *Now what the — !* Kit thought.

He stepped forward again. Again he was prevented from going through the gate. *Oh, no,* he thought. *They've blocked this, too!*

Frustrated, Kit reached out and put his hand up against the gate. But it went through. *Okay,* Kit thought, *so that's not the problem* — He pressed himself forward against the worldgate interface, very slowly. His face went through; his arms went through; he could see what was on the other side, feel the cold of the Martian atmosphere against his face. But he couldn't go farther. Something about chest-level was stopping him.

Kit backed up, realizing what it was. His manual wouldn't pass. It knew he was banned, and it wasn't going anywhere.

Kit cursed under his breath. There was nothing he could do for the moment but reach into his jacket pocket, take out the manual, and very slowly and carefully bend down to leave it leaned up against the inside wall of Carmela's closet, where it would be unlikely to get kicked through the gate by accident. *It'll be safe enough here.* He pulled out his antenna-wand, stuck it experimentally into the gate: it at least passed. *So I won't be unarmed. And I'm still a wizard — it's not like the manual is* required *on the road.* But all the same Kit felt unnerved at the thought of going to another planet equipped only with the very basic set of spells he had memorized: life support and so forth.

Getting back wouldn't be a problem: he'd programmed the gate to produce an automatic portal for him three hours from now, picking him up at the border between the City of Shamask and the Martian wilderness. *I'll be back before anyone even knows I'm gone . . . and if I get into some kind of trouble, I can always yell for Ronan or Darryl, or even Neets.* But any thought of what might cause such a need, or of the explanations he would make to the others regarding what he was doing and why, seemed very far away. Right now the imperative of getting to Mars overrode everything else. In the back of his mind, Khretef was fretting, worrying, desperate to get back. Aurilelde needed them, needed *him*, before the trouble started ... and Khretef seemed very sure that it would start. He also seemed very sure that they were — *he* was — was the only one who could stop it. *We stopped it once before*, Khretef's voice said in the back of his head. *But we can't linger. We need to get going!*

Kit nodded, let out one last breath of nervousness and guilt, passed through the gate, and the closet went dark behind him.

Nita came down for breakfast the next morning feeling very wrung out and weary of mind, for reasons she couldn't fully understand. Granted, there'd been a lot going on lately, and the seemingly endless drudgery of the end of the school year had been wearing her down. And now there was this craziness with Kit as well. *Banned. I can't believe it. What's the matter with him?*

Coming down the stairs, Nita suddenly found herself thinking, as she'd kept finding herself doing lately, about Ponch. Obviously Kit missed him most of everybody, but it was difficult, sometimes, to look at Kit and realize that that constant, black presence was not ever again going to appear galloping along at his side. *We've been losing so much stuff lately*, Nita thought. *This has not been a great year. First Mom, then Ponch . . .* She sighed, thinking of how she had heard her mom say sometimes that "these things come in threes." *Well, I hope they don't! Two's more than enough for me, thanks. Especially if losing Ponch is part of what's left Kit acting so weird. What are we going to* do *about him?*

In the kitchen, she yawned and put the kettle on to make tea. *Listen to you,* she said to herself. *So depressed, and the day hasn't even started yet! It's probably blood sugar.* It was true that over the past couple of days she hadn't been eating well: there'd been too much going on. *Really need to do something about that.* She leaned back against the kitchen counter, waiting for the water to boil. It was just beginning to produce its pre-boil rumbling when Dairine came wandering into the kitchen in one of those shin-length T-shirts she favored. "You're up early," Nita said.

Dairine yawned, then looked at Nita with vague annoyance. "Unlike some people, who have a half day today for the completely unfair reason that they're older than me," she said, "I have school this morning. But if I get a head start on some of the things I need to do, I can leave early and get back to Wellakh."

Nita nodded, turning her attention back to the kettle. "So things are going okay?"

"Dad's lightened up, if that's what you mean." She opened the fridge and got out a quart of milk, then started foraging in one of the cupboards for cereal and came out with a box of her preferred oaty loops.

"Good," Nita said.

Dairine threw her an oblique look. "When I'm working . . . how much is he seeing of what's going on?"

Nita felt inclined to shy away from the question, but that would cause more trouble later. "Go ask him to show you. It's physical stuff mostly: movements, video." She raised her eyebrows at the slowness of the kettle and reached over to turn the stove up higher. "He's interested, but not in an unhealthy way. So however you've been handling the content with him, you're doing good."

Dairine nodded, got down a cereal bowl from the cupboard, and poured the bowl almost entirely full of oat loops. "How are you planning to fit any milk in that?" Nita said.

"Magic," Dairine said drily. "Back in a moment."

Dairine wandered out through the kitchen again, heading back upstairs to her bedroom. The milk carton that she'd left poised in midair now popped itself open, tilted, and started pouring milk into the cereal.

Nita watched this minor demonstration of expertise with interest, waiting for the milk to overflow: but it didn't. The cereal in the bowl rose just high enough for some of the little oat *o*'s to teeter at the bowl's edges without actually falling out. *She's good*, Nita thought, amused. *Can't take that away from her . . .*

Dairine came thumping down the stairs again and appeared in the dining room completely dressed, with her school backpack thrown over her shoulder, and her manual and a copy of *Three Men in a Boat* in one hand. "Oh, and by the way," Dairine said as she came back into the kitchen and grabbed the milk carton out of the air, closing it and shoving it back into the fridge, "there's a dinosaur in the backyard to see you."

Nita stared at Dairine as she slammed the refrigerator door shut, dislodging a few of the magnets stuck to the outside of it. "What?"

"A dinosaur," Dairine said, stooping to pick up the magnets and put them back on the fridge door, then fumbling around in the silverware drawer for a spoon. "Really big lizard? Goggly eyes? Skin all lit up in fluorescent colors like someone who's really pissed off about something? That kind of dinosaur."

"Oh, my god," Nita said, and ran toward the back door. "Oops —" She ran back to the stove, shut off the heat under the kettle, and then plunged outside.

Sure enough, at the rear end of the backyard, there was Mamvish, crouching in the spell-shielded area under the sassafras saplings and the big wild cherry tree. "Mamvish!" Nita said. "*Dai stihó!* What's up?"

"Apparently," Mamvish said, fixing one eye so intently on Nita that it actually held still, "your friend Kit. What's he doing on Mars?"

She stared. "What? He can't be on Mars. He's banned."

"Exactly," Mamvish said. The colors under her hide swirled neon-bright. "He shouldn't be there at all. Yet somehow he is. Would you care to explain?"

The nearest eye was trained on her very hard. Nita's own eyes went wide. "What?" she said. "Are you suggesting I *helped?* I knew he was grounded! No way I'd take him up there: you think I'm crazy?"

"I have to ask," Mamvish said, "because you're his partner. You two are quite close, and have been through some . . . well, let's say some extraordinary experiences together: experiences that might tempt one of you to break the rules for the other's sake."

Nita shook her head, hardly knowing what to say. *Close, yes, but* this *close? No! . . . Well, maybe yes! But not this time.* And that obscurely pained her. She gulped, trying to get some control over herself. "Mamvish," Nita said, "look, sure, sometimes he's gone off the rails and I've gone after him to pull him back on. But he's done the same for me. Anyway, if you think I took him to Mars, I didn't! I didn't even know he was banned till last night, and I haven't heard from him since then. And now he's — Where *is* he??"

"Since you two are normally so close," Mamvish said, "I'd hoped you might be able to give me a better idea, as we're having difficulty locating him precisely. His location is being obscured by local factors —"

Nita scowled. "I just bet it is . . ."

Mamvish turned to stare at her with the other eye. "Do you know something I should know?"

"Probably yes," Nita said. "But it would help a lot if you can stop assuming I'm guilty before I can explain my innocence!"

Mamvish looked stricken. "I'm sorry," she said. "Terrible changes have begun up there, and I'm on my way to deal with them, but it's no excuse for me to deal unfairly with you. Come along and tell me what's been happening. You're saying you don't know how Kit got to Mars?"

Nita shook her head. "Unless one of the guys took him — But Darryl said he wouldn't do that."

"As did Ronan," Mamvish said.

"Then unless he —" Nita shut her mouth as the idea came to her. "Oh, my god. Carmela's closet!"

Mamvish looked at her strangely. "A closet? That's some kind of room in your house?"

"Not my house. Kit's. His sister — you remember, she was at the Crossings when that trouble broke out? The Crossings administration gave her a spinoff worldgate as part of her compensation. It's strictly mechanically managed. I guess if Kit used it —" Then she shook her head. "We don't have to stand here guessing: we can find out from Kit's manual. Let me get mine and I'll tell you what's going on."

"Good," Mamvish said. "Hurry. And when we're there, be ready to help, because this is likely to be difficult —"

Nita burst out in a sweat on hearing a wizard of Mamvish's experience and power levels saying that something was likely to be difficult. "Sure, half a sec, let me go get my stuff —"

She was running toward the house when her father came out and met her halfway by the backyard gate, peering over it and down toward the end of the backyard. "Okay," he was saying to himself as Nita ran up to him, "she wasn't exaggerating. A dinosaur.

Nice color scheme; didn't know they came like that."
He looked at Nita. "Please tell me it's not an herbi-
vore. I just got the new peonies planted out . . ."

"I don't know about the peonies," Nita said, "but
when we get back you'd better hide the tomatoes."
She started to push past him.

He stopped her and handed Nita her backpack.
"That white wand of yours," he said, "your manual,
your phone, a sandwich. Sorry, there wasn't time for a
Thermos. I'll call school if you're late. Mars again?"

"Mars!" she said, grabbing the stuff from him,
kissing his cheek, and running back down the yard to
where Mamvish waited. As she went, Nita could just
hear him mutter, "I wonder what the real estate prices
there are like?"

Seconds later, they were there. Nita's breath went out
of her again, the sheer range of Mamvish's power taking her once more by surprise.

The problem was that the Mars where they now
stood, outside the City of the Shamaska, was not quite
the one Nita had been expecting. Yesterday, the city
through which she had walked had been an ephemeral
thing — plainly a construct of wizardry, partly resur-
rected from the deeps of time, partly from fiction and
illusion. This, however, was a city standing proudly
out in view for anyone to see — including any number
of satellites, and telescopes, and whatever else might be
looking this way. And there was air here: thinner than
Earth's, but breathable. Streams were flowing through
the red landscape, and they were real —

"This wasn't here yesterday," Nita whispered to Mamvish. "Or not like this."

"Not in the present, you mean," Mamvish said. "A memory? A reconstruction?"

Nita was unsure about the fine distinctions and now was wishing she'd bugged Kit's manual a lot sooner. "It wasn't just Kit's imagination," Nita said as she looked around, "or his memories. Someone else's, too . . ."

And then she stopped. Mamvish . . . had changed. Suddenly the giant saurian was gone. In her place was a giant ten-legged creature, also faintly saurian-looking and big enough for a number of humans or large humanoids to ride on in a line, for the length of the "wheelbase" was considerable. A long, high neck and small fierce-toothed head; blunt, flat feet somewhat like a camel's, good for running on the legendary Martian sands; a long, straight deinonychus-like tail for balance — Nita had to rummage around in memory for the name of the creature: it had been a while since she'd read the Burroughs books. *A thoat. She's turned into a thoat. Well, that's weird! But she doesn't look concerned . . .*

Mamvish looked sideways at Nita. "The other Kit?"

Nita shook her head. "It's like there was an earlier version of him."

"A more ancient incarnation?"

"Not sure. You should check what I got out of his manual."

Mamvish's eyes shifted to and fro for a moment.

Then she looked at Nita with some concern. "What you've done to his manual," she said, "is very creative . . . and potentially very expensive."

"I know." They started walking down the white road toward the City. "I'm not wild about it, either."

"And a reincarnation it may indeed be," Mamvish said, "though not in the usual style. More of an archive function, though it needs closer analysis." She didn't say anything for a moment as they walked along. Then she glanced at Nita again. "But you're also thinking that he's involved with someone who's another version of you?"

Nita grimaced. "I don't know about involved . . ." *Oh, yes, you do,* said the back of her mind. "He was — He was definitely attracted to her."

The look in the eye on that side of Mamvish's new, smaller head was unreadable. But now she gazed forward at the city again, noting the water and the blueness of the sky. "This effect is spreading," Mamvish said. "Detailed analysis is going to have to wait. For the moment —"

The whole of her hide blazed with Speech-symbols, swirling, burning. Mamvish gestured with her tail, and the fire of the symbols ran out of her, through the ground, straight out to the horizon, and seemingly up to the sky, running straight to the zenith. Sky and earth flared briefly: then the spell-flare vanished.

Nita stared at Mamvish as the spell expired. Mamvish was eyeing the ground with a dubious expression. "Interesting," she said. "Some resistance —"

She waved her tail. "No matter," Mamvish said.

"Come. They know we're here now. But for the time being, no one on Earth will see what's happening."

They started walking again. Nita stared at Mamvish. "You just put a visual shield around *the entire planet?*"

"It's going to take some holding," Mamvish said, sounding aggrieved. "There's resistance. And there shouldn't be. But I thought this would get more complicated before it became less so. Let's go see what these people think they're doing."

They continued their walk up the broad, paved way toward the city gates. About halfway there, Nita started feeling undressed. She looked down at her sweatshirt and jeans —

Or where they should have been. They were a lot less "here" now. It wasn't that the ornaments and delicate draperies, the gems and gleaming precious metals weren't pretty in a very exotic way. But for Nita, the thought of anybody seeing her dressed like this, especially Kit, immediately brought on a blush.

Mamvish glanced at her. "What's the matter?"

"I, uh —" Nita grabbed at what was draped around her hips and passed for a skirt, at least in places. It was hard to get hold of, more like being dressed in faded blue-denim fog than anything else — and its opacity was subject to change without notice. "This isn't exactly, I mean, it's not what I usually —"

"Oh, come on, Nita," Mamvish said as she ambled along, "it's their reality . . . for the moment. We must play here if we're to win here. What is it your people say? Snort it up?"

"Suck it up," Nita said, and suited the action to the word, pulling in her stomach. *It only hangs over a little bit,* she thought. *And the top doesn't really look that bad. If there was just a little more fog between the metal bits, it might actually —*

"You need to stop allowing yourself to get so self-absorbed," Mamvish said as they got closer to the gates. "You're a wizard! You should be well past the point in your practice where body taboos are an issue. You've been off-world enough now, spent time on the High Road: act the dignity of your role and stop looking like a nervous teenager!"

I am *a nervous teenager!* Nita thought. But she said nothing more for the moment, just concentrated on trying to walk tall. Her mother always used to say to her, *When you're embarrassed, make yourself taller. It covers.*

And the covering, Nita thought as she tried to get rid of the last vestiges of panic, *is exactly what I need about now!* The chilly wind was playing with the long, diaphanous draperies about her hips, and no attempt of Nita's would get them to lie down. Finally she gave up trying. She had everything she needed. What had happened to the sandwich she wasn't sure, but her manual was in a little pouch hanging on the right side of her low-slung belt, and her wand was in an elaborately chased metal sheath on the left. *And Mamvish is right. I'm a wizard. Clothes don't make any difference to that!* Though she was left uncertain whether the goosebumps she was suffering were due to the clothes or her emotional state . . .

Mamvish paused. "What is it with the gravity here?" she said, shuffling her feet and glancing around her. "I don't feel quite right. Synesthesias of some kind . . ."

Nita stopped and gave her a look. "What?"

"I don't know what's causing it," Mamvish said, "but it's as if —" She looked down at her feet.

Her mouth dropped open. Her eyes wiggled as if they were trying to go around. Nita, caught off guard, tried to choke down her laughter, and failed. "Wait a minute. You mean you didn't *notice?*"

A growl started rumbling somewhere inside Mamvish. "What — *am* — I?"

"You're a thoat. They're —" *Oh, god, how can I say it? Never mind, just look at her face —!* "In the stories, they're a beast of burden. Not very smart. People ride them . . ."

The growl got louder. It took Nita a few moments to get control of her laughter. "Come on, Mamvish!" Nita said. "You ought to be past being shape-proud by now! A wizard like you has the power to look like anything she wants, and you ought to know the seeming's not the self." She started snickering again. "So act the dignity of your role. Snort it up!"

The thoat eyes could be surprisingly expressive. They flared with annoyance, and then there was a brief flurry of furious tantrum-based foot-stamping, even more impressive with all a thoat's legs than it had been with Mamvish's. Dust flew up from the pink-white Martian road until it almost concealed her. "This is so embarrassing, what if anybody ever hears about this, some kind of gratuitous insult, do they even know why I, how can this *possibly*, why do I even bother, don't these people know why I —"

Nita turned away, as there was no point in Mamvish being made worse by watching Nita fail to control her grin. *Increasing entropy locally is bad, bad,* bad. *She's a baby wizard still; don't laugh, don't laugh . . . !*

Nita got control of herself long before Mamvish did. But finally the stomping and muttering stopped, and Nita turned back to see Mamvish staring morosely at her thoat feet. "I suppose," she said, "it wasn't meant personally."

And what will she do if it ever turns out it was? I'm tempted to tell her . . . No, no, no! Nita kept her face straight. "Wouldn't know how it could be," she said, which was true.

"*Hmmmmmfffff,*" Mamvish said, a huge blown-out exclamation of resignation and annoyance. Then she put her head up high. "Work to do," she said. "Let's go do it."

"Bobo," Nita said as they got closer to the city, "what about your tap on Kit's manual? Is there anything about what's going on in there?"

The tap is not active at the moment: he could not bring it with him because of the ban. But there is some stored material that he was considering before he came. Information about persons, motivations . . .

"Let me have it all! And hurry up."

Nita quickly found herself blushing hot in increasing discomfort as she browsed through entirely too much of Kit's recent stream-of-consciousness. *But this is gonna be very useful, I can't deny that . . . even if this really is* not *stuff I want to be seeing . . . ! Never mind, just make the most of it —*

Shortly they came up to the great sheer metal gates and stood there for a moment, looking upward. The gates remained obstinately closed.

"Maybe they don't know we're coming . . ." Nita said. But immediately after she said it, she was certain that wasn't true.

"Oh, they know," Mamvish said. "I can hear them." She flourished her thoat tail. "So let's go see how this will proceed."

And the next second, they were standing in a high Tower room where light poured in from the pink-white sun overhead, and white clouds chased across that blue sky. And in the center of the room stood three people around a broad red sandstone bench: and a fourth one sat there on the bench, wearing at her throat a sharp oblong Shard of light burning fiercely violet even in the full light of day.

Gathered all around the sides of the great circular room were many men and women in the metal harness and light draperies of the Shamaska-Eilitt. All their dark eyes were turned to Mamvish and Nita as they walked up to the bench-throne, and Nita found it very strange to pass among them — like walking through a congress of living, breathing statues in all shades of gray, and all the faces smooth and immobile. Here and there among them were the green metal scorpions, sitting or crouching against the polished floor, watching the newcomers with all their eyes, scissoring their claws gently together. But most of Nita's attention was on the Throne. There was Iskard, and the dark Rorsik behind him, at a little distance, watching with a cold face; and standing next to the bench-throne, Khretef.

Kit! Nita insisted to herself: and she spoke to him silently. *Kit!* But he was gray and stony, dressed like one of them, looking like one of them, except that he looked like Kit as well. His eyes didn't react to hers when she looked into them: she was just another stranger walking in. And on the Throne sat Aurilelde, with the violet-blue fire of the Shard clinging to the smooth gray flesh above her gemmed metal bodice — and about her, an echo of its glow that was coming from something else, something inside her, the faintest possible rosy light —

Oh, no, Nita thought. *Mars's kernel. She's got the planet's kernel* inside her. *How long has that been there? And whose good idea was* that?! But as her glance went to the smug and triumphant-looking Rorsik, she thought she knew.

Mamvish stopped about six feet from the Throne and lifted her head. "In the Powers' names, and that of the One They serve," she said, "we are on errantry, and we greet you."

Some of those around the room bowed, but many looked at Mamvish and Nita with distrust, and the four around the Throne didn't move at all. Finally, Iskard said, "Fellow wizard, tell us what errand brings you here so that we may speed you on your way."

Nita's eyebrows went up, for in the Speech the response had so little genuine greeting in it that it nearly translated as "Don't let the door hit you in the fundament on the way out."

Mamvish blinked in reaction. Then she said, "On the Powers' behalf and as Species Archivist for this part of the Galaxy, I've come to investigate your appearance on this world, which has been vacant for some while under circumstances which we're investigating. Instances of self-archiving are also within my remit for investigation. Am I to understand that you are descendants of the people of Shamask-Eilith, formerly of this system and also called the First World?"

"We are not those people's descendants," Rorsik said, sounding outraged. "We *are* those people."

"You have, however, built or engineered new bodies for yourselves, to better suit yourself to this world when you reached it."

"Such was our right," Iskard said. "A species has the right to survive."

"But not to interfere with another species' survival," said Mamvish. "You must be aware that there is another planet in this system populated with life forms wearing bodies similar to the ones you've engineered for yourselves."

"We know that perfectly well," Rorsik said.

"You should also know, then, that that culture is both *astahfrith* — generally unaware of wizardry — and *asdurrafrith*." It was the Speech-word for a species that hadn't yet openly met alien species or

didn't yet believe in them. "The works you're enact-
ing here at the moment — I speak of the extensive res-
urrection of former environmental conditions across
the planet — endanger the psychological and physical
well-being of that planet. Do you accept that?"

"We not only accept it," said Rorsik, "but we
embrace it. The other planet is no concern of ours. If
they are not strong enough to accept the return of the
People of the First World to the system where we
were the First Life, then they should learn such
strength. Or possibly vacate that world in favor of a
people better suited to occupy it."

Nita blinked, unable to believe what she was
hearing. "Kit," she said. "Listen to them! They're
talking about invading the Earth! *What are you doing
here with these guys?*"

Khretef shifted uneasily but said nothing.
Aurilelde looked at Nita with what was supposed to
look like understanding, but Nita didn't miss the
slight edge of contempt in the expression. "He came
to us first because I called him," she said. "Because he
was a fragment, as this was once a fragment" — she
touched the Shard that lay between her breasts —
"and is now reunited with the kernel from which it
was severed. For a long time the test lay waiting, while
all of us and our cities lay in stasis, and while Khretef's
soul waited and worked to be reborn. Finally he was.
And sure enough he found his way here along with
others — my hero, my warrior, my other half — and
took the test, and freed the power that we needed to

be alive again." She looked up at him and took his hand. "As Kit, he finished the quest that once was his bane: broke open the Nascence and brought home the Shard, the tool to use the Nascence's power."

Nita folded her arms, getting more annoyed by the moment at Aurilelde's manner. "There were more tests than just that one. And not just for boys."

"Those were of no concern to me," Aurilelde said. "Knowing what daughters of another world might make of the ancient Daughters' tales of past years mattered far less than finding the male wizard in whom our savior would lie hidden. Only to him and his kind would the real tests present themselves ... especially to the right one. And now that he has come again through him, we all live once more. And he lives as Khretef." She smiled up at him.

Khretef smiled back, which Nita found hard to bear. But she looked Aurilelde in the eye. "So nothing we found matters, huh?" she said. "Even the Red Rede —"

For a second Aurilelde's expression changed, as if she was at a loss. "You don't know what it means," Nita said. "Or not all of it. You *think* you do, though. You've convinced yourself that you understand it. I wouldn't be so sure."

Then she stopped, because she had no idea what she'd meant by that and was desperate not to be asked.

Aurilelde forced that superior smile again. "The Rede is no issue to me," she said. "Or our people. All that matters is changing this world so that we can live in it again."

"So," Mamvish said, "you will not stop."

Slowly Aurilelde stood up, looking at them. Nita was watching the Shard. *Has that dumped its power into the main body of the kernel now,* she wondered, *or is it just immaterially connected? If somebody could grab it* — But Aurilelde was laughing. "Stop? We will do no such thing! We've spent enough terrible endless years waiting trapped half alive in the cold and dark, waiting to be freed in a better time. That time has come! And if you think an overgrown *slessth* and a scrawny bad-mannered brat-child who was never even off her own planet until a few years ago are going to stop the rebirth of a mighty race that ruled this system hundreds of millions of years before your planet was even solid, then you'd better think again."

Nita's eyes narrowed. "One last time," she said. "Before we start dealing with you, I want to talk to Kit."

Aurilelde simply squeezed Khretef's hand, then smiled at Nita. "But you still don't understand, do you? He returned to us as soon as he was able to, some hours ago . . . and as soon as that happened, he was absorbed." She smiled up at Khretef again. "The more senior soul always has priority in any such meeting. It didn't take much doing: he was young and inexperienced, and not as wholly there as either of us are." She looked at Nita with what was perhaps meant to be kindness. "If you really want so to be with him," she said, "maybe you should consider submitting yourself to the same fate. I dare say I could fit you in somewhere."

Nita flushed with fury. But she knew what to do with that. "Don't count on it," she said.

"And why wouldn't I? Surely you can see my Khretef far exceeds the incomplete fragment you've fastened onto! He's a child of the First World, a warrior, a great wizard, greater than anything you or your poor Kit would ever have been. You two are just poor shadows. Khretef and I are the substance, the originals. And Khretef lived for me. He *died* for me! Whereas your little Kit seems merely to have been saved from dying for you once or twice. Sometimes even by you —"

Nita looked at Aurilelde and concentrated on holding still. "If you think you're holding some kind of moral high ground because somebody's died for you," she said, her voice shaking, "I've been there, and what you're displaying now looks nothing like it. And as for the possibility that I might want to make up any part of *you* —" She laughed. "*That's* not going to happen. So turn him loose, and then we'll talk about what happens to this planet."

Aurilelde regarded her quietly. "No," she said after a moment, "if that's your response, the talking's over. So, to wreak aright —" She made a casual gesture at Nita.

And the world upended itself around Nita and dumped her on the ground —

In desperate cold and freezing vacuum. Nita had just sense enough to instantly close her eyes and let out the breath she was tempted to hold. Then she got her life-support force field working again, just before something else happened all around her: a shudder, a strange feeling of change and negation —

She took an experimental breath, found that there was air, opened her eyes. She was sitting on red-brown dirt, out under an early dawn sky. *Why does this look familiar?* she thought.

She stood up, brushing herself off, and looked around. *Sunrise*, she thought. *That puts me, let's see —*

Nita glanced toward the southern horizon and froze. Between her and the pale, pinky Sun, something was rising up that filtered and dimmed that light. It was a wave, easily a hundred feet thick in this gravity, and easily a mile high. Up and up it reared, taller by far now than the mountain, even at that distance leaning up over Nita, leaning farther out, the great sparkling arch of it stretching out over the top of the crater basin and shadowing the mountains in it like a vast, downward-curving smoked-glass roof. The distant Sun was caught in the oncoming wave, flickering, flaring brighter briefly as the water sporadically lensed its light.

When the water burns —

But the Sun was struggling to shine now, the thickness of the wave obscuring it as it grew, putting it out.

From what seemed a million years ago, she heard

a scratchy bird voice, the voice of a scarlet macaw, saying: *Fear death by water!*

    Oh, no, Nita thought. *Oh, no. That dream . . . it* wasn't *a dream.*

    It's now.

Aurorae Chaos

NITA LOOKED SOUTHWARD across the vast impact basin at the oncoming wall of water. *There's enough water frozen on Mars to flood the whole planet thirty feet deep,* she remembered Kit telling her so many times that she had to threaten him with whacking to make him stop. *Now you could repeat it fifty times in a row and I wouldn't care,* she said to Kit, wherever he was, *as long as it was really you saying it!* But right now she had a more serious problem, because a significant portion of that water was apparently coming right at her. "Bobo," Nita said. "What is this I'm standing on?"

Oceanidum Mons, Bobo said. *It's not far from where you were before: toward the southwestern side of Argyre Planitia —*

Oh, no, Nita thought. *Then I didn't come here because the kernel had been here before. I came here because this was going to happen, and I saw it was coming. Because I was going to be here. Or supposed to be here — if there's a difference —*

And something else that was going to be here? Nita thought. *Or supposed to be here? The lake that was here before. And here it comes . . .*

"Well, screw it," Nita said. "If she thinks I'm going to hold still for this, boy is she wrong!" She reached down to her charm bracelet for a transit spell, started to recite it with some changes —

— and found herself being blocked.

Okay, Nita thought. *Shield-spell!* She started to enact her usual one —

It was blocked, too. Nita blanched. "Bobo, what's going on?!"

Someone managing the planet's kernel, Bobo said, *is disallowing the wizardry locally.*

"Can she do that??"

Unfortunately, Bobo said, *yes.*

Nita went hot with fury. *She wants me* dead*!* she thought. *And she wants me to stand here and watch it coming. That complete and total bitch!*

It wasn't that various Powers and principalities hadn't tried to kill Nita over time. But this was somehow much more personal, much more offensive, because she'd really been trying to understand this other person, only to have the understanding completely rejected . . . or used against her. Now Nita's rage was starting to boil over, and she did her best to get control of it — because it would be really useful, just so long as she *did* stay in control.

Nita breathed out and tried to get a grip. "Where's Mamvish?" she said.

Not on the planet, said Bobo. *She appears to have been forcibly removed. Possibly her return is also being blocked.*

She breathed out again. *I'm on my own, then,* Nita thought. *But boy, if I'd realized kernels were this powerful, I'd have studied them even harder than I did . . .* Nita watched the water coming, lifting higher, the wavefront bulking up and up as the water flowing into existence behind it pushed it higher in the light gravity. She shook her head, awed. *This would be one of the coolest things I ever saw,* Nita thought, *if it wasn't going to kill me.* She had maybe two minutes to figure out what to do, find a spell that would do the job, implement the spell, and turn it loose . . . and then, ideally, recover from it and get the hell out of here.

The wave was closer, climbing the sky. "Bobo, she can't disallow all wizardry, can she?" Nita said.

No. That would require power levels similar to Mamvish's. The blockage involves any transit or defensive spell.

"Okay, let's go on the offensive. Water magics . . ."

I have the ones you've been researching recently, Bobo said, *and all the other ones there are.*

Some of which probably look real impressive but might not work for me. The sweat was breaking out on Nita. *Where do I begin?*

And then she remembered sitting on the jetty with S'reee the other morning, which now seemed about a million years ago. *You should talk to Arooon,* S'reee was saying. *He knew Pellegrino . . .*

Nita gulped. "Bobo," she said. "The Gibraltar Passthrough wizardry —" *This is insane. But with all the insanity running around, what's a little more?*

There was a pause. *A big piece of work,* the peridexis said. *And the conditions here are very different.*

"Yes, they are," Nita said, "because the gravity's a lot less here! And look at it. All these highlands —" She stared around her. "This is perfect. It's like the underwater terrain where Pellegrino designed the spell to be used! And I don't have to control the whole body of water, just what's coming at me!" She grinned, briefly fierce. "Aurilelde thinks I'm stuck here; she's sure I can't gate out; she's counting on me not to be able to react in time —"

Another pause. *Fueling it,* Bobo said, *is going to cost you.*

"Being *dead* is going to cost me, too!"

Point taken. But Bobo still sounded extremely concerned.

"This is what you've been wanting to do for me," Nita said, "so get on with it. It's a big spell diagram. Lay it out!"

A second later the diagram was burning in lines of light all over the top of the massive tableland where Nita stood. "Big" didn't begin to sum it up. But Nita didn't let the size of it freak her: there was no time. She looked it over quickly and located the control nodes, as well as the specific lines and chords of the spell that needed her own name information written out along them. As she went to them, stepping carefully so as not to interrupt the design, Nita saw her name and other personal information flash into fire along the lines. She stooped to check them: found them complete.

Nita straightened up, saw the gigantic main wave-crest thundering closer. Lesser waves were running and splashing hugely along either side of the table-land. The memory of her previous visions of that wave was making her shiver. *But remember the cave,* she thought then. *You saw the scorpions get you once. And then you did something different, and it didn't turn out that way. Let it be that way now —*

The water kept coming, vast, roaring low. The frontal main wavecrest was still miles off — but not for much longer: the low gravity meant it could move a lot faster than it could on Earth. *Maybe another minute,* Nita thought. *Let's go.*

She walked to the middle of the spell. Away on its far side, almost exactly opposite her own name, she caught sight of another scrawl of characters in the Speech, in neither her own handwriting nor the peridexis's flawless printlike Speech-charactery. It was Angelina Pellegrino's signature, the autograph of the greatest hydromage of the last two centuries, a small, firm, elegant set of curves and curls. Nita, standing at the center of the circle, remembered how proud she'd been to discover that she, too, now had a spell named after her in the manual: that in however small a way, Callahan's Unfavorable Instigation now held the same kind of stature in the wizard's manual as a work of art like this, and had her signature on it. *And it won't be the last one,* she thought, watching that wall of water run at her. *Not if this works. Angelina, if you're around, watch this!*

The core of the spell was laid out around the center, where Nita was standing. She started reading in the Speech, one eye on the approaching water, speeding up her reading as the main wave drew closer more swiftly than she'd ever thought it might. She read faster. *Don't panic; just get the spell finished, then get your mind in the right shape to let the water through and tell it which way to go — !*

She read and read, faster and faster — *Two phrases left!* — as the inrushing wave towered higher and higher over her, as the Sun struggled its last against the tumbled-up dirt and stone trapped in the oncoming water, and the water on either side of the tableland rose higher and higher, and Nita was standing on an island in a raging sea. *One phrase left!* — as the main oncoming wave leaned over her like a curved glass roof, reaching out and out over her and the tableland and even the angry water beyond them. *Isn't light gravity neat? How can it possibly* do *that? It has to fall now, it* has *to, and here's the last phrase, five words, three, the last really long one —*

The wave fell.

And the wizardry leapt up at it from the tableland like a sword-edge of focused fire, splitting the wave vertically down the middle into two vast, downcurling sheets of water that fell crashing to left and right.

Nita dropped to her knees as the energy went out

of her in a blast like a fire hose. *Now I know why there aren't a lot of hydromages,* she thought as she pitched forward and supported herself on her hands, doing her best not to collapse, to stay conscious, because she *had* to stay conscious. Above her, the wizardry was pushing itself out into the body of water behind the split wave and curling into two gigantic tubular structures burning with light, each one finned inside with what the spell's précis had described as "tailored Venturi structures." Whatever those were: to Nita they looked like someone had taken the chambers out of a chambered nautilus and set the chamber walls around the tubes' walls in a spiral structure. The fins and the shapes of the tubes blazed as they lifted the water up and slowed it down, soaking up the fury of the extra energy that the tsunami had been about to dump on top of Nita and all the surrounding terrain.

She was gasping for air now, having to concentrate harder on staying conscious, staying focused. The thought of Kit was helping. *He has to be in there inside Khretef* somewhere. *He has to! No way he'd ever just let himself be absorbed, no matter how smart a wizard Khretef might be. And as for Aurilelde —* Nita breathed out, breathed in, getting her second wind, feeling less shattered. *But I'm getting angry again.* She looked up at the wave, no longer a wave anymore but a long, sinking slope, filling the impact basin around her rapidly but not in danger of killing her. *She may have control of this planet's kernel,* Nita thought, *but she can't just keep throwing stuff like that at me. In fact she has to be suffering now, no mat-*

ter how easy she tried to make that look. And control or no control, she's not a wizard —

Nita pushed herself up until she was kneeling upright again. The wave had sunk now almost to the level of the filling impact basin, and the whole huge space, at least the stretch of it that Nita could see from horizon to horizon, was full of water splashing back and forth like a bathtub in which the person submerged has moved too quickly. *It'll take care of itself now,* she thought. *The next stage will be ready to go in a few seconds. So get up and do the next thing before the reaction sets in. Hers will be setting in, too, and if you can push her into overloading herself before she understands what's happening —*

Nita got her feet under her, staggered, steadied herself. "Bobo," she said. "I want to see them. And I want them to see me. And the area around me for about a mile or so."

Remote visioning? I can handle that.

"What's the energy outlay like?"

Against what you just did? Negligible.

"Do it."

Nita stood as straight as she could. She didn't have to work at looking angry. A moment later, she was looking at the floor of the Scarlet Tower as if it were an island touching her own. All around it, the Shamaska stared at her in astonishment: and the four in the center were trying to maintain neutral expressions, and mostly failing. Aurilelde in particular was looking both horrified and enraged, and trying to cover it up.

"Well," Nita said, trying to sound as snotty and unconcerned as Dairine could on occasion, "*that* was pretty lame."

Aurilelde opened her mouth. Nita didn't give her a chance. "Yeah, yeah, impossible," she said. "Well, guess what, Miss Not-a-Wizard? *Not* impossible. And I am annoyed with you. Not Khretef, who is really Kit — Hi, Kit! — and not your poor dad; the One only knows which of you is running things, and I don't care. Not even Mister Rorsik behind you there; I don't know who he thinks he's running, and I don't have time to waste finding out. *You* dropped that wave on me and choked off transit and shield-spelling. So let's get serious."

She glanced over her shoulder. Behind her, their initial stage completed, the massive twin tubes of the Pellegrino passthrough were now slowly rearing up behind her over the city like the graceful bodies of two gigantic serpents — the wizardly containment field no more than a thin, shimmering skin that looked like it could let go at any moment. "Earth's premier hydro-mage," Nita said, "spent nine years of her life designing this wizardry to move huge volumes of water around between two oceans, under precise control. And I mean *precise* — not like the big crude kindergarten-sandbox stunt you just tried. But then you're not a wizard, and having one telling you how to dump a bucket of water over somebody's head isn't the same as actually under-standing what you're controlling. I, however, *under-stand* water because I work with it a lot. So you'd better believe me when I tell you that if you do not answer my challenge right now, I'm going to instruct one of the two ends of this wizardry to terminate right there in that room with you, and the other to terminate over the City of the Shamaska, and then I'll tell both of them to emit the same volume of water as you just dropped on me ... with approximately a hundred times the force. The City will be destroyed. And as for you personally, your bodies may be tough, but I'm betting many of you will die. And even if you don't, how pleasant will the very few Shamaska survivors find life in this world when I've destroyed all your lovely, comfy tech, and your pretty city, and forced you to roam the surface of Mars digging up raw materials and building things from scratch?"

The three men around the Throne looked nervously from Nita to Aurilelde. "You would never do such a thing!" Aurilelde cried. "You are a wizard — wizards cannot —"

"Wizards *can*," Nita said. "*Watch me!* I told you, I am *annoyed*. You are screwing with life on my planet generally and my life personally ... and I'm willing to pay the price for dealing with you once and for all. You want to prevent me smashing you and your little toy city all over the mountainside? Then you, Aurilelde, meet me right here, and you and I will have it out. You have a kernel. I have everything else. Let's find out who really rules Mars." And she grinned a nasty grin that she did not have to borrow from Dairine. "Should be fun." Then she allowed some scorn to show. "Unless you're scared, of course."

Khretef was trying to stop her, but Aurilelde

leaped to her feet, a murderous expression on her face. The white-hot fury would have looked astonishing on someone so young, except that Nita had Dairine for a little sister and was used to such displays. "I have *no* fear of you! You cannot take my world, or my Khretef, or my City —"

"Actually, I can," Nita said softly. "Come down here and stop me . . . if you dare." And she turned her back on them. *Bobo? Kill it.*

The view into the City vanished. Nita glanced at the passthrough wizardry. "How long will it hold there?" she said.

Approximately twenty-eight minutes. Then your backlash will kick in.

Nita rubbed her face, feeling the shakes starting, and tensed herself: she didn't dare let them take hold. "I need some height," she said. "She was able to stop local spelling partly because I was too close to the ground, where a kernel's power is most effective — close to the body of the planet. It'll be weaker up high. She'll be limited to exploiting magnetic fields and microgravity and wind and such, and she won't have had enough time to get proficient with those. I just need to wear her down and get close, and then —"

Physical confrontation?

"Crude and ugly," Nita said, "but though I hate to admit it, occasionally effective. So let's go skywalking."

Hi, Kit!

He had been dozing uneasily in the darkness, caught in a dream from which he couldn't wake and through which he couldn't sink into deeper sleep. But the words caught him out of the darkness, pushed him toward waking.

He caught just a glimpse of the world through Khretef's eyes: the room at the top of the Scarlet Tower, the Shamaska people gathered there — and in the midst of it all a single non-Shamaska figure, slender, erect, and dangerous-looking. Over everything loomed vast twin serpents of water, poised and waiting on her word. He caught the gleam of her eyes, angry, but somehow still with a hint of amusement in the anger: everything under control, even though she was also deadly tired and scared.

Neets!

Hi, Kit!

— the image shut down. Fear darkened everything around him. But at least he knew his name again. For a few moments there, he'd lost it.

Kit looked around him in the darkness, hunting for a way out, for any ray of light. There was none. He might as well have been in a hole in the ground, the dirt shoveled in, tamped down. . . . *A grave. That's what this is like* . . .

It was a freaky image, one he pushed away. *It's only if I accept it that I'm going to be stuck here,* he thought. Yes, it was hard to think: there was pressure all around him to give it up, let it go, no way out . . . and the darkness itself seemed to have weight. But time's weight wasn't enough to keep a wizard down, not unless he let it. And the weight of intention wasn't enough, either. *I've got some intention of my own —*

As if in response, the darkness pushed down harder on him. But Kit had something to hold up against it: the image he'd just caught, the glimpse of Nita. *She's hot,* Kit thought in surprise. *Just how exactly have I failed to notice that Neets is hot?* Maybe it was because she didn't throw it around or make a weapon of it, the way some of the girls at school did, or tried to. Maybe it was because Kit was so busy just being her friend and not wanting to add anything extraneous to the equation. When the spell was already balanced, you didn't go hanging extra elements on it just because you could —

And maybe I was just a little bit chicken about it? Kit thought. Because this admission would complicate things — no question about it. Maybe life was nice and comfy and safe without this complication, at a time when a lot of things had not been comfy or safe for either of them — so that Kit hadn't wanted to rock the boat. *And maybe that's why I've been giving Darryl and Ronan so much grief.*

But the sight of her there, looking deadly — and extremely competent and wizardly and pissed off and, well, frankly, kind of magnificent —

Kit blushed. Then he swore at himself. *Later for that. Right now we've got problems!* And there was somebody else besides Khretef who was part of the "we." The realization was strangely exciting. *Now all I have to do is get the hell out of here so I can be some use to her. Because I got her into this —*

"You can't!" said a gigantic voice that was both Khretef's and his own — and for that reason, strangely difficult to argue with. "Too much is riding on it! The fate of our people, their past *and* their future —"

He's trying to drown you out, Kit thought. *Don't let it happen. Stand up; get real; get focused. You still have a body. Even if you don't,* fake *it that you have a body!*

Kit felt around him. For a scary few seconds there was nothing to be felt in the darkness. *Nothing's here, I'm not here —*

Cut that out! Yes, I am! And slowly he felt a floor under him — or talked himself into believing there was one. *Which is it? Doesn't matter. Wizardry's about persuasion, and sometimes the one you've got to persuade is yourself. Let's go, floor!*

It was there: he could feel it against his hands. He was sitting on it. Kit got his feet under him, got up. "Khretef?" he shouted. "This has got to stop!"

"Yes, it does. At *your* end! Stop fighting it: let what's fated happen!"

Kit clenched his fists as the pressure of the darkness came down on him again, and he braced himself against it. It was tough: he felt strangely hollow, as if he had no access to wizardry.

"You don't," said that weird dual voice. "Your power is mine now . . . and it's being passed to someone who can make the best use of it."

Kit's eyes narrowed. There were ways to do that legally: any wizard could act as power source for someone else's spell. But the procedure required consent. "No way!" he shouted. "I'm not playing this game!"

"You consented when we blended a little while

ago," said the voice. "Too late now. Why fight with yourself? It's over."

The darkness kept pressing down, a physical force, hard to resist. But Kit flashed on something else — one of his gym teachers, Mr. Thorgesen, who'd been coaching him on weights this last semester. Kit had started out hating this part of gym but had suddenly realized that there was a skill involved, a matter of balance and leverage very like some acts of wizardry, and almost against his will he'd started to get into it. *And will's the issue* — "It's not just a dead weight," Mr. T. kept saying. "Work out where the leverage is and use it to your best advantage —"

"I'm not fighting with myself!" Kit said, pressing up, feeling for the points of leverage in the other's mind. And suddenly, in bizarre alliance, it was Mr. Mack helping him here, too, helping him find the leverage point. *What matters is thinking yourself into those people's heads. Imagine how the world looked to them! Their lives, their troubles. That's how what they do starts to make sense* — "*I'm* me! And Nita's Nita! We are not just little fragments of you guys, like the Shard's a fragment of the kernel! We've got our own lives, and they're not yours! But you people are all about being fragmented and broken up. You see *everything* that way! And you really need to get past the blind spot, because you're ruining any chance for your own lives to be whole things that aren't broken!"

For the first time Khretef didn't seem to have an answer ready. Kit could feel his uncertainty, like a splinter of light piercing the gloom. It actually *was* a splinter of light: the room in the Tower, right now, where Nita stood challenging the furious Aurilelde, and then vanished. "You've got it backwards!" Kit said as Aurilelde vanished, too. "We're not the ones who're like you: you're the ones who're like *us*. We're what you could be if you weren't stuck in the past and in the middle of this dumb thing where your people hate each other! And your two sides have been hating each other so long, I bet you don't even remember what started it in the first place!"

"That's nonsense!" Khretef shouted. And then for just a shocked second he was silent. The silence told Kit that Khretef couldn't find anything to say, and however screwed up he might be, Khretef was still wizard enough not to want to lie —

"It's true, and you know it is!" Kit said, both sad for Khretef's people's sake and yet triumphant to know that his guess was true. "Whatever got you guys fighting, it's so long ago that you can't remember. Which means it also shouldn't *matter* anymore! And you've got the sense to see that. But Aurilelde doesn't! She's the one who scared you into trapping me in here, isn't she? And now she's going to take this mess through to its illogical conclusion. Lots of people on Earth will die when our world's status quo gets destabilized by what's happening here. The Eilitt and the Shamaska will keep right on killing each other. Everything will get worse. This isn't your dream of everything working out for the best. This will be a *nightmare*. Put a stop to it, Khretef! Let me go!"

There was a long, unhappy silence. "It's too late now," the voice said. "It's started . . ."

The skywalking Nita had in mind didn't involve actual walking, as in the various exploits using hardened air. From the manual Nita had pulled a spell that persuaded local gravity to ignore her for a while, wrapping it around her like a blanket so that it dissolved into her body. Another price to be paid later — and not too much later. *I'll worry about that in half an hour,* Nita thought as she more completely undid gravity's effects on her mass and drifted ever more quickly upward. Normally this kind of spell was a fair amount of work, which was why wizards didn't overdo it. But she was in a hurry, and the effort would have a specific use in what she was doing . . . so Nita soared, and enjoyed it. *Since who knows how much time I'm going to have to enjoy afterwards?*

She reached an altitude of about thirty thousand feet above Argyre Planitia and just hung there, savoring the view. High above her, Mamvish's cloaking-spell was holding: it was too far above the planetary kernel's range for Aurilelde to interfere with it, and too powerful for Khretef or Iskard to alter, even if they wanted to. Down below, though . . . water, water was everywhere. It was stunning. Nita thought of how it would be someday when people from Earth or wherever started terraforming this terrain slowly and responsibly. When there was an atmosphere again, when there was enough heat held in to keep water liquid, enough to grow plants . . . she could imagine what it would look like. But even now the huge flow and rush of water across the landscape was beautiful. Chains of crater lakes flashed in the sunlight: water was rushing down the sides of Valles Marineris in waterfalls six miles high; the southern polar basins were flooding, flashing the Sun back in a bloom of light —

— and a small, dark shape there, suddenly, between Nita and the water — drifting closer, her veils of smoke and her smoky hair wreathing weightless around her up here in the almost-nonexistent air: Aurilelde.

Nita let herself drift closer to Aurilelde, holding out her hands, ready. Normally she didn't believe in grandstanding during her spells, and dramatic gestures weren't for her. But perception could count for a great deal in a wizards' duel.

Nita gulped hard at the thought that that was exactly what she was now embarked upon. It was not a situation you normally invited. Wizardry itself could become cranky at the concept of being used against itself without good reason. And she wasn't sure that even having Bobo on her side would necessarily mean she was going to prevail in this contest. The phrase "grudge match" kept rising in her mind, and Nita had to keep pushing it away.

Aurilelde was drifting closer to Nita now. Nita assumed an amused smile while stretching out her senses to learn the one thing that she most desperately needed to know: that the kernel was still indeed here, and complete. *It's all here, and it's still inside of her.*

"So you can feel it," said Aurilelde. "You're more talented than I thought."

"Any *wizard* can feel it," Nita said. "And are you insane to actually allow someone to talk you into putting a planet's kernel inside your body? Don't you know what that will *do* to you?"

"Rorsik has told me what it will do to *you*," Aurilelde said. "That's sufficient."

Nita shook her head. "Bad advice," she said. "The kind of management you get from internalization is short-lived. And management isn't anywhere near mastery. Down on the ground, it might have been enough. Up here?" She laughed softly. "Let's see what you've got, because the about-to-be-ex-Khretef can't help you anymore."

"On the contrary," Aurilelde said in her mind, cold and furious. "He's helped me all he needs to. And he's taken your little ghost-Kit's power and shown me how to use it to manage the planet's non-gravitic forces: the magnetic fields, the upper winds. So now the problems are all yours. Does the ground suit?"

Nita frowned. In a wizard's duel, the phrase acquired a meaning past the usual one; it was tantamount to offering the other wizard a choice of weapons. "Aurilelde," Nita said, "that's not a question you have the right to ask me! You're just piggybacking on a wizard's talents. If you were one of us, you'd be concerned about the responsibility that goes with the power. But you just want your own way. You don't care about what happens to anyone else."

Aurilelde gave her a furious look. "I care! I care about Khretef! More than anything —"

"No, you don't," Nita said. "And if you did, that would be another problem." She clenched her fists. "I really don't want to do this —"

"That's apparent," Aurilelde said, laughing. "You hate the thought of fighting to keep him! You want me to just give him up and walk away."

Nita shook her head. "One of us has to be grown up about this, and I guess it gets to be me. Despite the fact that you're about five billion years old —"

Aurilelde glared at her, furious. "I am *not!*"

Nita had to grin. *And name-calling is so unproductive usually . . .* "Okay. Four point five billion, give or take an eon . . ."

"And you just want back what you think belongs to you!" Aurilelde said. "Khretef told me what he could hear in Kit's mind. You never let him be what he wanted to be! It was always about what *you* wanted, what *you* feared. But when he started to find a new life, a different world, you wanted no part of it: it bored you! Only when you thought it might take him from you did you start to become interested, and then you pushed yourself in —"

Nita was about to start arguing hotly about how this wasn't true. But she stopped herself. "This is about what you're about to do to my home planet. It isn't about him —"

"It's *all* about him!" Aurilelde cried. "It's *only* about him! To try to pretend otherwise is a lie. And wizards don't lie. Do you?"

Nita let herself drift more closely to Aurilelde, trying not to make it look like she was doing it on purpose. But as she did, through her tenuous connection to Mars's kernel, she could feel the planet under her shiver uneasily, as if about to turn in its sleep. It wasn't a feeling she liked. "You're trying to tell me," Nita said, "that I'm just jealous of you. There's an easy lie. Even easier for somebody who's not a wizard. But even if you and Khretef are so much older than us, that doesn't give you the right to do whatever you like with Kit's soul! And if you or Khretef have actually *done* what you say you have" — she found suddenly that she was shaking — "then it's better we should *all* die, right here and now. The One will sort us out, reincarnation or no reincarnation. I know what Timeheart is, if you don't!"

Aurilelde's expression was going back and forth between stricken and furious — and then the horror shifted permanently to rage. Nita, drifting just a little closer, thought again of the good old cartoon idiom about getting an opponent angry so they'd make a mistake. Aurilelde was making it already. *Just let me close enough to you to get a good grip and pull that kernel out of you* — But Aurilelde wasn't angry enough. One last thing was needed. "I wonder, though," Nita said, "whether someone who died for you once might just see how you're behaving now and say, 'Did I die for her, or did she just let me go out and be killed so she could have *this* — the power to rule the planet?'" For she could feel the tremor down below them starting to grow. "'And when this poor Kit came along, she used him the same way, and let his soul be lost so she could keep this power for herself — '"

"No!"

"And then he'll say, 'How long do *I* have? When she realizes the truth, she'll find another way to get rid of me —'" Nita was now staring into Aurilelde's eyes from only a few feet away —

"No, no, *no!*" Screaming, Aurilelde lunged at Nita. Nita grabbed for her, but Aurilelde hurled herself backward and away in reaction, raising her arms. Underneath the two of them, the surface of the planet started going hazy. *Dust storm?* Nita thought, and then realized the truth. *No! Marsquake!*

The planet's crust was beginning to convulse, great ripples starting to spread away from the spot beneath them. Craters were cracking across, water flooding down into the crevasses; elsewhere vast blocks and slabs of stone were jolting upward out of the crust —

Olympus Mons wasn't affected yet, but Nita had no idea how long that would last. *She doesn't realize what she's capable of with that thing inside her,* Nita thought, horrified. *She doesn't realize that the kernel's more than just a planet's physical rules, but its spiritual affiliations, the myths and stories others wind into it, all tangled up together.* Aurilelde didn't realize what was happening to her. She was *becoming* Mars itself, a mad Mars: not a god of war, but a goddess, and a goddess scorned —

And in her craziness she'll pull the whole planet apart, Nita thought, horrified. She could feel the tremors propagating farther down into the crust, the strains in the planet's mantle increasing. *It'll just shatter!* At first the pieces wouldn't go far: they'd settle into another great asteroid belt. *But orbits elsewhere in the system will be destabilized! And Earth's closest —*

Twenty-four minutes, Bobo said.

Nita swallowed and headed directly for Aurilelde. "If you're trying to get at me that way," Nita said to her, "you're going to have to get a lot more personal —"

That was when the blow hit Nita and slammed her tumbling up toward space. "Think so?" Aurilelde said. "Then we'll just give you your wish."

Around Nita, now choking in the vacuum, suddenly freezing, the pitiless darkness closed in. . . .

In the darkness, Khretef's voice was saying, "It doesn't matter, anyway. When they're done, when Aurilelde's won, we'll be one forever. Why should this be so bad?" Khretef was almost pleading. "We were so alike, anyway, almost the same . . ."

Standing there by himself in the dark, holding off its ever-increasing pressure, Kit shook his head. "We have things in common, sure!" he said. "We're alive! And you and me, we're in the service of Life: you took the Oath! We're on the same side! So why are you trying to rub me out? Wizards don't destroy things without good reason! Wizards keep things going, they fix what's broken, they don't throw other living beings out just because they're in the way!"

"But Aurilelde says —"

"Aurilelde's not a wizard, Khretef! She's a seer,

yeah, but even seers don't always see straight. Especially if they're scared! She's scared for you, and she's letting that warp the way she sees what has to happen! You can't just let her pictures of how the world ought to be erase yours. It's as bad as what she's told you that you've got to do to me!"

"That's wrong," Khretef said. "That has to be wrong — you don't understand —"

Once again that uncertainty made Kit sure he was right. "She got it backwards, buddy," Kit said. "She foresaw us, me and Nita, and she saw that we were somehow the answer to Mars's problem. No news there: every wizard's the answer to some problem of the universe's! But she also saw that everything was going to have to change for you guys in some big weird way, and that scared her. She started concentrating on the parts of the vision she could bear to look at, and screened out the rest. She saw she needed a wizard's power to bring Earth's wizards into the picture. She saw herself at the center of it, protecting her dad and her people, even protecting you. So you gave her access to your power. And now you just feel dumb because you can't take it back without a fight, and fighting her's the last thing you want to do!"

The silence in the darkness was anguished. Finally the voice spoke again, and this time it was far less Kit's, far more Khretef's. "She was so sure," he said. "Even when I started becoming uncomfortable about letting her share my own power..." Kit could feel Khretef's shame at that remembered discomfort: how could he deny any part of himself to the love of his life? "And then she said, 'The other's coming: give me his power if you can't give me yours! It won't matter; he's just another you. And think what it will mean. No more fighting. The end of the other side's threats, at last and forever —'"

"The old story," Kit said. "And not Aurilelde's voice, either. You know who wrote *that* dialogue! You didn't invent war: the Lone Power did! One of its favorite tools — because war's the easy way out of conflict, and *not* having wars, having enough compassion and smarts to stay out of them, is real hard work! Getting into the other guy's mindset is real tough to do in the first place, and it's hard to stay there. Lots easier to decide that the other guy's so different from you that there's no hope for him. That he's going to hate you forever, and for the sake of your peace of mind, he's better off dead." The image of that dark splotch on the Korean peninsula, where the light suddenly stopped, was flaring at the back of Kit's mind: and Khretef saw it, too, laid out before them in the darkness as Kit had seen it while sitting on his Earthwatching rock on the Moon. "But it doesn't have to be that way, Khretef! *Break the pattern and poke the Lone One in the eye!*"

There was a long silence. "They'll say I'm a traitor to both sides," Khretef whispered. "Again! And I'll be betraying Aurilelde, too —"

"Brother, you've got to do *something*," Kit said. "You can't just sit here and let this go on! It's not just your world, and your people — all of them, the Eilitt and the Shamaska. It's Earth, too, billions of people whose lives are going to get completely screwed up because of what's happening here if it's not stopped! You're a wizard. You know how it has to go! You can love Aurilelde all you like, but if you don't act now, the Lone Power's just going to sit there laughing at how you gave It just what It wanted while you were sure you were doing the only thing you could —"

Another long and desperate silence. "What do I do?" Khretef said finally.

"*Let me go!*" Kit said. "I'll do what I can for you and Aurilelde, I promise, but right now we've got two whole worlds to worry about. *Let me out of here!*"

The silence continued. Then the pressure against which Kit had been straining started to let up. From deep inside the darkness, Kit felt a shift in the power underlying the place. The feeling started slowly transmuting into a weird stretching, as if something was fastened to Kit's skin and his bones, pulling him painfully out of shape. Kit set his teeth, tried to deal with the pain as it worsened, became intolerable —

It stopped.

It's not working, Khretef said silently, as if inside Kit's head again. *It's too late. For both of us . . .*

Nita tried to blink, couldn't. She gasped for air, shivering with the frost that had formed on her skin in just a few seconds of airless darkness. *Bobo?*

She hit you with a chunk of hardened atmosphere, the peridexis said. *I was just able to keep your shields in force at minimum, because you weren't entirely unconscious. You got lucky. Stay conscious, or I can't be of any use to you!*

Nita brushed away ice, blinked until her eyes worked again, and turned to face Aurilelde, who was hanging there in the darkness and laughing. "You see?" she said. "You have no *idea* what I can do. With the kernel — and the power of a wizard whose will is in abeyance — I can do things you can't imagine!"

Nita was starting to get really steamed now. "What, hitting somebody with a brick?" Nita said. "*That's* unimaginable? Heaven forbid I should get really creative with you, then. Let's keep it simple." *Because all that bluffing down there aside, I really don't want to run the risk of killing you and maybe screwing up the kernel forever —*

She reached her hands out into the space around her. *Dust,* she thought. The space around the planet was full of it. Nita called it to her, whispering in the Speech. *Dust, come help your mother-world, because if this space case has her way, there won't be a solid place for you to fall back on: you'll be left floating out around here by yourself forever in the dark till Jupiter eats you or you fall into the Sun! Come lend me a hand here, get solid, get real —*

Seconds later Nita was almost obscured by a cloud of it. Aurilelde laughed at her. "You think you can hide that way?" she cried, and came at Nita. "Watch this —"

"By all means," Nita said, turning the spell loose, and swept one hand down at Aurilelde. The dust followed, clumping together, solidifying, and striking Aurilelde hard in the chest. The impact of the blow sent her plummeting toward the planet as if a giant hand had swatted her there.

Nita dived after her, intent on the kernel. *Have to work out how to do this. Don't want to hurt her, just have to get that kernel out of her! Got them out of walls and floors and planetary cores before: but those weren't alive. How do I do this without —*

Something struck Nita hard in the head. She jerked sideways, dazed for a moment, and just got a glimpse of the thing as it floated away on the rebound. It was a nickel-iron meteorite about the size of a walnut. Aurilelde, recovering too quickly from Nita's blow, had snagged it in passing and slung it at her. Nita put her hand up to her head, pulled it back and saw the blood, and went queasy. *Better quit being so nice and put a stop to this real quick before she hits you with something bigger. Like Deimos!*

Fortunately Mars's lesser satellite wasn't in the neighborhood, but there were other asteroid fragments nearby, and Aurilelde threw a number of those at Nita, missing as Nita dodged. Then she started using the weak Martian magnetic field itself on Nita. Strange lights started sparking at the back of Nita's eyes, and her ears started ringing as her nervous system complained about the abuse by the locally accelerated fields —

Would you please cut that out?! Nita said to the magnetic field: and as usual, preferring courteous wizardly persuasion to the crass ordering-around that Aurilelde was inflicting on it, the knots of magnetic flux assailing her dissolved. But by the time Nita's vision and sense of balance were back to normal,

Aurilelde was trying the hardened-air exploit on her again, this time simply sliding a block of it up under Nita and accelerating it. *Whoa!* Nita thought as the acceleration sharply increased. *Not good, we're heading for escape velocity here —!*

Nita let out an angry breath and simply pushed sideways off the block to drift free again in the microgravity: then spoke the phrase that would undo several vital strands of the antigrav spell she was wearing. *I'm trying to help you out here!* she said in the Speech to Mars's gravity well. *A little pull here, please? You've got some gravitational anomalies to spare —*

Her acceleration away from the planet slowed, ceased, then reversed direction. Nita dropped toward the planet's surface with increasing speed; she doubled over into a dive, straightening as she fell faster. *Doing end-runs around the kernel by sweet-talking local forces isn't going to stop this,* she thought. *Got to get my hands on that thing fast!* "Bobo, how're her energy levels holding up?"

She's strong, Bobo said. *She's got a whole planet to draw on.*

"Can't you do anything about it?"

Not without getting the kernel dissociated from her, Bobo said. *For the time being, she* is *Mars —*

Don't remind me, Nita thought, for down on the surface the dust was kicking up. *So how the heck do I get her to stop being Mars? If only for a few minutes —*

Another of those blocks of hardened air hit Nita and clouted her hard up into the borders of the atmosphere again. As she recovered and plunged downward again, Nita could see the destruction continuing, the desolation spreading as some old volcanoes woke up and new ones broke out like a fiery rash as the crust ripped and lava thrust up from the depths. Fueled by the power Aurilelde's kernel-connected rage was feeding to the wizardry running loose on the planet; oceans were coming real out of the past; Valles Marineris was slowly flooding, running over with ancient water beyond its ability to drain out into the northern ocean basins. Mars was tearing itself apart in fire and water. "Stop it, Aurilelde!" Nita shouted at her as she got close to Aurilelde again. "You can't do this!"

"I can!" Aurilelde yelled back. "And I will! If only to teach you what I can do and *you* can't — what I can have and *you* can't! Khretef is *mine!* He was always mine! We don't need this world! Yours will do just as well. When this world's gone, and we've taken yours, we'll live there and he'll be mine again! Mine forever —"

Nita kept heading toward her. *Angry isn't working! Just tell her the truth* — "Nothing's forever, Aurilelde!" she shouted. "You may not be a wizard, but Kit is, and Khretef is, and they both know that entropy's running, and sooner or later, everything dies." Nita's eyes started to sting. "The people you love die, and love may be enough to slow down the death sometimes, or even reverse it for a while — but not every time, and not forever!" She thought of her mother, of Ponch, and then had to wipe her eyes. *Oh, damn it, I thought I was through with this! I guess not for a while yet.* It won't work. Kit will die someday, yeah! I may be there to see it: I've already almost seen it once or twice." She wiped her eyes again, but anger was getting the better of her now. "But that's more than you can say — because where were *you* when Khretef died? Off somewhere safe. Let him handle the danger, huh? Not your business, Princess? That's not how love works!"

Aurilelde laughed scornfully as she arrowed toward Nita again. "As if *you* know anything about love! Your idea of physical intimacy is punching Kit in the shoulder —"

Nita flushed hot. "Well, looks like I know more than you do, because I don't have to keep *my* boyfriend in a cage! That's what you're trying to build for Khretef. You'll stamp out all your enemies — meaning his people, mostly — and then rule Mars or Earth or whatever with him at your side. *Chained* there! Because the life you're awake in now scares you too much to ever let him go; he's the only thing that makes you feel safe. It's not love holding you to him now: it's fear! And Khretef knows that! But he means to stay with you anyway, because he's sorry for what the fear's turned you into —"

The completely stricken look spreading across Aurilelde's face told Nita that this was all the truth, her visionary talent perhaps picking up on something Kit knew. Nita shivered.

"No! He stays with me because he loves me —"

"Oh, he'll let you think that," Nita said, angry. "Because he's a hero, like Kit, he's willing to be locked up in that cage with you forever. That's his business. But I will not let Kit stay locked up in there, too!"

Aurilelde slowly dropped her hands and just hung there on the borders of space, a look of increasing horror spreading across her face. Nita, watching, hardly dared to breathe, even to move.

It was hard to just wait and give Aurilelde this one last chance to get it right, even with the memory of that voice screaming, *I don't need this world: yours will do as well!* It was so easy to think, *You're a hopeless case: nothing to do with you but throw you out of the game!* But the Rede had said, *To wreak aright | she must slay her rival* — And that had to mean the scared and angry Aurilelde who was ready to tear a planet apart to get her way. *She has to have the chance to reject that option, or this won't work* —

The moment stretched as Aurilelde drifted, and the back of Nita's mind became an uproar of her own fears, for Earth, for Kit. *We're wasting time. She'll never turn! Just put her out of her misery while she's off balance and get on with saving one world if not two* — Nita swallowed. *Bobo*, she said silently, *this is it. Let's have that routine for getting a kernel out of a living matrix against its will* —

The peridexis showed Nita the structure of the spell. And as it did, Aurilelde raised her arms, her face shifting into a mask of fury, and launched herself toward Nita. A moment later her hands were around Nita's throat, squeezing.

Nita reeled back in shock bizarrely tinged with

embarrassment, since her personal force field was presently keyed toward protecting her from vast impersonal forces, not the kind of playground stuff that she might have expected from Joanne and her crowd back in the bad old days. But Nita had learned some techniques back then that still worked fine. She reached out and snaked her right arm over one of Aurilelde's and under the other, then angled the arm up to twist her attacker's arms free. Aurilelde tried to get another grip, but before she had a chance, Nita grabbed both her wrists in one hand, then described a quick line of hard light around them with one index finger. The thin strand of force field knotted itself tight.

That second was all Nita needed. Inside Aurilelde, the visionary gift showed her the tangle of light that was what she wanted. As Aurilelde struggled and screamed, *"No!,"* Nita finished saying the spell the peridexis had passed her, and plunged her hand straight into Aurilelde's chest.

Aurilelde screamed. So did Nita, so close to the pain and so much in sync with it: for the kernel she gripped was all tangled up with Aurilelde's soul. She could even hear Kit scream, too: through Khretef he was as caught up in this as Nita.

Not — much longer! Nita thought, panting with pain. *At least — I've got hold of the kernel. Now all I need to do — is get it out —* But that was going to be the hard part. She made sure of her grip on the tangle of hot, rusty light buried inside Aurilelde. This wouldn't be easy: the wizardry that had implanted it there was complex, elegant, and very tough.

But so are you! she heard Kit say from somewhere. *Go!*

Nita grinned in triumph and desperate hope. She clenched her fist around the kernel, braced herself, spoke the final word of the spell's second part, and yanked out what she held.

The kernel came free. Nita fell backward with the flash of pain that went through her opponent. Crying out in shock and anguish, Aurilelde plummeted toward the planet. But Nita had no time for her right now. All her attention was on the brilliant interwoven tangle of profoundly ancient wizardry that was the kernel of the planet Mars. The impression she'd gotten of it earlier, of reddish light, was correct: thousands of strands and cords of wizardry, all keyed to the planet's gravity and mass and composition and construction, were writhing and glowing in the tangle of power as it flowered out to its full volume, a beachball-size mass of rose and rust and blood and sunset colors. But they were in chaos, the tangle of terrible power now jittering and buzzing in fury that was a residue of Aurilelde's.

Traumatized, Nita thought. *And why not, after where it's been stuck and what it's been through?* She threw a glance down at the planet. Half of it was obscured now by the fury of dust being kicked up by the worsening quakes. *Bad. Let's go —*

Nita took a deep breath, then sank her hands into

the kernel, concentrating. One strand very deep in the kernel, near its nucleus, controlled geological and crustal activity, and that one was singing like a plucked string, still resonating with Aurilelde's rage. Nita grabbed for it, tried to calm it down.

But the kernel had already been locked too long in relationship with Aurilelde's soul for the relationship to quickly come undone. Furious at having been ignored and mismanaged for so long and now further enraged at being tampered with by yet another stranger, the kernel resisted Nita. But it was now in the hands of a wizard who'd gone through some difficult schooling in kernel management techniques — unlike Aurilelde, whose control over it had been strictly second-hand a matter of half-understood instincts, half-remembered advice, and wishful thinking. *What you need with these things is understanding,* Nita thought. *And figuring them out always wins out over just plunging around feeling stuff . . .*

In Nita's grasp, the kernel jumped and struggled, indignant at the sudden change of control, trying to leap away and return to where it had been moments before. "Oh, no," Nita said softly. "You are *not* going there!" She clutched it, hanging on, working her right hand in to close around that one shrieking string of the kernel through which she could feel the earthquakes rippling across Mars's crust. She gripped that string hard, damping it down. "Stop being so angry!" she told it. "There's no point in it. It's all over now. Just calm down —"

It ignored her. "Just stop it," Nita told it. "*It's going to be all right!* Let go of it and *calm down!*" And slowly, slowly, under force of mind, under furious intention, and right through Nita's fear for Kit, the vibration gradually began to settle down, fading, letting go. The string stopped singing. Nita glanced down at the Martian surface. It would be a long while before the dust settled. But under the surface, she could now feel the residual transverse waves of the earthquake dying away, going quiet.

She let out a long, scared breath.

Twelve minutes, Bobo said. *Meanwhile, don't you think you've forgotten something?*

Nita glanced down. Bright in the light of the Sun behind her, like a falling star, a tiny figure was accelerating toward the planet's surface. For just a moment, thinking of what Aurilelde had intended for Kit and for the Earth, a nasty, satisfied anger flared up in Nita. *If she does land a little too hard to survive, well, maybe she had it coming. The* Rede *did say:* — yet to wreak aright, / she must slay her rival — *And if she didn't, then maybe I* . . .

Nita hung there, silent. *No,* she thought. *Prophecy is fine, but it doesn't* have *to happen* . . . "Sorry," she said to someone she was sure was watching, "not today . . ." and dived after Aurilelde.

The Shamaska was falling uncontrolled, tumbling. Nita easily beat her down to ground level at Argyre Planitia — now a sprinkling of islands in a broad, round sea that was slowly draining through many outlets at its edges — and alighted on one to wait for her. Nita felt around in the kernel's interior for the controls for local gravity and planetary mass. *There they are,* she thought, and made a couple of simple but significant changes.

High above her, Aurilelde's fall began to slow: by the time she was perceptible as a body with arms and legs, several hundred feet up, she had decelerated to a slow drift. "Bobo," Nita said, "I need the usual transit spell. Put the far end down inside the Scarlet Tower —"

Right, the peridexis said. *Nine minutes . . .*

"Until I collapse?" Nita said.

Unless you do it sooner.

Nita gulped. She was starting to feel those shakes again as the circle of the transit spell appeared on the tableland in front of her. *Never mind,* she thought. *Not just yet —*

Aurilelde was falling toward the center of the circle. Nita checked the integrity of her personal force field, making sure it was set for physical attack and weaponry now. "Collapse this after we're both through," she said, and stepped in.

Meridiani Planum

Nita's second step came down on the polished floor of the Tower. The Throne was empty. A hubbub of scared, angry voices was bouncing around inside, but it went hushed as they registered Nita's sudden presence.

She headed for the Throne and the three men standing there, the kernel in her hands. They stared at her: Iskard in shock, Khretef in horror, Rorsik in rage.

"That is ours!" Rorsik cried. *"Give it back!"*

Nita stared at him, then looked at Khretef. "You see what *he* cares about," she said, jerking her head at Rorsik.

Khretef hurried toward her. "Where is Aurilelde?"

Behind Nita, Aurilelde fell out of the air and bounced gently to the floor.

Khretef rushed to her. Nita ignored those two for the moment. "This is *not* yours!" she said to Rorsik. "It belongs to Mars. And you haven't done a whole lot today to prove that you ever ought to be given access to it, so if I were you, I'd just shut up. Especially since *you* put her up to this."

Rorsik opened his mouth, shut it again.

"And as for you," Nita said, turning her attention to Iskard, "*you* really need some father lessons. I'm sure it's nice for you to run the city! Maybe you even really do have your people's interests at heart. But you let *this* guy talk you into endangering your daughter's life so she could use the kernel to wipe out your enemies. You know what? She would have destroyed the planet doing it! She was halfway there already. And then you forced Khretef into doing things he wouldn't otherwise have wanted to do, because otherwise you wouldn't let him and Aurilelde hook up. Which was *really* nasty and sick. One wizard subverting another like that? One wizard getting another one to bend the Oath way out of shape for his own purposes? What got into you? Then again, don't tell me. I think I can guess."

She was getting angrier by the moment, and shakier, but Nita was intent on seeing this through to its logical conclusion before she fell over. "You don't understand!" Iskard said to her, coming toward her. "We dared not allow the Eilitt to obtain an advantage over us! Their wizards were doing exactly the same kind of thing, seeking control of the kernel, trying to —"

"You stop *right there*," Nita said, holding up the kernel, "because I'm just about ready to hose you and your city off the face of Mars like dog poop down the driveway!"

Iskard froze where he was. "I'm sick of your excuses and your fighting!" Nita said. "And I'm sick of wizards who're so blinded by how much they've hated each other for umpty million years that they're willing to forget that they took an Oath never to *do* crap like this! So you're about to get a taste of your own medicine." Nita staggered, straightened again. "There's a full implementation of a transoceanic pass-through hanging over your heads right this minute, and I'm in a mood to use it if I don't get my partner back *right now*. If I go, too, when the hard rain comes down, big deal, because life without Kit doesn't look so hot right now! And I'm betting I'd be doing the universe a service in getting *you* people off the books. For Kit and me, 'cause our Oaths are in place, I'm betting there's always Timeheart. Whereas for you, the Lone Power only knows where you'll wind up, and I can't bring myself to care. *So?*"

Iskard looked back toward where Khretef was helping Aurilelde up. He sat down dully on the Throne with a thump, like a man defeated. "It cannot be undone," he said.

"Wrong answer," Nita said softly. "Try again."

In her hands, the kernel flared with furious fire, now reflecting her own mood quite clearly in an eye-hurting carmine blaze that made the Shamaska around her wince and flinch away. Nita turned around and looked back toward Khretef and Aurilelde. "Well?" she said to Khretef.

Aurilelde, slumped again Khretef, wouldn't look at her. Khretef, kneeling beside her, was doing his best to hold himself straight, but his shame was evident. "I could hear his voice inside me before," he said, miserable, "but I can hear him no more. If I had known that another wizard would die because of me —"

"Your problem was that you didn't think he *was* another wizard!" Nita said. "Rorsik talked her into believing that he was 'just' another version of you. And she talked you into believing it." She glared at him, wobbling again. "I'm sorry for you, but right now that's not going to be good enough —"

In her hands the kernel flamed even brighter. The Shamaska standing around the room began to flee for the exits: one of them was Rorsik.

Nita stood there with the kernel, feeling the big backlash from the passthrough and the smaller ones from her other exertions inexorably catching up with her. *I'm out of ideas,* she thought, as the shaking got worse. *They really can't do anything. I don't know what to do! Where do we go from here?*

How about we start with not panicking? Kit said inside her head.

Nita's head snapped up. And quite abruptly there was a multicolored dinosaur standing in the middle of the room . . . and next to her, a young blond woman with a baby in a chest sling and a parakeet sitting on her head.

"Mamvish!" Nita said — and then sat down on the ground, quite hard, even considering the low gravity. The surroundings started to blur. *No —!* "Mamvish, they've got Kit! What about Kit —?"

The massive head swung toward her. Suddenly

Nita could see clearly again: energy poured into her in a rush, and she got to her feet again, though unsteadily.

Colleague, hold your nerve! Mamvish said way down inside her. *I think I got the one thing we needed before they threw me out —*

From beside Mamvish, Irina looked over at Nita with an extremely neutral expression — but Nita thought she could see an edge of amusement on it as Irina's eyes fell on the kernel. *At least you didn't drop it,* Irina said.

Do you want it —?

No. Just be quiet for a moment and let's see how this develops.

But Kit!

"First things first," Mamvish said to the room at large. The general rush for the exits had stopped where it was with the appearance of the two new arrivals. "It's as I thought: what we have here is an incomplete archival." And she looked at Khretef. A storm of fiery Speech-characters flared under her skin.

Khretef screamed and went down on hands and knees, and the hair rose on the back of Nita's neck, because the scream had two voices in it, one of them Kit's. Khretef collapsed, fell flat to the floor, writhed and twisted, rolled away —

— and left a body behind him, dressed as he was, but not gray-skinned.

"*Kit!*" Nita cried, and ran to him.

He was getting to his knees as she reached him. "Whoa," Kit said as Nita helped him up one-handed. "That was . . . *so* interesting."

"We're not done with the interesting stuff yet," Nita muttered.

Kit looked around the room, saw Irina and Mamvish standing there, and shivered all over. "Yeah, I bet," he said. And he glanced over at Aurilelde. "You mind if we put some distance between us and her?"

Nita smiled a grim half-smile. "No problem." They headed over toward Mamvish.

Irina was making her way toward the Throne, where Iskard still stood, and to which Rorsik had just slowly returned. The baby, apparently asleep, took no notice of any of this. The yellow parakeet, however, glared at the two Shamaska, rustled its wings, and made an angry scolding sound as its mistress stopped and folded her arms.

"My name is Irina Mladen," she said. "I am the Planetary Wizard for Earth. I speak for our world, but also for the system's other Planetaries, who vest their joint authority in me at this time as presently the system's most senior among equals. In the Powers' names and the name of the One they serve, I greet you with reservation, and with regret at the sanction I have come to impose."

Her voice was chilly, and Nita shivered all over at the sound of it. "What sanction?" Rorsik said. "What are you talking about?"

Iskard had gone pale even for someone of the Shamaska's stony complexion. Now he put out a hand to try to stop Rorsik from saying anything further. But Irina merely gave Rorsik a look, then turned her attention back to Iskard.

"Regardless of being a wizard for much of your lifetime and fully cognizant of the responsibilities the Art requires of its practitioners," Irina said, "you have allowed your people in general, and other wizards and talents under your management in particular, to enter into courses of action that have recklessly endangered the conduct of life on an entire neighboring world." She turned that cool regard on Khretef, who along with the faint and miserable Aurilelde he was half carrying had now come up alongside the Throne. "In your case, you must be clear that we do understand the terrible urgency of *hwanthaet* that you've been experiencing. The condition can cause irrational responses in even the most stable species when it becomes acute, and we are therefore willing to consider it to a limited extent as an extenuating circumstance for you personally —"

"What's *hwanthaet*?" Kit muttered under his breath.

Nita shook her head.

"But this consideration does not exonerate you for your own errors of judgment and lapses in wizardly conduct," Irina said. "And we have yet to determine whether further sanctions need to be taken against you personally and, if so, what form they should take."

She turned away from Khretef and Aurilelde, glancing just briefly at Kit and Nita as she did so. "Meanwhile," she said to Iskard and Rorsik, "as rulers of this city, immediate responsibility for the actions of its inhabitants falls on you. You" — and she indicated Iskard — "were the deviser of the superegg-based conditional stasis and revival routines, called by you the Nascence, which induced matter/spirit hibernation for you and the City of your kindred the Eilitt, and then brought them out of stasis again. Your actions since then have all flowed from a desire to destroy that other City —"

"They have been trying to do the same to us!" Rorsik cried. "They have been trying to destroy us since the First World was young —"

"And you haven't been making any serious attempts to stop that trend," Mamvish said. "Rather, you've been intent on keeping it going. You have repeatedly failed to question your own motives and assumptions as the Art requires."

"By irresponsible use of both wizardry and science, you've seriously damaged the normal developmental progress of this planet," Irina said. "If major intervention had not taken place, you would have caused significant psychological damage to the inhabitants of the third planet as well. And though you've been the aggressors here, it's not realistic to assume — bearing in mind the past actions of your enemies — that they wouldn't eventually try to do something very similar if the opportunity arose." Irina let out an aggrieved breath. "Therefore sanction will be imposed forthwith upon your cities generally, and upon the major actors personally."

A terrible silence fell in the room.

"You have two options," Mamvish said. "You can elect to be rafted to another solar system and resettled on a new world. There the Art will be withdrawn from you, and you will be left to your own devices until the One sees fit to release wizardry into your world once more."

"Why should we go to any other solar system? This one is *ours!*" Rorsik shouted. "We were the First People, the originals. We are the true Masters of this system, whatever power you may claim! All of this only comes now because you weaklings desire the use of this world for yourselves, for your —"

And Rorsik suddenly fell silent. His face got quite dark gray, his mouth worked, but not another sound came out of him.

Irina raised her eyebrows. "Or," she said, "if a majority of your people have come to agree with this being, then you may elect to be locked again into the same state of stasis in which you lay until your recent revival. Your dormancy site will be guarded and spell-locked until all other species in this system for whom your discovery would be an issue have reached a sufficient level of cultural maturity for the discovery of your presence no longer to be problematic. At that time your stasis will be broken and your suitability for settlement on this planet will be reevaluated."

The silence in the room, if possible, grew even more deadly. "Even the first option will require that you return to stasis for a while," said Mamvish, "because though there are thousands of planets that might suit you, coming up with the best match will take time — and there's no chance whatsoever that we'll leave your species at large on this planet or anywhere in this system until your new home is found and prepped."

Iskard stood quiet for some time, considering. Finally, still looking pale, he lifted up his head. "We cannot and will not leave this system," he said. "We are the First People, and you have no right to force us to leave for some strange new home elsewhere."

"It may not seem that way to you," said Mamvish. "But the Powers That Be see it differently. Primacy of development doesn't imply either moral or spiritual primacy in any species, in any system. I've seen many come and go: and rarely, I'm sad to say, have I seen a people less considerate of other species, or more hate-filled toward its own, as you folk. By your recent actions you've forfeited the right to live your lives as you've been living them. You will therefore continue them somewhere else . . . or you will not continue them at all until far into the future."

Nita was watching Iskard's face, waiting for him to see sense. But no change showed there at all. "Do what the Powers command you," he said at last. "But never hope to get us to agree to it."

Irina glanced over at Mamvish and exchanged a long look with her. Nita felt something itching at the back of her mind, but the sensation passed. To Kit, she said silently, *You getting the same feeling from these guys that I am?*

They'd sooner be dead than do it anybody else's way, Kit said. *So sad.*

Nita looked at him with some surprise. *They just*

did to you what they did, she said, *and you can still be*
sorry *for them?*

Kit shrugged. *It's not so much them,* he said. *I was*
one of them for a little. Maybe I get it . . .

He stepped out into the middle of the gathering.
"Irina," Kit said.

She looked at him in surprise.

"They can't help it," he said. "The stasis was terrible for them; I could feel it when I was inside
Khretef. It wasn't just like being asleep and not
dreaming: they could feel it all. Time didn't go by
faster to them: it went slower. They could feel every
minute, every second." He looked over at Khretef.

The Eilitt wizard bowed his head. "It made them
worse," Kit said. "They were angry before . . . and
when they came out now, they were a little crazy. I
caught some of that, maybe." Kit looked embarrassed.
"But it's not entirely their fault. And . . ." He looked
more embarrassed still. "They still know how to love
each other. But being scared about whether they're
going to survive at all can really get in the way . . ."

Irina was watching Kit with some perplexity.
"Kit," she said, unfolding her arms enough to shift the
baby-sling, "they *can't* stay in the system as it's now
constituted while they're free and able to act. The
Powers have withdrawn that right from them. And
they won't accept rafting out, or stasis until the situation changes —"

"I know," Kit said. "But there's another way."

Irina and Mamvish looked at each other, then
back at Kit. "What?"

"Timeslide," he said. "Into the past."

Irina gave him an odd look, then glanced over at Mamvish. Mamvish's eyes on both sides were going around.

"To reposition a sanctioned species far enough back not to be a threat to the timelines of associated planets," Mamvish said, "would take a tremendous amount of power. Even for a Planetary and a Species Archivist."

"What if the power wasn't so much of a problem?" Kit said.

He looked, not at Iskard or Rorsik, but at Khretef. "What if you were here," Kit said, "but long, long ago, before anybody on Earth was able to notice you? Millions of years back? No carbon-based species lasts that long." He looked at Mamvish: one eye fixed on him in a way that suggested he was right. "And nobody would have to go into stasis. Your cities could be relocated here on the planet in real time . . ."

Khretef looked at Kit oddly. "But the Eilitt would still try to attack us . . ."

"Not if your relocation was in time as well as space," Kit said. "Put one city down in one spot . . . And the other one, five hundred thousand years away . . ."

Irina was looking at him now, and the expression was more thoughtful. Once again she glanced over at Mamvish, and Nita felt that odd itching at the back of her mind.

It ceased. Iskard now was looking at Kit as if he couldn't understand why Kit was being so helpful.

"If this could be done..." Iskard said. "We would accept it."

Irina turned to Kit, looking troubled. "I'm a Planetary, Kit," she said, "not one of the Powers That Be. The problem with this is finding enough energy to fuel the spell. Pushing thousands of living beings and the mass of two ancient cities back a million years or two would require —" She shook her head.

"Wait," Kit said. "Just wait, okay? I need to transit back to my house." And then he looked annoyed. "By the way, since these guys were doing *hwanthaet* or whatever it is on me to make me so crazy to be back here, can I please be ungrounded?"

Irina gave him a dry look. "Go," she said, and waved a hand.

Kit vanished.

He appeared in his kitchen and turned to head toward the back door — and found that standing there, looking at him wide-eyed, with yet another armful of laundry, was Helena.

"Uh —" Kit said.

To his great relief, the look with which his sister was favoring him was more bemused than scared or angry. "So that noise is traditional, then," she said.

"Huh?"

"When you appear," Helena said. "It's in the mutant comic books, too. 'Bamf!'" And she then started looking even more bemused. "Does this mean the comics people actually *know* mutants?"

"Uh... they might," Kit said.

Helena nodded, apparently pleased at having worked this out for herself. She started heading toward the cellar stairs with her laundry, then paused as something occurred to her. "When you appear out of nowhere like that," she said, "there's no chance you could appear where somebody else already *is*, is there? Like, you know, a transporter accident?"

Kit was briefly annoyed, then realized it was a fair question. "No. There's an automatic offset, it —" He stopped, as there was no point in explaining the safeguards built into the spell: Helena was thinking in a different idiom now, and he was just going to have to get used to it. "It can't happen. Don't worry about it."

"Okay." Helena headed for the stairs and was halfway down them as Kit stepped down onto the landing and reached in among the coats and so forth to pull out what he'd come back for. Helena stopped on the stairs, looked up at the glowing thing that Kit was carefully unwinding from the hook where it had been hanging.

"What's that? Oh, don't *tell* me!" Helena said, sounding genuinely impressed. "Wonder Woman's magic lasso? Is that real, too?" And then she paused. "I thought it was supposed to be gold."

Not for the first time when dealing with one of his sisters, Kit was left briefly speechless.

Helena got a musing look. "And if that can be real, maybe other stuff from the comics could be real, too? Like—I can't remember: what are those guys called who have the green glowy rings? Like them.

Wouldn't it be great if there *was* this interplanetary brotherhood with all kinds of creatures, you know, banding together and using their powers to fight evil . . ."

She sighed, then smiled at Kit. "Never mind, I know, it's probably more secret stuff," Helena said, turning and heading down the stairs again. "Guess I've just got to get used to it. What a world." She moved out of sight, and Kit heard the clunk of the washer's lid being opened. "I should really start getting back into comics. My brother the mutant . . ."

Kit stared down at her, dumbfounded: then heaved a sigh and vanished again.

Back on Mars, Kit went to Irina and handed her what he'd brought from home.

Irina took the long, slender, pale cord from him — and started, her eyes wide. In its sling, the baby woke up. On her head, the parakeet was shocked into the air and fluttered there for several moments before settling again and staring down at what she held.

Irina ran the cord through her hands, noting — as did everyone else — the way the faint bluish glow about it overrode every other light in that great room. As she moved her hands apart while holding it, the cord stretched: the glow got brighter.

"It was my dog's," Kit said. "Before he . . . graduated . . . he really used to get around. Other universes, other times . . . Sometimes a lot further. This leash was the only way I could keep up with him. Anchor one end of it in one reality, fasten it to something in another — and it'll pull the other thing through."

Mamvish came over to look at Ponch's old leash. It had been powerful enough when Kit had used it for doggie-walking before the affair with the Pullulus earlier in the year. What it would be able to do now, after having been even briefly affiliated with the canine version of the One, even Kit could only guess.

But apparently Irina had some idea. She closed her eyes for a moment, then opened them again, letting out a long, surprised breath and glancing over at Mamvish. "This artifact," she said, "has a power rating even bigger than yours. I wouldn't have thought it possible."

Mamvish swung her tail. "And it's built for transits," she said. "With this, and your power and mine, we can pull it off. I'd say the solution suits."

Irina turned back to Kit. "You understand that probably it won't survive this wizardry."

Kit nodded. "I don't need it anymore. And Ponch sure doesn't. If it can do some good here . . . let's go."

After that it seemed to Nita that things happened nearly as quickly as her decommissioning of the passthrough wizardry had. There was a brief consultation about temporospatial coordinates, and then a transit out to the city limits, past the farthest buildings, at the end of the white road. Mamvish and Irina stood there conferring to resolve the last few issues, while Iskard watched from the road.

Kit had taken Khretef off to one side, and together the two of them stood for a good while looking down at Kit's manual while Kit turned the pages, shifting from section to section as he constructed a spell. After a few moments he pulled a long glowing string of speech-characters out of the manual — a deactivated spell, set for storage and later use by another wizard.

Nita watched Kit checking the center section of the spell one last time before passing it to Khretef, and knew what it was. Her mouth went dry at the prospect of handing another being so much personal information. *But it's his business* . . . And Khretef, too, looked at the spell with some disquiet: but also, Nita thought, with a touch of guilt. He and Kit exchanged a long glance before Khretef took the spell and made it vanish into his own unseen version of the manual: and he bowed to Kit, quite deeply.

Finally Kit headed back to where Nita waited. "He's got what he needs to build into the Nascence," Kit said as they joined her. "So the superegg'll recognize me and behave the way it ought to, and start all this going." He glanced over at Irina, who nodded at him. "Irina and Mamvish have stoked the Nascence wizardry up so it can't be cracked by any amount of brute-force wizardry in backtime . . . and they've stuck a heavy-duty cloaking routine on it so they won't recognize the presence of their own wizardry in the superegg when we find it on the uptime leg."

Nita realized that Irina was looking at her. For a moment she didn't understand — and then she realized what was needed. "I have to give her what you did, don't I?" she said. "Enough of my personal information for Aurilelde to link to her own . . . so that the congruency between us is complete, and all this works out the way it should . . ."

Kit didn't say anything.

. . . *But why wouldn't I?* Nita thought. *To make all this come out all right.* She nodded at Irina. Irina nodded back, turned away.

And only then did it occur to Nita, with a shock, that this would mean it hadn't actually been Aurilelde who Kit had been so attracted to. It was her . . .

"It is a great gift to them," Khretef said. "We will not forget you — who helped us when you had little reason to."

"I had the same reason any wizard had," Kit said. "You just had . . . a little memory lapse. With some assistance."

From a little distance away, where she'd been standing looking rather forlorn, Aurilelde came up to clutch Khretef's hand.

For a long time it seemed as if she wouldn't look at Kit or Nita. But finally she stole a glance at them. "You know that I had to —" she said: and then she fell silent.

Nita sighed and shook her head. "It all worked out in the end," she said. "You were scared, and at times like that it's hard to think straight. Don't be afraid anymore, okay? And you two be happy together."

Khretef and Kit were exchanging glances. "Cousin," Khretef said holding a hand out, "brother — I'm sorry."

Kit took his arm. "You think you screwed up?" he said. "You should have seen some of mine. Go on. And take care of her."

"Time, Kit," Irina said.

Kit stepped back. Khretef and Aurilelde and Iskard stepped back as well, in the direction of the city.

Irina raised her hands; in them was the leash, knotted into a circle. She threw the leash into the air. It hovered there and began to stretch into a circular line of light, widening, growing —

The leash ascended, growing with astonishing speed, becoming a circle yards wide, tens of yards, hundreds: finally nearly a mile in diameter, still stretching as it rose. Then, high above the City of the Shamaska, centered over it, the burning circle began to fall. As it did, the space that it enclosed began to go misty. It fell farther, and the uppermost towers of the City were no longer there, vanishing as if some invisible shade were being drawn down over them, obscuring the view. Then the city proper vanished; next the buildings around them. Finally Nita saw Aurilelde turn to Khretef, and the circle dropped to the ground only a few feet away —

Everything was gone. The shoulder of Olympus Mons stood bare in the afternoon: and slowly, from high clouds up in the dusty sky, a little snow started to fall.

Mamvish and Irina stood there watching the snow come down. After a moment, Irina turned to them and let out a long breath. "It took," she said. "And at the other city site as well. They're positioned where we intended . . . far from each other in time and space."

Mamvish flourished her tail, looking around. "Well," she said, "we have a lot of work to do. We're going to have to do extensive time-patching on this whole environment to get rid of the seismic damage and the water . . ."

"You'll be wanting to call in all your Mars teams, then," Irina said. And she looked at Kit. "I'd suggest, though, that for the moment you sit this out. The wizardry that connected you and Khretef will need some time to fade."

"And *that* was why he was so crazy?" Nita said, starting to feel wobbly again.

"Yes," Irina said. "Among other things. Which is why the energy outlay for the normally rather illegal thing you did to his manual has been subsidized, and I've arranged for you to be forgiven."

Kit stared at Nita. "What did you do to my manual?"

Nita rubbed her eyes. "Later," she said. "Right now, I really, really need a nap."

Together, they vanished.

Elysium

IT TOOK MORE THAN A NAP before Nita was ready to do much of anything the next day. Her dad had gotten her off the final day of school, citing family business — which was true enough — but once she got home, she slept straight through into the next morning. It was mid-evening before she and Kit had a chance to get together with Irina and Mamvish to review the events of the weekend.

Her father set out the lawn chairs and the barbecue kettle in the shielded part of the backyard and sat there drinking iced tea with Kit's mama and pop and Tom and Carl. Across from them, the Powers' Archivist (too large to do anything but sprawl among the lawn chairs) and Earth's Planetary relaxed with Nita, Kit, Dairine, Carmela, Ronan, and Darryl, debriefing them on the fine details of the last few days and filling in missing ones.

Mars had been fairly quickly repaired, since the

necessary timeline-patching started almost immediately after the Cities were gone. The power requirements of the patching spells had meant that a lot of wizards had to be called in to assist, but now everything was once again dry except for carbon dioxide snow, and all the planet's water was back where it belonged, frozen under the crust or at the poles. However, there were still endless minor details to sort out.

"So the 'blue star' was Earth," Carmela was saying to Dairine: "that was these guys getting involved. And 'the word long lost,' that was the Shard —"

"How's that a word?" Dairine said, unconvinced.

"It's a pun in the Speech. One term for a single word in the Speech is *shafath*, a fragment of a longer expression, get it?"

"Yeah, but what about the 'spoke by the watcher' thing? How can you 'speak' a fragment of anything?"

Carmela sighed, looked up at Mamvish. "It's true," Mamvish said, "there is a verb form of *shafath* as well: *shafait'*, to *use* a fragment —"

Dairine rolled her eyes. "Forget it," she said. "It's just another of these symbolic poems that can mean anything. Give me the concrete stuff any day."

Carmela was starting to look annoyed. "Okay, I'll give you this," Dairine said. "This stuff about the watcher, the silent yearning for the lost one found, blah de blah de blah, fine, that was Aurilelde and Khretef. He was dead while everybody else was in stasis. Then when Kit showed up, he got unlost and started looking for the Shard again. But 'she must slay her rival'? Just who was her rival? Because nobody got slain! You should find somebody to complain to, because this prophecy is substandard."

Behind Dairine, Ronan and Darryl were utterly failing to control their snickering. Dairine glared over her shoulder at them; and they both got extremely interested in Darryl's WizPod.

Carmela was scowling. "'Mela, you did a great job on that," Carl said, "but we may never know exactly what it meant." He stretched his legs out. "Oracular utterances all over this galaxy have at their heart the need to be able to stretch to a lot of different interpretations, so that as temporospatial conditions change around them, they'll still be suitable . . ."

"And whatever the prophecy might have meant," Kit's pop said, "there'll be Martians after all." He paused, trying to sort the tenses out. "Will have *been* Martians?"

Irina let out a long breath. "*Were* Martians," she said. "But not anymore."

That made Kit look up. "*What?*"

Mamvish exchanged a one-eyed look with Irina, then glanced back to Kit. "Well, naturally we checked the backtime history once the relocation was completed," she said. "But they didn't last very long, as it happens: only seventy thousand years . . ."

Nita thought suddenly of the odd itching she'd felt in the back of her brain. "You were discussing that possibility right then. When we were setting the timeslide. And you already suspected things were going to turn out this way."

Irina sighed. "Yes," she said. "The Shamaska-Eilitt may indeed have been the system's oldest species, which meant it was no surprise that they were also showing signs of being *uvseith*. A diagnosis which this outcome has now confirmed."

Carmela frowned. "'Moribund'?"

Irina cocked an eye at her. "Yes," she said. "The word's far more emphatic in the Speech, of course." She glanced over at the parents. "It says a species has only a short time to survive."

"Some species simply can't live long off the planet that engendered them," Mamvish said. "Their own personal kernels are wound up too closely with the planet's. In the case of the Shamaska-Eilitt, their own bodies' kernels were irreparably damaged when their planet was destroyed. Long-lived as they were, they were already doomed."

"And they were in denial about it," Irina said, "which happens all too frequently in such cases. The problem with their body change after the destruction of Shamask-Eilith wasn't that the Martian climate changed . . . though it did. It was that they were never really suited to live anywhere but on their own world, and *any* change would have killed them in time. Moving to a new world only made the problem worse, speeding up the damage they were doing themselves. And as Kit confirmed, the stasis made it worse still: some of the irrationality we saw from them would definitely have been a result of holding themselves in their already-damaged state for so long. Had they succeeded in moving to Earth, they wouldn't have lasted long there, either."

"So they *would* have invaded Earth eventually," said Nita's dad, "and Earth would have killed them." He took a drink of his iced tea. "Sounds familiar, somehow. Archetype?"

Irina nodded slightly. "Hints and warnings of what would have been or may yet be do slip into myth and popular culture from the deep past and the possible future," she said. "It's a hall of mirrors, the universe: in the spiritual sense, anyway. And sometimes it's hard to tell which end of time the images and reflections belong to."

She glanced over at Kit. "That's the cause of the *hwanthaet* you were caught up in — the timeloop proximity syndrome. To be repeatedly positioned near the effect end of a timeloop when you were also involved in the cause, but before the cause has happened, or when it's just starting to execute — well, the human brain's circuitry doesn't take well to that. You got off pretty lightly, though, in the physical sense: it helps to be young. And the Powers wouldn't come down on you too hard for infractions that you committed due to the after effects of the good deed you were about to do in the past."

Kit's pop blinked at that. "Sounds like you need a whole different language for this kind of thing."

"It's a subset of the Speech," Mamvish said. "Intratemporal syntax takes a while to learn. But some species pick it up entirely too quickly." She looked with amusement at Nita and Kit.

Nita, now sitting cross-legged on the ground in jeans and a cropped top and feeling very relieved to be that way again instead of in filmy, glittery Shamaska women's wear, was paging through her manual, looking at the revisions that had been made over the last day. Now she looked up at the more senior wizards. "Irina," Nita said, frowning, "this is weird. When I checked the manual before, it said the kernel had been missing for half a million years. But now it says it hasn't been missing after all."

Irina looked over Nita's shoulder at her manual. "Oh, I see," she said. "Tom, you didn't enable her need-to-know updates."

Tom rolled his eyes. "It *has* been busy around here lately, what with recovering from the Pullulus and so forth . . ."

Irina gave him an amused look. "Oh, stop it," she said. "That wasn't a critique. Anyway, you've just had your end-of-decade evaluation: you know where you stand."

She glanced up from the page to Nita again, and Nita saw that the open page had already changed its content. Now she was looking at a comment box that said, *Temporal adjustment emendation: timeline shift. Previous timeline details archived, viewable on need-to-know basis.*

She shook her head and smiled. "When everything settles down, Time's arrow is always seen to run straight," Irina said. "After the solution you three came up with yesterday, the kernel's always been present on Mars in real time —"

"Though blocked away from the inhabitants' use," Mamvish said. "Jupiter's Planetary kept a light-patch on it while the Shamaska-Eilitt were there."

Irina nodded. "But the manual still remembers the previous timeline."

"As well as the solution you and Khretef arrived at," Mamvish said. "The binding power inherent in Ponch's leash let us set aside, in the timeslide, the additional power to build the superegg, to lock the Cities' stasis so that it couldn't be interfered with, and for Khretef to encode the Nascence with the personal data that would be needed to lead you to Mars, and impel you to bring the future about. And the past."

"A past that worked," Nita said. "One where Aurilelde wouldn't be afraid anymore, and would be able to have the Red Rede written in a way that would produce *this* result. Instead of the one her fear of losing Khretef had been showing her . . ."

She glanced over at Irina, who was gazing at her with a strangely assessing expression. "And it actually worked," Nita said.

Irina nodded and had a drink of her iced tea, finishing it. "Yes, it did," she said. "Since we're all sitting here, and the world's more or less as we left it . . . and we're not all speaking Martian."

"So she really became Nita — or like Nita — in a way," Kit's pop said. "The way Kit's counterpart became like him."

"That's right."

"Smart choice," Nita's dad said, and got up to stir the charcoal.

Kit was looking thoughtful. "But which really came first?" he said. "What we did, or what they did?"

"Oh, please," Ronan said, rubbing his face. "It's the chicken-or-egg thing again. And you get completely different answers depending on whether you ask the chicken or the egg."

"Let it go, your Kitness," Darryl said, stretching. "Life's too short. Let's stick to playing with the future. *Soooo* much more malleable."

"What happens to the kernel now?" Nita said. "There are still no Martians to manage it. Or no Martians again . . ."

"The kernel's at large in the body of the planet. But I'll be keeping an eye on it," Irina said.

"One more thing for you to do," Mamvish said. "As if you don't already have enough!"

Irina shrugged and smiled; the parakeet started idly nibbling her hair. "It'll be easy enough to keep in tune until Mars gets new tenants, some of whom will be wizards and can take on the job. People from here, or from somewhere else — who knows? Earth won't be *astahfrith* forever."

She sighed. "But for the moment it is, and there are problems that need to be tended to." Irina stood up, smiling at Nita's father. "Mr. Callahan — thanks so much. It's been a pleasure." She picked up her baby, which was lying nearby snoozing in a carrier seat: the parakeet on Irina's shoulder ruffled its feathers up and made a few little scratchy noises. "*Dai,* cousins," she said, and vanished without so much as a breath of breeze.

Mamvish, too, stood up. "I too have a few things to deal with," she said. "Friends, cousins —"

"Oh, goodness, I almost forgot. Wait a moment," Nita's dad said, and got up, heading for the house. A minute or so later he was back with a plastic carrier bag from one of the local supermarkets, looking to be stuffed very full of something heavy.

Mamvish's eyes started to go around in her head as she looked toward Nita's father. Nita, seeing this, poked Kit and Dairine and gestured for them to get out of the way.

"Oh, cousin!" Mamvish said. Nita's father held up the bag to her, and Mamvish took it from him with some haste. "You are my *friend!*"

"Stop by again in a couple of weeks," Nita's dad said. "The new crop will need some thinning."

Mamvish's grin went right around her face. A moment later she, too, was gone.

Nita shut her manual and put it away, looking over at Tom. "So," she said.

"So that's it," Tom said. "Nice job, you two." And he gave Kit an amused look. "Even the part when you went around the bend. Not entirely your fault, and not nearly as far as you might have gone . . . so all is forgiven, and we're all done."

Nita reached out for her own iced tea. "*Are* we done?" Nita said. "The Lone Power hasn't turned up yet."

Tom smiled slightly and looked down into his own iced tea. "It hasn't? You sure about that?"

Nita sat still and thought about that for a moment.

"Uh-huh," Tom said. He pushed back in his chair and looked at his iced tea as if something might jump out of it. "Far be it from me to generalize about wizardry," he said, "or the way it affects people. But it's not uncommon for the younger wizard to see the Art, in the early part of his or her practice, as a very stratified thing: all blacks and whites, instead of the shades of gray that start to manifest themselves later in the way you see the world. It's not that we're *not* in a massive battle of good against evil. Of course we are! But that's just one of many ways to characterize the fight. When you're getting started, there's a tendency to simplify things while you're trying to work out how to classify all the weird new data you have to handle. And when you're simplifying everything that way — and fueling that perception with the considerable power of a new wizard — very often you wind up forcing that kind of very straightforward, in-your-face, physically obvious role on the Lone Power."

"Whoa, whoa, wait a minute!" Nita stared at him. "*We're* forcing *It?*"

Tom nodded. "The youngest wizards really don't have any sense of how tremendous their power is, right out of the gate, and maybe that's for the best. They just *use* it . . . and a surprising amount of the time, they win, even though they've compelled the Lone One to come out of hiding and confront them in the only way that gives It a chance of success when they're at such power levels: direct physical intervention. That's where it's always weakest . . . for to manifest so directly, you need matter. And the Lone Power, being hung up on what It considers the essential superiority of spirit, really hates matter."

Tom smiled slightly, glancing at the various parents, who were listening with interest. "Later on, as a wizard's power decreases and his mastery of the complexities of the Art increases, the Lone One's able to make more inroads into his life in the way it does with non-wizardly people: using a lot less power, but also being a lot more subtle." He looked at Nita and Kit and the other younger wizards. "Don't think this makes It any less dangerous! You see how close It came to getting a result on Mars that would have absolutely delighted It, just by working underhandedly and using people's own habits and weaknesses against them — sometimes even their strengths. Death and destruction on two worlds: the poor dupes doing the Lone One's work for It, while It sits back and laughs."

Tom shook his head. "This time, just in time, Kit got smart. So did you." Tom looked up at Nita from under his brows, his eyes glinting. "And so did Khretef. Together you found your way past the pitfalls the Lone Power hoped you'd be blind to, because you'd dug them yourselves. That's always one of our great strengths, as wizards: we're committed to looking out for each other, each seeing the thing the other is blind to. The tricky part is convincing each other that 'blind' doesn't necessarily mean 'stupid.'"

He sighed and looked at the bottom of the glass. "But sometimes we get lucky," he said. "This last time, we all did. You kids especially. So now we get to relax."

Nita's dad reached down by the chair and picked up the iced-tea jug, filled Tom's glass again. "Even you?"

Tom laughed. "I've got enough time off next weekend to want to talk to you about some landscaping."

Nita got up and headed toward the house. Kit came along after her, catching up with her where she had paused to look at the spark of red light hanging low in the sky.

Nita glanced at it as he came up behind, then went back to gazing at Mars. "I'm not sure I got smart," she said under her breath. "It felt completely like luck to me."

Kit stared at her. "Neets, are you kidding? Think what you did with that passthrough —"

"If I hadn't had Bobo to help, I could never have done it. You should've seen the size of that spell —"

Kit shrugged. "So? You used what you had. You used what you *remembered* you had. And what you had enough power to pull off. Every wizard does that every day with their manual or whatever they use . . ."

Nita thought about that. "I was the one who was kind of late about getting smart," Kit said then. "Seemed like it took me forever to figure out that not only was Aurilelde's take on everything all wrong, but so was Khretef's. Even a wizard's perceptions of wizardry can get screwed up under the right circumstances. Khretef was too busy believing everything Aurilelde told him. Aurilelde was too busy believing what her father told her . . ."

"And he was busy believing what Rorsik told

him." Nita shook her head. "And with that whole Shamaska versus Eilitt thing going on, nobody was thinking straight about anything. Except you, eventually."

"They were too busy believing in stuff to look at what was true," Kit said. "I just hadn't been stuck in the middle of it for as long as they had."

Nita nodded, leaning back against the fence. "So, no Martians after all . . . that's got to come as a letdown."

"Yeah," Kit said. But he didn't look away from the red star burning up there. "Still . . . it's a neat place, and it needs taking care of. I'm not going to dump it just because its backstory's changed . . ."

Looking up at it, Nita nodded. "Yeah," she said. "Besides, there are still some craters up there that don't have names . . ."

She was expecting a snicker, but none came. After a moment she got a strange feeling and turned to find Kit watching her. "What?" she said.

"Charcoal's ready," Kit said. "Don't you want a burger?" And he headed back to the group at the rear of the backyard.

Nita smiled slightly and followed him.

Much later, in the dark, someone spoke Nita's name.

She woke up in the middle of the night and turned over, eyes open in the dark. *What?*

But no one was there to have said anything. Nita sighed. *Just another of those dreams,* she thought. She closed her eyes again, completely worn out but for the moment also completely happy. *Nothing to do tomorrow,* she thought. *School's over. This is so great! I can sleep as late as I want. And I'm going to start that all over again right now . . .*

But perversely it didn't happen. Outside her closed eyes, she could tell that there was light. *I hate this,* Nita thought, resigned. *This has been one of those sleeps where you wake up and you don't feel like you've been to sleep at all.* She felt vaguely cheated, but there was no point in trying to go back to sleep under these circumstances. She sighed and opened her eyes again.

Red dirt all around her, and stones and rust-beige rubble, and a light dusting of snow —

Nita sat up and stared around her. Her first thought was that Dairine had finally gotten around to getting revenge on her for sending her bed to Pluto that time. But as Nita looked around, she started getting the slightly rainbowy, shivery feeling around the edges of things, what Tom called the "temporal aberration," that told her this wasn't a real physical experience: it was vision. *Oh, okay,* she thought, and got up. *Let's see what this is about.*

There was no mistaking the view; this was Kit's preferred landing spot on Mars, at the top of Elysium Mons. Nita stood there feeling under her bare feet the cool gritty dust of another world. *This is what visions are really good for,* she thought, *not having to worry about force fields, or the real temperature, or whether you brought enough air . . .* The morning around her felt no chillier than an early spring morning on Earth. The Sun was just up and actually felt warm on her skin.

Overhead the sky was lightening, swiftly going from violet to blue. Silhouetted against it, a couple of hundred yards away where the tableland dropped off, Kit was standing, looking southward across the plains of Elysium Planitia. Nita just watched him for a moment, then felt a draft and looked down at herself.

Oh, no, she thought, seeing the gossamer draperies again, and the gleaming wrought and gemmed metal of the bodice. *I have* got *to talk him out of this look for me: it does* not *work!!* But second thoughts did intrude, and surreptitiously Nita glanced down. *Well, okay,* maybe *the top isn't bad —*

Down by her foot she saw a small rock that she recognized. Nita reached down to pick it up. "So," she said to it, "what's new up here?"

Water snow and gas snow, said the rock. *And then some changes in the terrain.* It sounded bemused.

"Yeah, I just bet," Nita said, and put the rock carefully down. "Later . . ."

She wandered over to where Kit was standing. He, too, was in "Martian" harness and metallic kilt, his wand stuck in his belt, and he was gazing across at the spires of the city that from this height could just be glimpsed away many miles to the south, where the highlands of Aeolis Mensae ran down to the plains of Elysium. "It's a nice location," Kit said. "Pretty close to the equator: the weather's as good as anywhere on the planet . . ."

And without warning they were standing up somewhere high in that city, looking down at the proud, calm people in the streets, and the little busy flying craft zipping around among the towers, more of the Shamaska going about their business. Nita looked over her shoulder and saw that the spot where they were standing was a terrace of the Scarlet Tower: and toward them came gracefully bounce-walking two people, a Shamaska female and an Eilitt male. Behind them a multi-legged, many-clawed green lizard creature was scrambling along to keep up on the polished floor.

"We thought we might see you here eventually," Aurilelde said, smiling at Nita and Kit as they got closer. "We're so glad you came!"

"Just look at it," Khretef said to Kit. "It's grown." He gestured toward the City's outskirts. "There have been plenty of raw materials to work with: it's a rich world. We'll do well here."

"You're running things now?" Kit said to him.

Khretef nodded. "In more ways than one. I'm the Master of the City here now, it seems. Iskard didn't want the position: he was tired. And happy to pass rule to Aurilelde once we'd moved and were finally safe in our new home, for the stress of the old life had taken its toll. He's got a place in the uplands now."

"And he's been so glad that there's no need to fear the Eilitt anymore," Aurilelde said. "We all have. Now we can be at peace at last." She looked at Nita with embarrassment. "Fear can make you do such terrible things. I can't believe how I was thinking . . ."

If I were awake, Nita thought, *you'd better believe*

I'd have something to say about that! But this didn't
seem to be the place or the time. "It was all a long time
ago," Nita said. "Or a long time from now. Let's just
forget about it. It turned out okay in the end . . ."

They looked out across the City. Khretef's
scorpion-pet now caught up with them, put his front
end up under one of Kit's hands, and wriggled like a
puppy. Kit looked down at it, grinning, and scratched
it on top of the head between the eyes. After a
moment it came over to her, and Nita looked down at
it, now bemused that she could ever have seen these
creatures as strange or threatening. And then she
caught something in its eyes, a familiar look —

I get around, said the large Presence behind the
look. *There are a lot more kinds of dogs in the universe than just the Earth ones.*

Nita smiled at him, then looked over at Khretef and
Aurilelde. "So the story has a happy ending," she said.

"Ending? I don't know that I'd call it that,"
Aurilelde said. "We have our whole lives ahead of us."

Knowing what she now knew, Nita held her smile
in place and said nothing. But Khretef, who had been
exchanging some silent comment with Kit, now
caught her eye. "And besides," he said, "even a short
life would be a good one in this world. Once you find
happiness, why sit around worrying that it might not
last forever? You make what you can out of it. No
point in worrying away the gift . . ."

He looked out to the horizon. Nita followed his
glance . . . and realized she was not looking at the
Mars of half a million years ago. Looking northward,

Nita saw that Elysium Planitia was no dry plain any longer, but a mighty sea: against the vast empty northern horizon, Elysium Mons stood up lone and splendid on its tremendous low-lying pedestal-island, silhouetted against the rose-colored afternoon. To either side of the highlands, great waterfalls poured down through chasms in the upper tablelands, draining the upland lakes around the craters Lasswitz and Wien. *Not our Mars,* Nita thought. *Not exactly theirs, either. But the one they found together after their time on Mars finally ended...*

Kit put out a hand to Khretef. *"Dai stihó,"* he said. "You found your way through. Good luck with the rest of it."

"And to you, brother," Khretef said, clasping Kit's arm. "Watch over your world."

Nita looked at Aurilelde's outheld hand, and took it in the same clasp. "Take good care of him," she said.

"It was all I ever meant to do," she said. "I lost my way, but you two helped me find it again."

Aurilelde and Khretef each raised a hand in farewell and turned away, heading for the Tower, with Khretef's scorpion-pet scrambling after them. "So there goes the first real Wizard of Mars," Nita said. "But who knows, maybe not the last . . ."

"Huh?" Kit was startled out of his silence. "Stop listening to me think."

"I wasn't!" Nita said. "It's just kind of funny. For a while there I thought you were going to ask Irina for the position."

Kit shook his head and grinned, gazing out over

the city. "Naah," he said. "I've got a planet. These guys needed a spare. I'm glad it was here for them."

Nita nodded. "I forgot to ask them what happened to Rorsik."

Kit shrugged. "He was all about fear. Either he's gotten himself past that, or he's found himself some other patch of eternity to be scared in."

Nita nodded. "Meanwhile," Kit said, "something I forgot to ask you."

"What?"

"Just what was it you called me back there?"

She shook her head. "Back there *where?*"

"You remember. Back at Argyre Planitia, when you were telling Aurilelde you didn't have to keep yours in a cage."

Nita stared at him, bewildered — then realized what he was talking about, and took a very deep breath.

"My boyfriend?" she said. And then Nita felt like cursing at herself for the way her voice squeaked with stress on the second word, turning it into a question.

Kit just looked at her. "Took you long enough," he said. He grinned at her and vanished.

Nita's eyes went wide: then narrowed with annoyance — and relieved delight.

"I'm gonna *get* you for that!" she said, and went after him.